STEVE SKROCE
WRITER · ARTIST

DAVE STEWART
COLORIST

FONOGRAFIKS
LETTERING & DESIGN

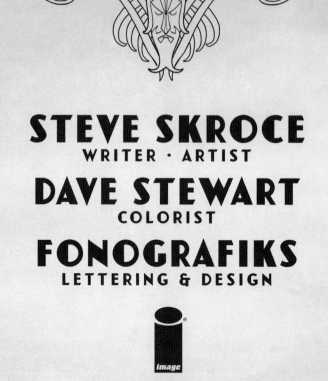

IMAGE COMICS, INC.

ROBERT KIRKMAN
Chief Operating Officer

ERIK LARSEN
Chief Financial Officer

TODD McFARLANE
President

MARC SILVESTRI
Chief Executive Officer

JIM VALENTINO
Vice President

ERIC STEPHENSON
Publisher / Chief Creative Officer

COREY HART
Director of Sales

JEFF BOISON
Director of Publishing Planning
& Book Trade Sales

CHRIS ROSS
Director of Digital Sales

JEFF STANG
Director of Specialty Sales

KAT SALAZAR
Director of PR & Marketing

DREW GILL
Art Director

HEATHER DOORNINK
Production Director

NICOLE LAPALME
Controller

IMAGECOMICS.COM

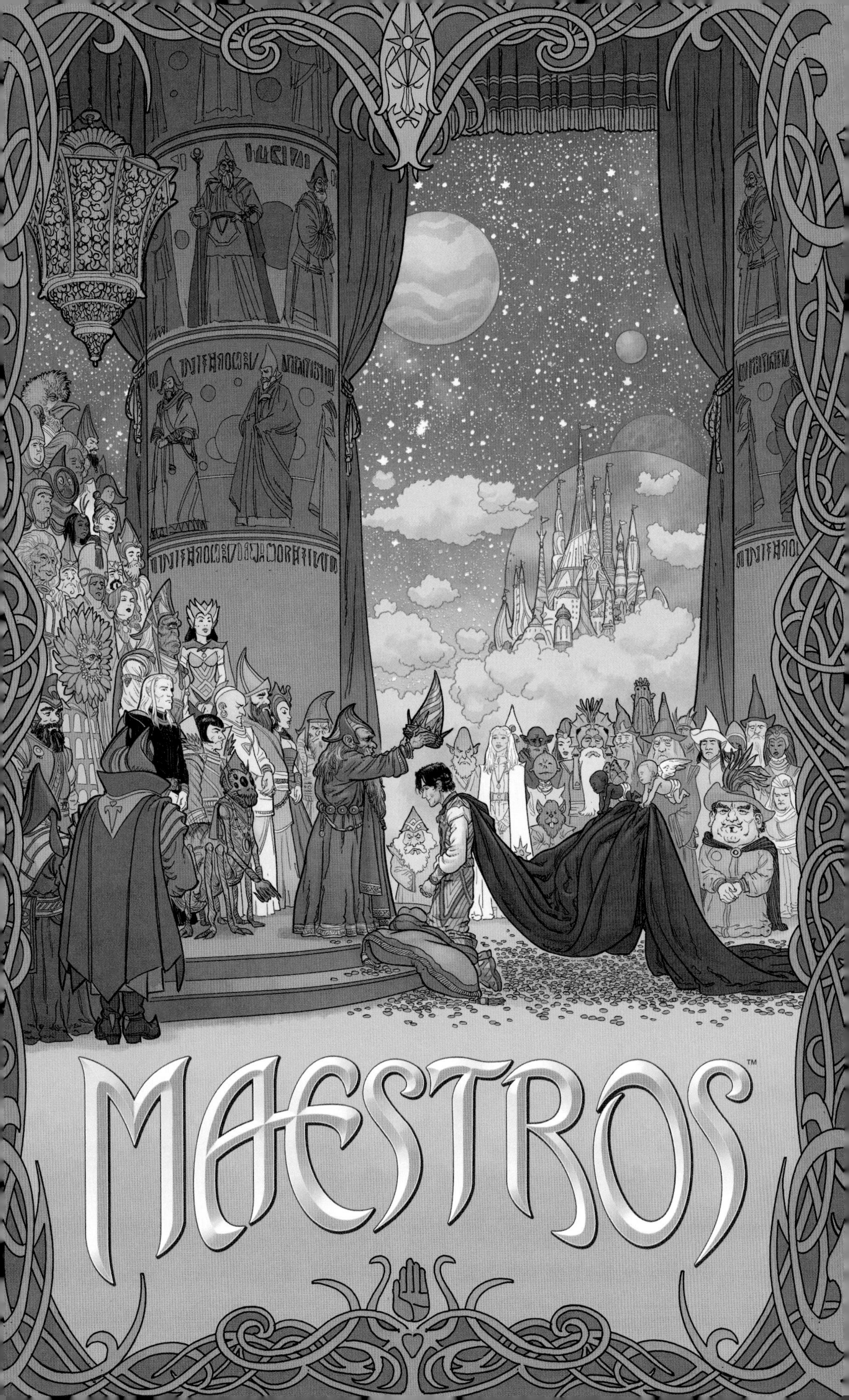
MAESTROS™

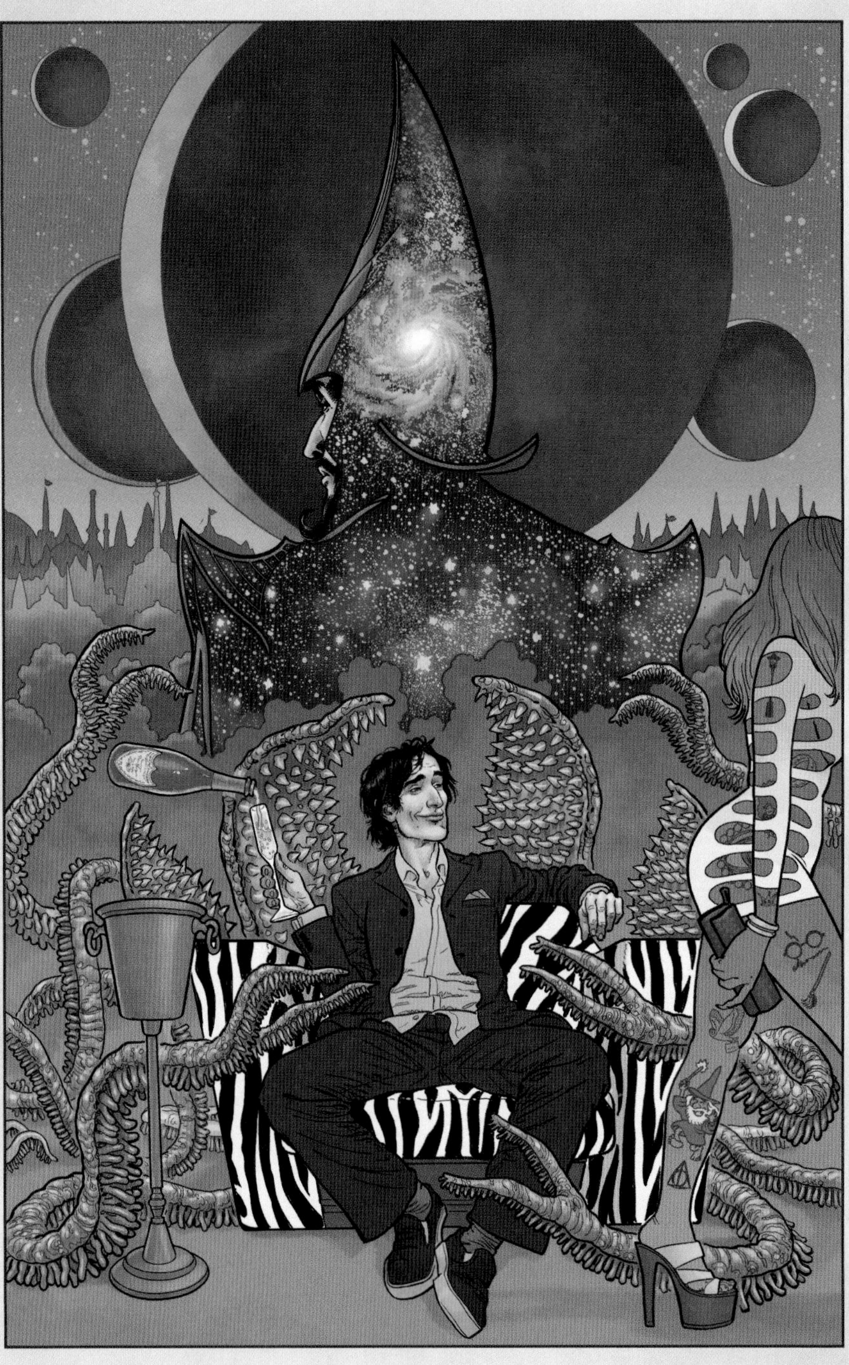

CHAPTER ONE

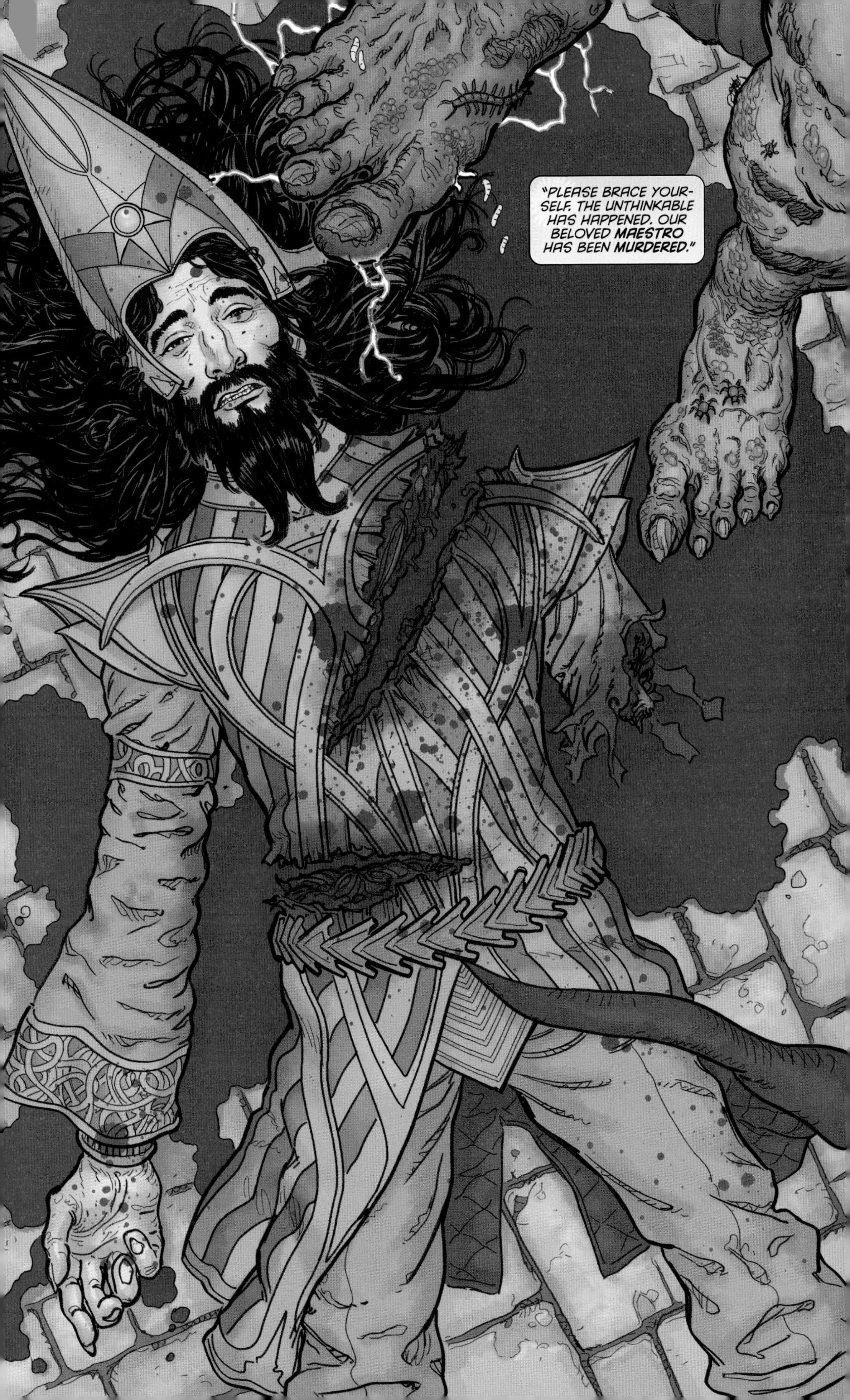
"PLEASE BRACE YOURSELF. THE UNTHINKABLE HAS HAPPENED. OUR BELOVED **MAESTRO** HAS BEEN **MURDERED**."

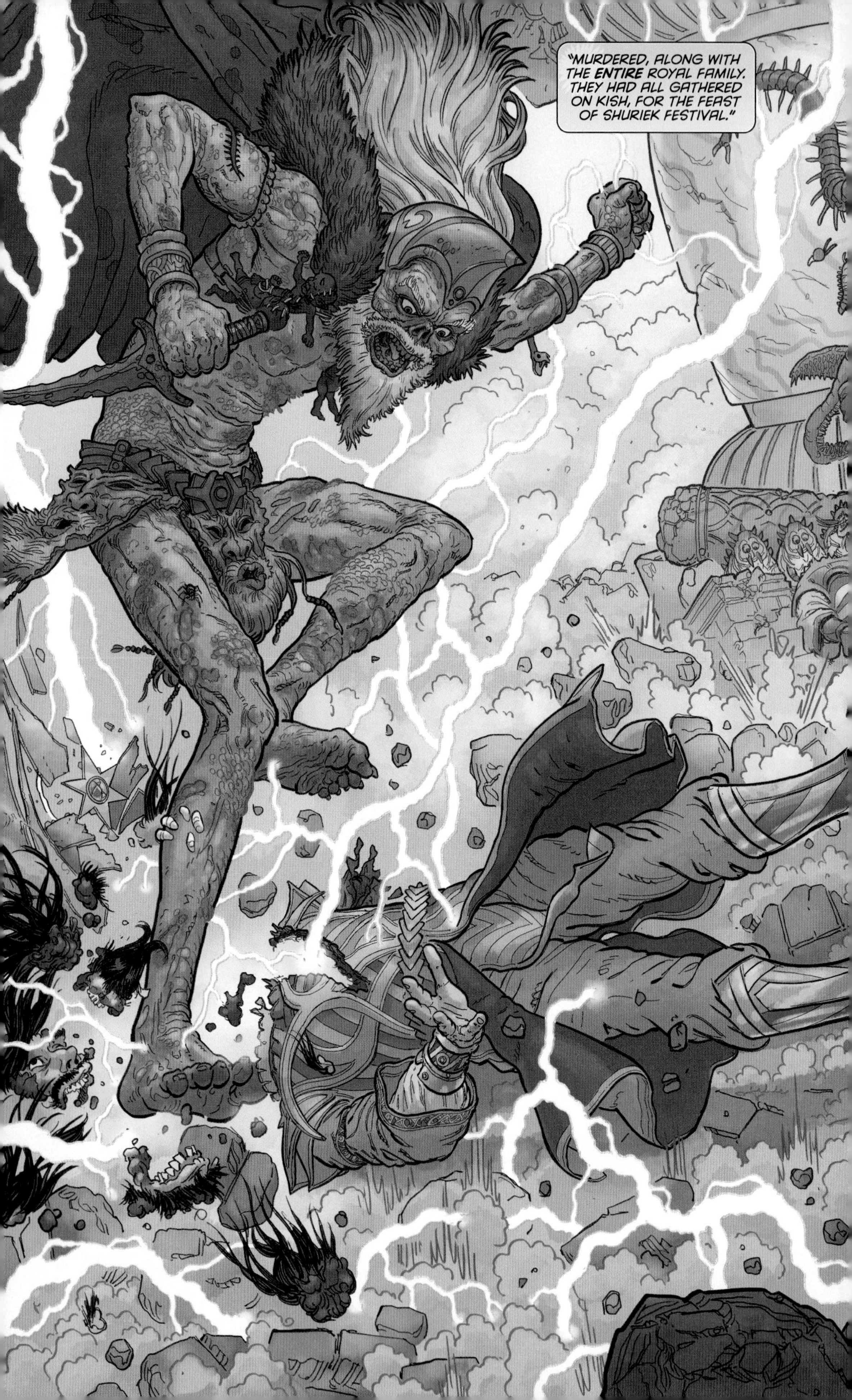
"MURDERED, ALONG WITH THE ENTIRE ROYAL FAMILY. THEY HAD ALL GATHERED ON KISH, FOR THE FEAST OF SHURIEK FESTIVAL."

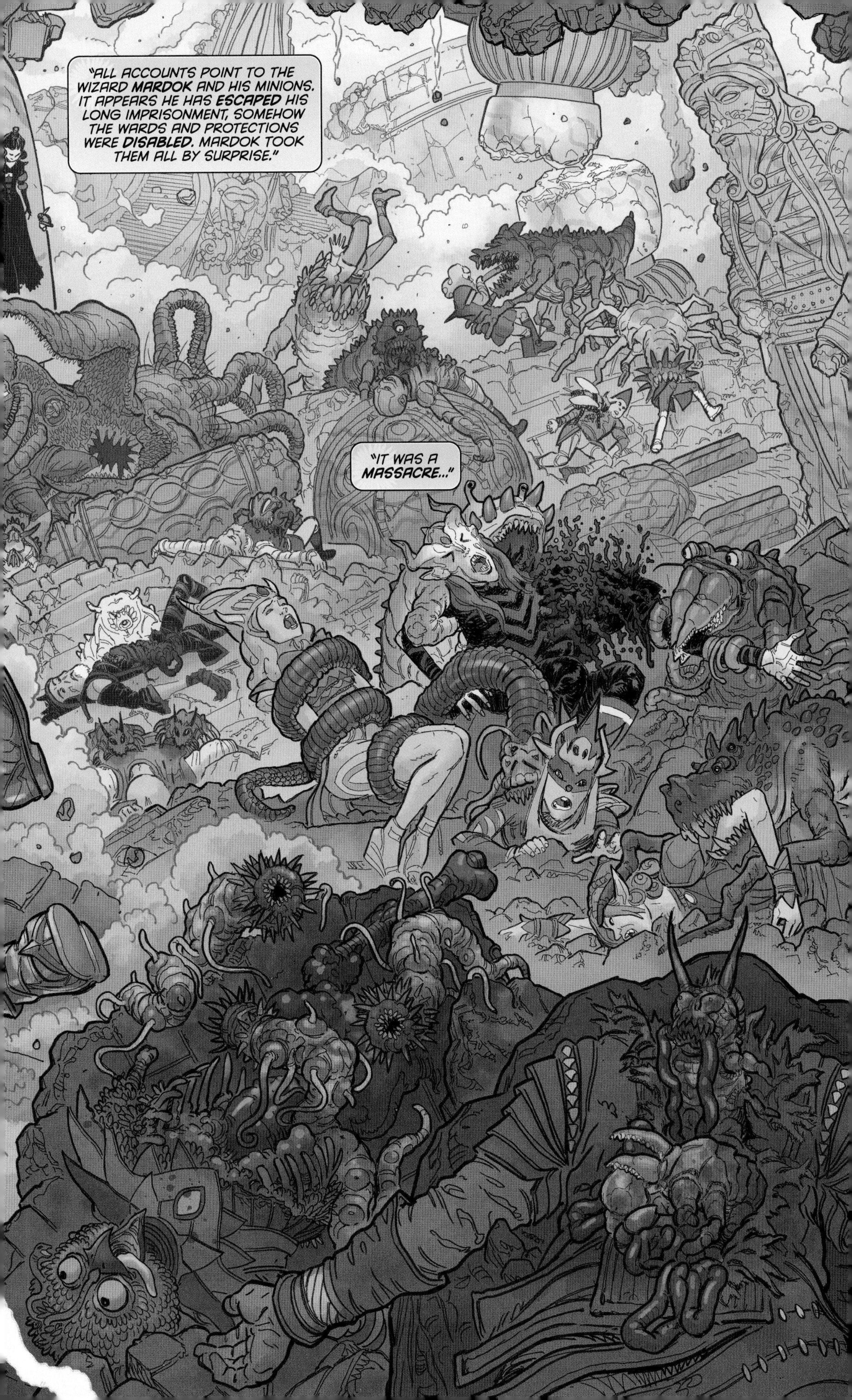
"ALL ACCOUNTS POINT TO THE WIZARD MARDOK AND HIS MINIONS. IT APPEARS HE HAS ESCAPED HIS LONG IMPRISONMENT, SOMEHOW THE WARDS AND PROTECTIONS WERE DISABLED. MARDOK TOOK THEM ALL BY SURPRISE."
"IT WAS A MASSACRE..."

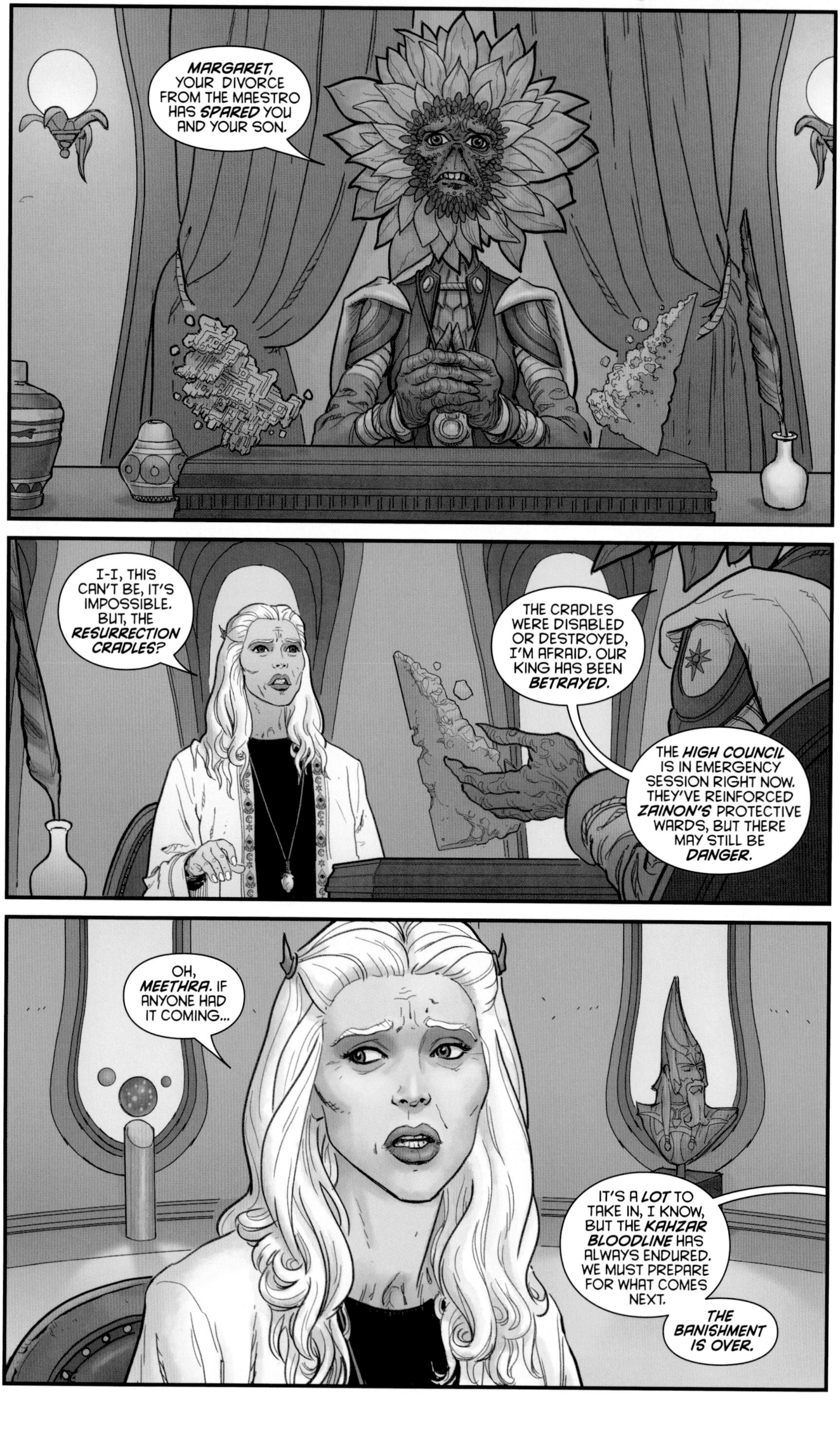

MARGARET, YOUR DIVORCE FROM THE MAESTRO HAS SPARED YOU AND YOUR SON.
I-I, THIS CAN'T BE, IT'S IMPOSSIBLE. BUT, THE RESURRECTION CRADLES?
THE CRADLES WERE DISABLED OR DESTROYED, I'M AFRAID. OUR KING HAS BEEN BETRAYED.
THE HIGH COUNCIL IS IN EMERGENCY SESSION RIGHT NOW. THEY'VE REINFORCED ZAINON'S PROTECTIVE WARDS, BUT THERE MAY STILL BE DANGER.
OH, MEETHRA. IF ANYONE HAD IT COMING...
IT'S A LOT TO TAKE IN, I KNOW, BUT THE KAHZAR BLOODLINE HAS ALWAYS ENDURED. WE MUST PREPARE FOR WHAT COMES NEXT.
THE BANISHMENT IS OVER.

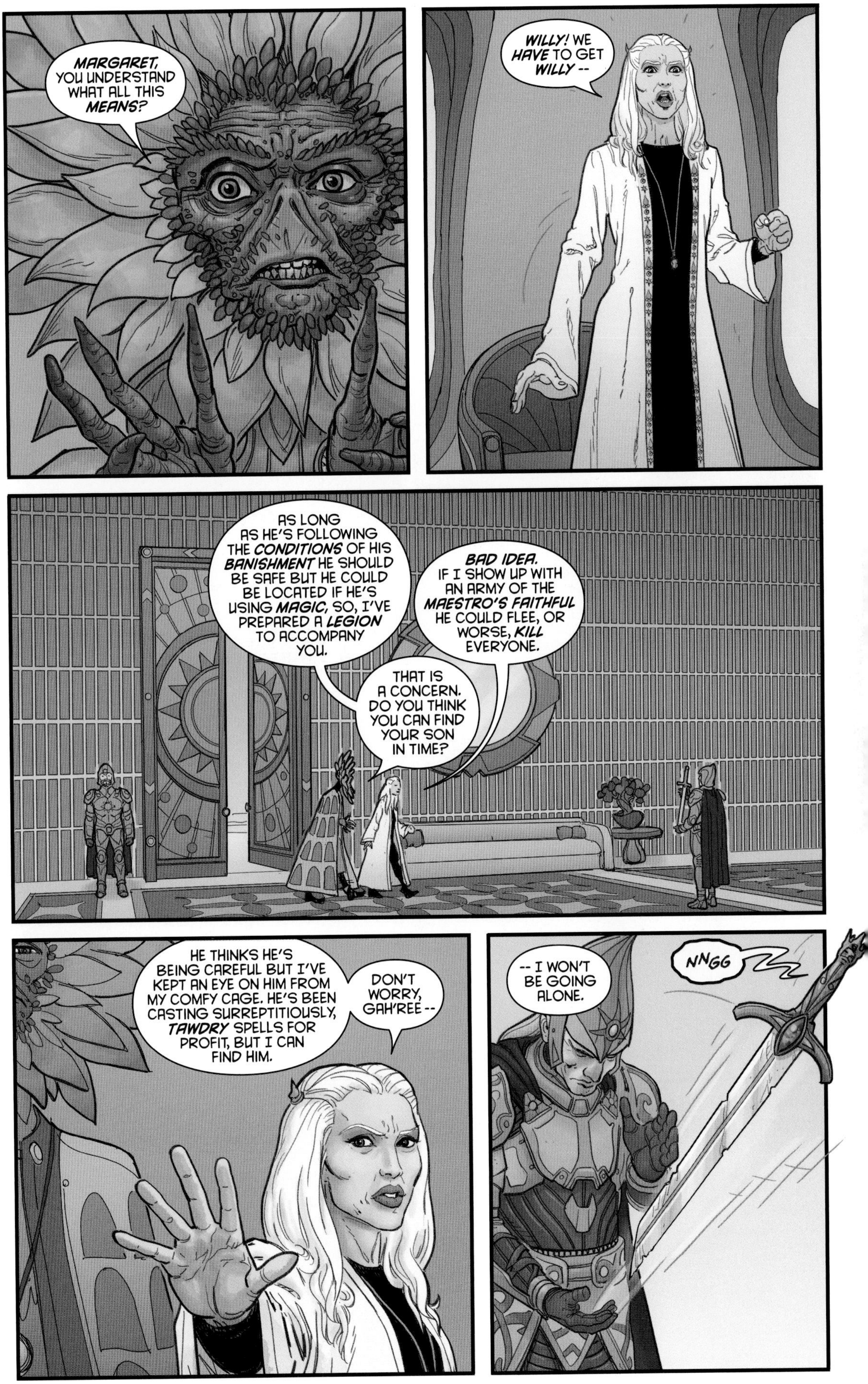

MARGARET, YOU UNDERSTAND WHAT ALL THIS MEANS?
WILLY! WE HAVE TO GET WILLY --
AS LONG AS HE'S FOLLOWING THE CONDITIONS OF HIS BANISHMENT HE SHOULD BE SAFE BUT HE COULD BE LOCATED IF HE'S USING MAGIC, SO, I'VE PREPARED A LEGION TO ACCOMPANY YOU.
BAD IDEA. IF I SHOW UP WITH AN ARMY OF THE MAESTRO'S FAITHFUL HE COULD FLEE, OR WORSE, KILL EVERYONE.
THAT IS A CONCERN. DO YOU THINK YOU CAN FIND YOUR SON IN TIME?
HE THINKS HE'S BEING CAREFUL BUT I'VE KEPT AN EYE ON HIM FROM MY COMFY CAGE. HE'S BEEN CASTING SURREPTITIOUSLY, TAWDRY SPELLS FOR PROFIT, BUT I CAN FIND HIM.
DON'T WORRY, GAH'REE --
-- I WON'T BE GOING ALONE.
NNGG

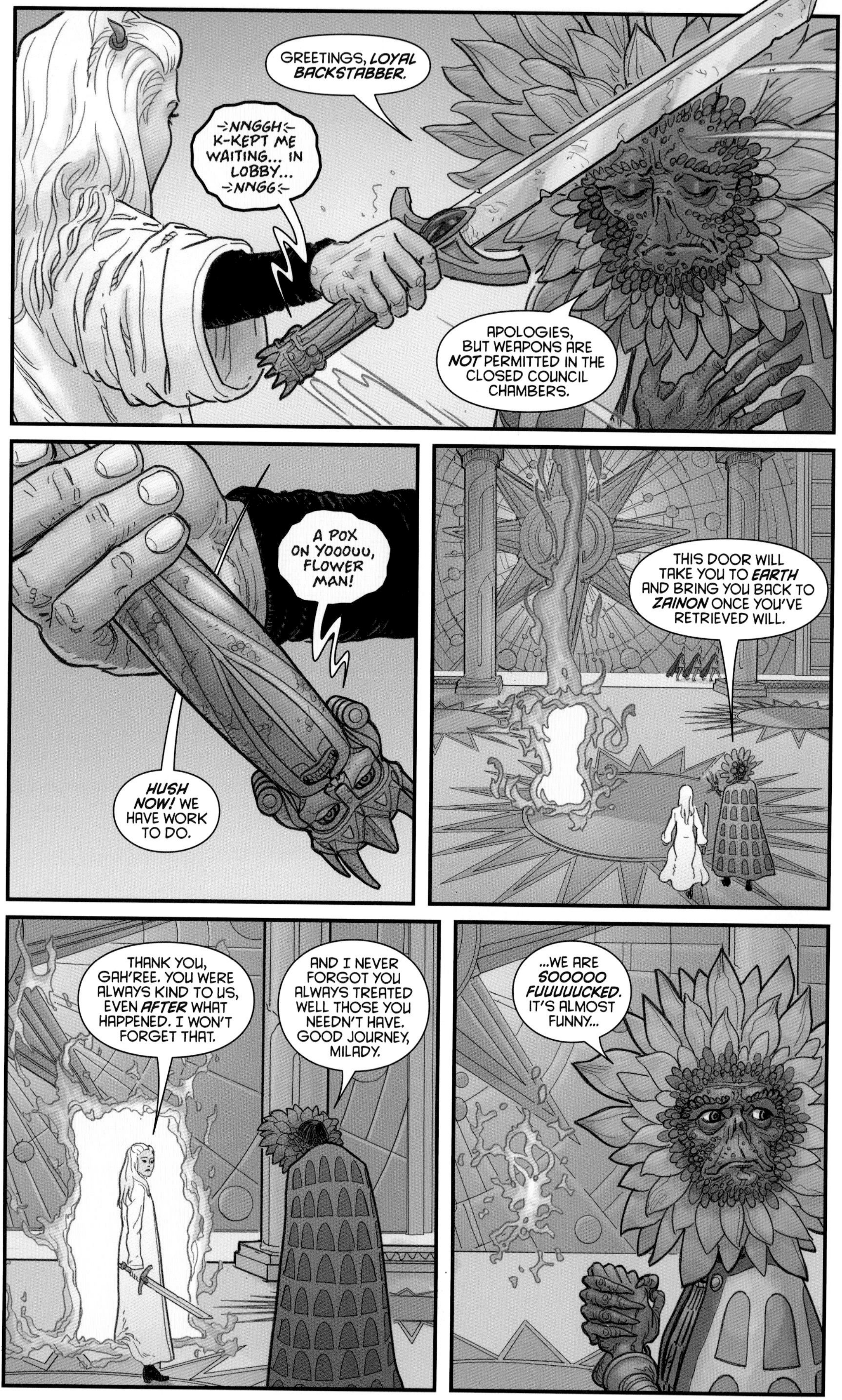
GREETINGS, LOYAL BACKSTABBER.
-NNGGH- K-KEPT ME WAITING... IN LOBBY... -NNGG-
APOLOGIES, BUT WEAPONS ARE NOT PERMITTED IN THE CLOSED COUNCIL CHAMBERS.
A POX ON YOOOUU, FLOWER MAN!
HUSH NOW! WE HAVE WORK TO DO.
THIS DOOR WILL TAKE YOU TO EARTH AND BRING YOU BACK TO ZAINON ONCE YOU'VE RETRIEVED WILL.
THANK YOU, GAH'REE. YOU WERE ALWAYS KIND TO US, EVEN AFTER WHAT HAPPENED. I WON'T FORGET THAT.
AND I NEVER FORGOT YOU ALWAYS TREATED WELL THOSE YOU NEEDN'T HAVE. GOOD JOURNEY, MILADY.
...WE ARE SOOOOO FUUUUUCKED. IT'S ALMOST FUNNY...

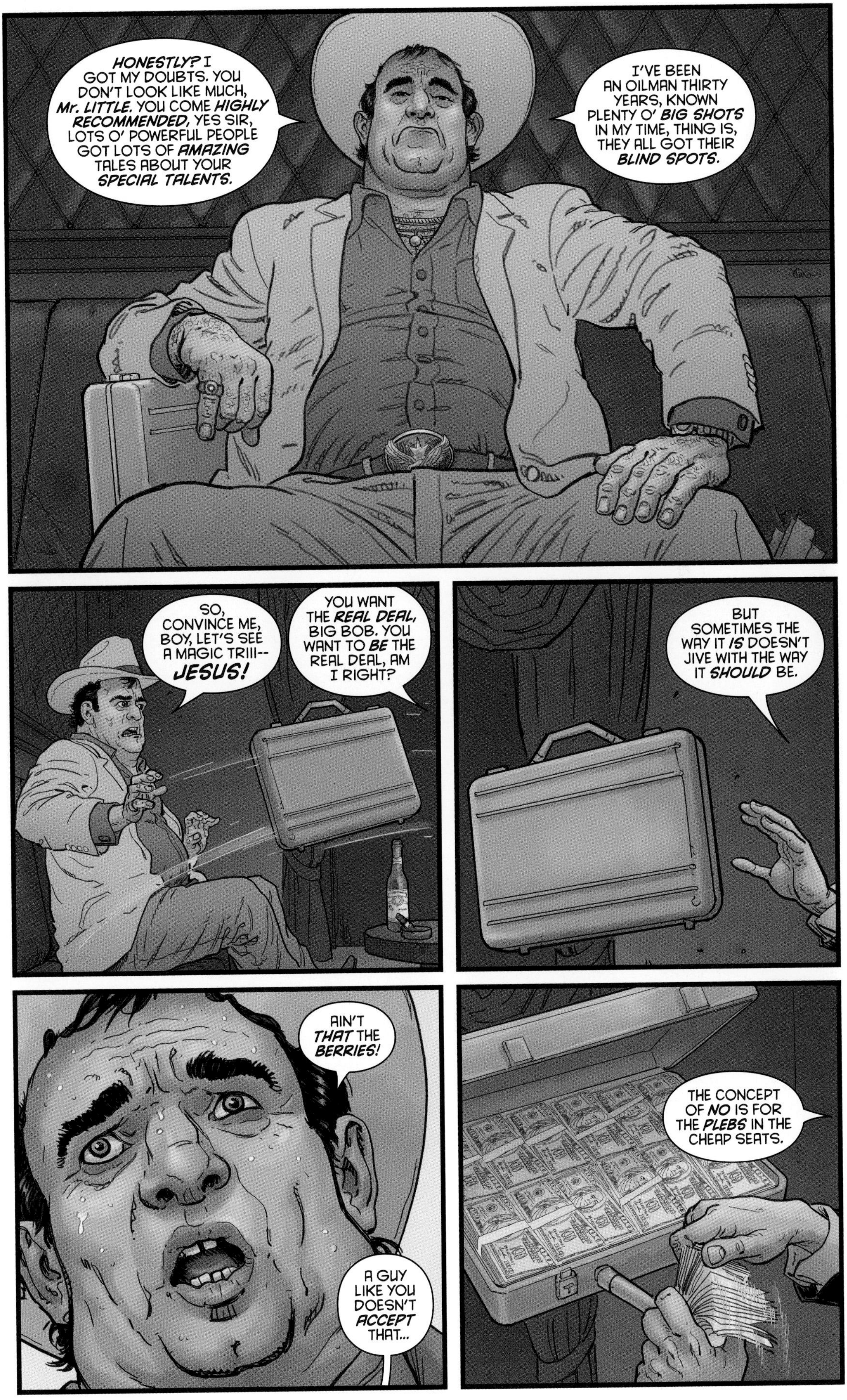
HONESTLY? I GOT MY DOUBTS. YOU DON'T LOOK LIKE MUCH, Mr. LITTLE. YOU COME HIGHLY RECOMMENDED, YES SIR, LOTS O' POWERFUL PEOPLE GOT LOTS OF AMAZING TALES ABOUT YOUR SPECIAL TALENTS.
I'VE BEEN AN OILMAN THIRTY YEARS, KNOWN PLENTY O' BIG SHOTS IN MY TIME, THING IS, THEY ALL GOT THEIR BLIND SPOTS.
SO, CONVINCE ME, BOY, LET'S SEE A MAGIC TRIII-- JESUS!
YOU WANT THE REAL DEAL, BIG BOB. YOU WANT TO BE THE REAL DEAL, AM I RIGHT?
BUT SOMETIMES THE WAY IT IS DOESN'T JIVE WITH THE WAY IT SHOULD BE.
AIN'T THAT THE BERRIES!
A GUY LIKE YOU DOESN'T ACCEPT THAT...
THE CONCEPT OF NO IS FOR THE PLEBS IN THE CHEAP SEATS.

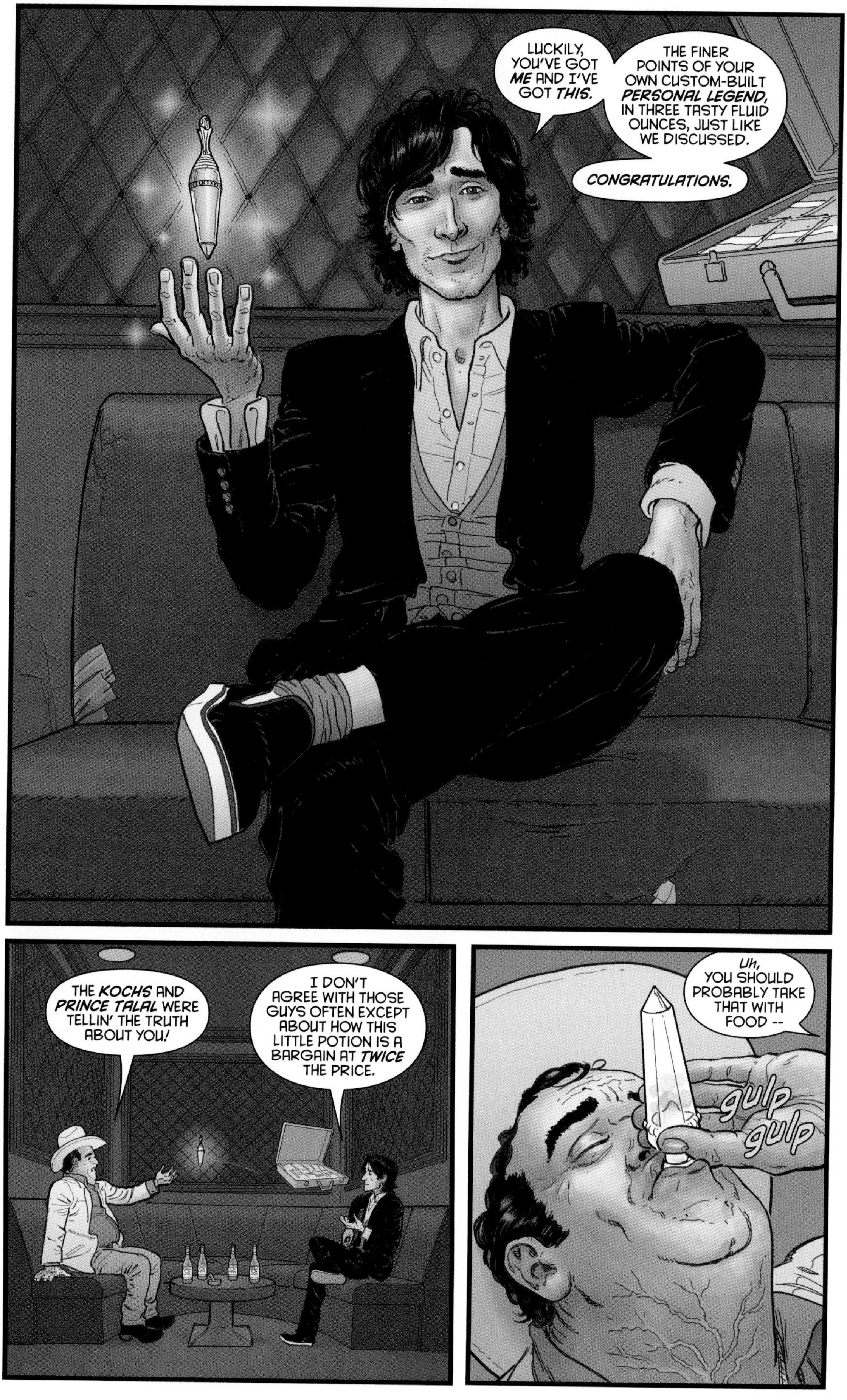
LUCKILY, YOU'VE GOT ME AND I'VE GOT THIS.
THE FINER POINTS OF YOUR OWN CUSTOM-BUILT PERSONAL LEGEND, IN THREE TASTY FLUID OUNCES, JUST LIKE WE DISCUSSED.
CONGRATULATIONS.
THE KOCHS AND PRINCE TALAL WERE TELLIN' THE TRUTH ABOUT YOU!
I DON'T AGREE WITH THOSE GUYS OFTEN EXCEPT ABOUT HOW THIS LITTLE POTION IS A BARGAIN AT TWICE THE PRICE.
UH, YOU SHOULD PROBABLY TAKE THAT WITH FOOD --
gulp gulp

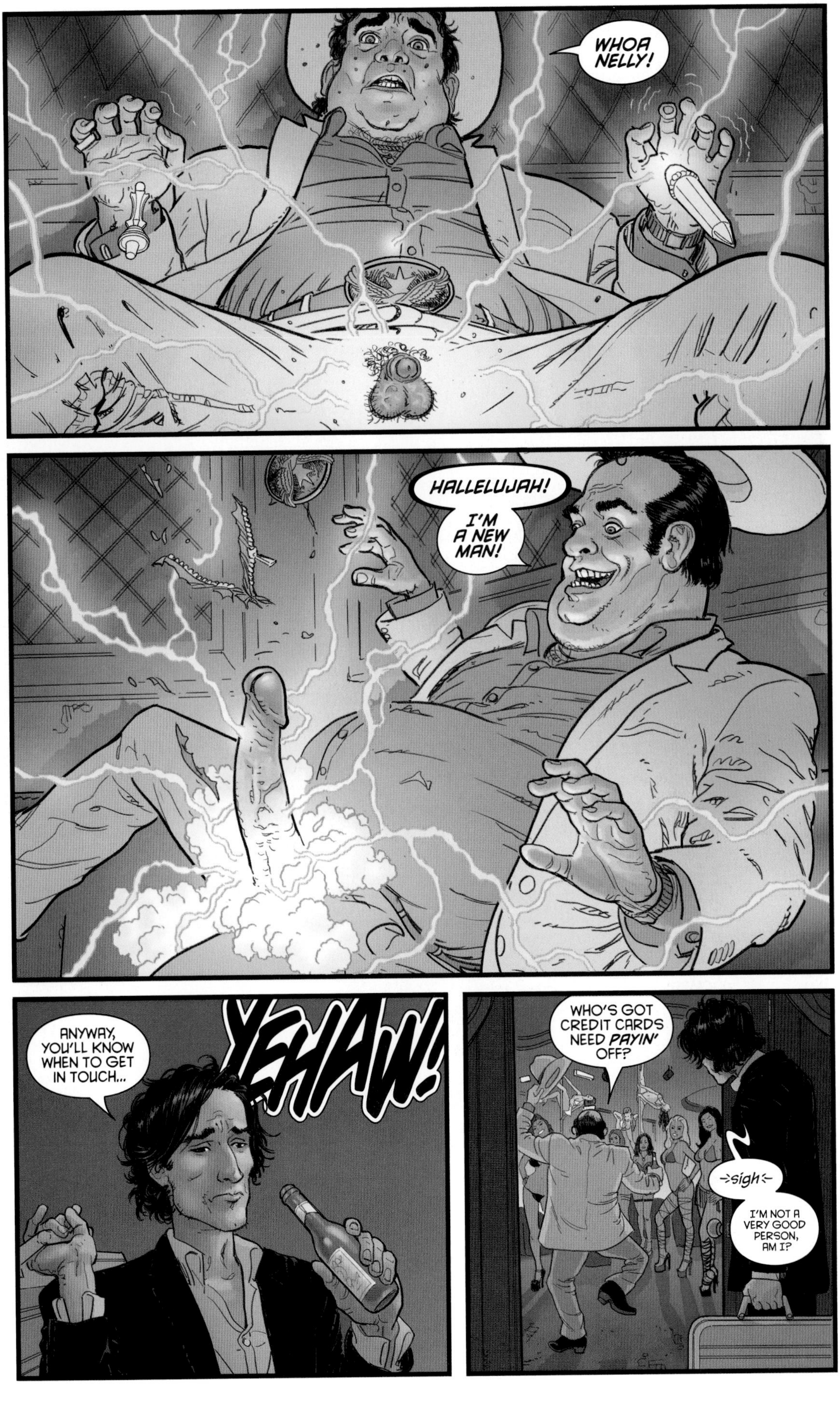
WHOA NELLY!
HALLELUJAH!
I'M A NEW MAN!
ANYWAY, YOU'LL KNOW WHEN TO GET IN TOUCH...
YEHAW!
WHO'S GOT CREDIT CARDS NEED *PAYIN'* OFF?
sigh
I'M NOT A VERY GOOD PERSON, AM I?

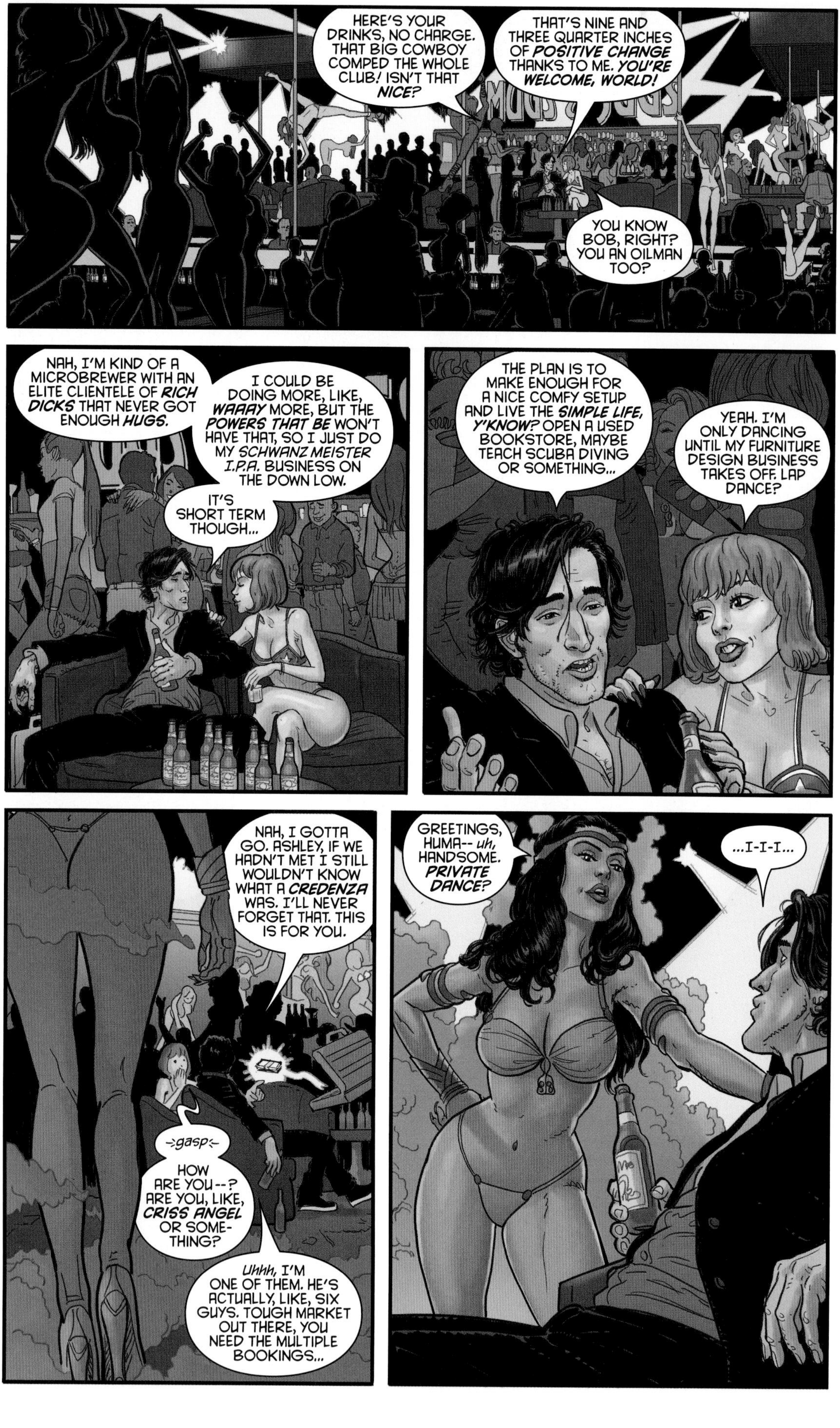
HERE'S YOUR DRINKS, NO CHARGE. THAT BIG COWBOY COMPED THE WHOLE CLUB! ISN'T THAT NICE?
THAT'S NINE AND THREE QUARTER INCHES OF POSITIVE CHANGE THANKS TO ME. YOU'RE WELCOME, WORLD!
YOU KNOW BOB, RIGHT? YOU AN OILMAN TOO?
NAH, I'M KIND OF A MICROBREWER WITH AN ELITE CLIENTELE OF RICH DICKS THAT NEVER GOT ENOUGH HUGS.
I COULD BE DOING MORE, LIKE, WAAAY MORE, BUT THE POWERS THAT BE WON'T HAVE THAT, SO I JUST DO MY SCHWANZ MEISTER I.P.A. BUSINESS ON THE DOWN LOW.
IT'S SHORT TERM THOUGH...
THE PLAN IS TO MAKE ENOUGH FOR A NICE COMFY SETUP AND LIVE THE SIMPLE LIFE, Y'KNOW? OPEN A USED BOOKSTORE, MAYBE TEACH SCUBA DIVING OR SOMETHING...
YEAH. I'M ONLY DANCING UNTIL MY FURNITURE DESIGN BUSINESS TAKES OFF. LAP DANCE?
NAH, I GOTTA GO. ASHLEY, IF WE HADN'T MET I STILL WOULDN'T KNOW WHAT A CREDENZA WAS. I'LL NEVER FORGET THAT. THIS IS FOR YOU.
-gasp-
HOW ARE YOU --? ARE YOU, LIKE, CRISS ANGEL OR SOME-THING?
Uhhh, I'M ONE OF THEM. HE'S ACTUALLY, LIKE, SIX GUYS. TOUGH MARKET OUT THERE, YOU NEED THE MULTIPLE BOOKINGS...
GREETINGS, HUMA-- uh, HANDSOME. PRIVATE DANCE?
...I-I-I...

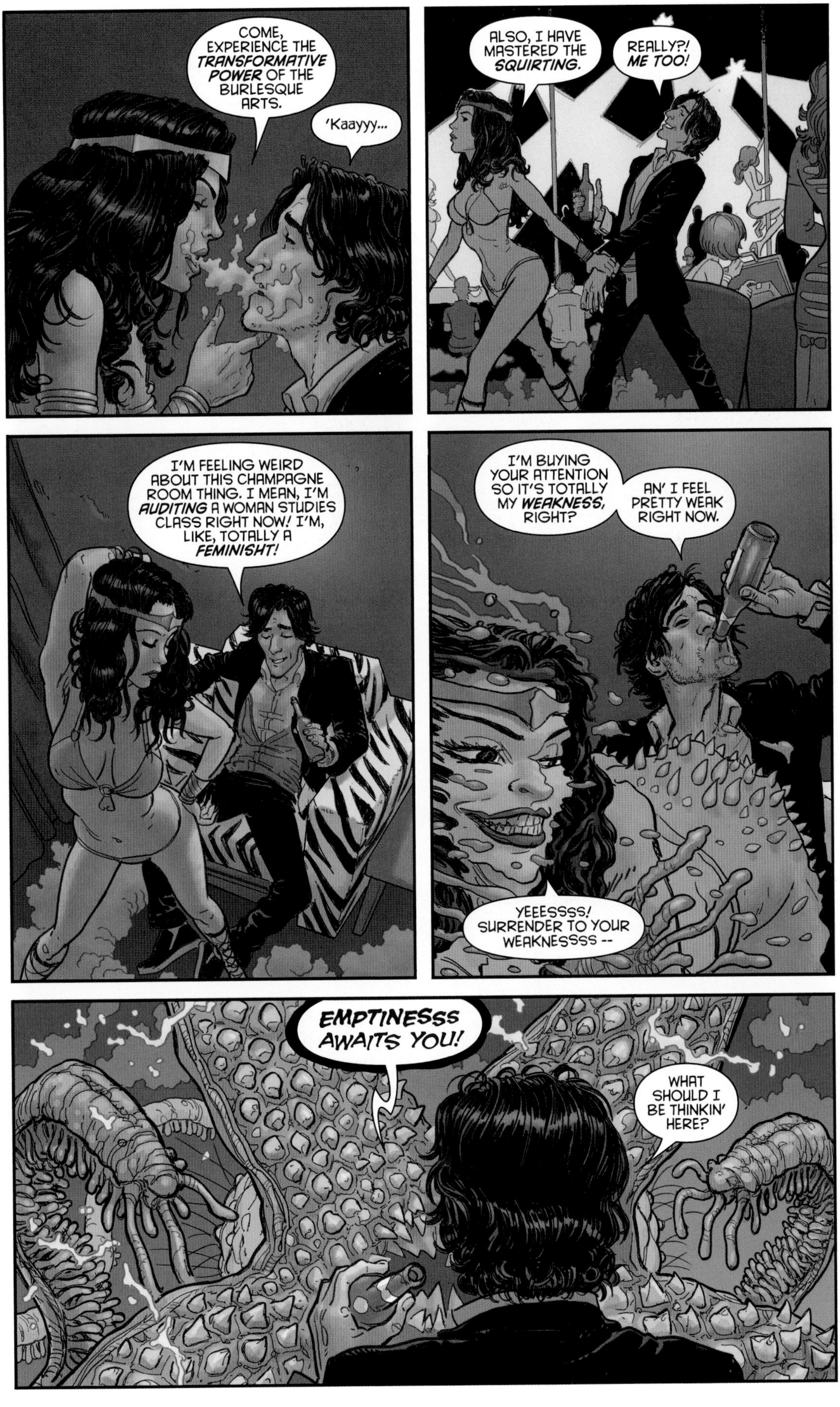
COME, EXPERIENCE THE TRANSFORMATIVE POWER OF THE BURLESQUE ARTS.
'Kaayyy...
ALSO, I HAVE MASTERED THE SQUIRTING.
REALLY?! ME TOO!
I'M FEELING WEIRD ABOUT THIS CHAMPAGNE ROOM THING. I MEAN, I'M AUDITING A WOMAN STUDIES CLASS RIGHT NOW! I'M, LIKE, TOTALLY A FEMINISHT!
I'M BUYING YOUR ATTENTION SO IT'S TOTALLY MY WEAKNESS, RIGHT?
AN' I FEEL PRETTY WEAK RIGHT NOW.
YEEESSSS! SURRENDER TO YOUR WEAKNESSSS --
EMPTINESSS AWAITS YOU!
WHAT SHOULD I BE THINKIN' HERE?

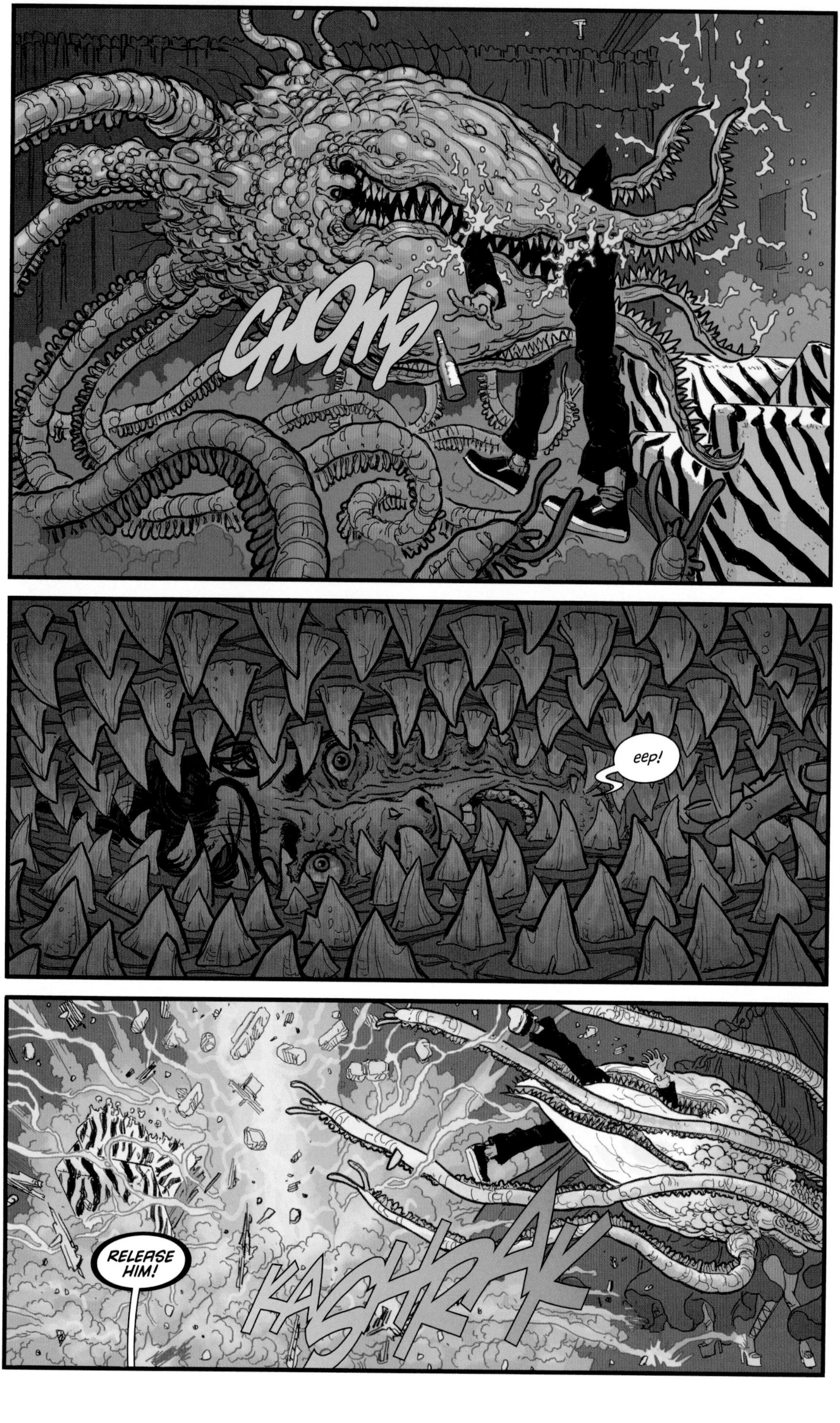
CHOMP
eep!
RELEASE HIM!
KASHRAK

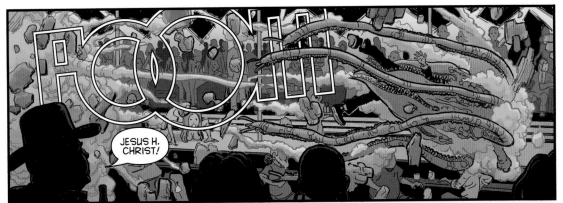

JESUS H. CHRIST!

-gurgle-

Hngg!

GET AWAY FROM MY SON!

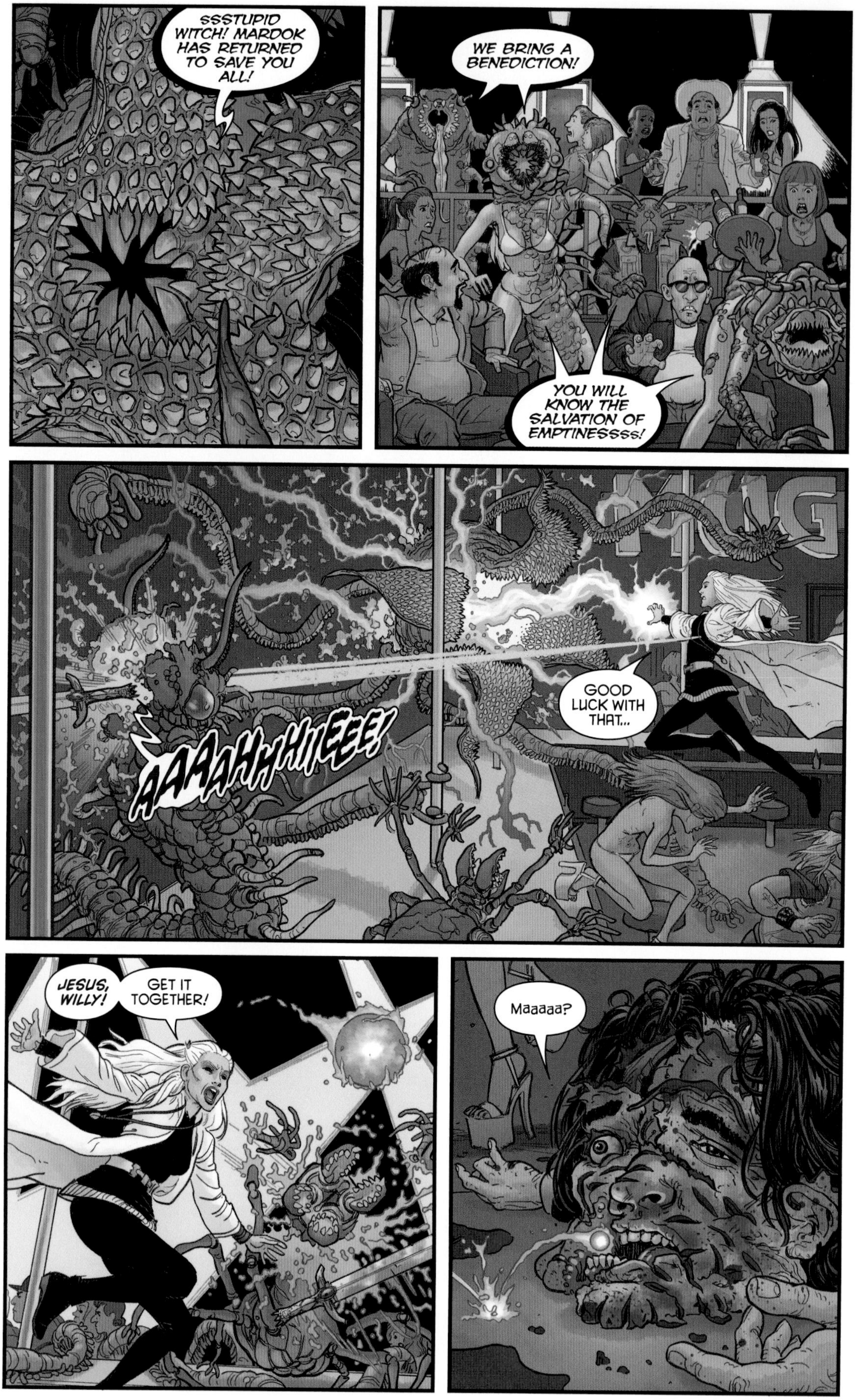
SSSTUPID WITCH! MARDOK HAS RETURNED TO SAVE YOU ALL!
WE BRING A BENEDICTION!
YOU WILL KNOW THE SALVATION OF EMPTINESSsss!
AAAAHHHIIEEE!
GOOD LUCK WITH THAT...
JESUS, WILLY!
GET IT TOGETHER!
Maaaaa?

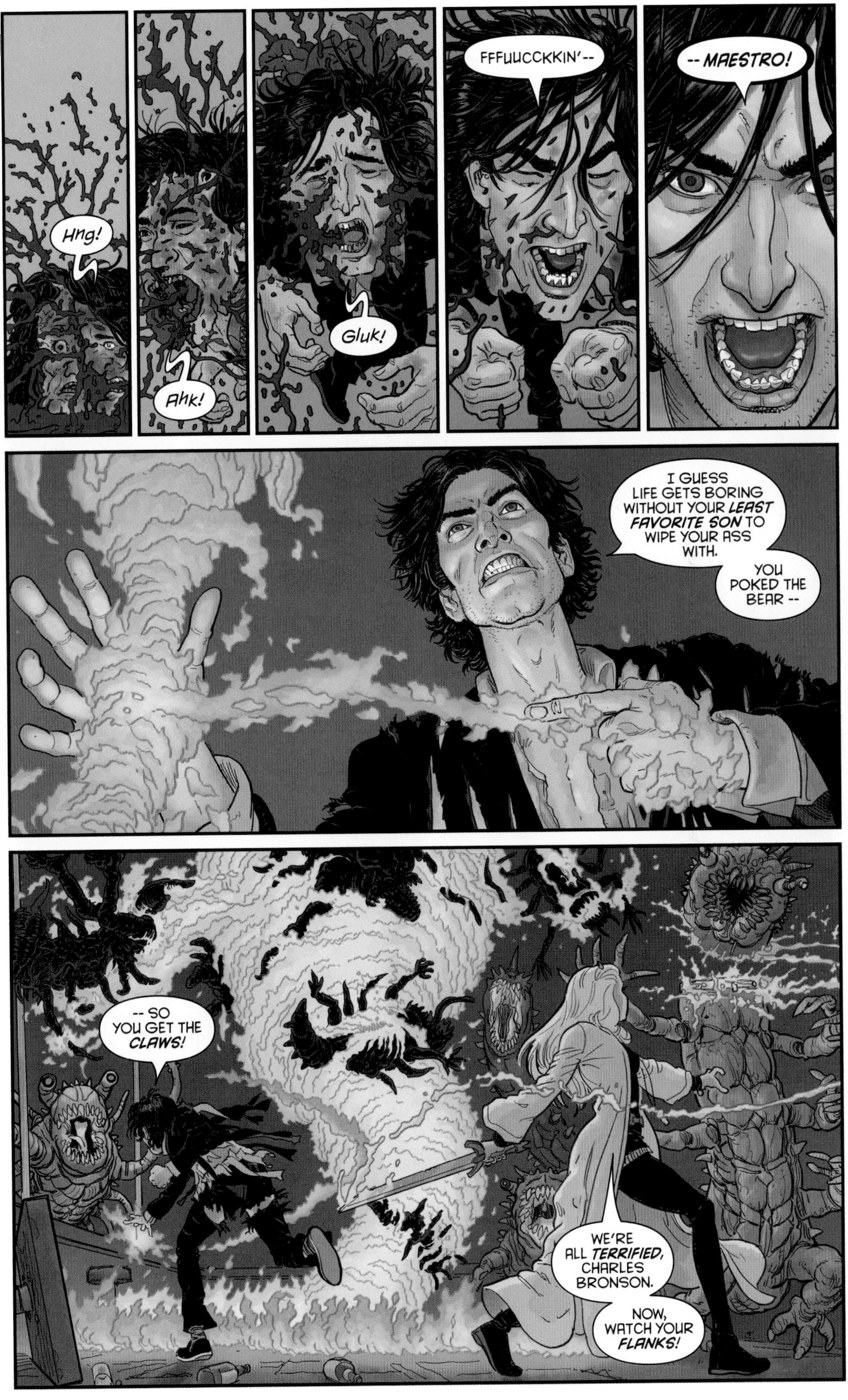

Hng!
Ahk!
Gluk!
FFFUUCCKKIN'--
-- MAESTRO!
I GUESS LIFE GETS BORING WITHOUT YOUR LEAST FAVORITE SON TO WIPE YOUR ASS WITH.
YOU POKED THE BEAR --
-- SO YOU GET THE CLAWS!
WE'RE ALL TERRIFIED, CHARLES BRONSON.
NOW, WATCH YOUR FLANKS!

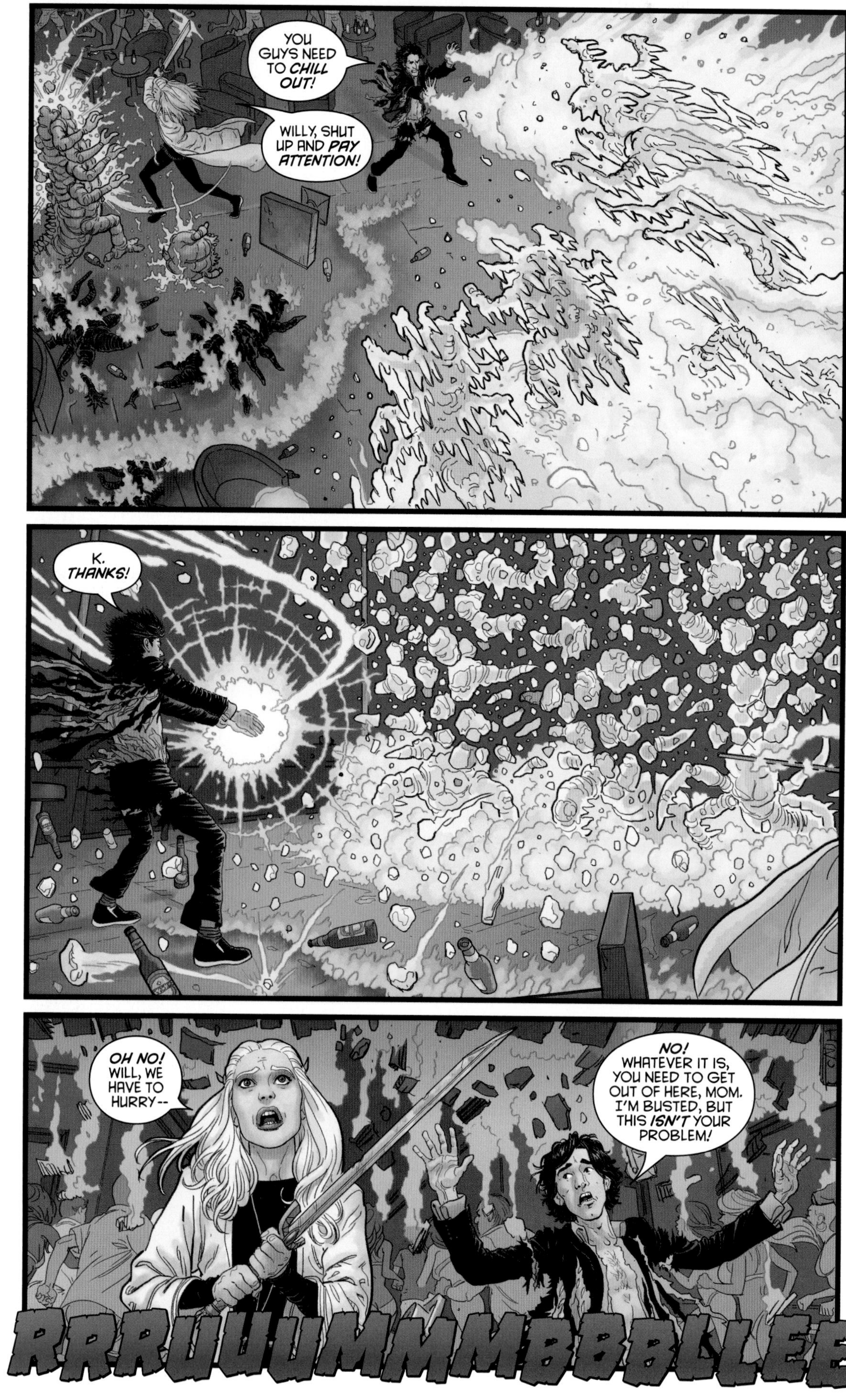
YOU GUYS NEED TO CHILL OUT!
WILLY, SHUT UP AND PAY ATTENTION!
K. THANKS!
OH NO! WILL, WE HAVE TO HURRY--
NO! WHATEVER IT IS, YOU NEED TO GET OUT OF HERE, MOM. I'M BUSTED, BUT THIS ISN'T YOUR PROBLEM!
RRRUUUMMMBBBLLEE

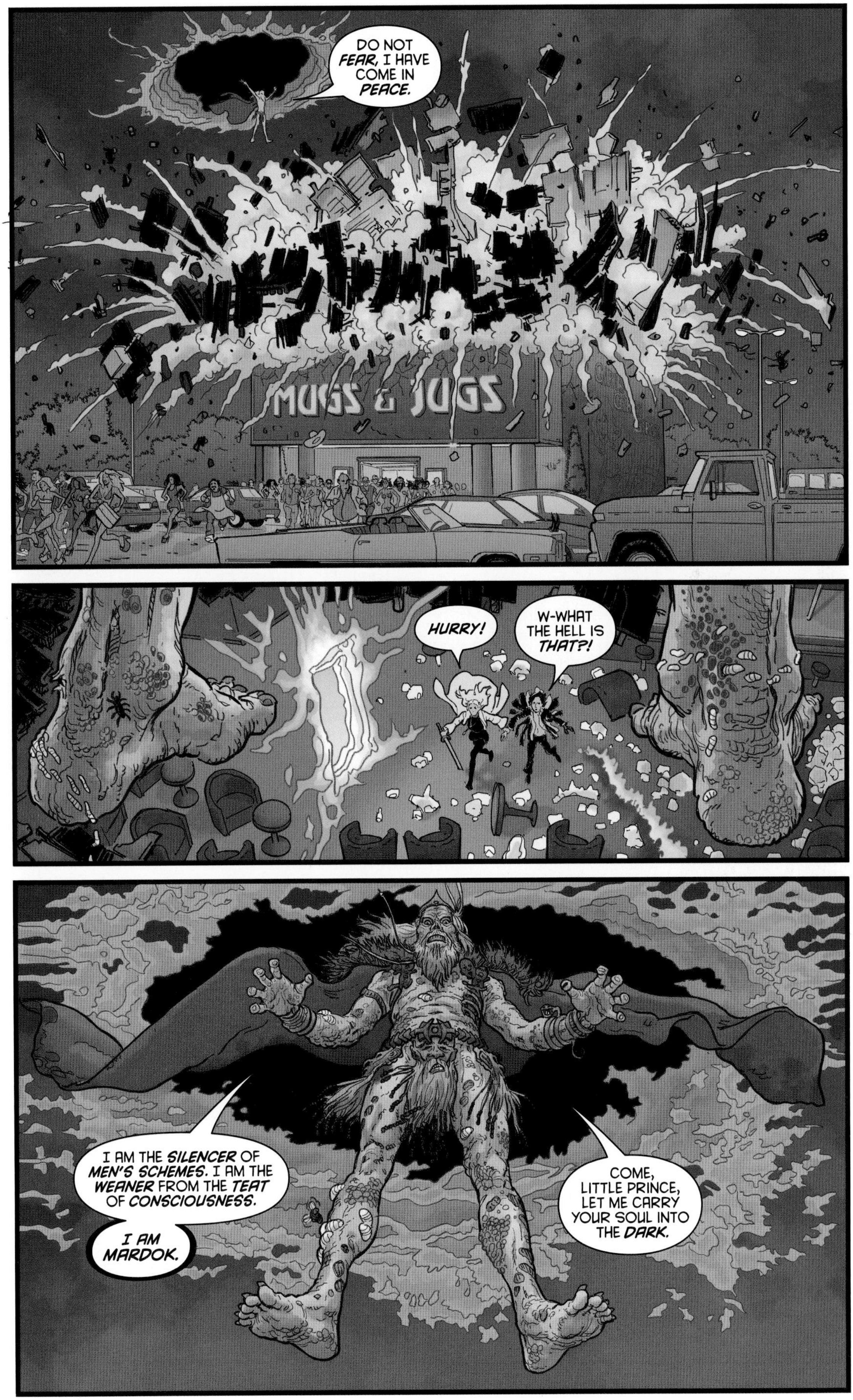
DO NOT FEAR, I HAVE COME IN PEACE.
MUGS & JUGS
HURRY!
W-WHAT THE HELL IS THAT?!
I AM THE SILENCER OF MEN'S SCHEMES. I AM THE WEANER FROM THE TEAT OF CONSCIOUSNESS.
I AM MARDOK.
COME, LITTLE PRINCE, LET ME CARRY YOUR SOUL INTO THE DARK.

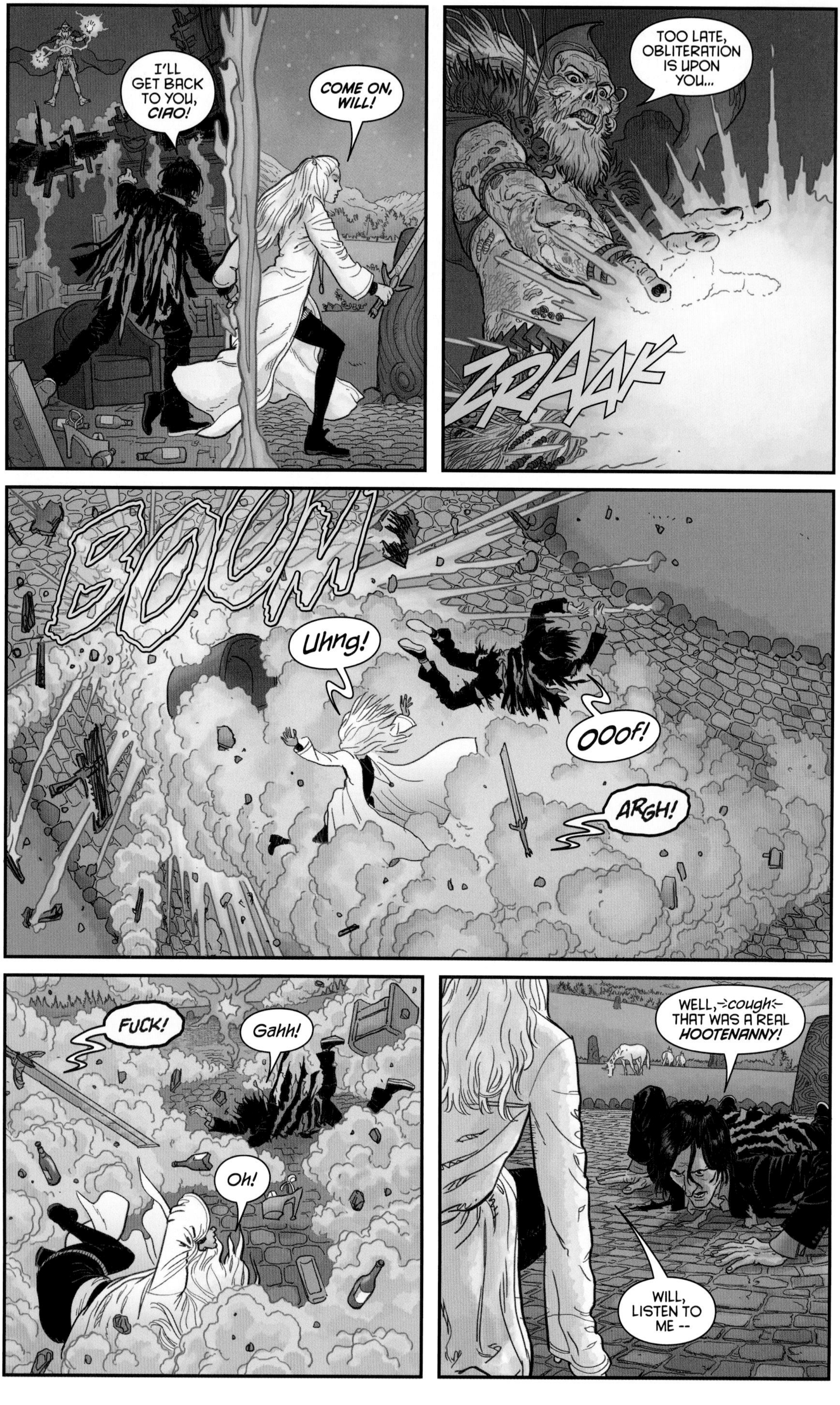
I'LL GET BACK TO YOU, *CIAO!*
COME ON, WILL!
TOO LATE, OBLITERATION IS UPON YOU...
ZRAAK
BOOM
Uhng!
OOOf!
ARGH!
FUCK!
Gahh!
Oh!
WELL, cough THAT WAS A REAL *HOOTENANNY!*
WILL, LISTEN TO ME --

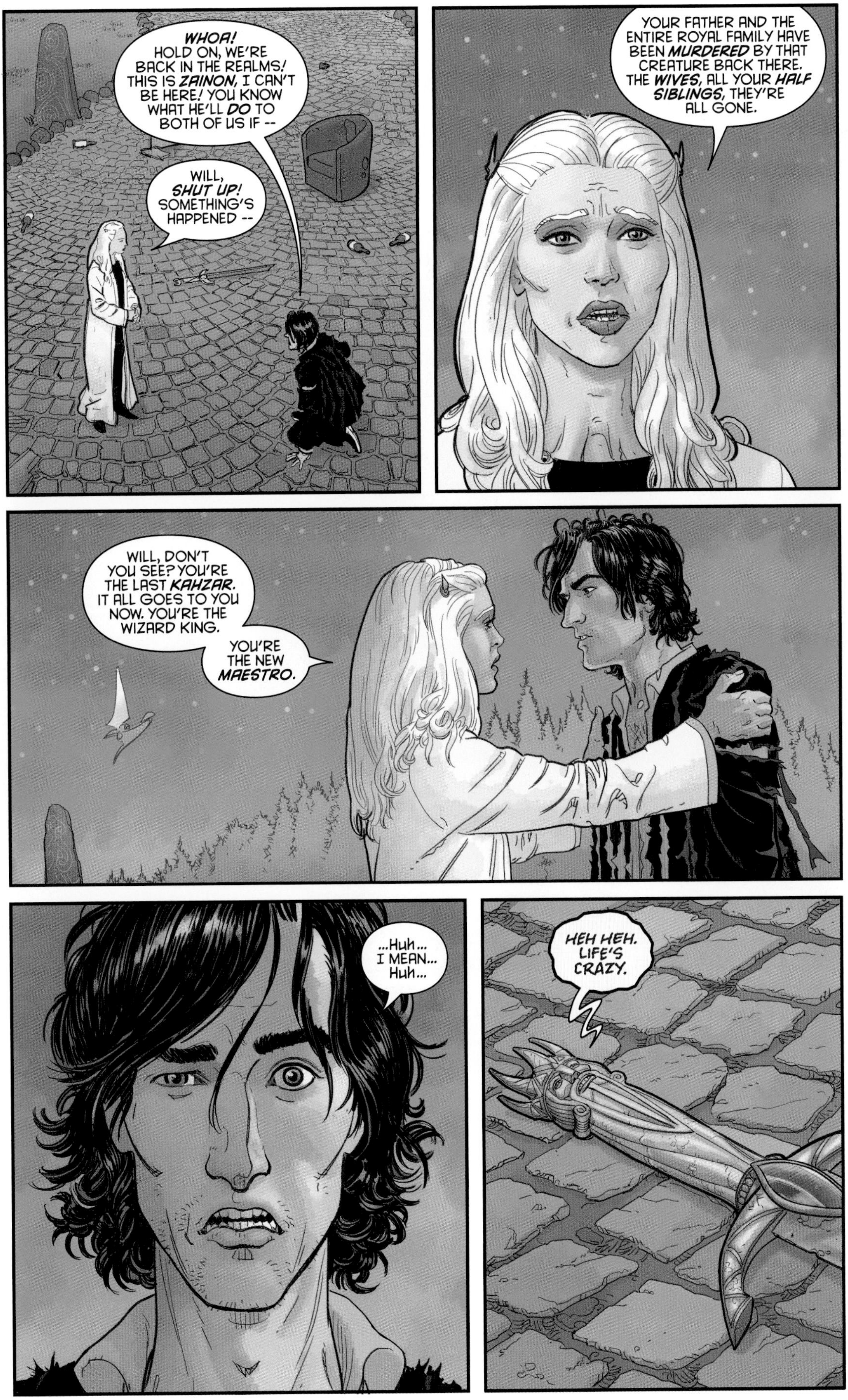
WHOA! HOLD ON, WE'RE BACK IN THE REALMS! THIS IS ZAINON, I CAN'T BE HERE! YOU KNOW WHAT HE'LL DO TO BOTH OF US IF --
WILL, SHUT UP! SOMETHING'S HAPPENED --
YOUR FATHER AND THE ENTIRE ROYAL FAMILY HAVE BEEN MURDERED BY THAT CREATURE BACK THERE. THE WIVES, ALL YOUR HALF SIBLINGS, THEY'RE ALL GONE.
WILL, DON'T YOU SEE? YOU'RE THE LAST KAHZAR. IT ALL GOES TO YOU NOW. YOU'RE THE WIZARD KING.
YOU'RE THE NEW MAESTRO.
...Huh... I MEAN... Huh...
HEH HEH. LIFE'S CRAZY.

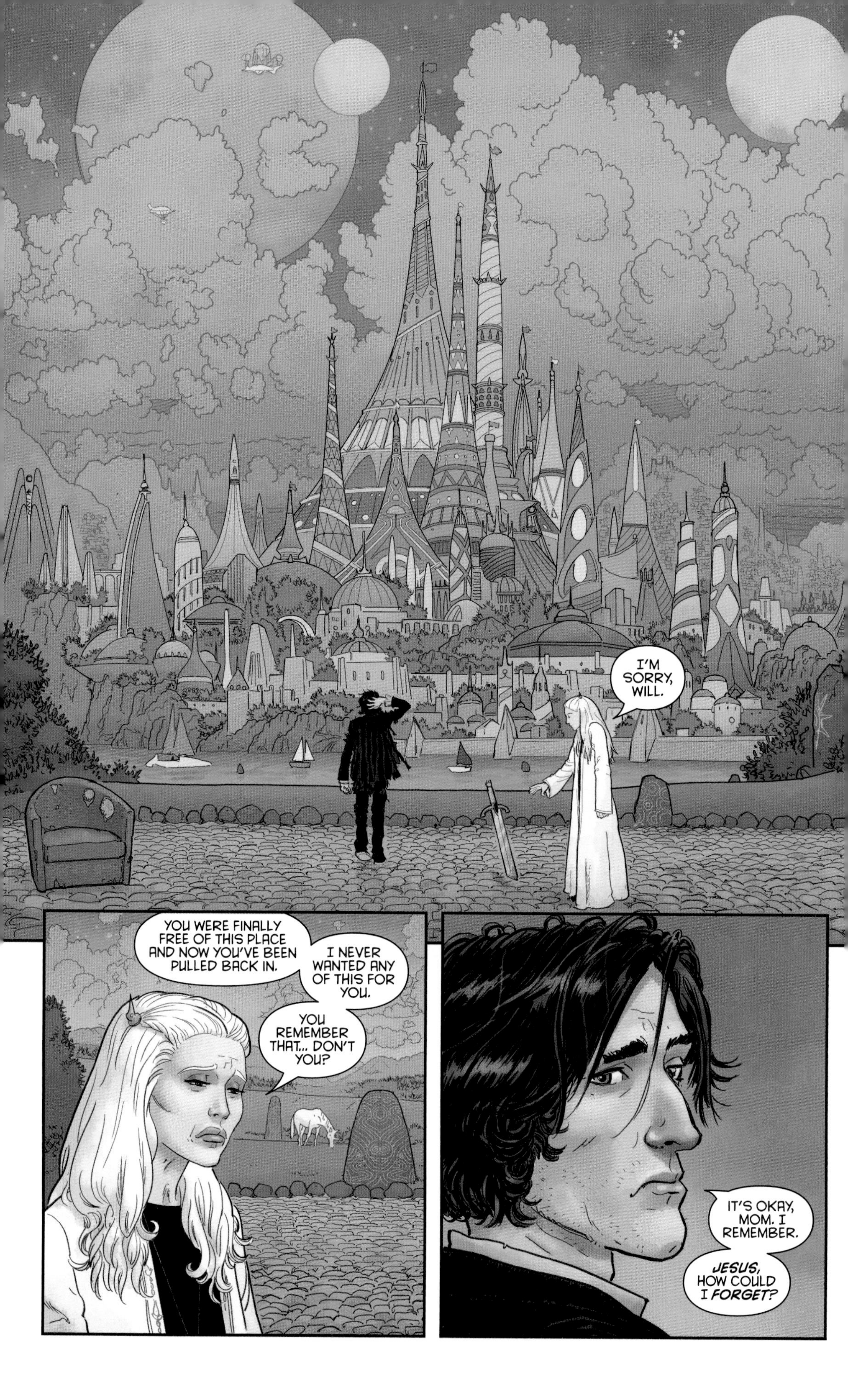
I'M SORRY, WILL.
YOU WERE FINALLY FREE OF THIS PLACE AND NOW YOU'VE BEEN PULLED BACK IN.
I NEVER WANTED ANY OF THIS FOR YOU.
YOU REMEMBER THAT... DON'T YOU?
IT'S OKAY, MOM. I REMEMBER.
JESUS, HOW COULD I *FORGET*?

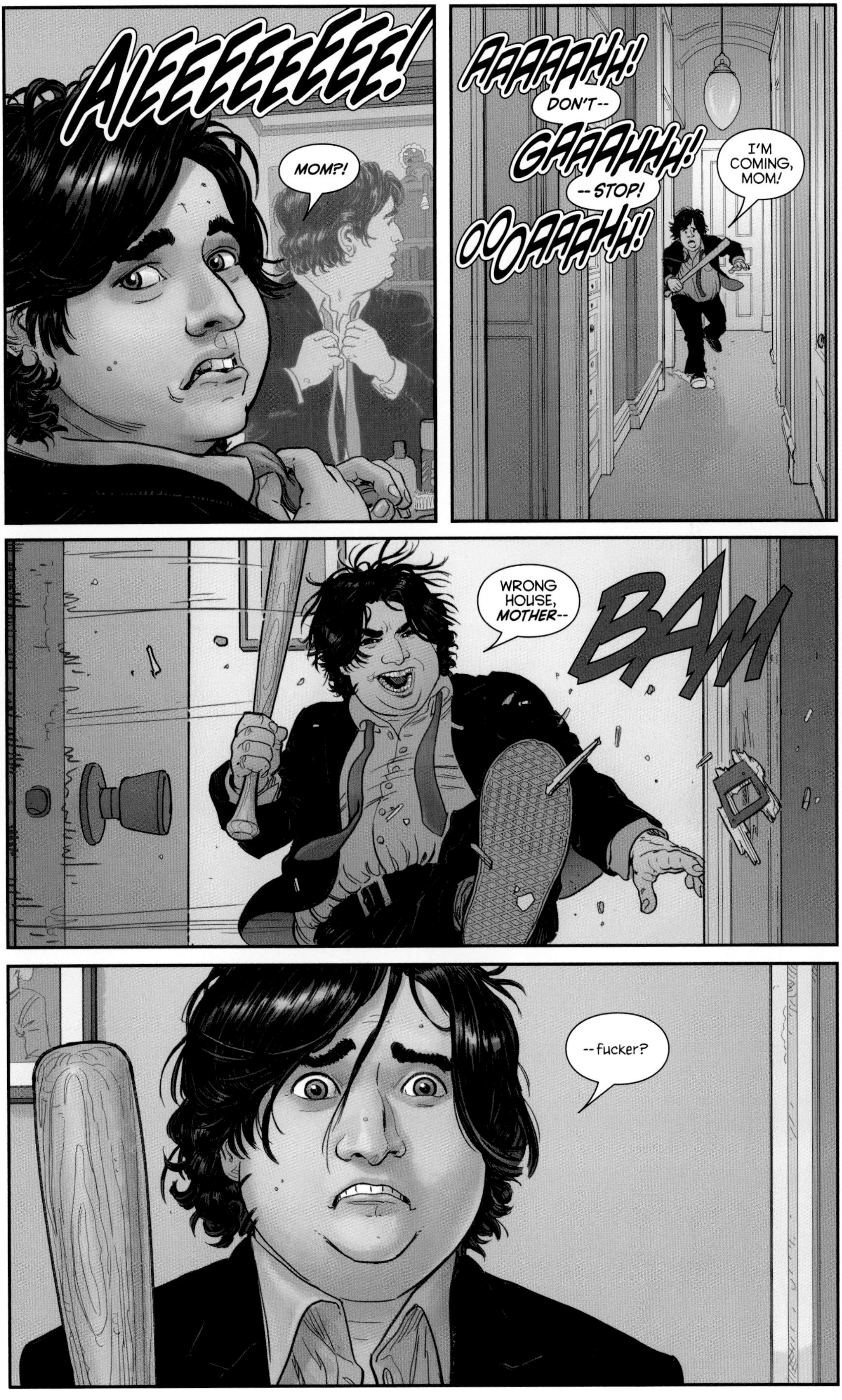
AIEEEEEEEEE!
MOM?!
AAAAAHH!
DON'T--
GAAAHHH!
--STOP!
OOOAAAAHH!
I'M COMING, MOM!
WRONG HOUSE, MOTHER--
BAM
--fucker?

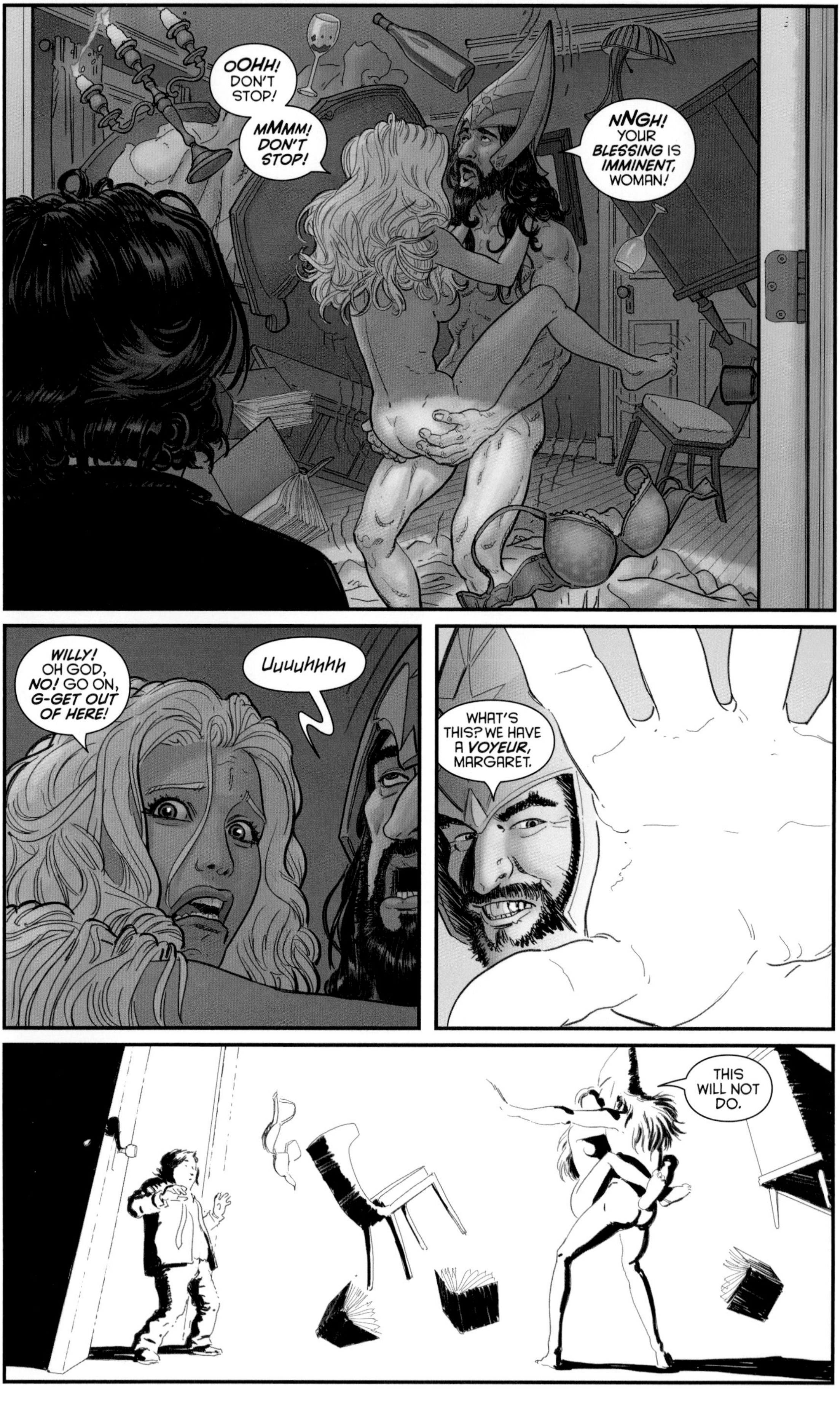
OOHH! DON'T STOP!
MMMM! DON'T STOP!
NNGH! YOUR BLESSING IS IMMINENT, WOMAN!
WILLY! OH GOD, NO! GO ON, G-GET OUT OF HERE!
Uuuuhhhh
WHAT'S THIS? WE HAVE A VOYEUR, MARGARET.
THIS WILL NOT DO.

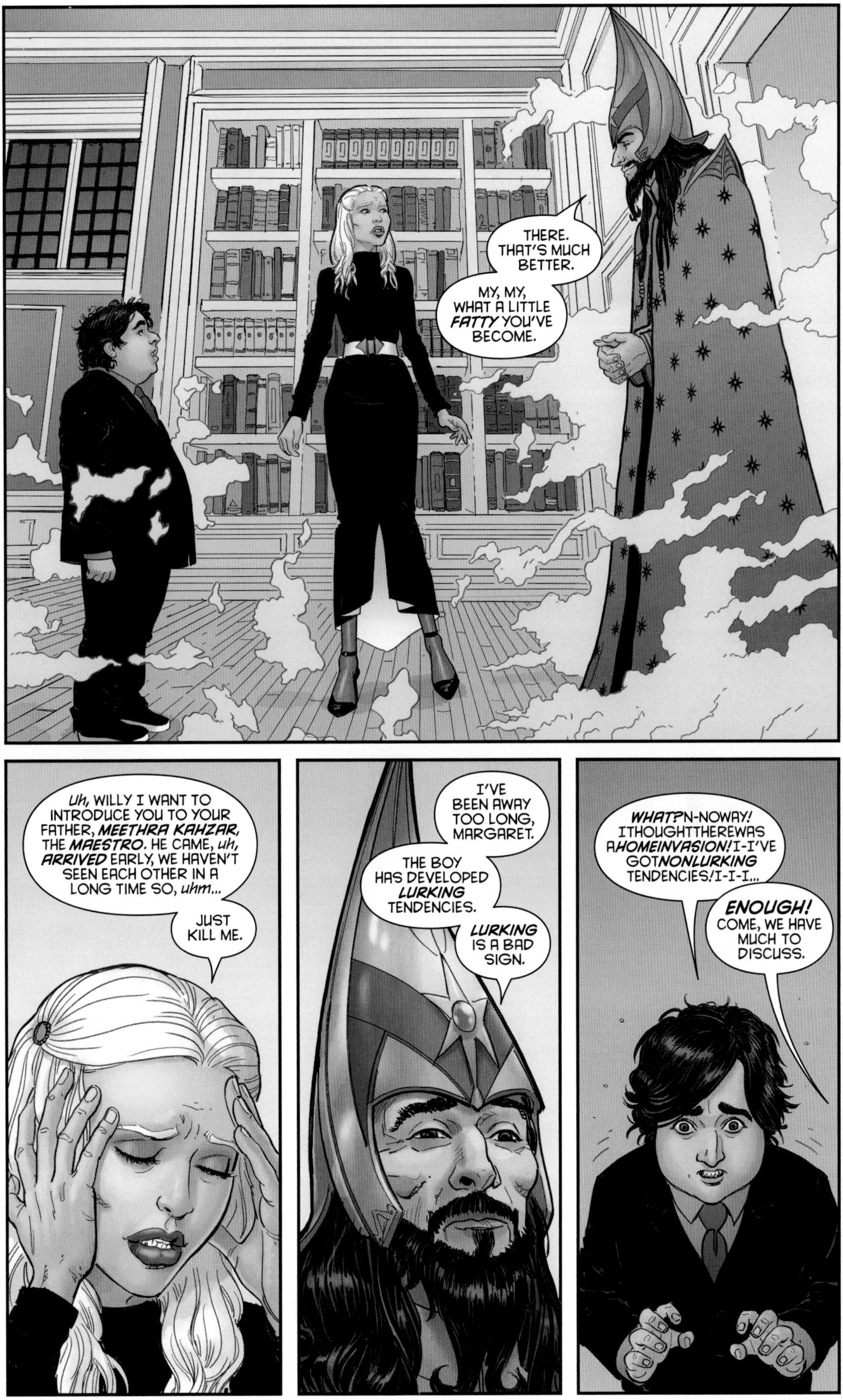

THERE. THAT'S MUCH BETTER.
MY, MY, WHAT A LITTLE FATTY YOU'VE BECOME.
UH, WILLY I WANT TO INTRODUCE YOU TO YOUR FATHER, MEETHRA KAHZAR, THE MAESTRO. HE CAME, UH, ARRIVED EARLY, WE HAVEN'T SEEN EACH OTHER IN A LONG TIME SO, UHM...
JUST KILL ME.
I'VE BEEN AWAY TOO LONG, MARGARET.
THE BOY HAS DEVELOPED LURKING TENDENCIES.
LURKING IS A BAD SIGN.
WHAT?N-NOWAY! ITHOUGHTTHEREWAS AHOMEINVASION!I-I'VE GOTNONLURKING TENDENCIES!I-I-I...
ENOUGH! COME, WE HAVE MUCH TO DISCUSS.

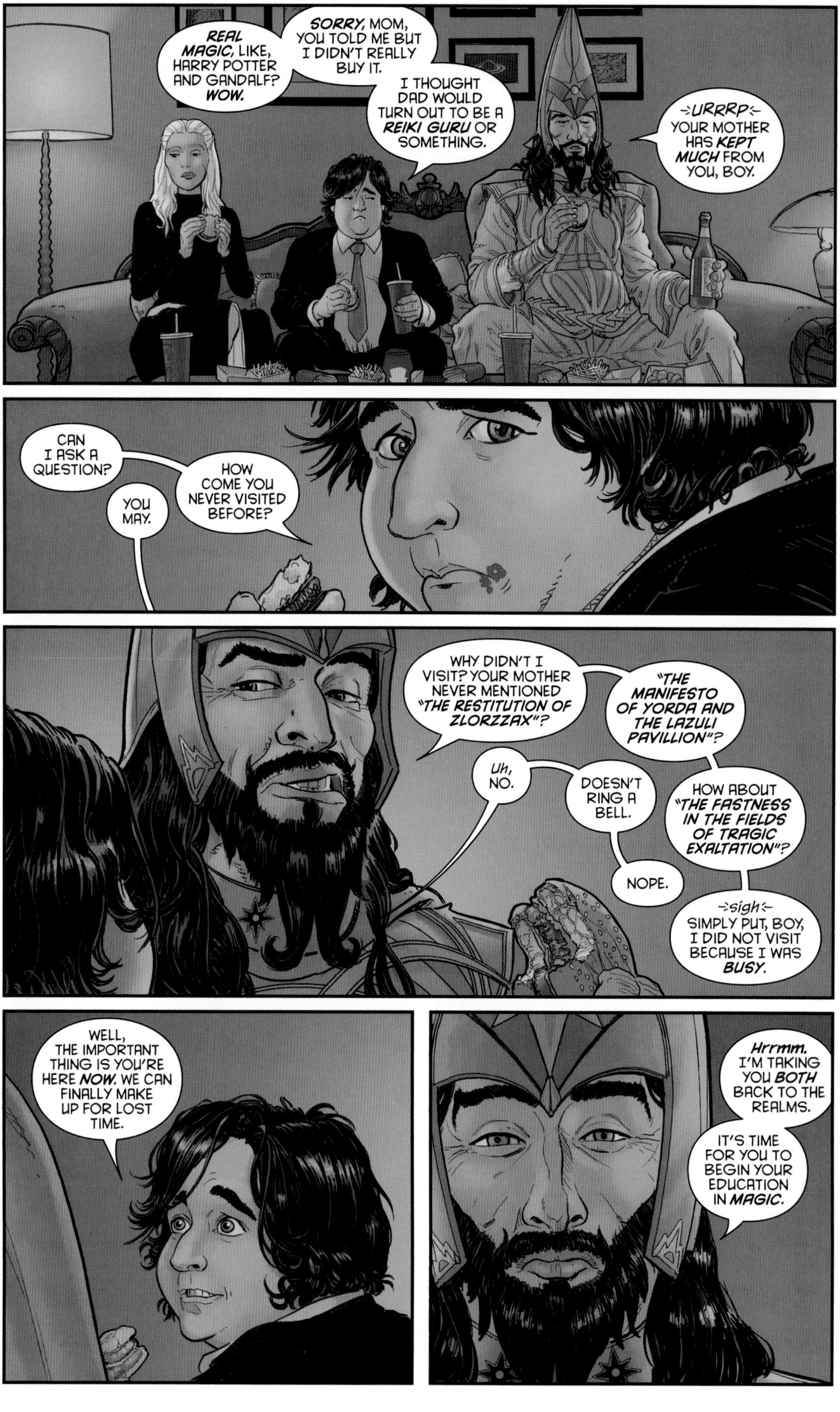
REAL MAGIC, LIKE, HARRY POTTER AND GANDALF? WOW.
SORRY, MOM, YOU TOLD ME BUT I DIDN'T REALLY BUY IT.
I THOUGHT DAD WOULD TURN OUT TO BE A REIKI GURU OR SOMETHING.
URRRP
YOUR MOTHER HAS KEPT MUCH FROM YOU, BOY.
CAN I ASK A QUESTION?
YOU MAY.
HOW COME YOU NEVER VISITED BEFORE?
WHY DIDN'T I VISIT? YOUR MOTHER NEVER MENTIONED "THE RESTITUTION OF ZLORZZAX"?
UH, NO.
"THE MANIFESTO OF YORDA AND THE LAZULI PAVILLION"?
DOESN'T RING A BELL.
HOW ABOUT "THE FASTNESS IN THE FIELDS OF TRAGIC EXALTATION"?
NOPE.
sigh
SIMPLY PUT, BOY, I DID NOT VISIT BECAUSE I WAS BUSY.
WELL, THE IMPORTANT THING IS YOU'RE HERE NOW. WE CAN FINALLY MAKE UP FOR LOST TIME.
Hrrmm. I'M TAKING YOU BOTH BACK TO THE REALMS.
IT'S TIME FOR YOU TO BEGIN YOUR EDUCATION IN MAGIC.

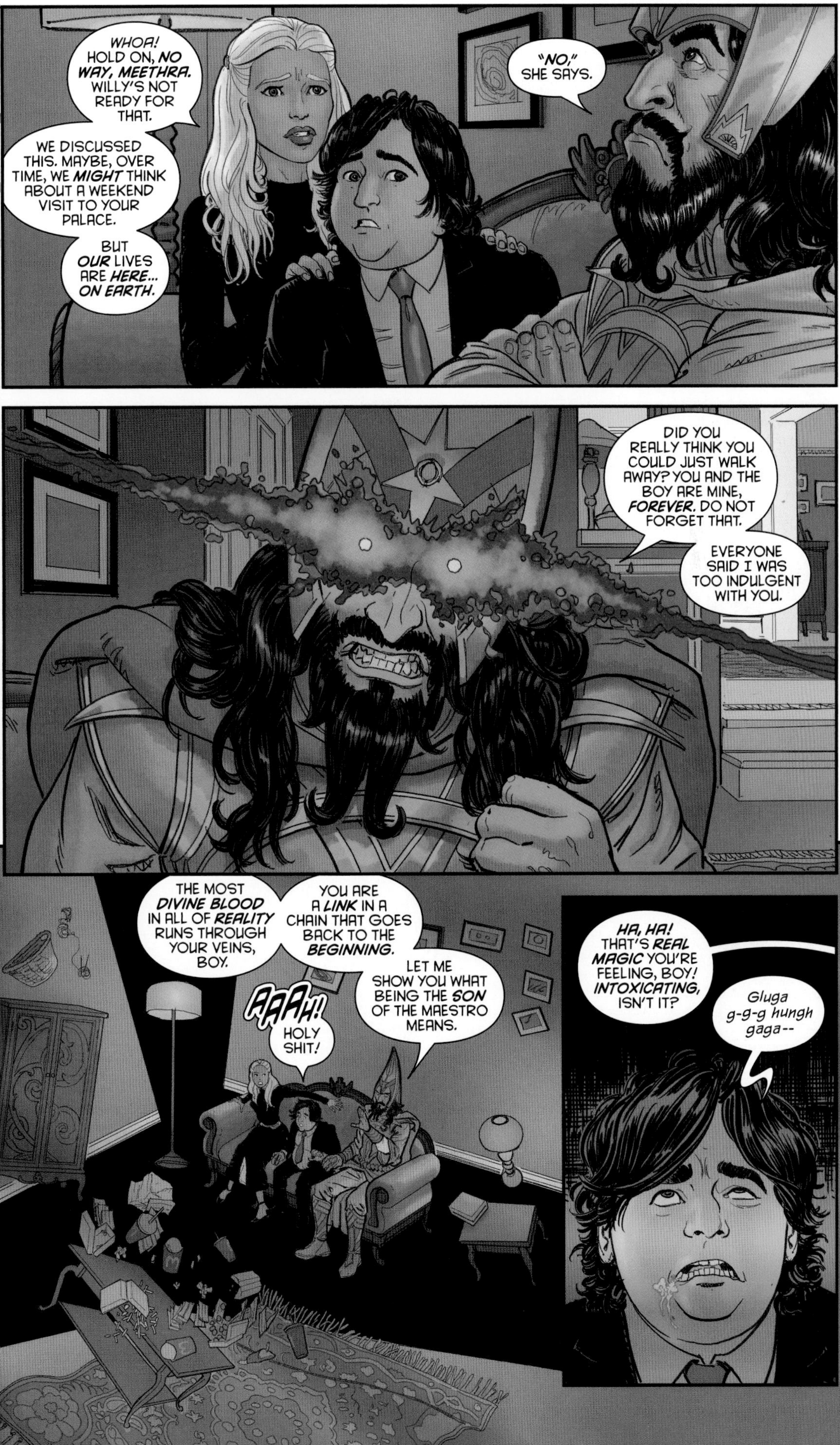
WHOA! HOLD ON, NO WAY, MEETHRA. WILLY'S NOT READY FOR THAT.
WE DISCUSSED THIS. MAYBE, OVER TIME, WE MIGHT THINK ABOUT A WEEKEND VISIT TO YOUR PALACE.
BUT OUR LIVES ARE HERE... ON EARTH.
"NO," SHE SAYS.
DID YOU REALLY THINK YOU COULD JUST WALK AWAY? YOU AND THE BOY ARE MINE, FOREVER. DO NOT FORGET THAT.
EVERYONE SAID I WAS TOO INDULGENT WITH YOU.
THE MOST DIVINE BLOOD IN ALL OF REALITY RUNS THROUGH YOUR VEINS, BOY.
YOU ARE A LINK IN A CHAIN THAT GOES BACK TO THE BEGINNING.
LET ME SHOW YOU WHAT BEING THE SON OF THE MAESTRO MEANS.
AAAH! HOLY SHIT!
HA, HA! THAT'S REAL MAGIC YOU'RE FEELING, BOY! INTOXICATING, ISN'T IT?
Gluga g-g-g hungh gaga--

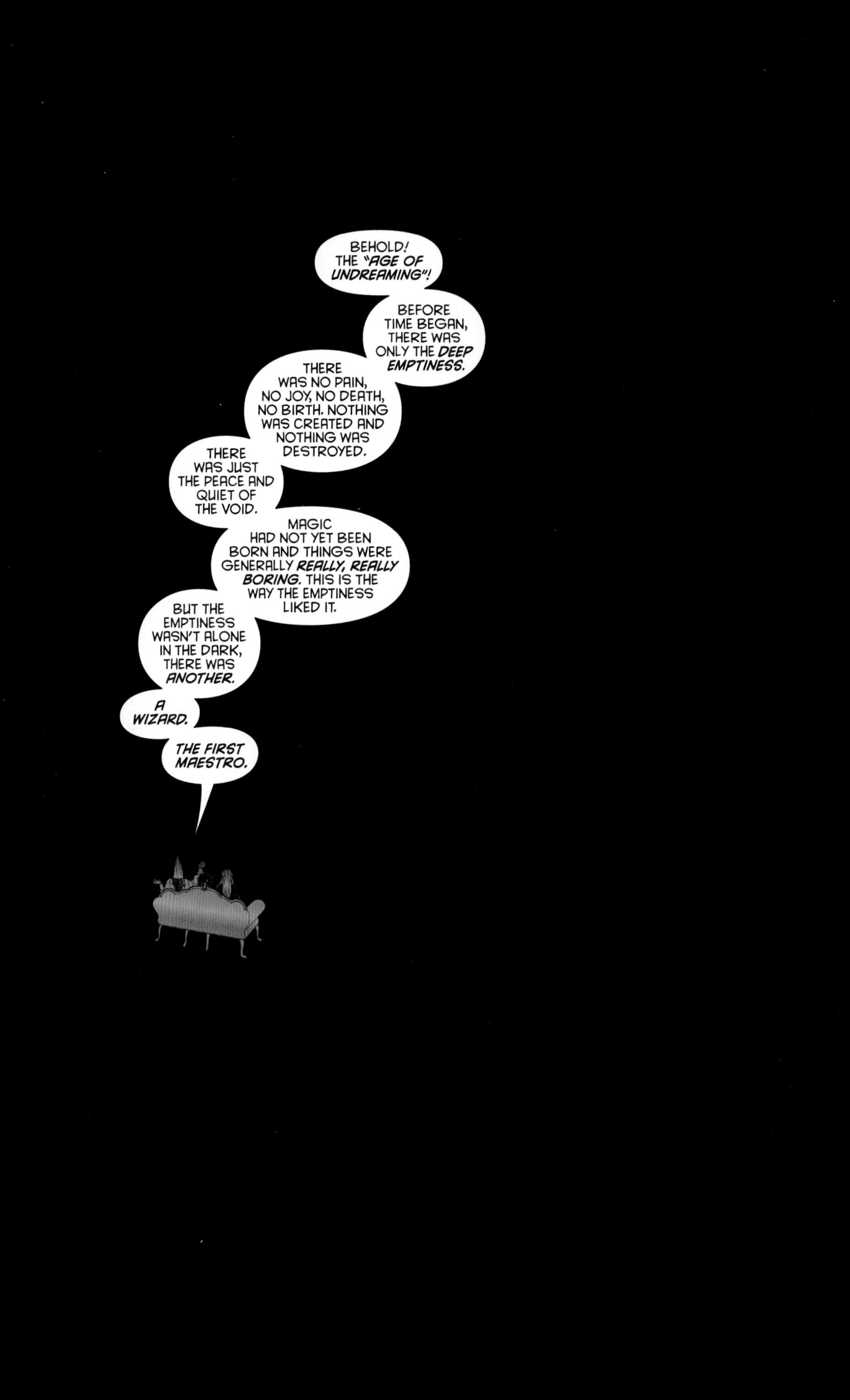
BEHOLD! THE "AGE OF UNDREAMING"!
BEFORE TIME BEGAN, THERE WAS ONLY THE DEEP EMPTINESS.
THERE WAS NO PAIN, NO JOY, NO DEATH, NO BIRTH. NOTHING WAS CREATED AND NOTHING WAS DESTROYED.
THERE WAS JUST THE PEACE AND QUIET OF THE VOID.
MAGIC HAD NOT YET BEEN BORN AND THINGS WERE GENERALLY REALLY, REALLY BORING. THIS IS THE WAY THE EMPTINESS LIKED IT.
BUT THE EMPTINESS WASN'T ALONE IN THE DARK, THERE WAS ANOTHER.
A WIZARD.
THE FIRST MAESTRO.

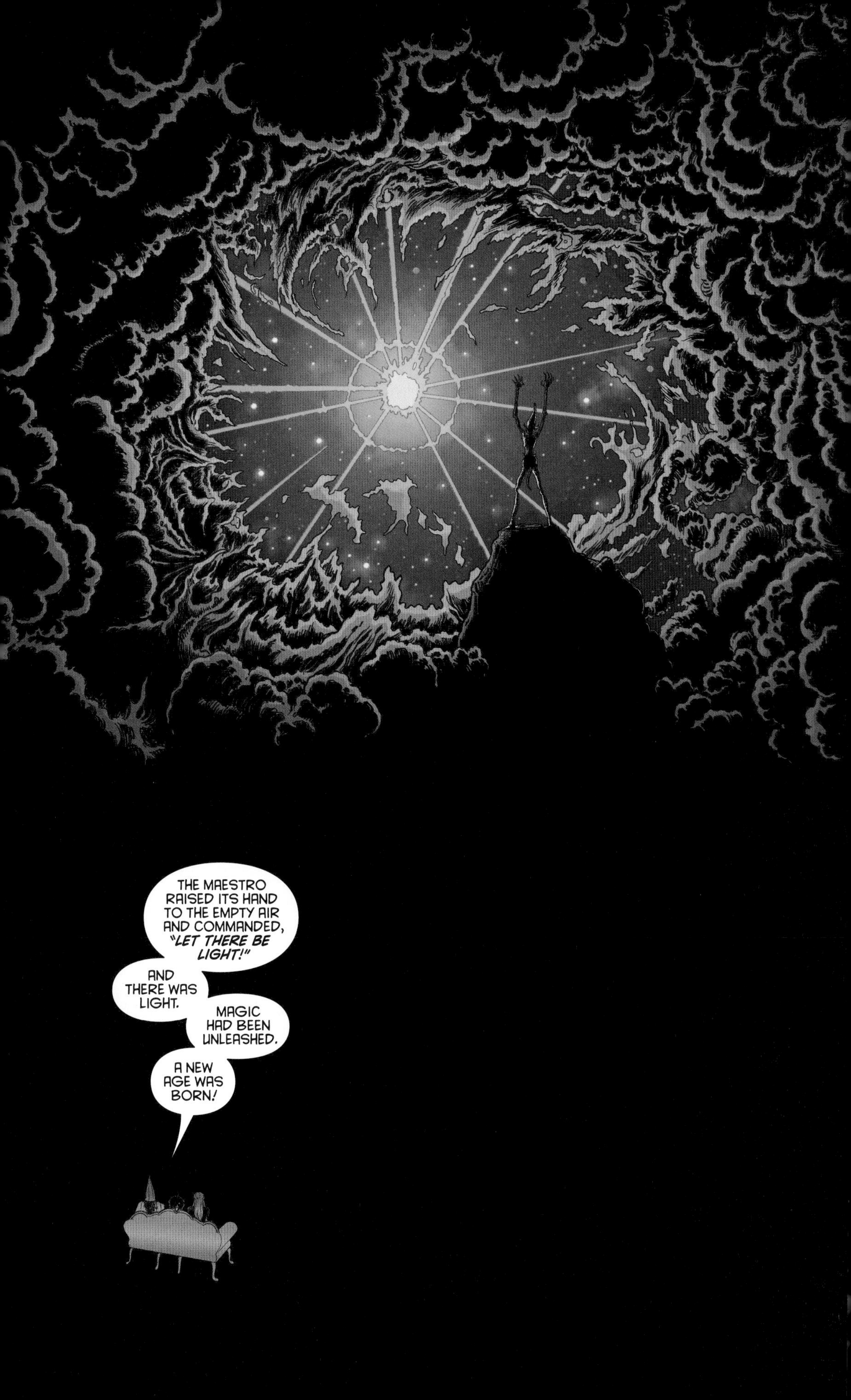
THE MAESTRO RAISED ITS HAND TO THE EMPTY AIR AND COMMANDED, *"LET THERE BE LIGHT!"*
AND THERE WAS LIGHT.
MAGIC HAD BEEN UNLEASHED.
A NEW AGE WAS BORN!

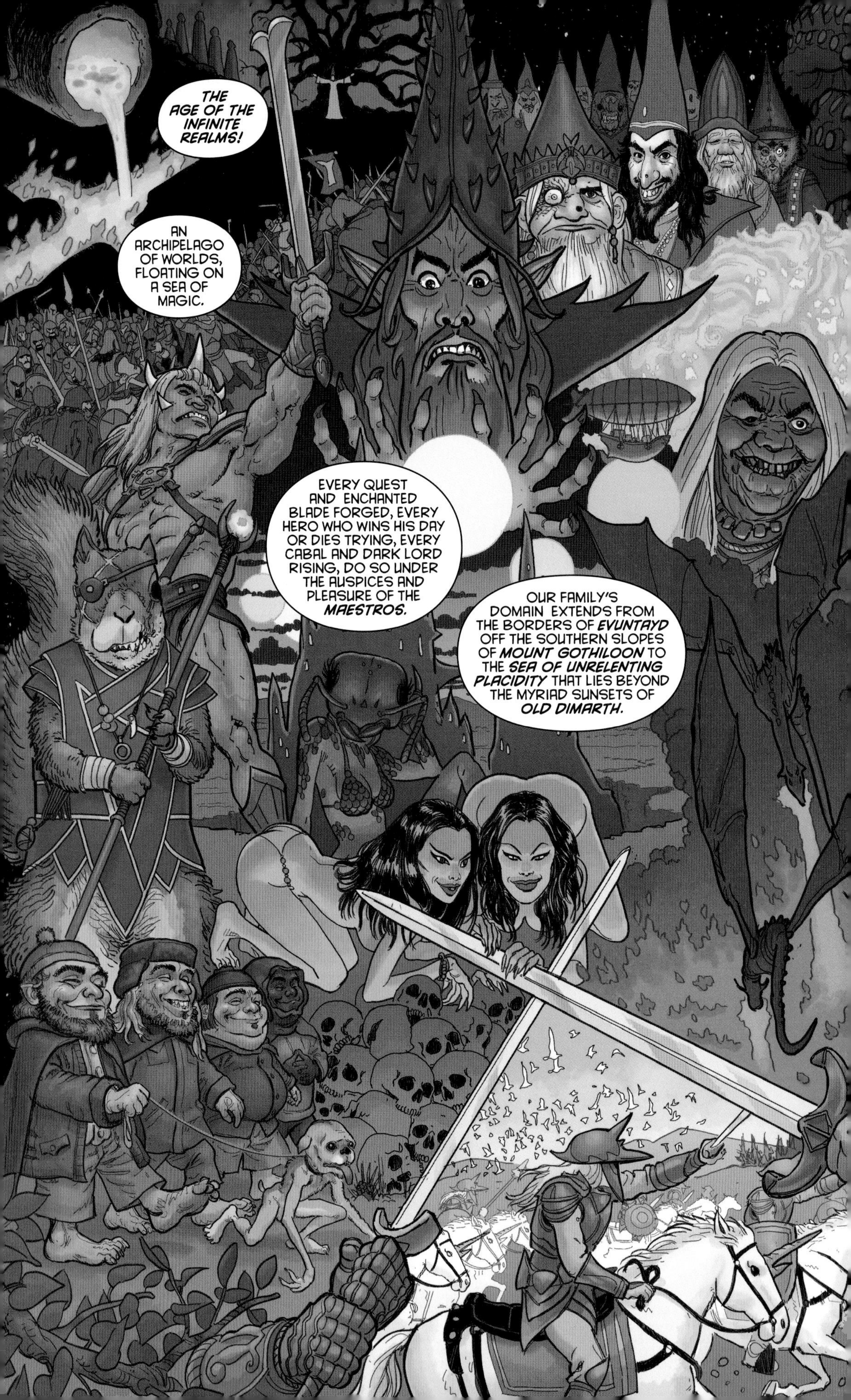
THE AGE OF THE INFINITE REALMS!
AN ARCHIPELAGO OF WORLDS, FLOATING ON A SEA OF MAGIC.
EVERY QUEST AND ENCHANTED BLADE FORGED, EVERY HERO WHO WINS HIS DAY OR DIES TRYING, EVERY CABAL AND DARK LORD RISING, DO SO UNDER THE AUSPICES AND PLEASURE OF THE MAESTROS.
OUR FAMILY'S DOMAIN EXTENDS FROM THE BORDERS OF EVUNTAYD OFF THE SOUTHERN SLOPES OF MOUNT GOTHILOON TO THE SEA OF UNRELENTING PLACIDITY THAT LIES BEYOND THE MYRIAD SUNSETS OF OLD DIMARTH.

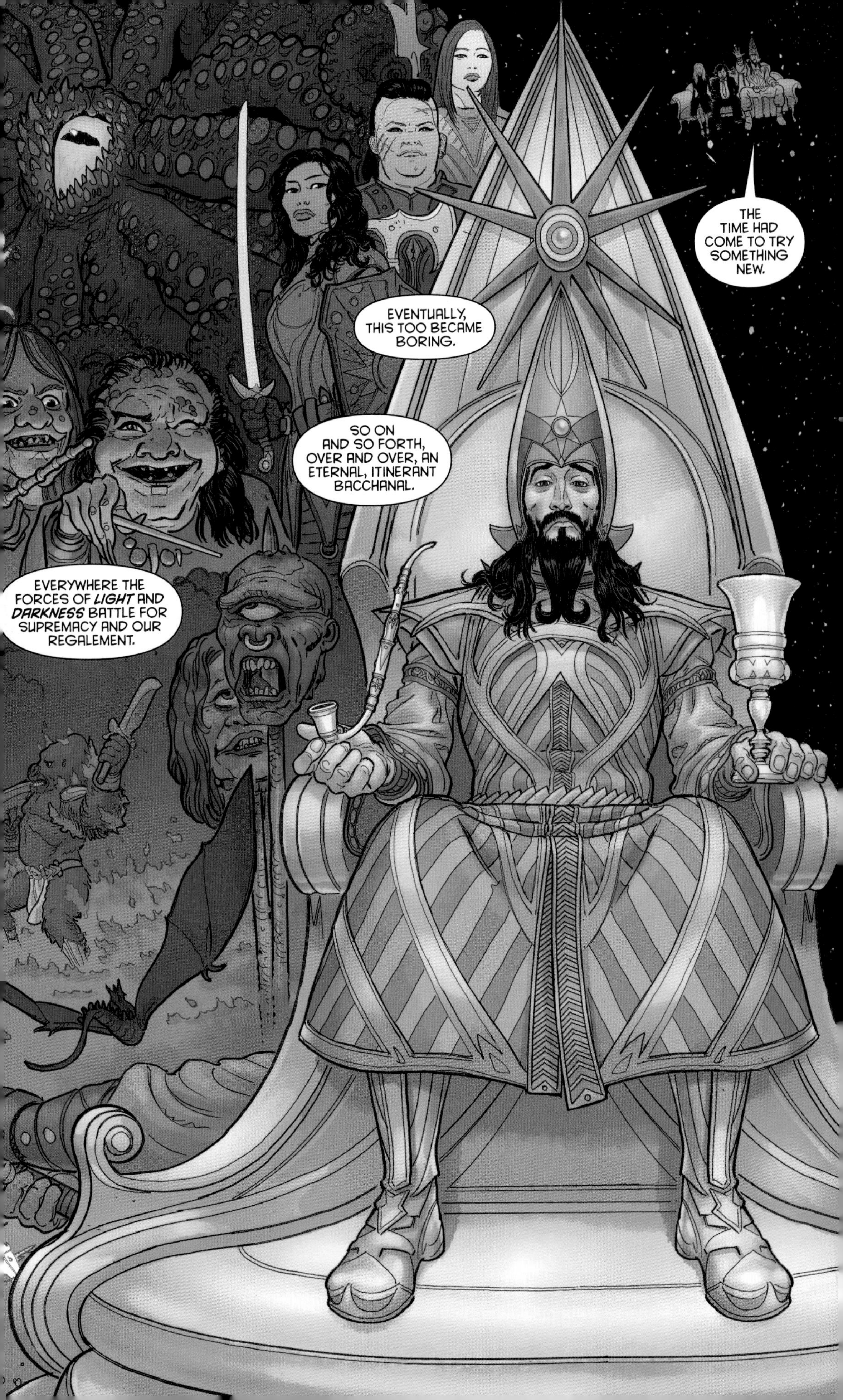
EVERYWHERE THE FORCES OF *LIGHT* AND *DARKNESS* BATTLE FOR SUPREMACY AND OUR REGALEMENT.
SO ON AND SO FORTH, OVER AND OVER, AN ETERNAL, ITINERANT BACCHANAL.
EVENTUALLY, THIS TOO BECAME BORING.
THE TIME HAD COME TO TRY SOMETHING NEW.

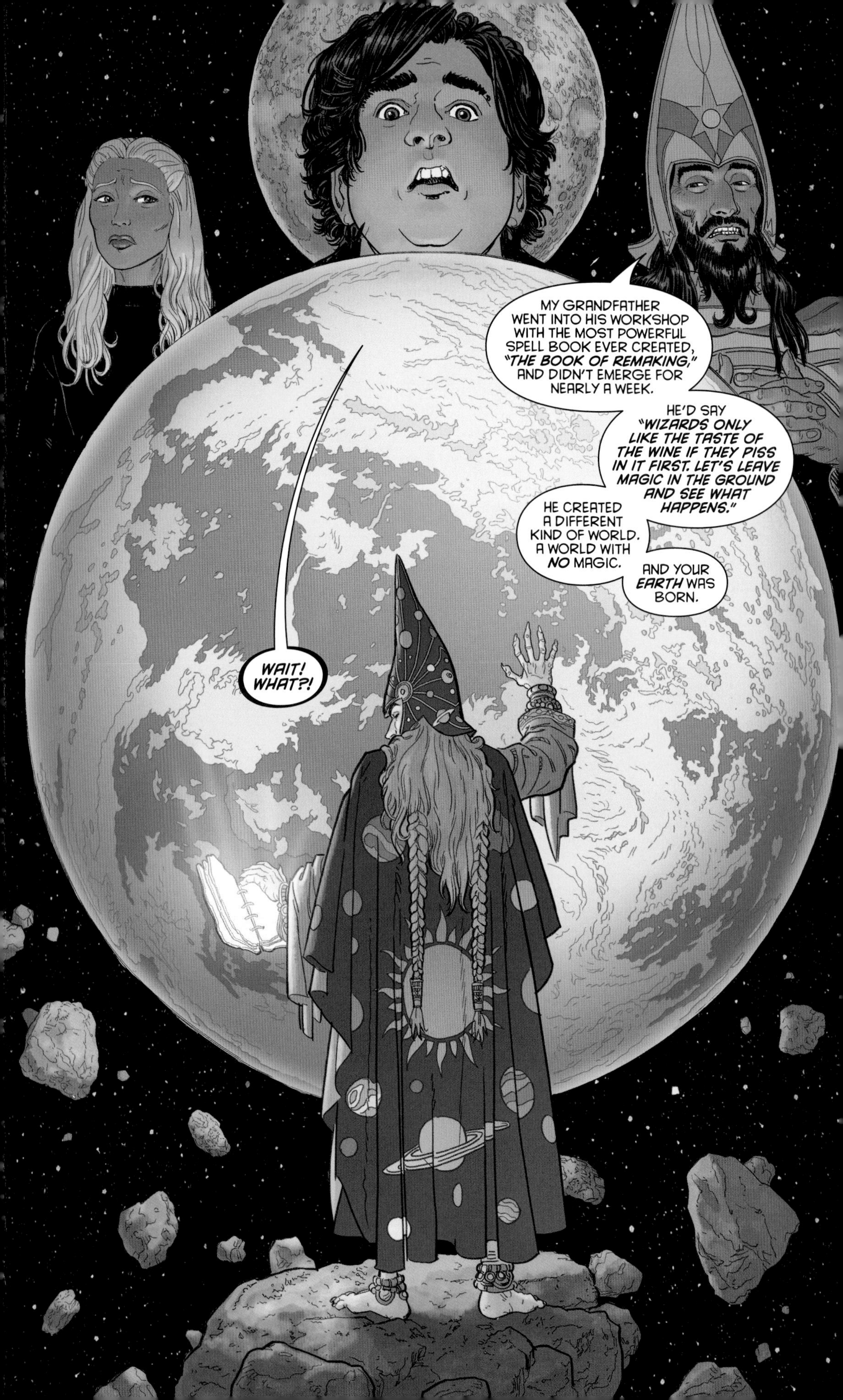
MY GRANDFATHER WENT INTO HIS WORKSHOP WITH THE MOST POWERFUL SPELL BOOK EVER CREATED, "THE BOOK OF REMAKING," AND DIDN'T EMERGE FOR NEARLY A WEEK.
HE'D SAY "WIZARDS ONLY LIKE THE TASTE OF THE WINE IF THEY PISS IN IT FIRST. LET'S LEAVE MAGIC IN THE GROUND AND SEE WHAT HAPPENS."
HE CREATED A DIFFERENT KIND OF WORLD. A WORLD WITH NO MAGIC.
AND YOUR EARTH WAS BORN.
WAIT! WHAT?!

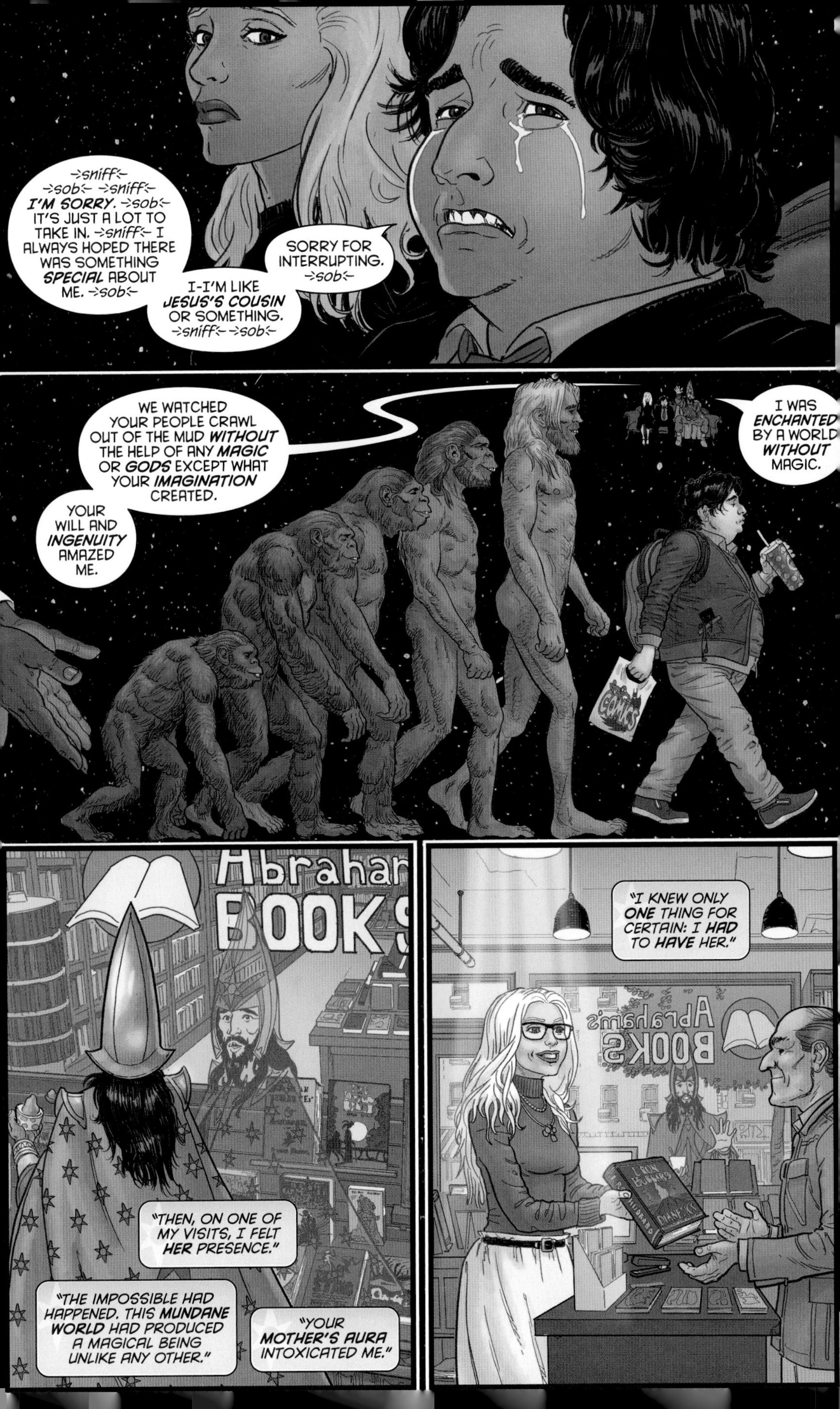

–>sniff<– –>sob<– –>sniff<– I'M SORRY. –>sob<– IT'S JUST A LOT TO TAKE IN. –>sniff<– I ALWAYS HOPED THERE WAS SOMETHING SPECIAL ABOUT ME. –>sob<–
I-I'M LIKE JESUS'S COUSIN OR SOMETHING. –>sniff<– –>sob<–
SORRY FOR INTERRUPTING. –>sob<–
WE WATCHED YOUR PEOPLE CRAWL OUT OF THE MUD WITHOUT THE HELP OF ANY MAGIC OR GODS EXCEPT WHAT YOUR IMAGINATION CREATED.
YOUR WILL AND INGENUITY AMAZED ME.
I WAS ENCHANTED BY A WORLD WITHOUT MAGIC.
COMICS
"THEN, ON ONE OF MY VISITS, I FELT HER PRESENCE."
"THE IMPOSSIBLE HAD HAPPENED. THIS MUNDANE WORLD HAD PRODUCED A MAGICAL BEING UNLIKE ANY OTHER."
"YOUR MOTHER'S AURA INTOXICATED ME."
"I KNEW ONLY ONE THING FOR CERTAIN: I HAD TO HAVE HER."

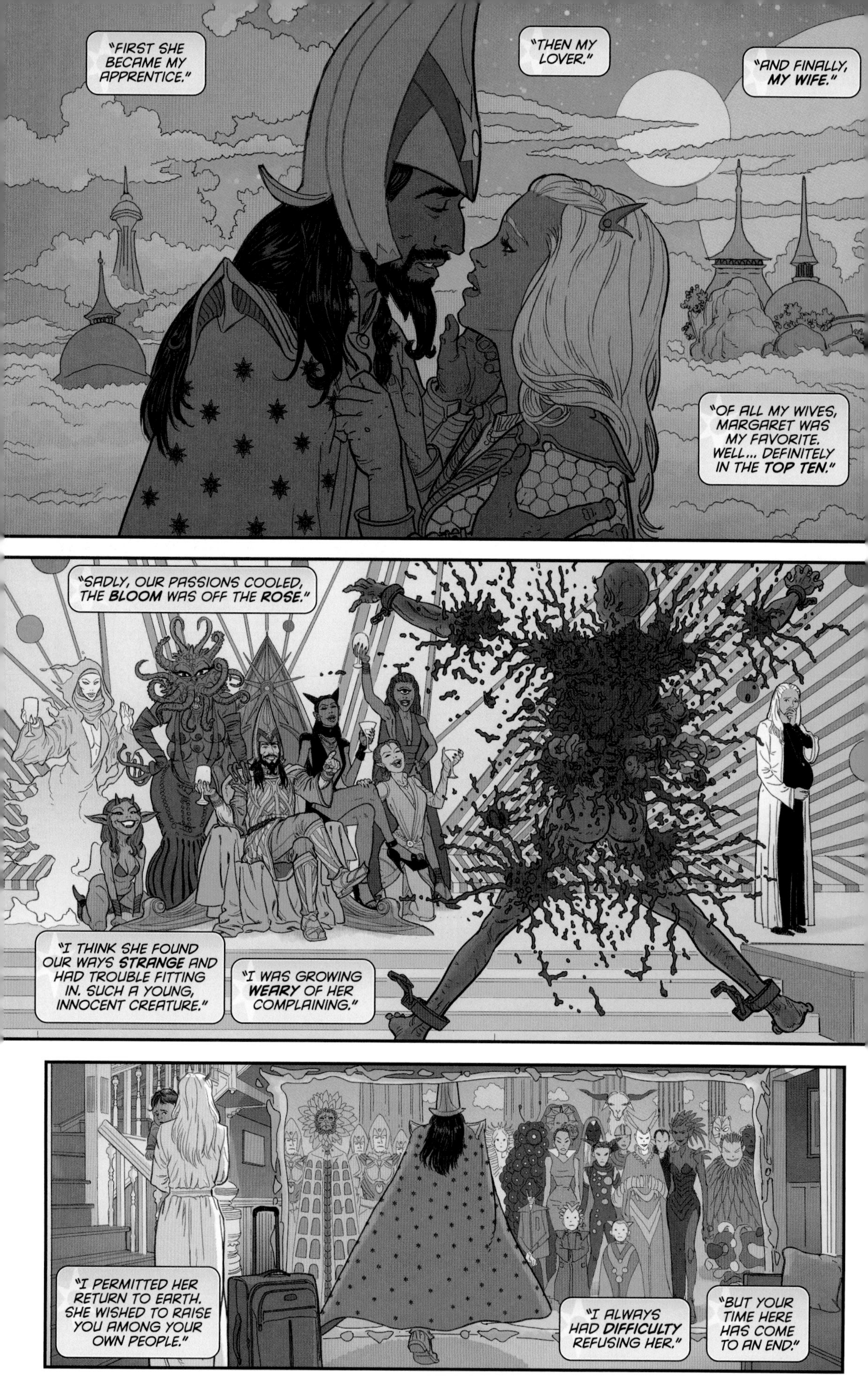
"FIRST SHE BECAME MY APPRENTICE."
"THEN MY LOVER."
"AND FINALLY, **MY WIFE.**"
"OF ALL MY WIVES, MARGARET WAS MY FAVORITE. WELL... DEFINITELY IN THE **TOP TEN.**"
"SADLY, OUR PASSIONS COOLED, THE **BLOOM** WAS OFF THE **ROSE.**"
"I THINK SHE FOUND OUR WAYS **STRANGE** AND HAD TROUBLE FITTING IN. SUCH A YOUNG, INNOCENT CREATURE."
"I WAS GROWING **WEARY** OF HER COMPLAINING."
"I PERMITTED HER RETURN TO EARTH. SHE WISHED TO RAISE YOU AMONG YOUR OWN PEOPLE."
"I ALWAYS HAD **DIFFICULTY** REFUSING HER."
"BUT YOUR TIME HERE HAS COME TO AN END."

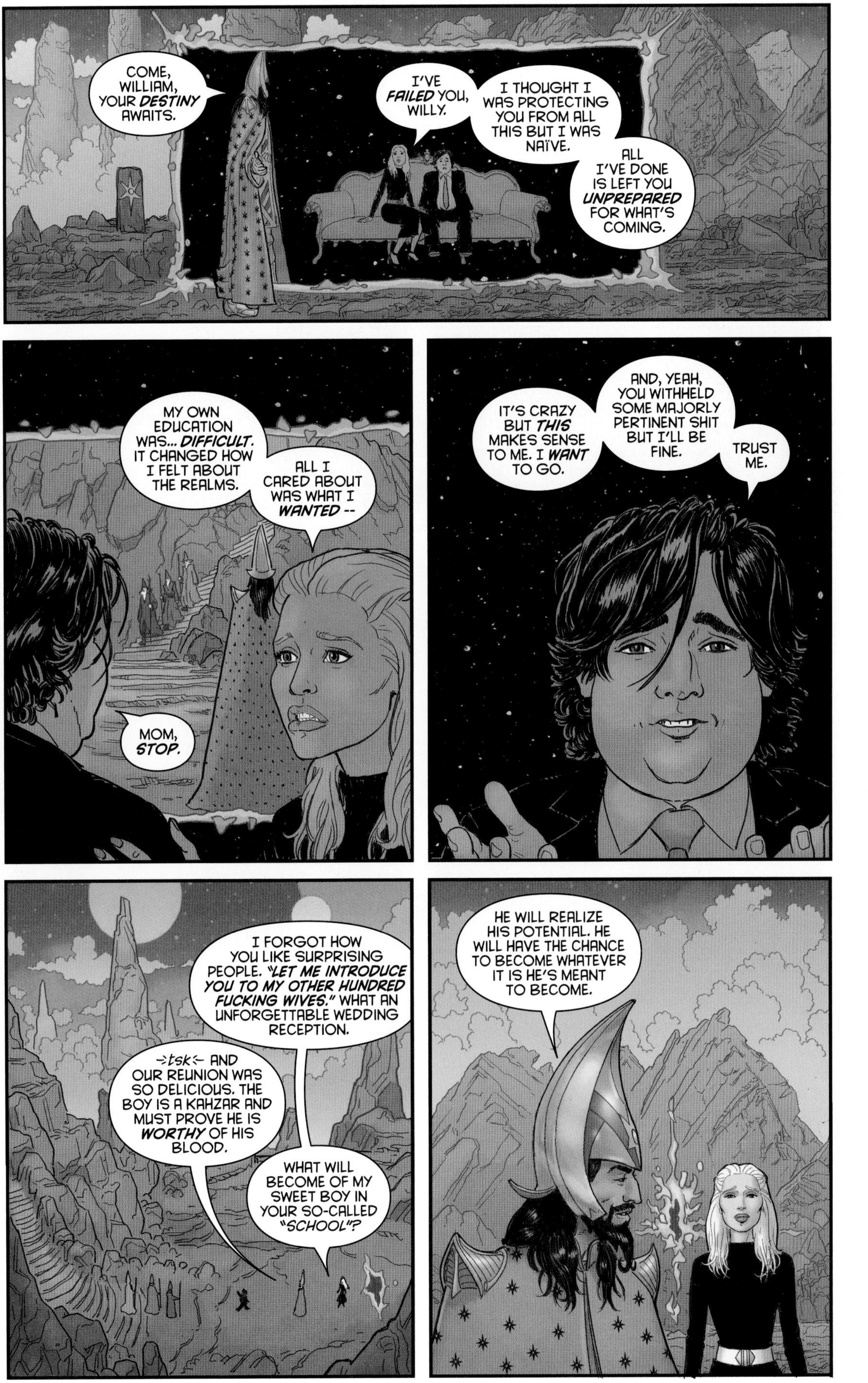
COME, WILLIAM, YOUR DESTINY AWAITS.
I'VE FAILED YOU, WILLY.
I THOUGHT I WAS PROTECTING YOU FROM ALL THIS BUT I WAS NAÏVE.
ALL I'VE DONE IS LEFT YOU UNPREPARED FOR WHAT'S COMING.
MY OWN EDUCATION WAS... DIFFICULT. IT CHANGED HOW I FELT ABOUT THE REALMS.
ALL I CARED ABOUT WAS WHAT I WANTED --
MOM, STOP.
IT'S CRAZY BUT THIS MAKES SENSE TO ME. I WANT TO GO.
AND, YEAH, YOU WITHHELD SOME MAJORLY PERTINENT SHIT BUT I'LL BE FINE.
TRUST ME.
I FORGOT HOW YOU LIKE SURPRISING PEOPLE. "LET ME INTRODUCE YOU TO MY OTHER HUNDRED FUCKING WIVES." WHAT AN UNFORGETTABLE WEDDING RECEPTION.
tsk AND OUR REUNION WAS SO DELICIOUS. THE BOY IS A KAHZAR AND MUST PROVE HE IS WORTHY OF HIS BLOOD.
WHAT WILL BECOME OF MY SWEET BOY IN YOUR SO-CALLED "SCHOOL"?
HE WILL REALIZE HIS POTENTIAL. HE WILL HAVE THE CHANCE TO BECOME WHATEVER IT IS HE'S MEANT TO BECOME.

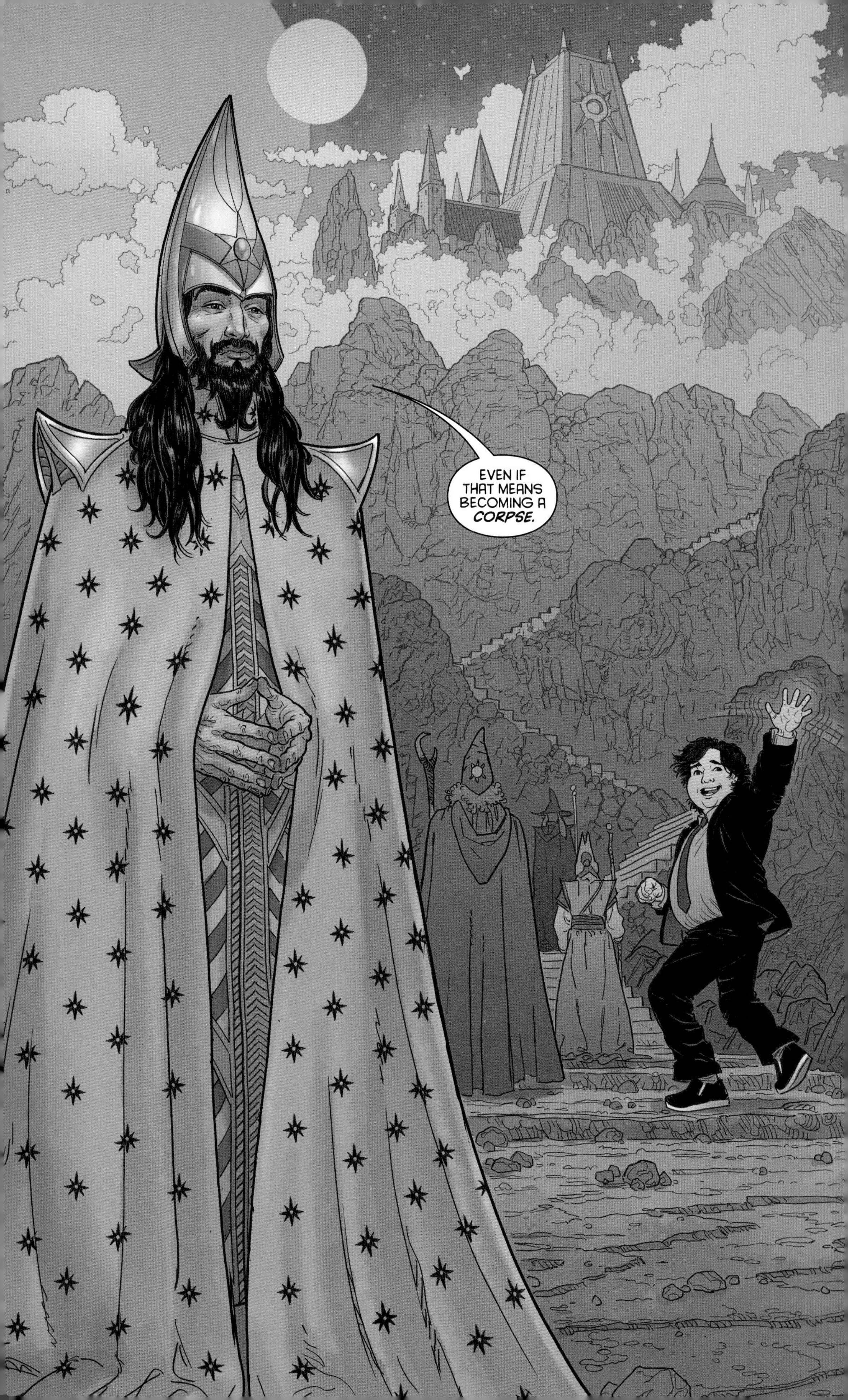
EVEN IF THAT MEANS BECOMING A *CORPSE.*

CHAPTER TWO

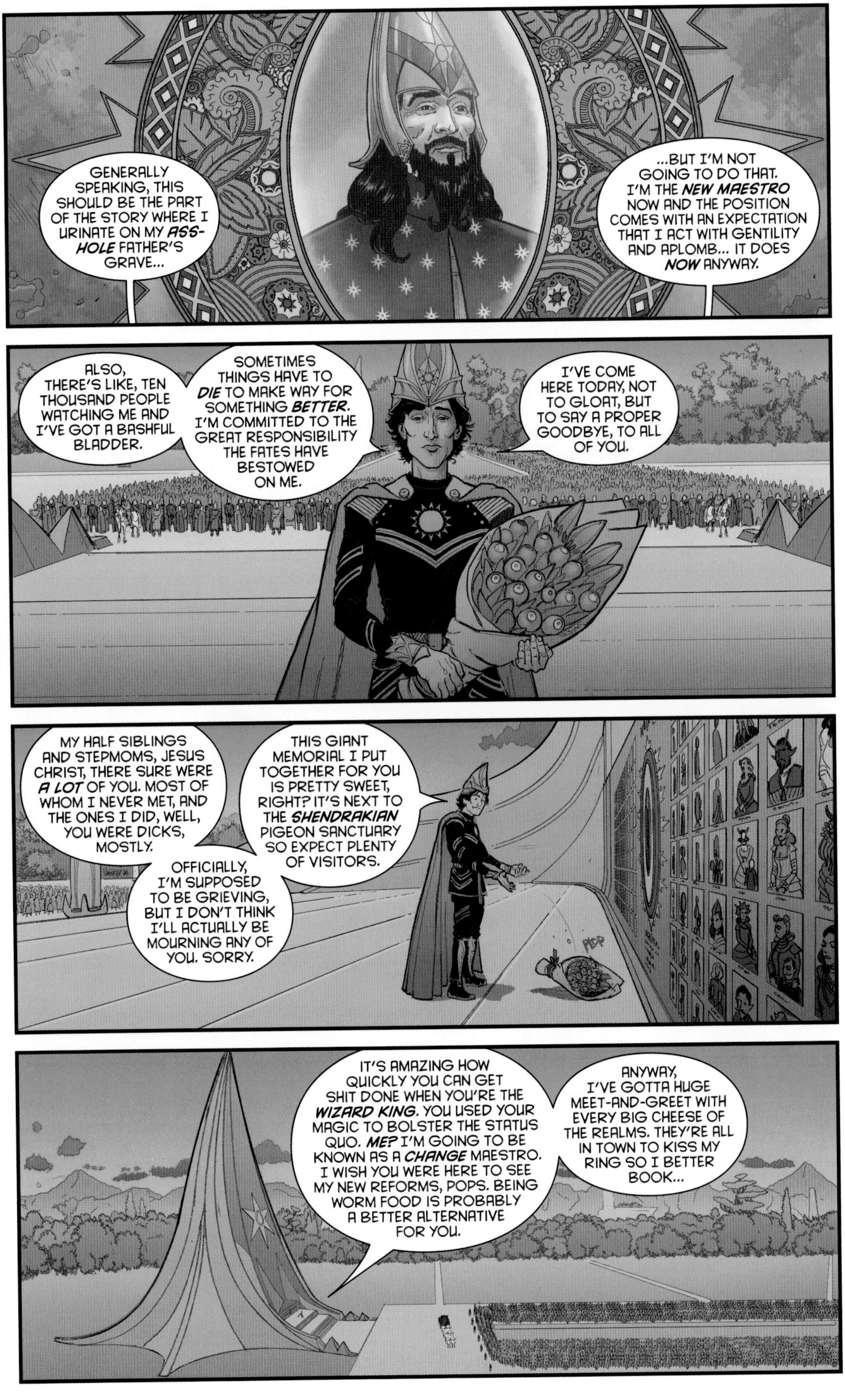
GENERALLY SPEAKING, THIS SHOULD BE THE PART OF THE STORY WHERE I URINATE ON MY ASS-HOLE FATHER'S GRAVE...
...BUT I'M NOT GOING TO DO THAT. I'M THE NEW MAESTRO NOW AND THE POSITION COMES WITH AN EXPECTATION THAT I ACT WITH GENTILITY AND APLOMB... IT DOES NOW ANYWAY.
ALSO, THERE'S LIKE, TEN THOUSAND PEOPLE WATCHING ME AND I'VE GOT A BASHFUL BLADDER.
SOMETIMES THINGS HAVE TO DIE TO MAKE WAY FOR SOMETHING BETTER. I'M COMMITTED TO THE GREAT RESPONSIBILITY THE FATES HAVE BESTOWED ON ME.
I'VE COME HERE TODAY, NOT TO GLOAT, BUT TO SAY A PROPER GOODBYE, TO ALL OF YOU.
MY HALF SIBLINGS AND STEPMOMS, JESUS CHRIST, THERE SURE WERE A LOT OF YOU. MOST OF WHOM I NEVER MET, AND THE ONES I DID, WELL, YOU WERE DICKS, MOSTLY.
THIS GIANT MEMORIAL I PUT TOGETHER FOR YOU IS PRETTY SWEET, RIGHT? IT'S NEXT TO THE SHENDRAKIAN PIGEON SANCTUARY SO EXPECT PLENTY OF VISITORS.
OFFICIALLY, I'M SUPPOSED TO BE GRIEVING, BUT I DON'T THINK I'LL ACTUALLY BE MOURNING ANY OF YOU. SORRY.
IT'S AMAZING HOW QUICKLY YOU CAN GET SHIT DONE WHEN YOU'RE THE WIZARD KING. YOU USED YOUR MAGIC TO BOLSTER THE STATUS QUO. ME? I'M GOING TO BE KNOWN AS A CHANGE MAESTRO. I WISH YOU WERE HERE TO SEE MY NEW REFORMS, POPS. BEING WORM FOOD IS PROBABLY A BETTER ALTERNATIVE FOR YOU.
ANYWAY, I'VE GOTTA HUGE MEET-AND-GREET WITH EVERY BIG CHEESE OF THE REALMS. THEY'RE ALL IN TOWN TO KISS MY RING SO I BETTER BOOK...

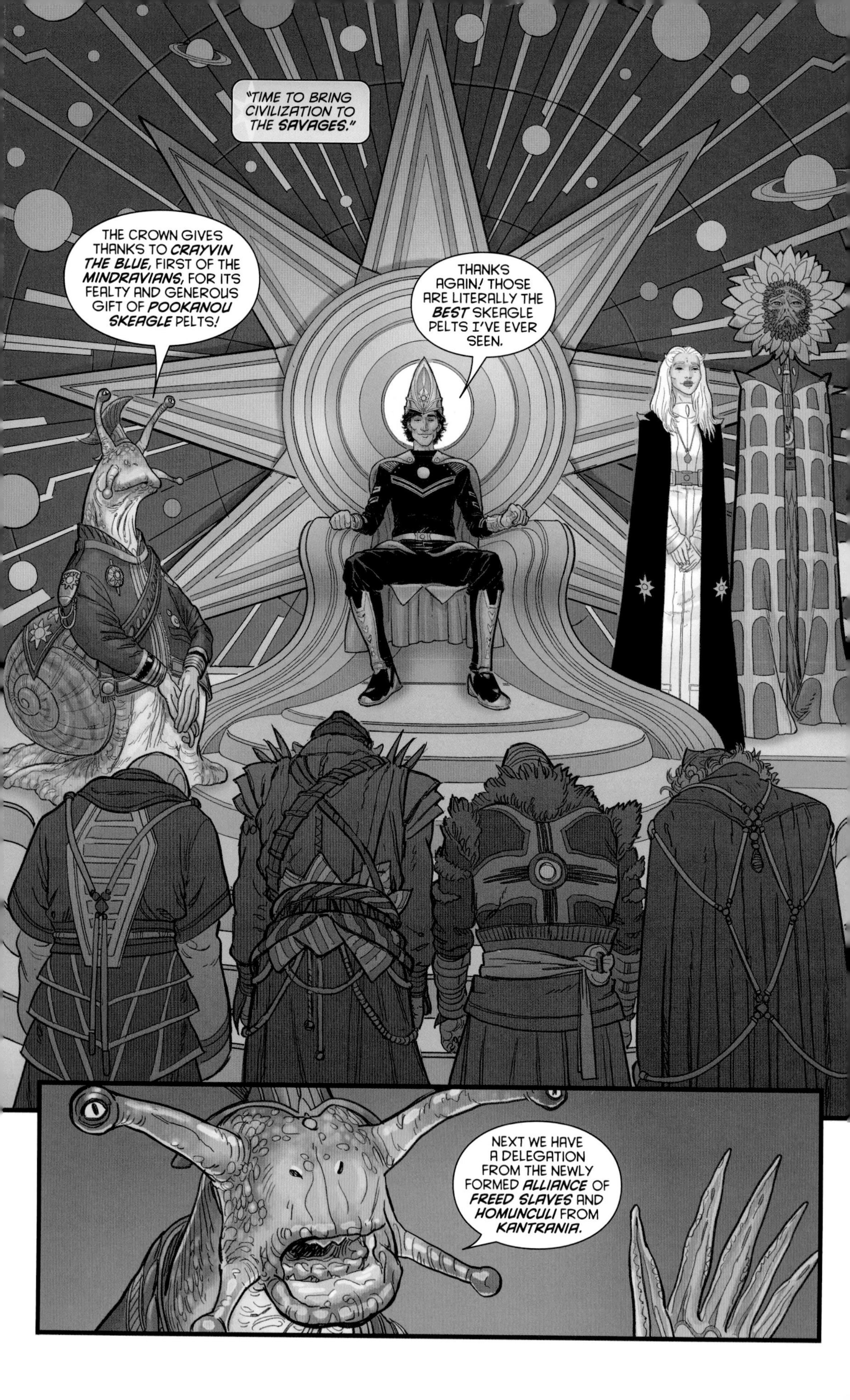
"TIME TO BRING CIVILIZATION TO THE SAVAGES."
THE CROWN GIVES THANKS TO CRAYVIN THE BLUE, FIRST OF THE MINDRAVIANS, FOR ITS FEALTY AND GENEROUS GIFT OF POOKANOU SKEAGLE PELTS!
THANKS AGAIN! THOSE ARE LITERALLY THE BEST SKEAGLE PELTS I'VE EVER SEEN.
NEXT WE HAVE A DELEGATION FROM THE NEWLY FORMED ALLIANCE OF FREED SLAVES AND HOMUNCULI FROM KANTRANIA.

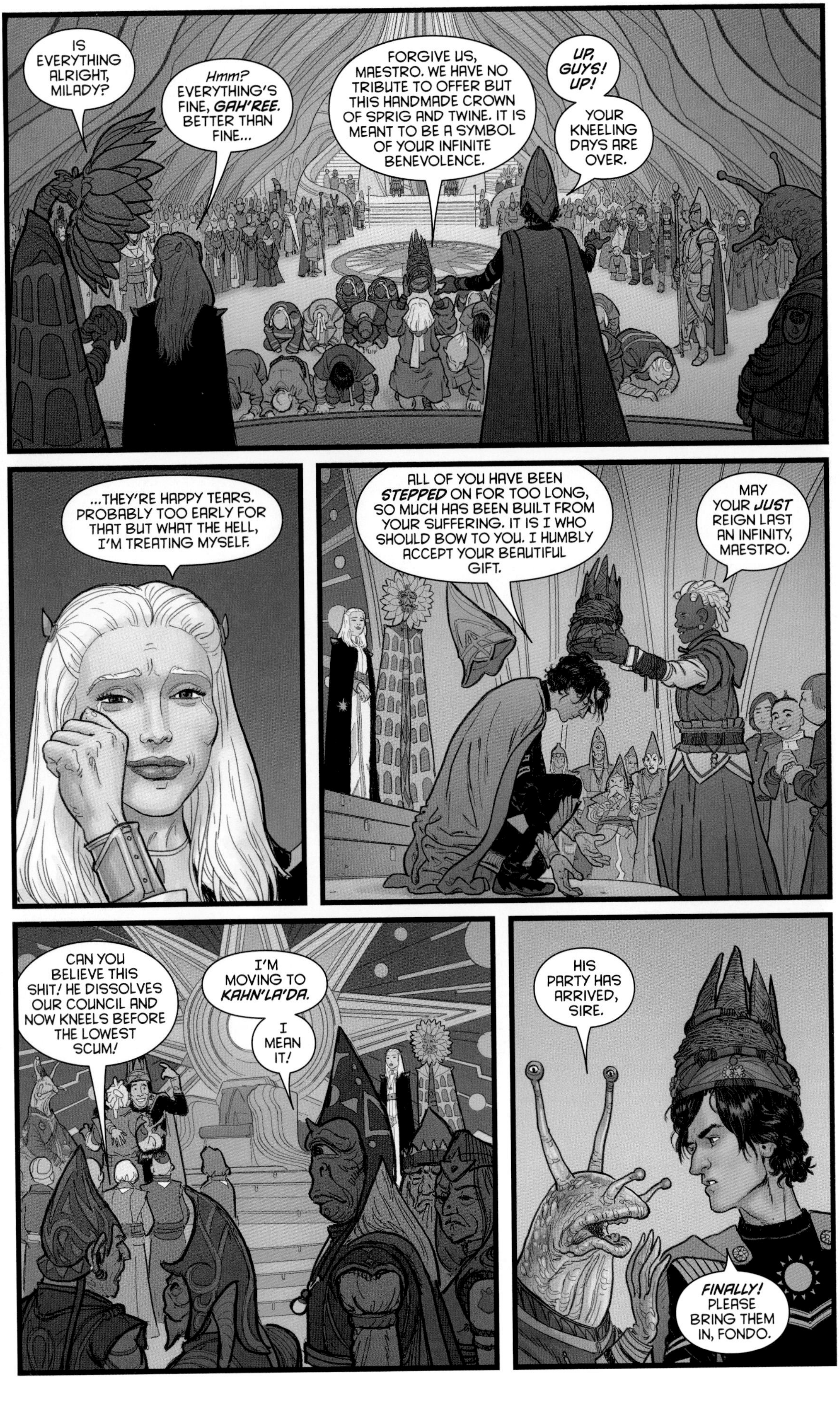
IS EVERYTHING ALRIGHT, MILADY?
Hmm? EVERYTHING'S FINE, ***GAH'REE.*** BETTER THAN FINE...
FORGIVE US, MAESTRO. WE HAVE NO TRIBUTE TO OFFER BUT THIS HANDMADE CROWN OF SPRIG AND TWINE. IT IS MEANT TO BE A SYMBOL OF YOUR INFINITE BENEVOLENCE.
UP, GUYS! UP!
YOUR KNEELING DAYS ARE OVER.
...THEY'RE HAPPY TEARS. PROBABLY TOO EARLY FOR THAT BUT WHAT THE HELL, I'M TREATING MYSELF.
ALL OF YOU HAVE BEEN ***STEPPED*** ON FOR TOO LONG, SO MUCH HAS BEEN BUILT FROM YOUR SUFFERING. IT IS I WHO SHOULD BOW TO YOU. I HUMBLY ACCEPT YOUR BEAUTIFUL GIFT.
MAY YOUR ***JUST*** REIGN LAST AN INFINITY, MAESTRO.
CAN YOU BELIEVE THIS SHIT! HE DISSOLVES OUR COUNCIL AND NOW KNEELS BEFORE THE LOWEST SCUM!
I'M MOVING TO ***KAHN'LA'DA.***
I MEAN IT!
HIS PARTY HAS ARRIVED, SIRE.
FINALLY! PLEASE BRING THEM IN, FONDO.

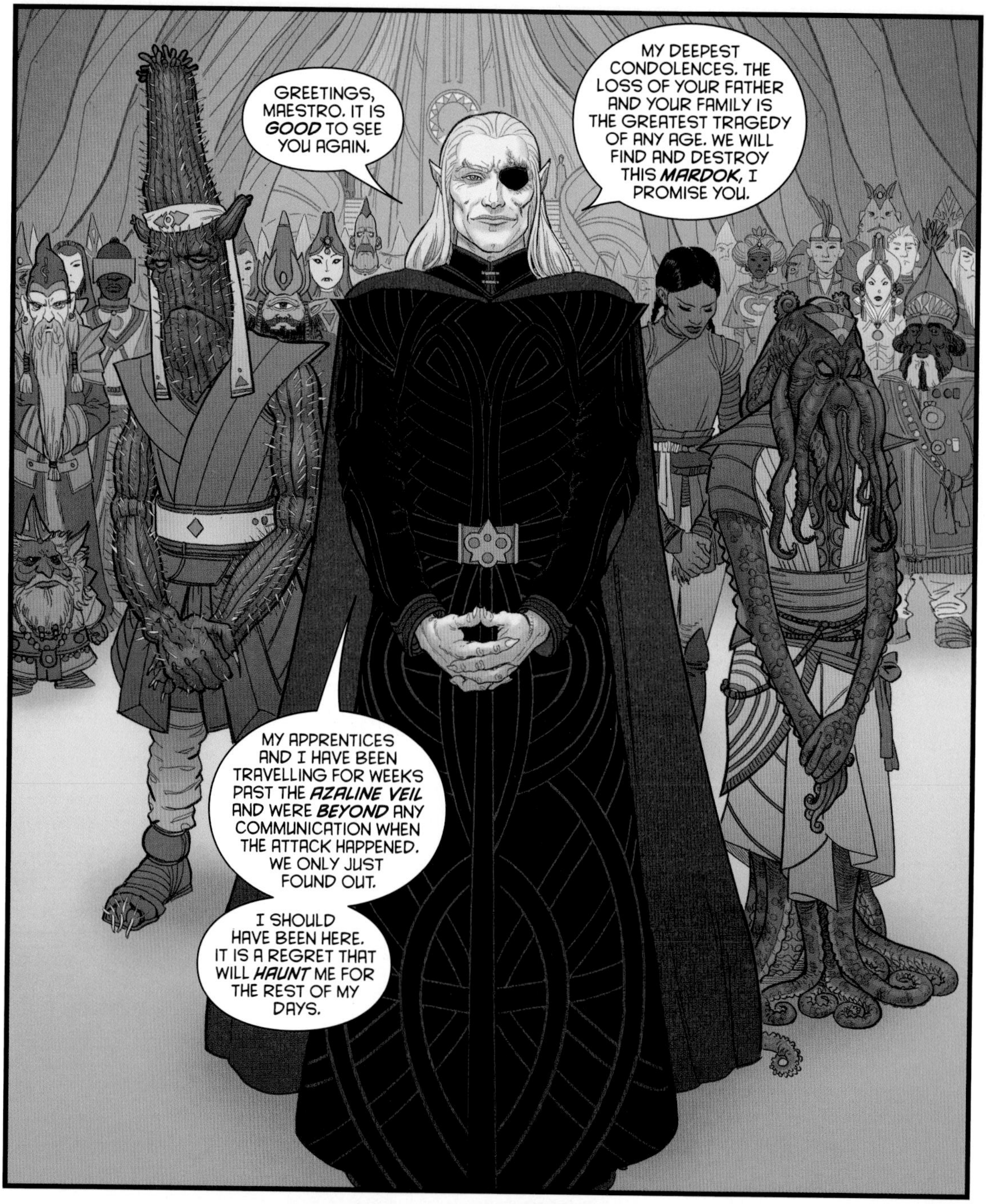
GREETINGS, MAESTRO. IT IS *GOOD* TO SEE YOU AGAIN.
MY DEEPEST CONDOLENCES. THE LOSS OF YOUR FATHER AND YOUR FAMILY IS THE GREATEST TRAGEDY OF ANY AGE. WE WILL FIND AND DESTROY THIS *MARDOK*, I PROMISE YOU.
MY APPRENTICES AND I HAVE BEEN TRAVELLING FOR WEEKS PAST THE *AZALINE VEIL* AND WERE *BEYOND* ANY COMMUNICATION WHEN THE ATTACK HAPPENED. WE ONLY JUST FOUND OUT.
I SHOULD HAVE BEEN HERE. IT IS A REGRET THAT WILL *HAUNT* ME FOR THE REST OF MY DAYS.

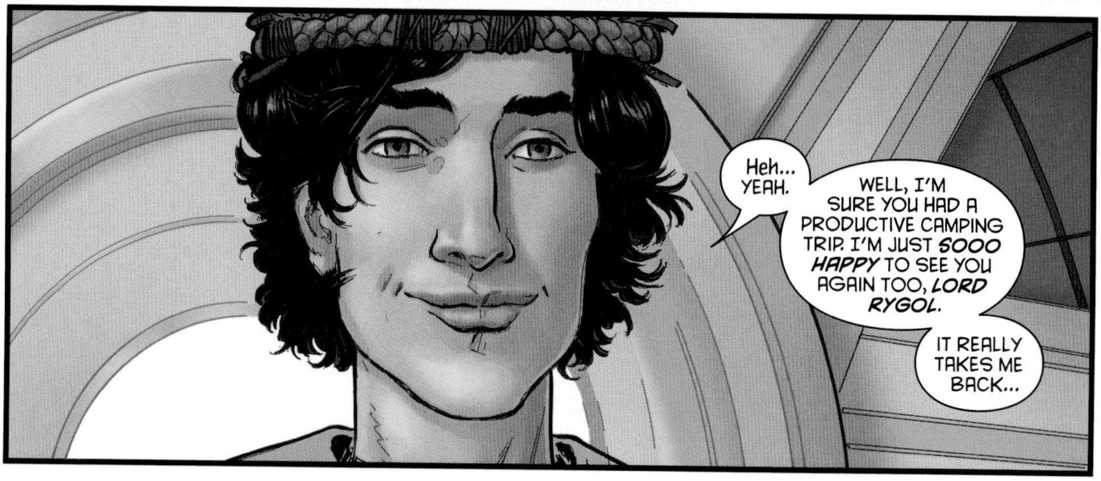
Heh... YEAH.
WELL, I'M SURE YOU HAD A PRODUCTIVE CAMPING TRIP. I'M JUST *SOOO HAPPY* TO SEE YOU AGAIN TOO, *LORD RYGOL*.
IT REALLY TAKES ME BACK...

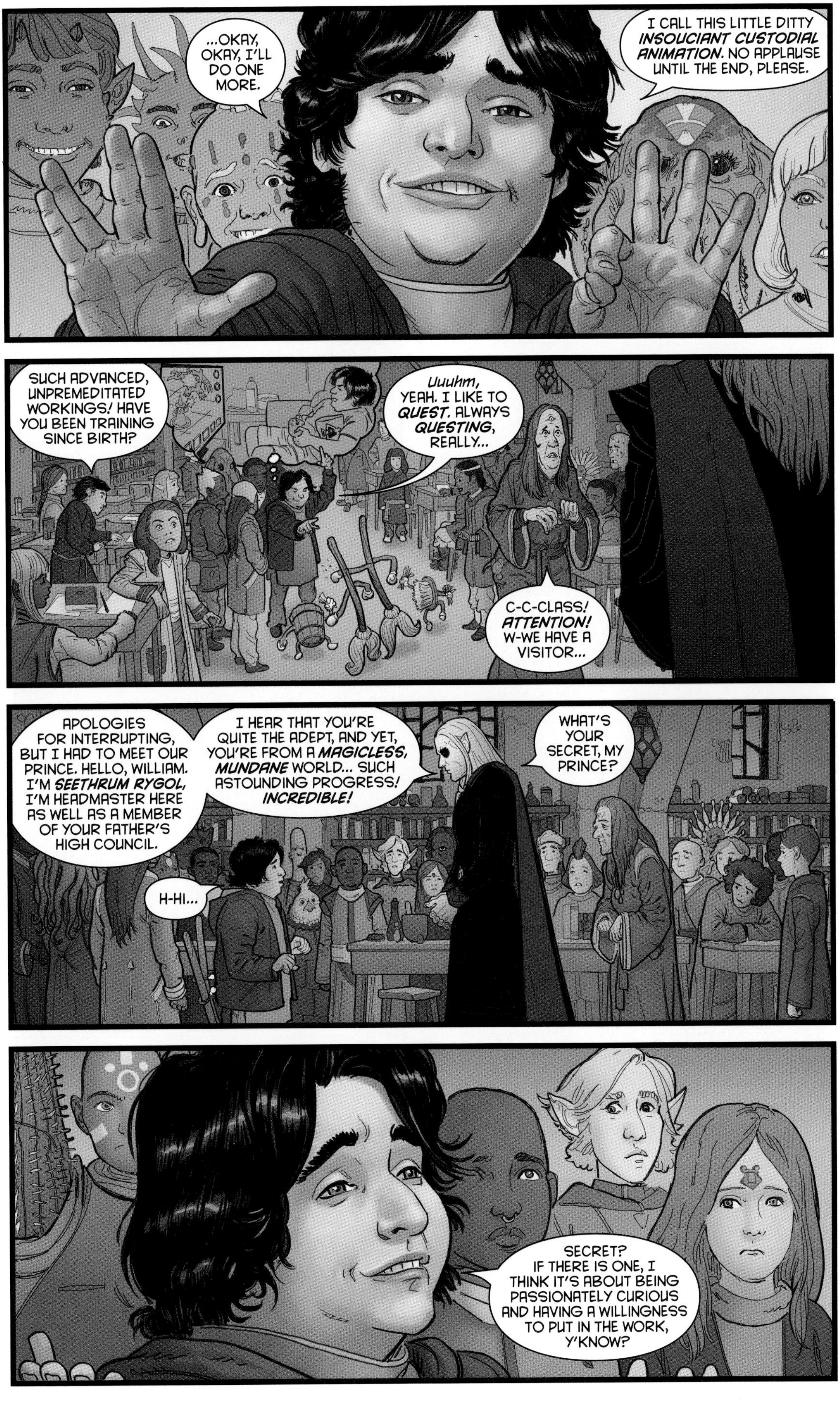
...OKAY, OKAY, I'LL DO ONE MORE.
I CALL THIS LITTLE DITTY *INSOUCIANT CUSTODIAL ANIMATION*. NO APPLAUSE UNTIL THE END, PLEASE.
SUCH ADVANCED, UNPREMEDITATED WORKINGS! HAVE YOU BEEN TRAINING SINCE BIRTH?
Uuuhm, YEAH. I LIKE TO *QUEST*. ALWAYS *QUESTING*, REALLY...
C-C-CLASS! *ATTENTION!* W-WE HAVE A VISITOR...
APOLOGIES FOR INTERRUPTING, BUT I HAD TO MEET OUR PRINCE. HELLO, WILLIAM. I'M *SEETHRUM RYGOL*, I'M HEADMASTER HERE AS WELL AS A MEMBER OF YOUR FATHER'S HIGH COUNCIL.
I HEAR THAT YOU'RE QUITE THE ADEPT, AND YET, YOU'RE FROM A *MAGICLESS, MUNDANE* WORLD... SUCH ASTOUNDING PROGRESS! *INCREDIBLE!*
WHAT'S YOUR SECRET, MY PRINCE?
H-HI...
SECRET? IF THERE IS ONE, I THINK IT'S ABOUT BEING PASSIONATELY CURIOUS AND HAVING A WILLINGNESS TO PUT IN THE WORK, Y'KNOW?

WHAT HAVE WE HERE?

A DINGUS FROM YOUR HOME WORLD, YES? I ACCOMPANIED YOUR FATHER ON A VISIT THERE. I THOUGHT IT AN ACRID, FILTHY PLACE BUT I WAS AMAZED BY WHAT YOUR PEOPLE *BUILT,* AND WITHOUT MAGIC.

SUCH *IMAGINATION* AND *INGENUITY.*

GAH!

RIP!

I SEE YOU'VE BROKEN INTO THE ARCHIVE AND USED THE DEVICE TO CAPTURE IMAGES FROM SOME RATHER ADVANCED SPELL BOOKS. I SUPPOSE TEACHING YOURSELF THESE SPELLS IS AT LEAST... SOMETHING.

~gulp~

Aw SHIT, GUYS! *MEA CULPA!* Heh heh...

THAT IS SOOOO WEIRD. THIS KIND OF THING IS *ROUTINE* BACK HOME!

REALLY, THIS IS JUST A BIG CULTURAL MISUNDERSTANDING. IT'S KIND OF HILARIOUS IF YOU THINK ABOUT IT, AM I RIGHT?

DECEIVER!

...FOOLS OF US ALL!

ADEPT! *Pfa!*

I FEAR WE'VE BEEN REMISS IN ASSIMILATING YOU TO OUR WAYS, BECAUSE OF THIS I'VE DECIDED ON *LENIENCY.*

DOES THAT SOUND FAIR, WILLIAM?

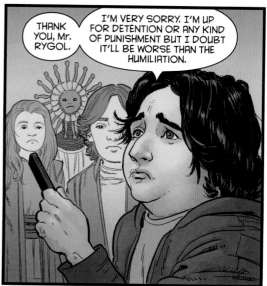

THANK YOU, MR. RYGOL.

I'M VERY SORRY. I'M UP FOR DETENTION OR ANY KIND OF PUNISHMENT BUT I DOUBT IT'LL BE WORSE THAN THE HUMILIATION.

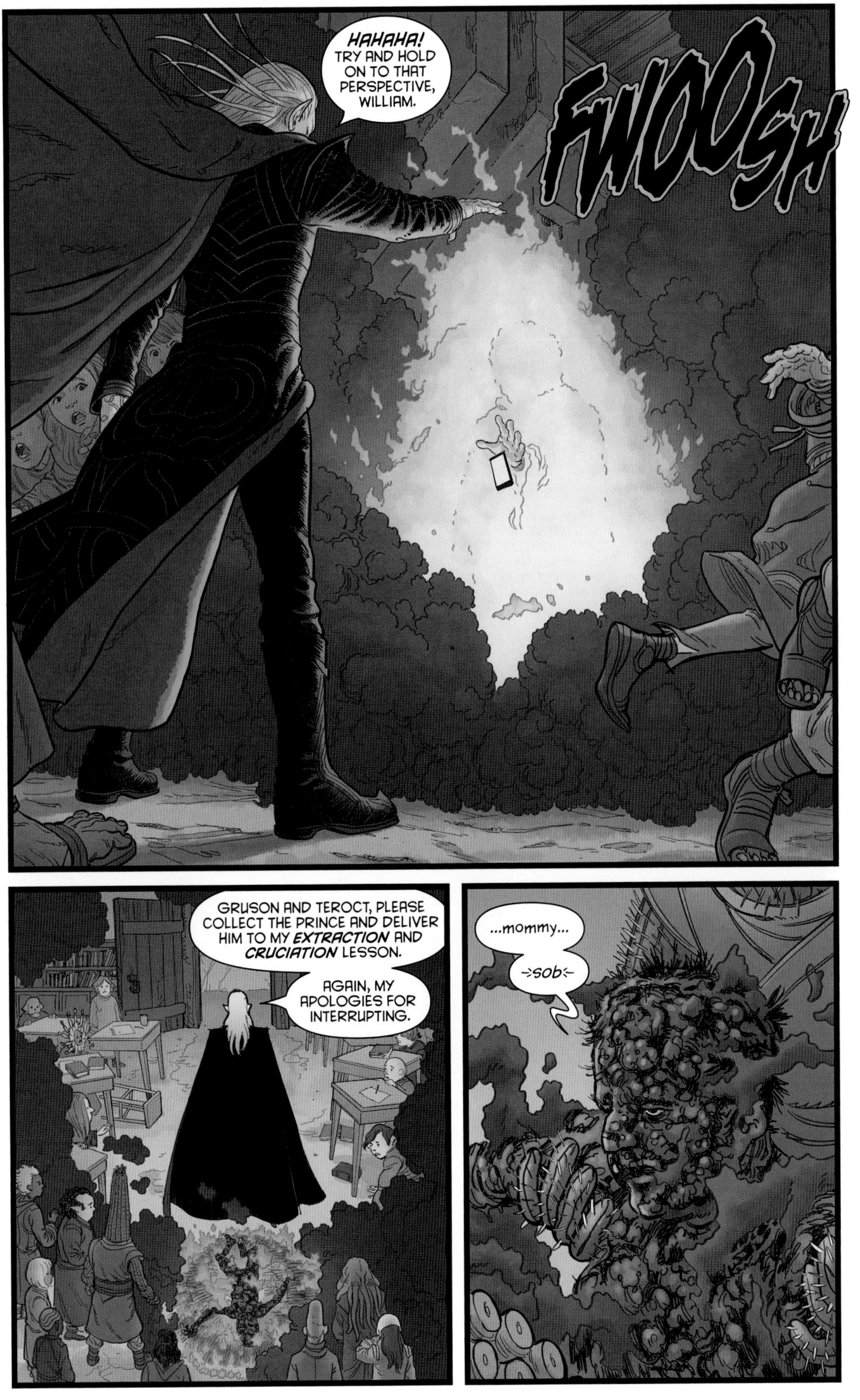
HAHAHA! TRY AND HOLD ON TO THAT PERSPECTIVE, WILLIAM.
FWOOSH
GRUSON AND TEROCT, PLEASE COLLECT THE PRINCE AND DELIVER HIM TO MY EXTRACTION AND CRUCIATION LESSON.
AGAIN, MY APOLOGIES FOR INTERRUPTING.
...mommy...
sob

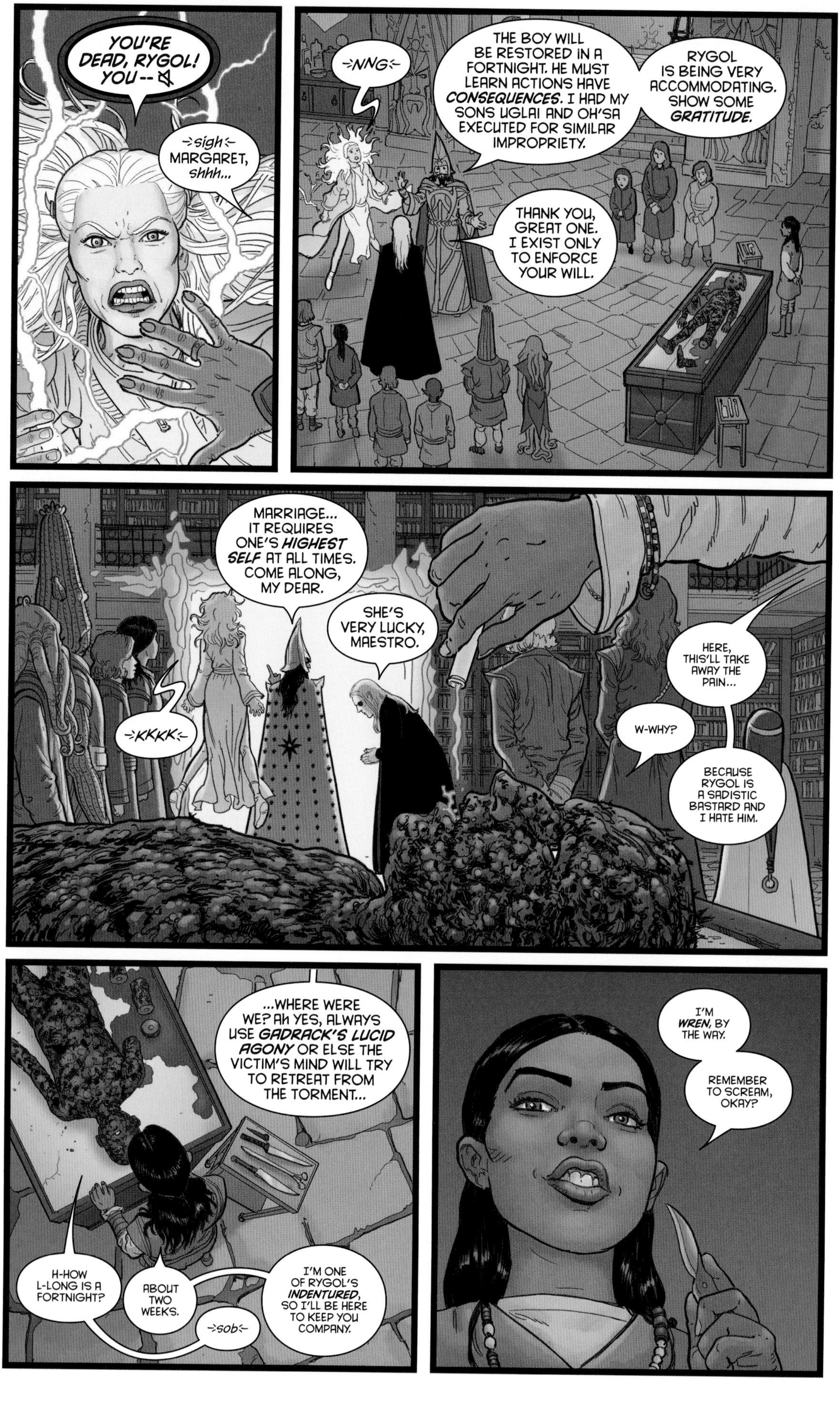
YOU'RE DEAD, RYGOL! YOU --
sigh MARGARET, shhh...
NNG
THE BOY WILL BE RESTORED IN A FORTNIGHT. HE MUST LEARN ACTIONS HAVE CONSEQUENCES. I HAD MY SONS UGLAI AND OH'SA EXECUTED FOR SIMILAR IMPROPRIETY.
RYGOL IS BEING VERY ACCOMMODATING. SHOW SOME GRATITUDE.
THANK YOU, GREAT ONE. I EXIST ONLY TO ENFORCE YOUR WILL.
MARRIAGE... IT REQUIRES ONE'S HIGHEST SELF AT ALL TIMES. COME ALONG, MY DEAR.
SHE'S VERY LUCKY, MAESTRO.
KKKK
HERE, THIS'LL TAKE AWAY THE PAIN...
W-WHY?
BECAUSE RYGOL IS A SADISTIC BASTARD AND I HATE HIM.
...WHERE WERE WE? AH YES, ALWAYS USE GADRACK'S LUCID AGONY OR ELSE THE VICTIM'S MIND WILL TRY TO RETREAT FROM THE TORMENT...
H-HOW L-LONG IS A FORTNIGHT?
ABOUT TWO WEEKS.
sob
I'M ONE OF RYGOL'S INDENTURED, SO I'LL BE HERE TO KEEP YOU COMPANY.
I'M WREN, BY THE WAY.
REMEMBER TO SCREAM, OKAY?

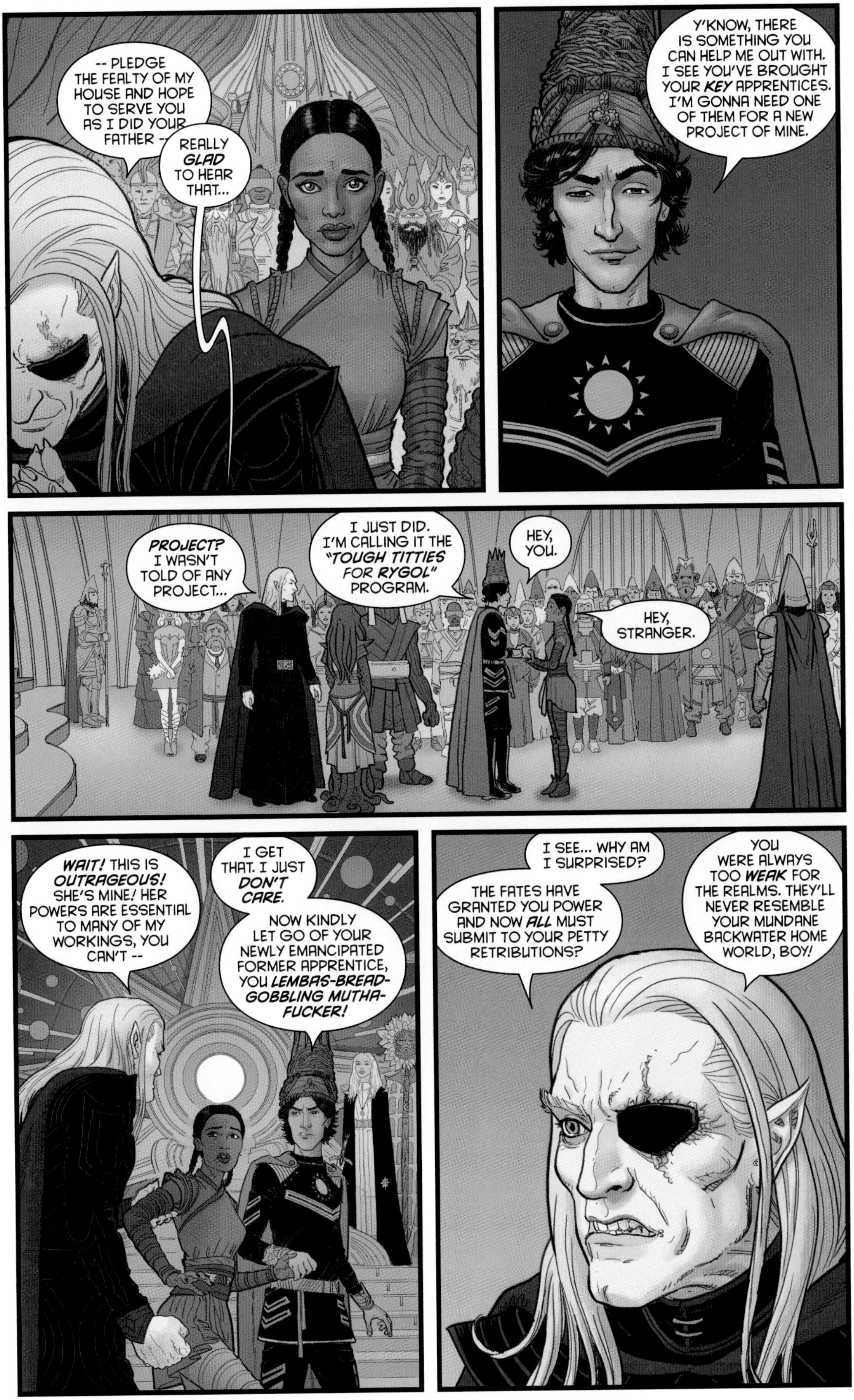
-- PLEDGE THE FEALTY OF MY HOUSE AND HOPE TO SERVE YOU AS I DID YOUR FATHER --
REALLY GLAD TO HEAR THAT...
Y'KNOW, THERE IS SOMETHING YOU CAN HELP ME OUT WITH. I SEE YOU'VE BROUGHT YOUR KEY APPRENTICES. I'M GONNA NEED ONE OF THEM FOR A NEW PROJECT OF MINE.
PROJECT? I WASN'T TOLD OF ANY PROJECT...
I JUST DID. I'M CALLING IT THE "TOUGH TITTIES FOR RYGOL" PROGRAM.
HEY, YOU.
HEY, STRANGER.
WAIT! THIS IS OUTRAGEOUS! SHE'S MINE! HER POWERS ARE ESSENTIAL TO MANY OF MY WORKINGS, YOU CAN'T --
I GET THAT. I JUST DON'T CARE.
NOW KINDLY LET GO OF YOUR NEWLY EMANCIPATED FORMER APPRENTICE, YOU LEMBAS-BREAD-GOBBLING MUTHA-FUCKER!
I SEE... WHY AM I SURPRISED?
THE FATES HAVE GRANTED YOU POWER AND NOW ALL MUST SUBMIT TO YOUR PETTY RETRIBUTIONS?
YOU WERE ALWAYS TOO WEAK FOR THE REALMS. THEY'LL NEVER RESEMBLE YOUR MUNDANE BACKWATER HOME WORLD, BOY!

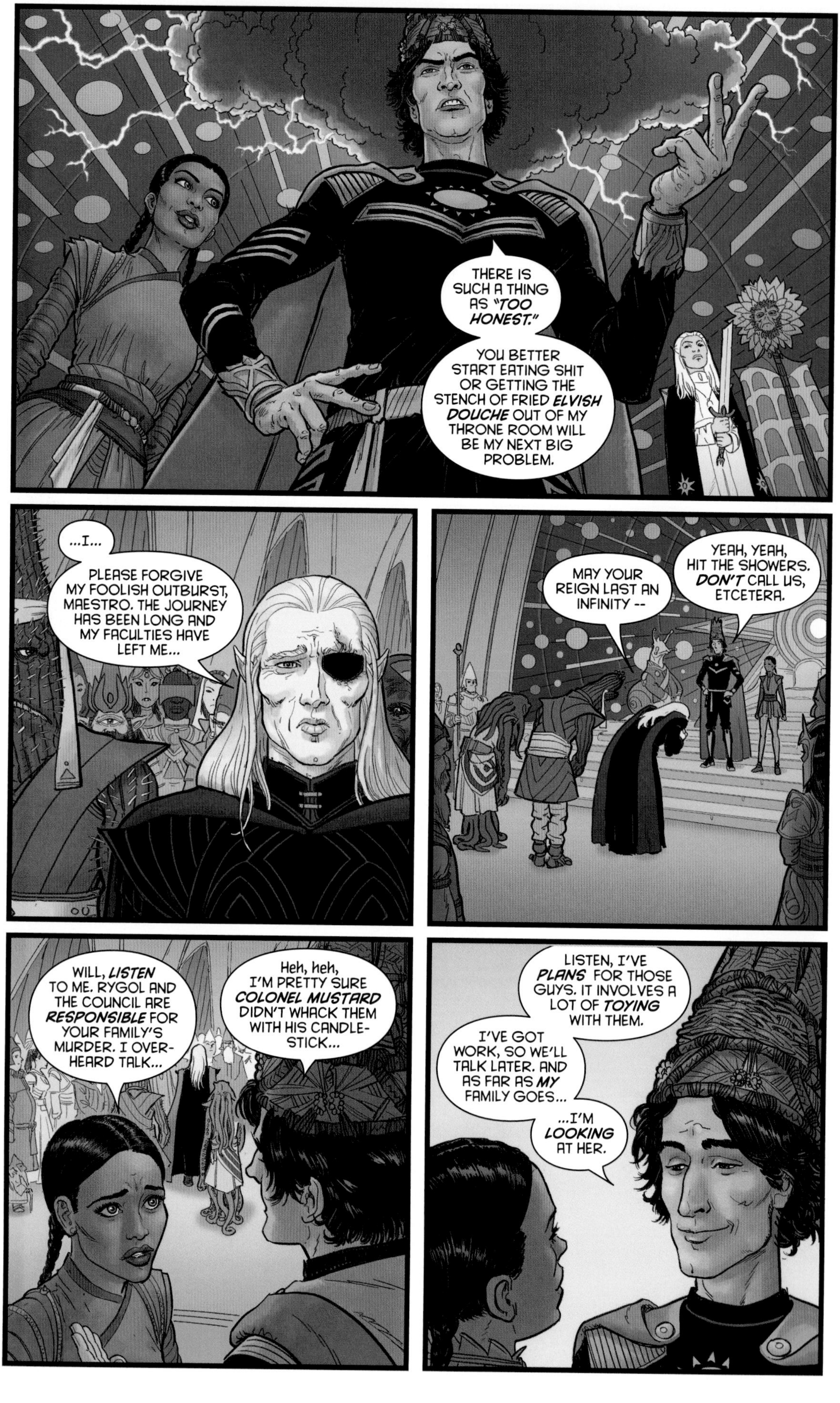
THERE IS SUCH A THING AS "TOO HONEST."
YOU BETTER START EATING SHIT OR GETTING THE STENCH OF FRIED ELVISH DOUCHE OUT OF MY THRONE ROOM WILL BE MY NEXT BIG PROBLEM.
...I...
PLEASE FORGIVE MY FOOLISH OUTBURST, MAESTRO. THE JOURNEY HAS BEEN LONG AND MY FACULTIES HAVE LEFT ME...
MAY YOUR REIGN LAST AN INFINITY --
YEAH, YEAH, HIT THE SHOWERS. DON'T CALL US, ETCETERA.
WILL, LISTEN TO ME. RYGOL AND THE COUNCIL ARE RESPONSIBLE FOR YOUR FAMILY'S MURDER. I OVERHEARD TALK...
Heh, heh, I'M PRETTY SURE COLONEL MUSTARD DIDN'T WHACK THEM WITH HIS CANDLESTICK...
LISTEN, I'VE PLANS FOR THOSE GUYS. IT INVOLVES A LOT OF TOYING WITH THEM.
I'VE GOT WORK, SO WE'LL TALK LATER. AND AS FAR AS MY FAMILY GOES...
...I'M LOOKING AT HER.

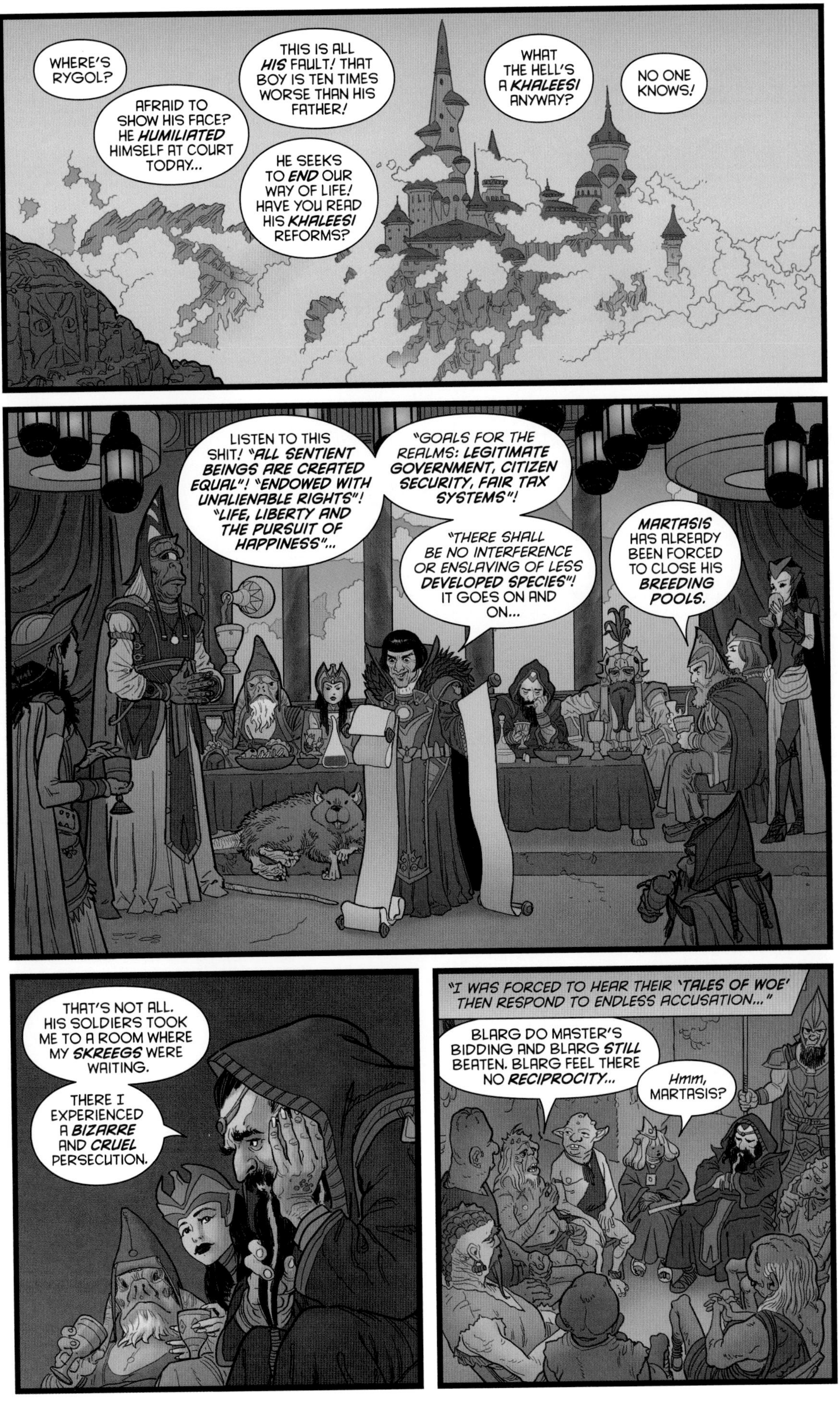
WHERE'S RYGOL?
AFRAID TO SHOW HIS FACE? HE HUMILIATED HIMSELF AT COURT TODAY...
THIS IS ALL HIS FAULT! THAT BOY IS TEN TIMES WORSE THAN HIS FATHER!
HE SEEKS TO END OUR WAY OF LIFE! HAVE YOU READ HIS KHALEESI REFORMS?
WHAT THE HELL'S A KHALEESI ANYWAY?
NO ONE KNOWS!
LISTEN TO THIS SHIT! "ALL SENTIENT BEINGS ARE CREATED EQUAL"! "ENDOWED WITH UNALIENABLE RIGHTS"! "LIFE, LIBERTY AND THE PURSUIT OF HAPPINESS"...
"GOALS FOR THE REALMS: LEGITIMATE GOVERNMENT, CITIZEN SECURITY, FAIR TAX SYSTEMS"!
"THERE SHALL BE NO INTERFERENCE OR ENSLAVING OF LESS DEVELOPED SPECIES"! IT GOES ON AND ON...
MARTASIS HAS ALREADY BEEN FORCED TO CLOSE HIS BREEDING POOLS.
THAT'S NOT ALL. HIS SOLDIERS TOOK ME TO A ROOM WHERE MY SKREEGS WERE WAITING.
THERE I EXPERIENCED A BIZARRE AND CRUEL PERSECUTION.
"I WAS FORCED TO HEAR THEIR 'TALES OF WOE' THEN RESPOND TO ENDLESS ACCUSATION..."
BLARG DO MASTER'S BIDDING AND BLARG STILL BEATEN. BLARG FEEL THERE NO RECIPROCITY...
Hmm, MARTASIS?

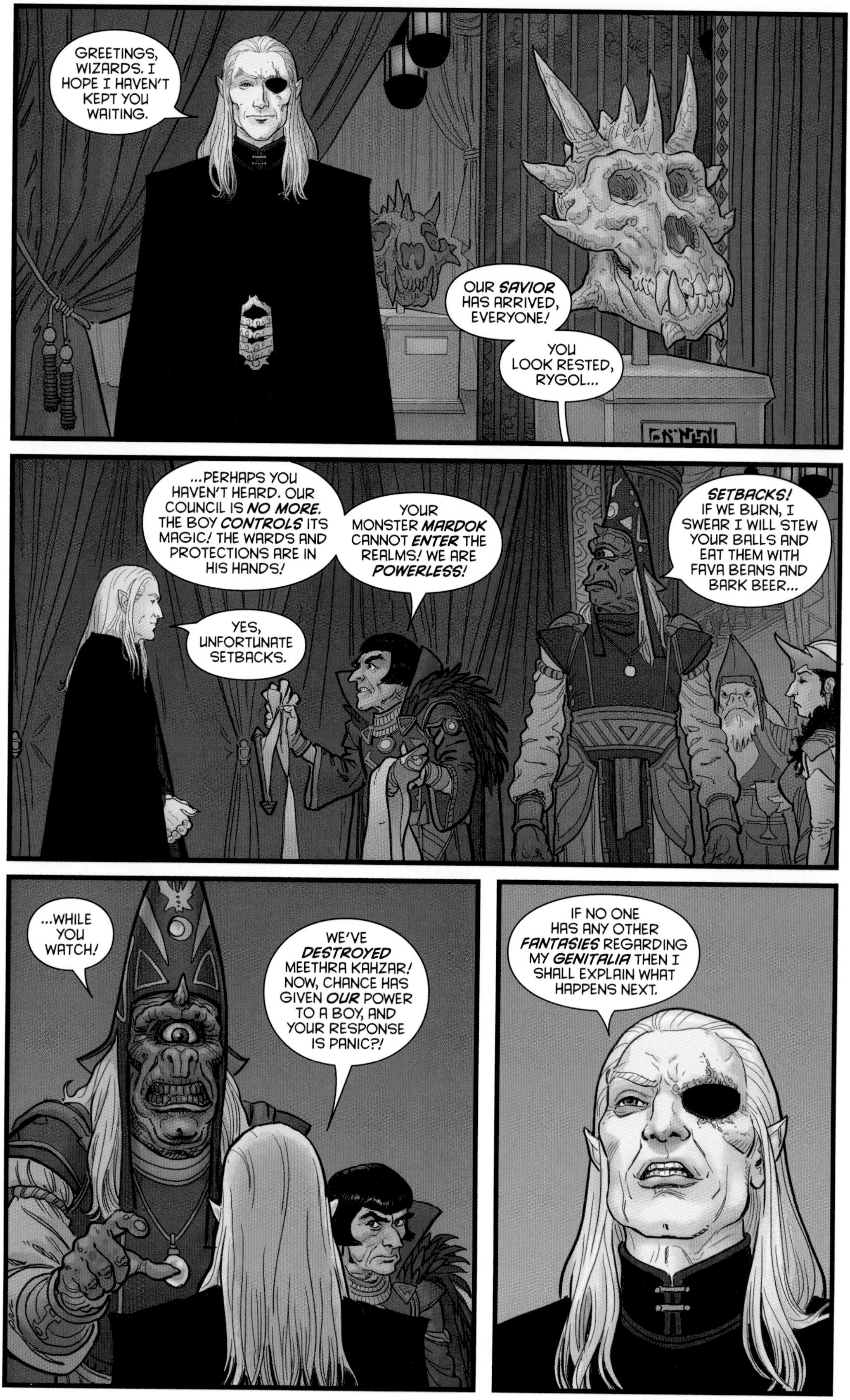
GREETINGS, WIZARDS. I HOPE I HAVEN'T KEPT YOU WAITING.
OUR *SAVIOR* HAS ARRIVED, EVERYONE!
YOU LOOK RESTED, RYGOL...
...PERHAPS YOU HAVEN'T HEARD. OUR COUNCIL IS ***NO MORE.*** THE BOY ***CONTROLS*** ITS MAGIC! THE WARDS AND PROTECTIONS ARE IN HIS HANDS!
YOUR MONSTER ***MARDOK*** CANNOT ***ENTER*** THE REALMS! WE ARE ***POWERLESS!***
YES, UNFORTUNATE SETBACKS.
SETBACKS! IF WE BURN, I SWEAR I WILL STEW YOUR BALLS AND EAT THEM WITH FAVA BEANS AND BARK BEER...
...WHILE YOU WATCH!
WE'VE ***DESTROYED*** MEETHRA KAHZAR! NOW, CHANCE HAS GIVEN ***OUR*** POWER TO A BOY, AND YOUR RESPONSE IS PANIC?!
IF NO ONE HAS ANY OTHER ***FANTASIES*** REGARDING MY ***GENITALIA*** THEN I SHALL EXPLAIN WHAT HAPPENS NEXT.

SAW SOME GREAT *HUSTLE* OUT THERE TODAY, *GARY!* KEEP IT UP!

IT'S *"GAH'REE,"* SIRE...

BE *GOOD,* YOU GUYS.

...I—I *SEE* MY HOME... O—ON A *HILL*... MY FAMILY...

BACKSTABBER CAN *ALMOST* REMEMBER WHO HE WAS, CAN'T HE?

DID I MENTION THAT *FREE* MUSIC THERAPY IS IN MY REFORMS? BACKY'S SESSIONS GAVE ME THE IDEA.

I DON'T KNOW... THE MUSIC SOOTHES HIM...

YES, DEAR, YOU TOLD ME.

WREN AND I WERE HAVING SUCH A NICE CATCH-UP...

...BUT I HAVE TO RUN.

Mmmmmmwa. YOU'RE SUCH A GOOD BOY.

MOOOOM! SHOW SOME *RESTRAINT,* JEEZ...

...WHERE HAS MY MUSIC GONE?

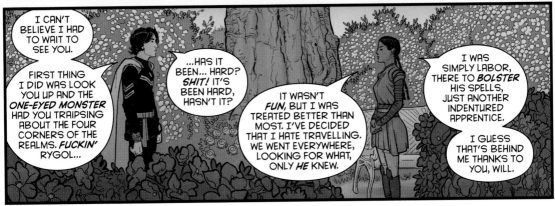

I CAN'T BELIEVE I HAD TO WAIT TO SEE YOU.

FIRST THING I DID WAS LOOK YOU UP AND THE *ONE-EYED MONSTER* HAD YOU TRAIPSING ABOUT THE FOUR CORNERS OF THE REALMS. *FUCKIN'* RYGOL...

...HAS IT BEEN... HARD? *SHIT!* IT'S BEEN HARD, HASN'T IT?

IT WASN'T *FUN,* BUT I WAS TREATED BETTER THAN MOST. I'VE DECIDED THAT I HATE TRAVELLING. WE WENT EVERYWHERE, LOOKING FOR WHAT, ONLY *HE* KNEW.

I WAS SIMPLY LABOR, THERE TO *BOLSTER* HIS SPELLS, JUST ANOTHER INDENTURED APPRENTICE.

I GUESS THAT'S BEHIND ME THANKS TO YOU, WILL.

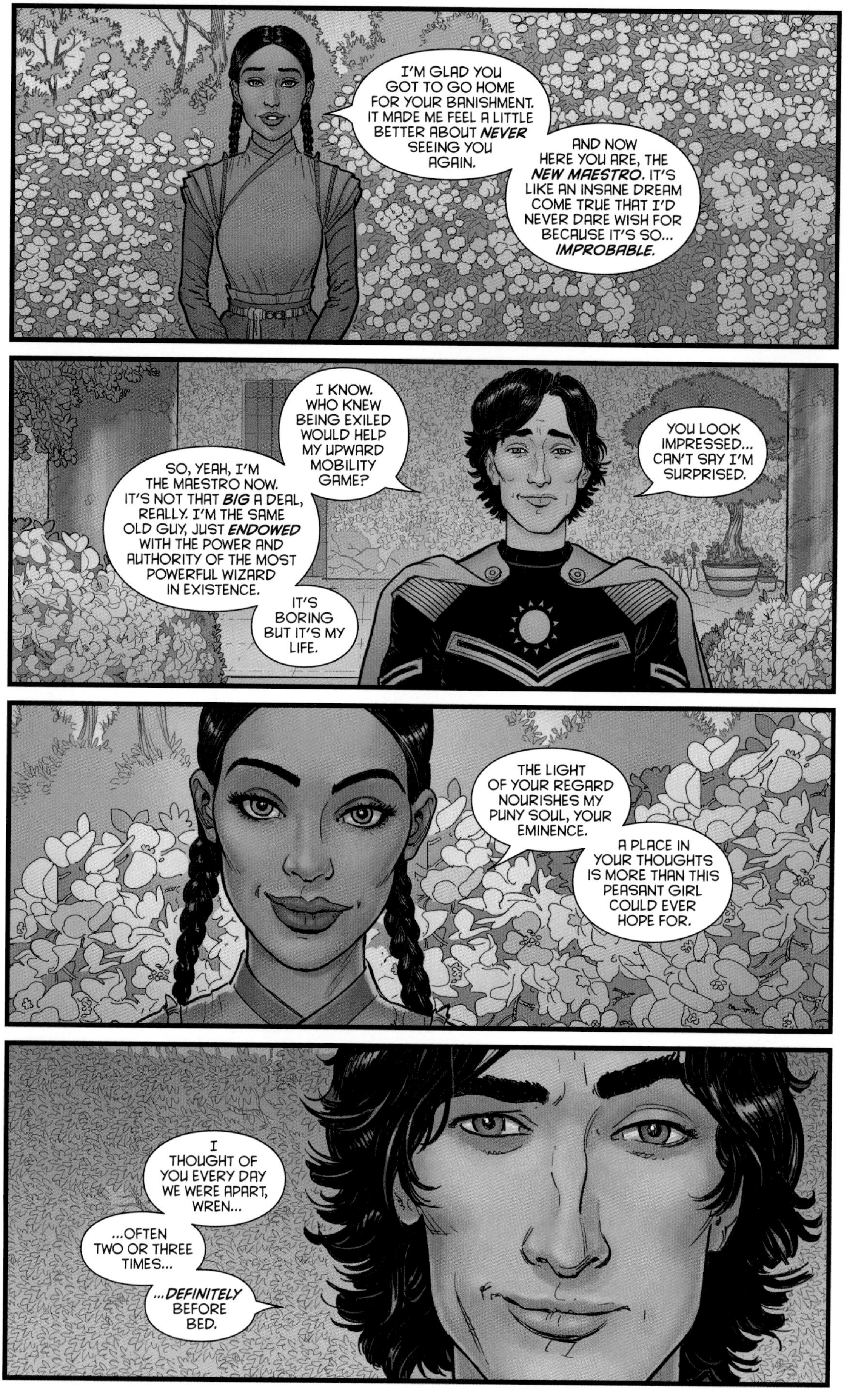
I'M GLAD YOU GOT TO GO HOME FOR YOUR BANISHMENT. IT MADE ME FEEL A LITTLE BETTER ABOUT NEVER SEEING YOU AGAIN.
AND NOW HERE YOU ARE, THE NEW MAESTRO. IT'S LIKE AN INSANE DREAM COME TRUE THAT I'D NEVER DARE WISH FOR BECAUSE IT'S SO... IMPROBABLE.
YOU LOOK IMPRESSED... CAN'T SAY I'M SURPRISED.
I KNOW. WHO KNEW BEING EXILED WOULD HELP MY UPWARD MOBILITY GAME?
SO, YEAH, I'M THE MAESTRO NOW. IT'S NOT THAT BIG A DEAL, REALLY. I'M THE SAME OLD GUY, JUST ENDOWED WITH THE POWER AND AUTHORITY OF THE MOST POWERFUL WIZARD IN EXISTENCE.
IT'S BORING BUT IT'S MY LIFE.
THE LIGHT OF YOUR REGARD NOURISHES MY PUNY SOUL, YOUR EMINENCE.
A PLACE IN YOUR THOUGHTS IS MORE THAN THIS PEASANT GIRL COULD EVER HOPE FOR.
I THOUGHT OF YOU EVERY DAY WE WERE APART, WREN...
...OFTEN TWO OR THREE TIMES...
...DEFINITELY BEFORE BED.

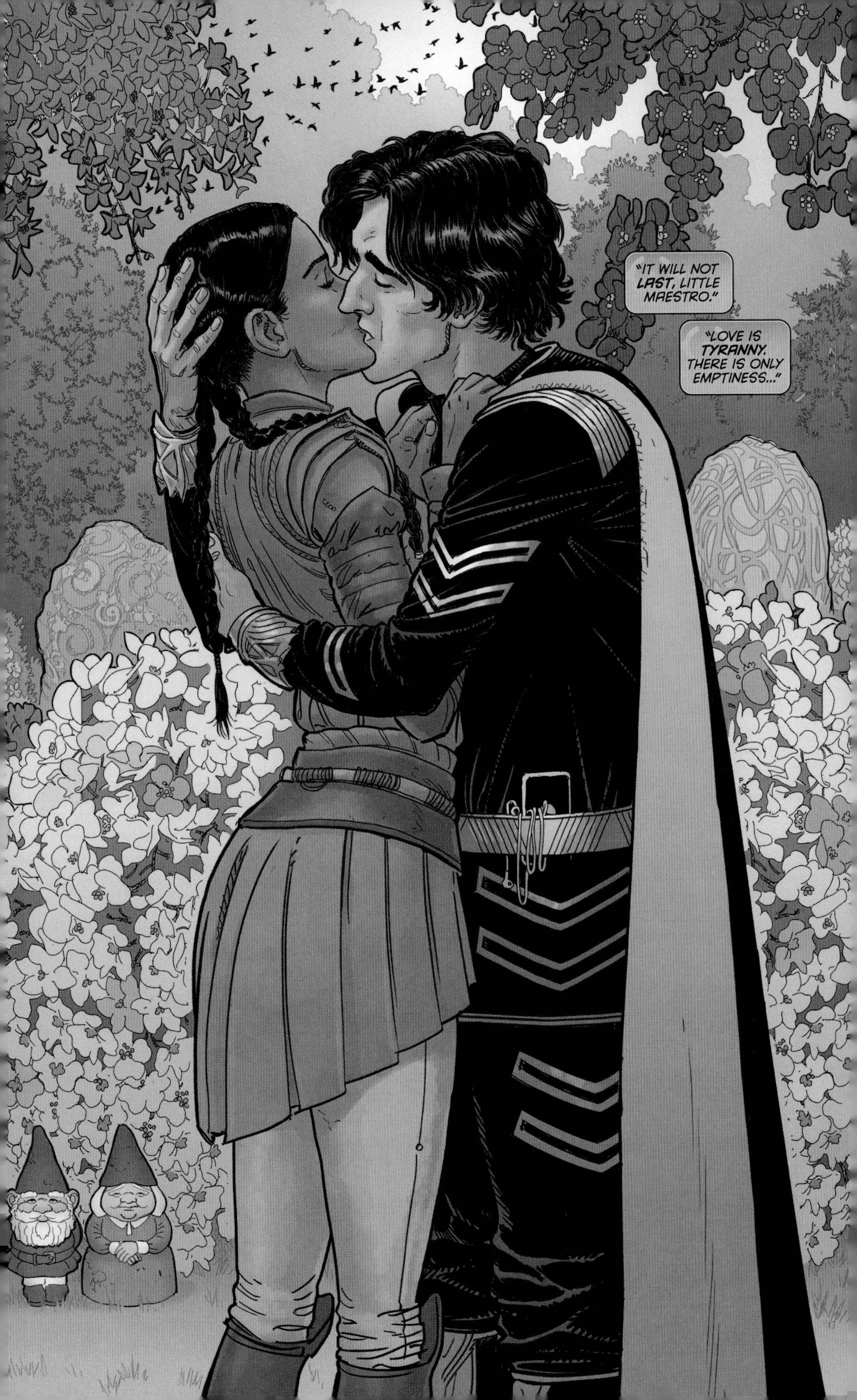
"IT WILL NOT LAST, LITTLE MAESTRO."
"LOVE IS TYRANNY. THERE IS ONLY EMPTINESS..."

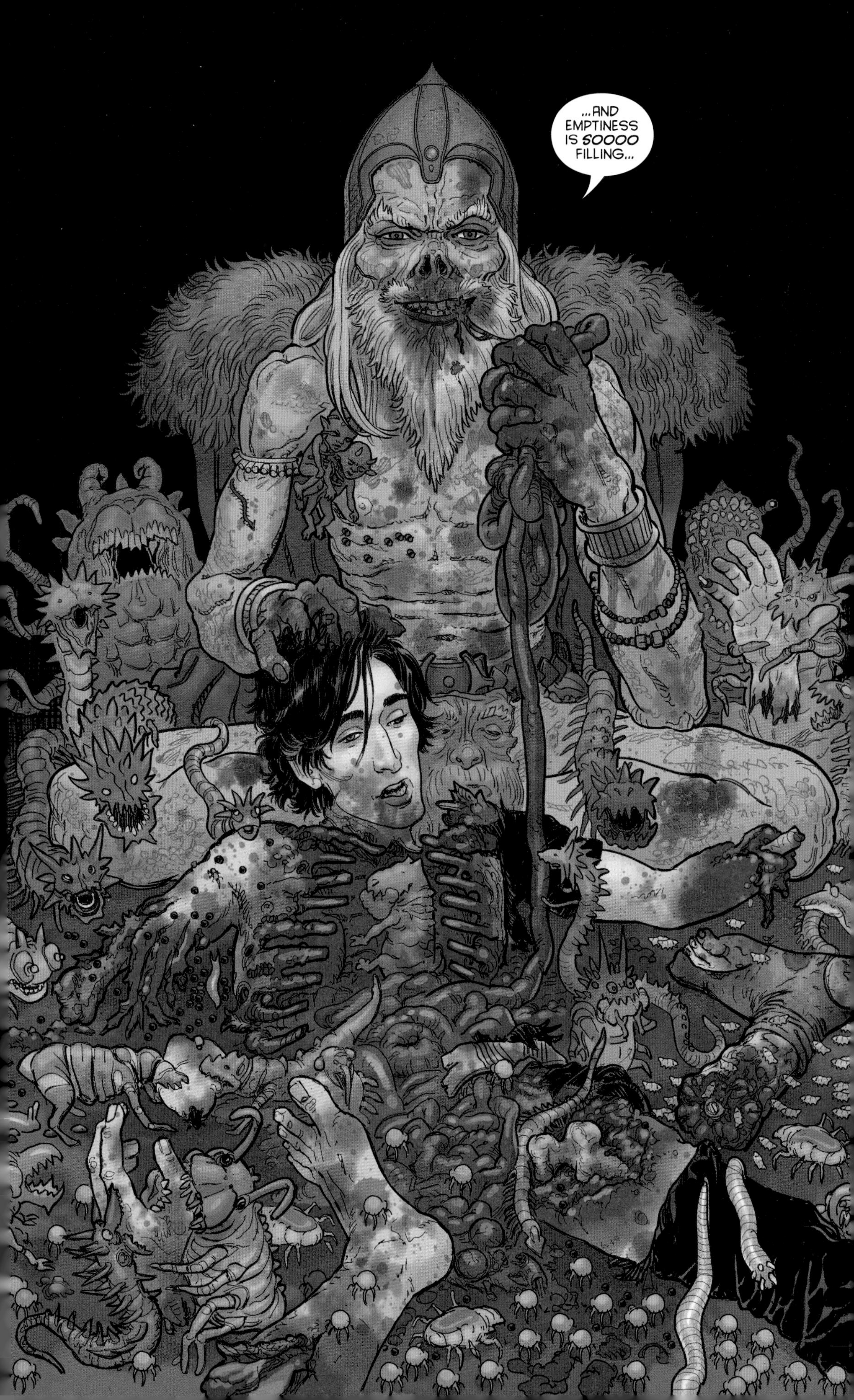
...AND EMPTINESS IS SOOOO FILLING...

AAAAAAHH!!

WILL, ARE YOU OKAY? WHAT'S HAPPENED?

IT'S NOTHING, JUST SOME *PTSD BULLSHIT*. GO BACK TO SLEEP.

WILL, EARLIER TODAY I READ *MUCH* OF YOUR KHALEESI REFORMS. IT WAS... COMPREHENSIVE.

THANKS. I WANTED TO INCLUDE *MORE* BUT I'VE ONLY BEEN AT IT A FEW WEEKS. REVISIONS ARE COMING.

MAYBE IT'S *TOO MUCH* TOO SOON...

WHAT? REALLY?

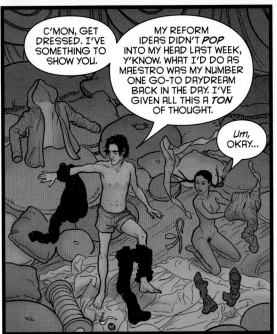

C'MON, GET DRESSED. I'VE SOMETHING TO SHOW YOU.

MY REFORM IDEAS DIDN'T *POP* INTO MY HEAD LAST WEEK, Y'KNOW. WHAT I'D DO AS MAESTRO WAS MY NUMBER ONE GO-TO DAYDREAM BACK IN THE DAY. I'VE GIVEN ALL THIS A *TON* OF THOUGHT.

Um, OKAY...

DURING MY EXILE, I MADE GOOD USE OF MY TIME. WELL, *MOSTLY* I DID.

I WENT BACK TO SCHOOL, I *AUDITED* A LOT OF COURSES -- *SOCIAL JUSTICE* COURSES -- AND NOW I'M *APPLYING* THAT KNOWLEDGE.

YOU ALREADY *SOUND* INSANE...

HERE'S WHAT I KNOW: *"WITH GREAT POWER COMES A SHIT-TON OF ASSHOLE BEHAVIOR."*

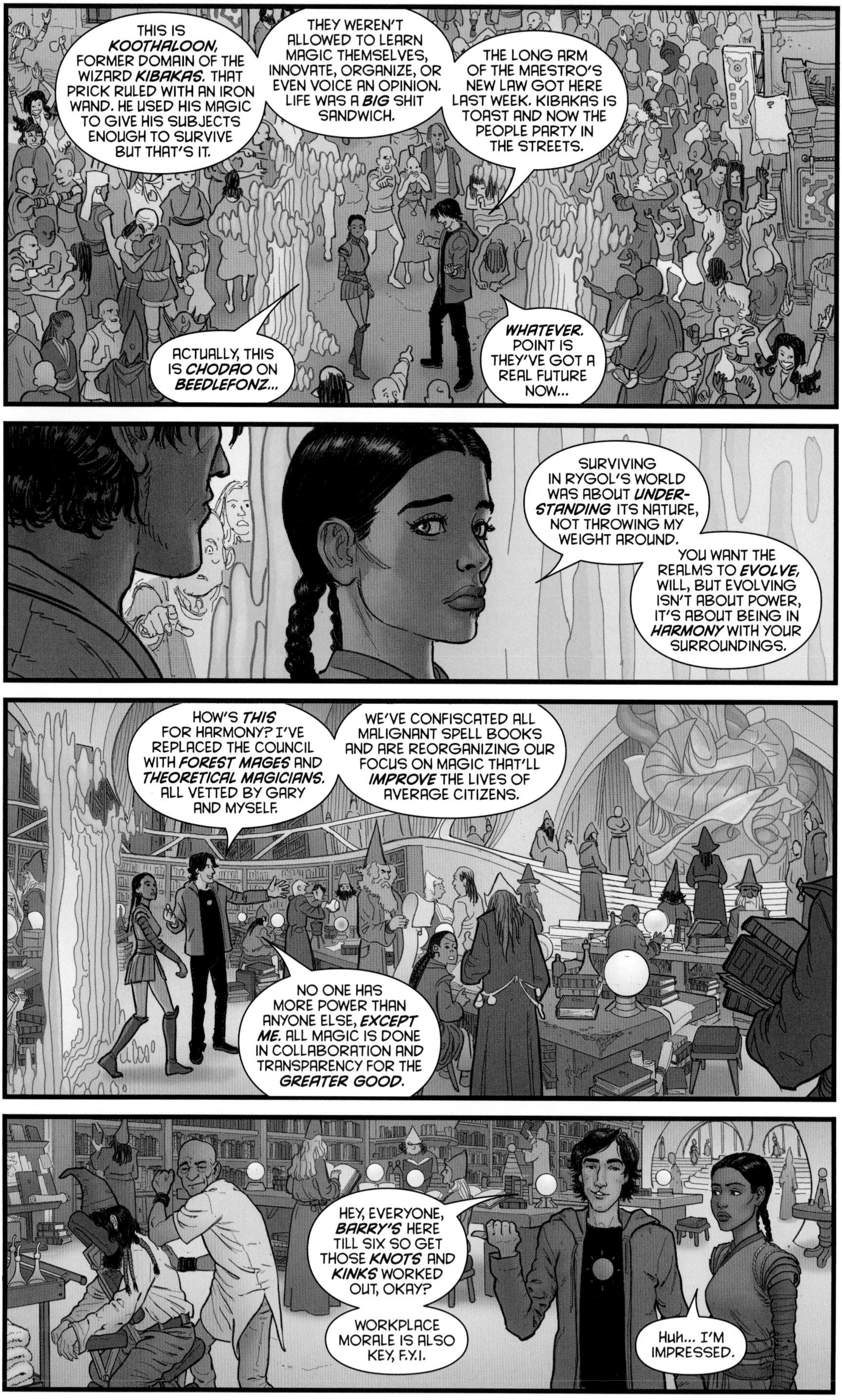
THIS IS KOOTHALOON, FORMER DOMAIN OF THE WIZARD KIBAKAS. THAT PRICK RULED WITH AN IRON WAND. HE USED HIS MAGIC TO GIVE HIS SUBJECTS ENOUGH TO SURVIVE BUT THAT'S IT.
THEY WEREN'T ALLOWED TO LEARN MAGIC THEMSELVES, INNOVATE, ORGANIZE, OR EVEN VOICE AN OPINION. LIFE WAS A BIG SHIT SANDWICH.
THE LONG ARM OF THE MAESTRO'S NEW LAW GOT HERE LAST WEEK. KIBAKAS IS TOAST AND NOW THE PEOPLE PARTY IN THE STREETS.
ACTUALLY, THIS IS CHODAO ON BEEDLEFONZ...
WHATEVER. POINT IS THEY'VE GOT A REAL FUTURE NOW...
SURVIVING IN RYGOL'S WORLD WAS ABOUT UNDER-STANDING ITS NATURE, NOT THROWING MY WEIGHT AROUND.
YOU WANT THE REALMS TO EVOLVE, WILL, BUT EVOLVING ISN'T ABOUT POWER, IT'S ABOUT BEING IN HARMONY WITH YOUR SURROUNDINGS.
HOW'S THIS FOR HARMONY? I'VE REPLACED THE COUNCIL WITH FOREST MAGES AND THEORETICAL MAGICIANS. ALL VETTED BY GARY AND MYSELF.
WE'VE CONFISCATED ALL MALIGNANT SPELL BOOKS AND ARE REORGANIZING OUR FOCUS ON MAGIC THAT'LL IMPROVE THE LIVES OF AVERAGE CITIZENS.
NO ONE HAS MORE POWER THAN ANYONE ELSE, EXCEPT ME. ALL MAGIC IS DONE IN COLLABORATION AND TRANSPARENCY FOR THE GREATER GOOD.
HEY, EVERYONE, BARRY'S HERE TILL SIX SO GET THOSE KNOTS AND KINKS WORKED OUT, OKAY?
WORKPLACE MORALE IS ALSO KEY, F.Y.I.
Huh... I'M IMPRESSED.

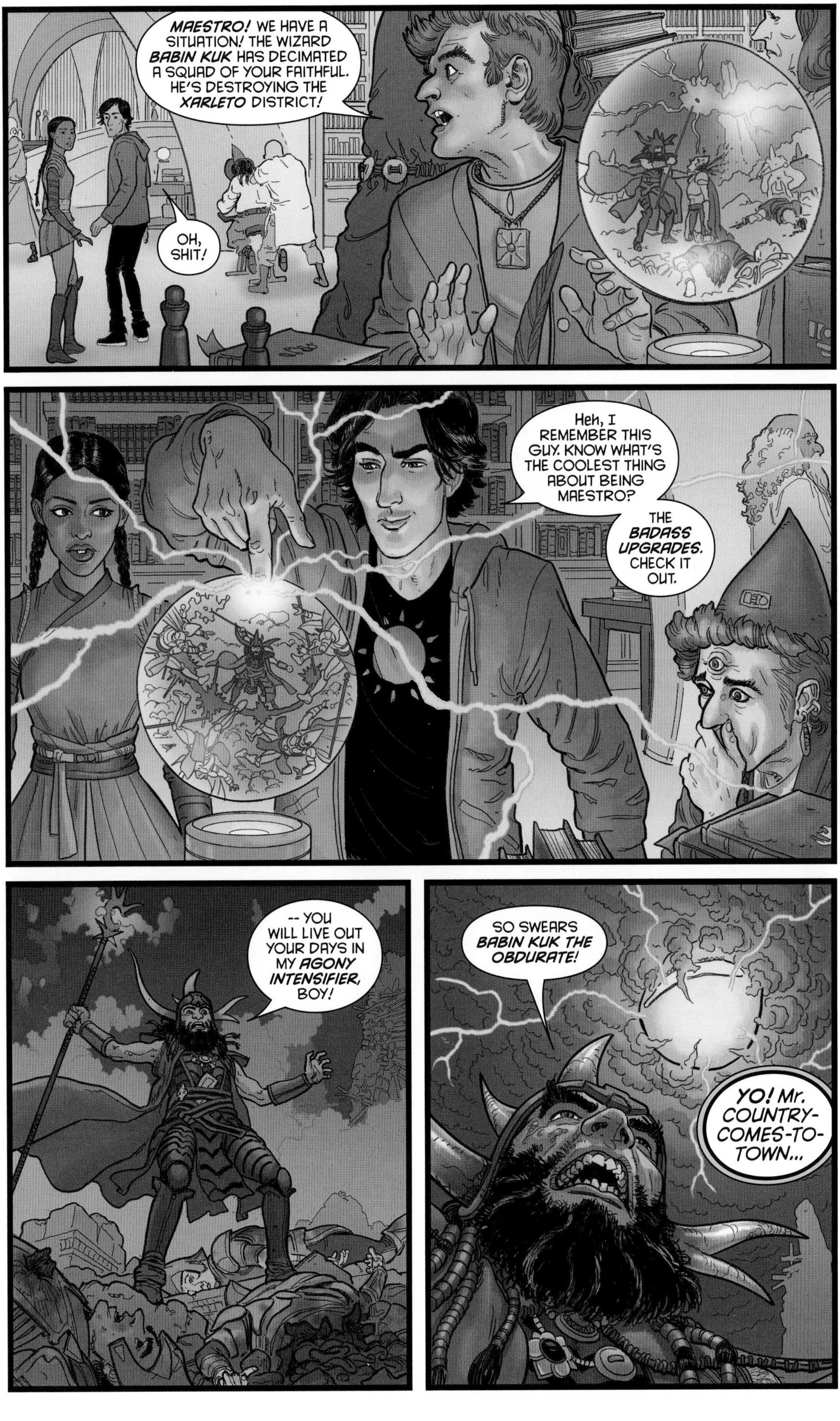
MAESTRO! WE HAVE A SITUATION! THE WIZARD BABIN KUK HAS DECIMATED A SQUAD OF YOUR FAITHFUL. HE'S DESTROYING THE XARLETO DISTRICT!
OH, SHIT!
Heh, I REMEMBER THIS GUY. KNOW WHAT'S THE COOLEST THING ABOUT BEING MAESTRO?
THE BADASS UPGRADES. CHECK IT OUT.
-- YOU WILL LIVE OUT YOUR DAYS IN MY AGONY INTENSIFIER, BOY!
SO SWEARS BABIN KUK THE OBDURATE!
YO! Mr. COUNTRY-COMES-TO-TOWN...

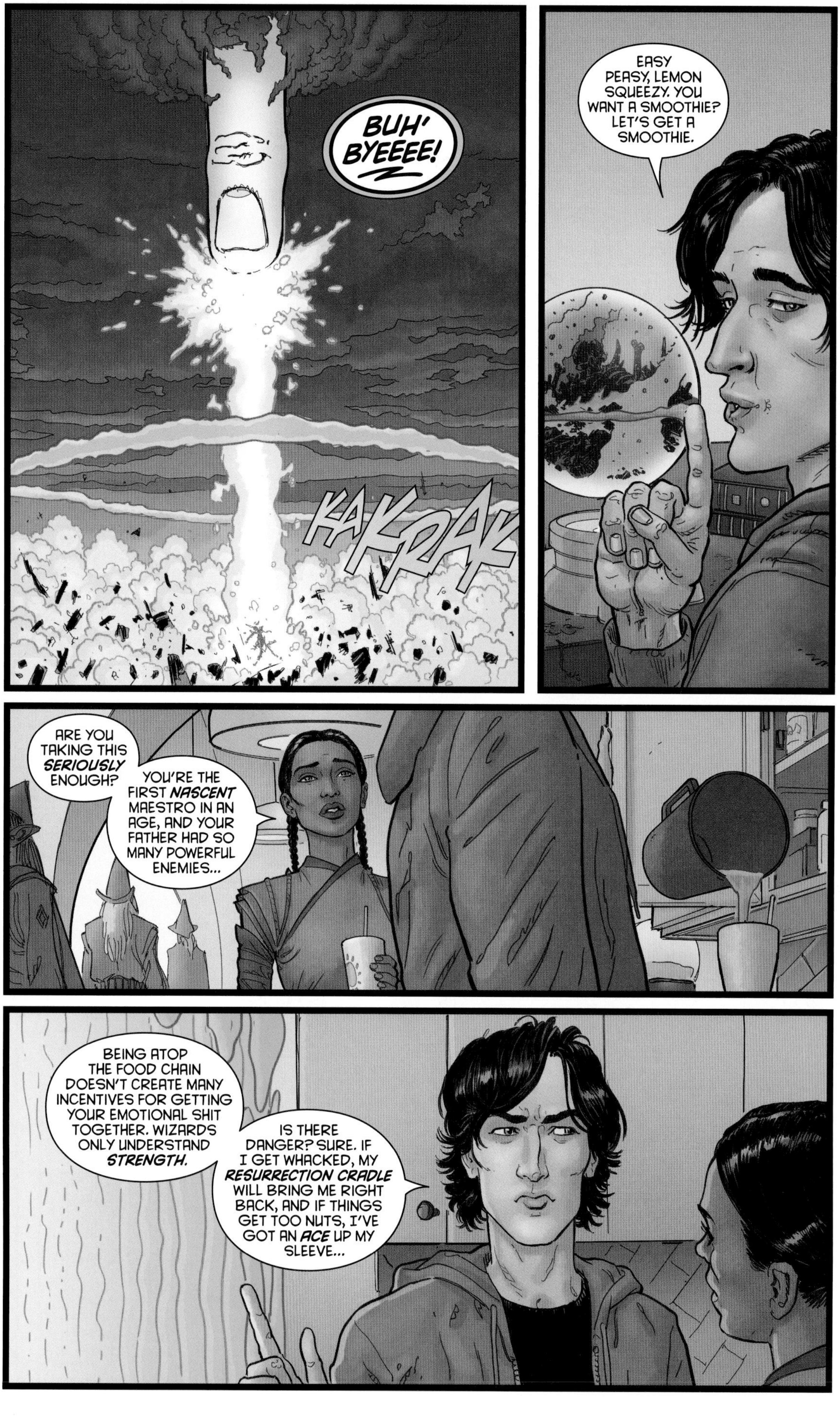
BUH' BYEEEE!
KAKRAK
EASY PEASY, LEMON SQUEEZY. YOU WANT A SMOOTHIE? LET'S GET A SMOOTHIE.
ARE YOU TAKING THIS SERIOUSLY ENOUGH?
YOU'RE THE FIRST NASCENT MAESTRO IN AN AGE, AND YOUR FATHER HAD SO MANY POWERFUL ENEMIES...
BEING ATOP THE FOOD CHAIN DOESN'T CREATE MANY INCENTIVES FOR GETTING YOUR EMOTIONAL SHIT TOGETHER. WIZARDS ONLY UNDERSTAND STRENGTH.
IS THERE DANGER? SURE. IF I GET WHACKED, MY RESURRECTION CRADLE WILL BRING ME RIGHT BACK, AND IF THINGS GET TOO NUTS, I'VE GOT AN ACE UP MY SLEEVE...

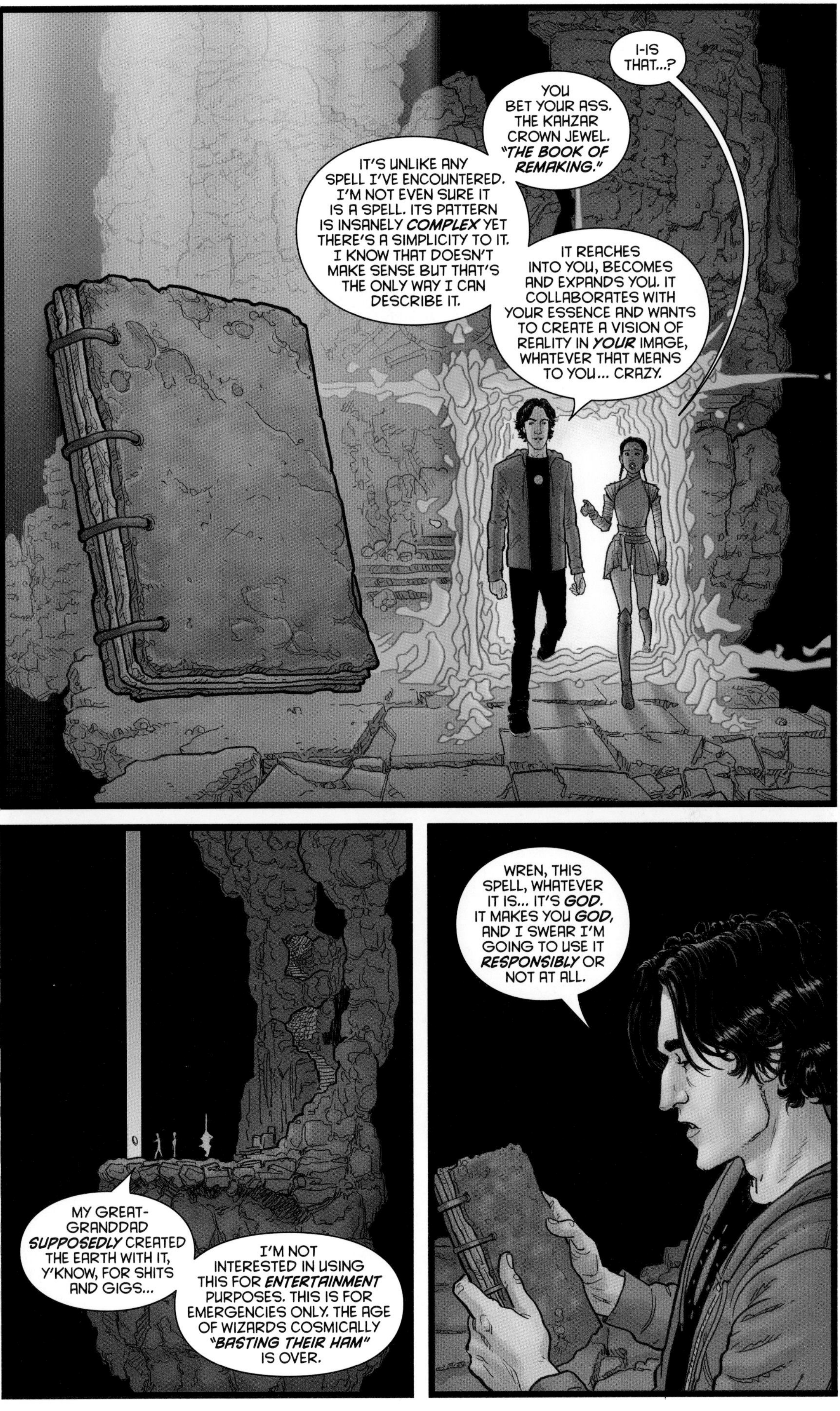
I-IS THAT...?
YOU BET YOUR ASS. THE KAHZAR CROWN JEWEL. *"THE BOOK OF REMAKING."*
IT'S UNLIKE ANY SPELL I'VE ENCOUNTERED. I'M NOT EVEN SURE IT IS A SPELL. ITS PATTERN IS INSANELY *COMPLEX* YET THERE'S A SIMPLICITY TO IT. I KNOW THAT DOESN'T MAKE SENSE BUT THAT'S THE ONLY WAY I CAN DESCRIBE IT.
IT REACHES INTO YOU, BECOMES AND EXPANDS YOU. IT COLLABORATES WITH YOUR ESSENCE AND WANTS TO CREATE A VISION OF REALITY IN *YOUR* IMAGE, WHATEVER THAT MEANS TO YOU... CRAZY.
MY GREAT-GRANDDAD *SUPPOSEDLY* CREATED THE EARTH WITH IT, Y'KNOW, FOR SHITS AND GIGS...
I'M NOT INTERESTED IN USING THIS FOR *ENTERTAINMENT* PURPOSES. THIS IS FOR EMERGENCIES ONLY. THE AGE OF WIZARDS COSMICALLY *"BASTING THEIR HAM"* IS OVER.
WREN, THIS SPELL, WHATEVER IT IS... IT'S *GOD*. IT MAKES YOU *GOD*, AND I SWEAR I'M GOING TO USE IT *RESPONSIBLY* OR NOT AT ALL.

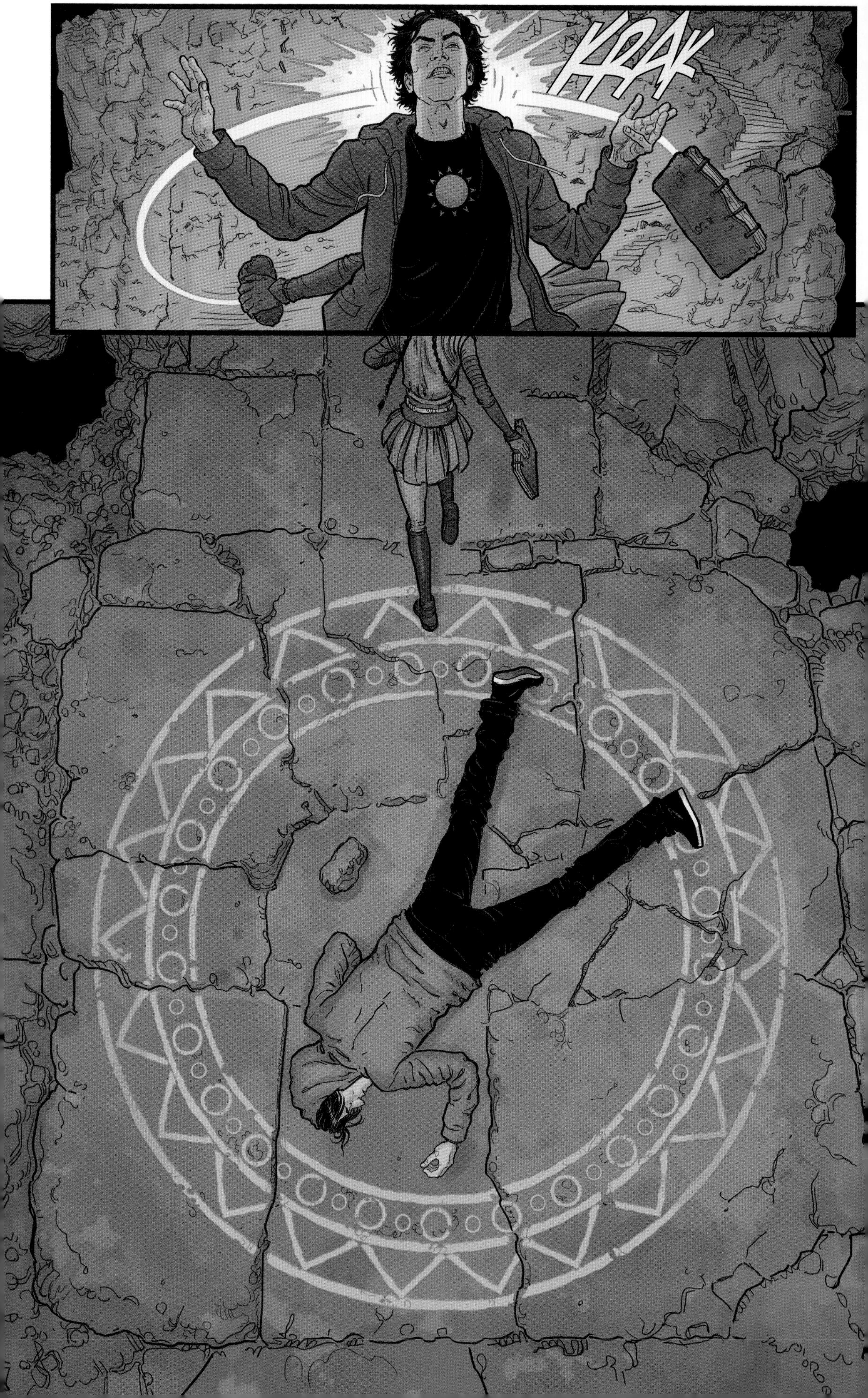
KRAK

CHAPTER THREE

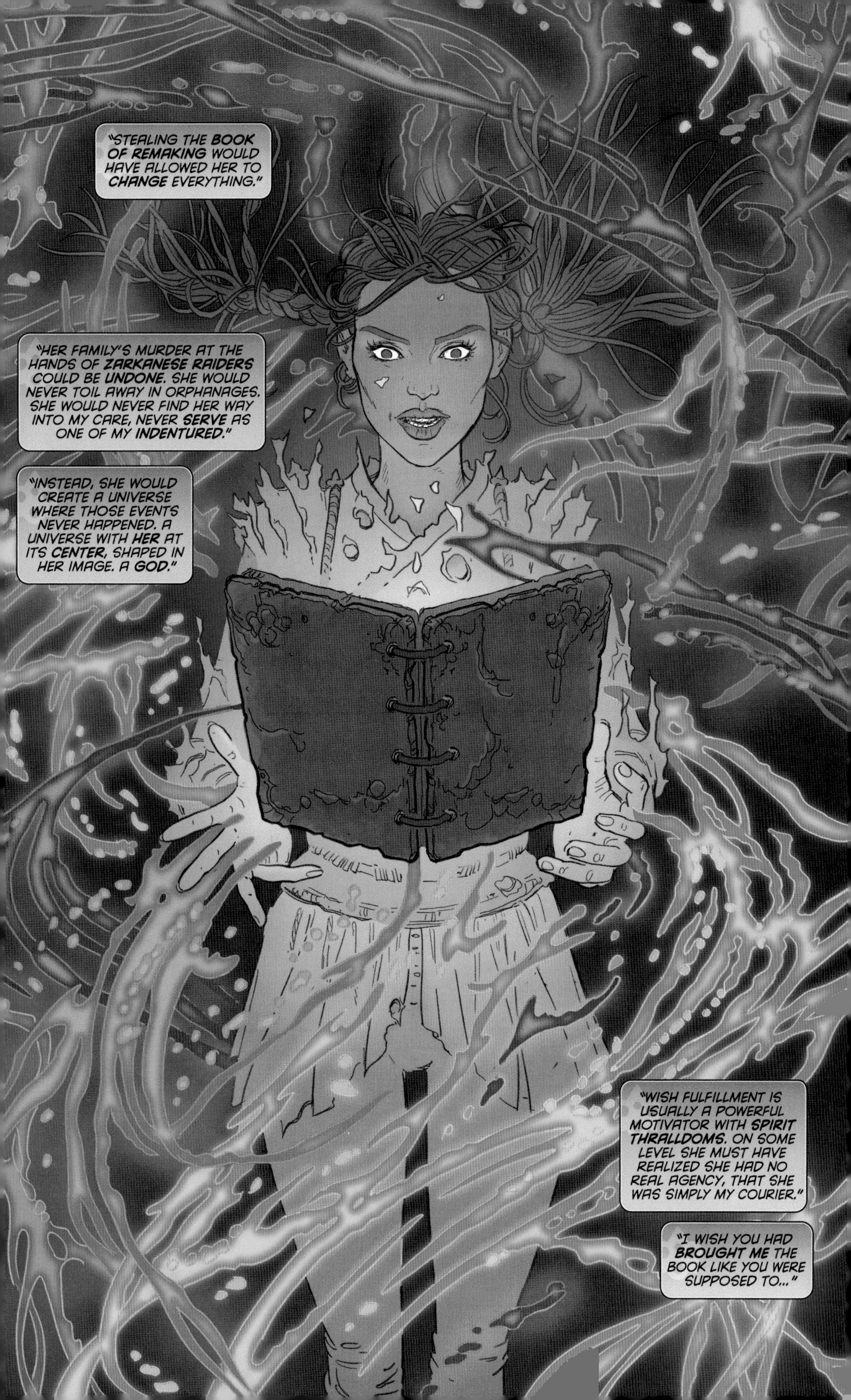
"STEALING THE BOOK OF REMAKING WOULD HAVE ALLOWED HER TO CHANGE EVERYTHING."
"HER FAMILY'S MURDER AT THE HANDS OF ZARKANESE RAIDERS COULD BE UNDONE. SHE WOULD NEVER TOIL AWAY IN ORPHANAGES. SHE WOULD NEVER FIND HER WAY INTO MY CARE, NEVER SERVE AS ONE OF MY INDENTURED."
"INSTEAD, SHE WOULD CREATE A UNIVERSE WHERE THOSE EVENTS NEVER HAPPENED. A UNIVERSE WITH HER AT ITS CENTER, SHAPED IN HER IMAGE. A GOD."
"WISH FULFILLMENT IS USUALLY A POWERFUL MOTIVATOR WITH SPIRIT THRALLDOMS. ON SOME LEVEL SHE MUST HAVE REALIZED SHE HAD NO REAL AGENCY, THAT SHE WAS SIMPLY MY COURIER."
"I WISH YOU HAD BROUGHT ME THE BOOK LIKE YOU WERE SUPPOSED TO..."

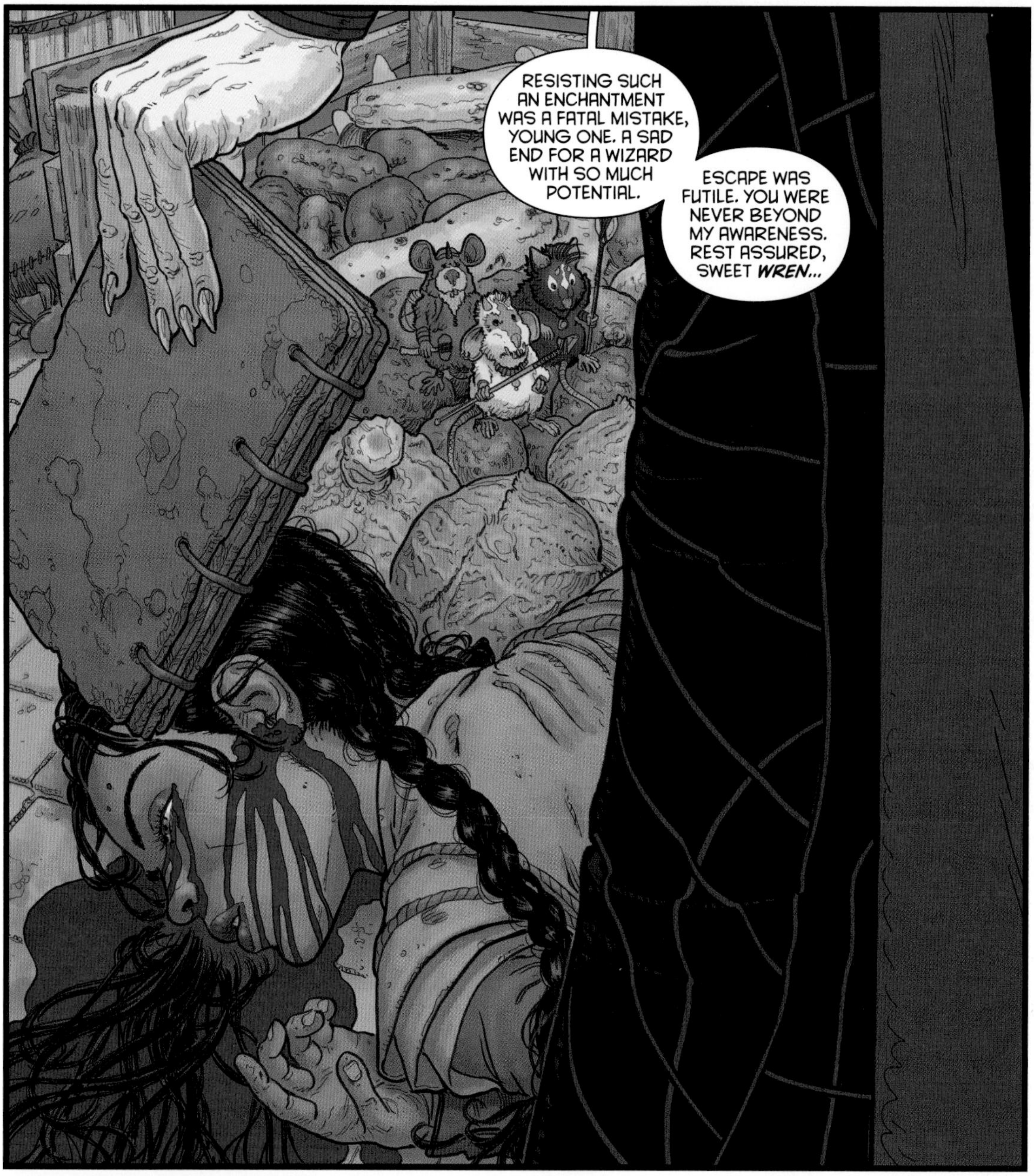
RESISTING SUCH AN ENCHANTMENT WAS A FATAL MISTAKE, YOUNG ONE. A SAD END FOR A WIZARD WITH SO MUCH POTENTIAL.
ESCAPE WAS FUTILE. YOU WERE NEVER BEYOND MY AWARENESS. REST ASSURED, SWEET *WREN*...

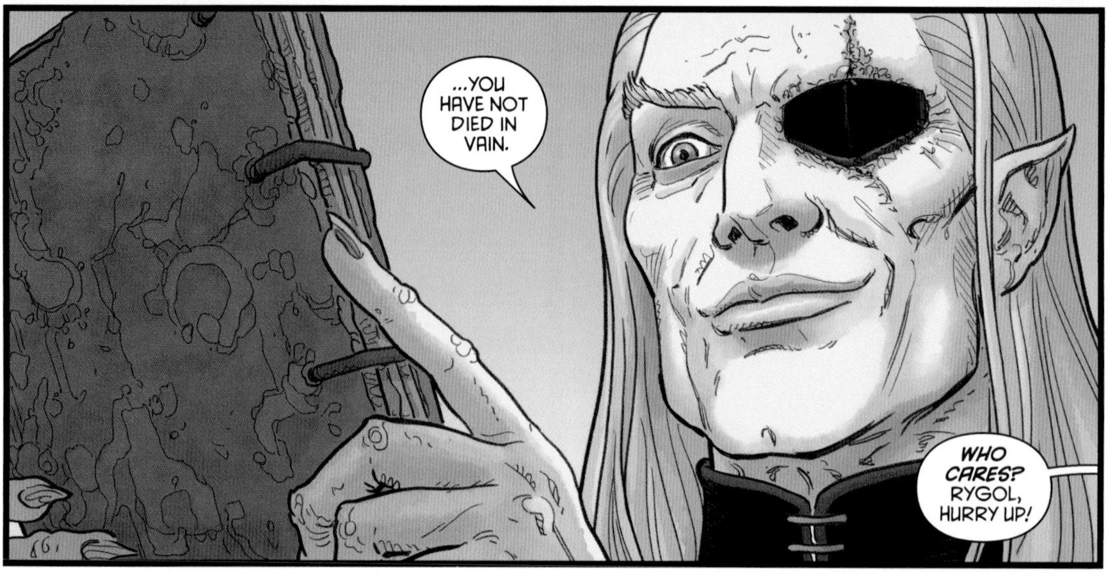
...YOU HAVE NOT DIED IN VAIN.
WHO CARES? RYGOL, HURRY UP!

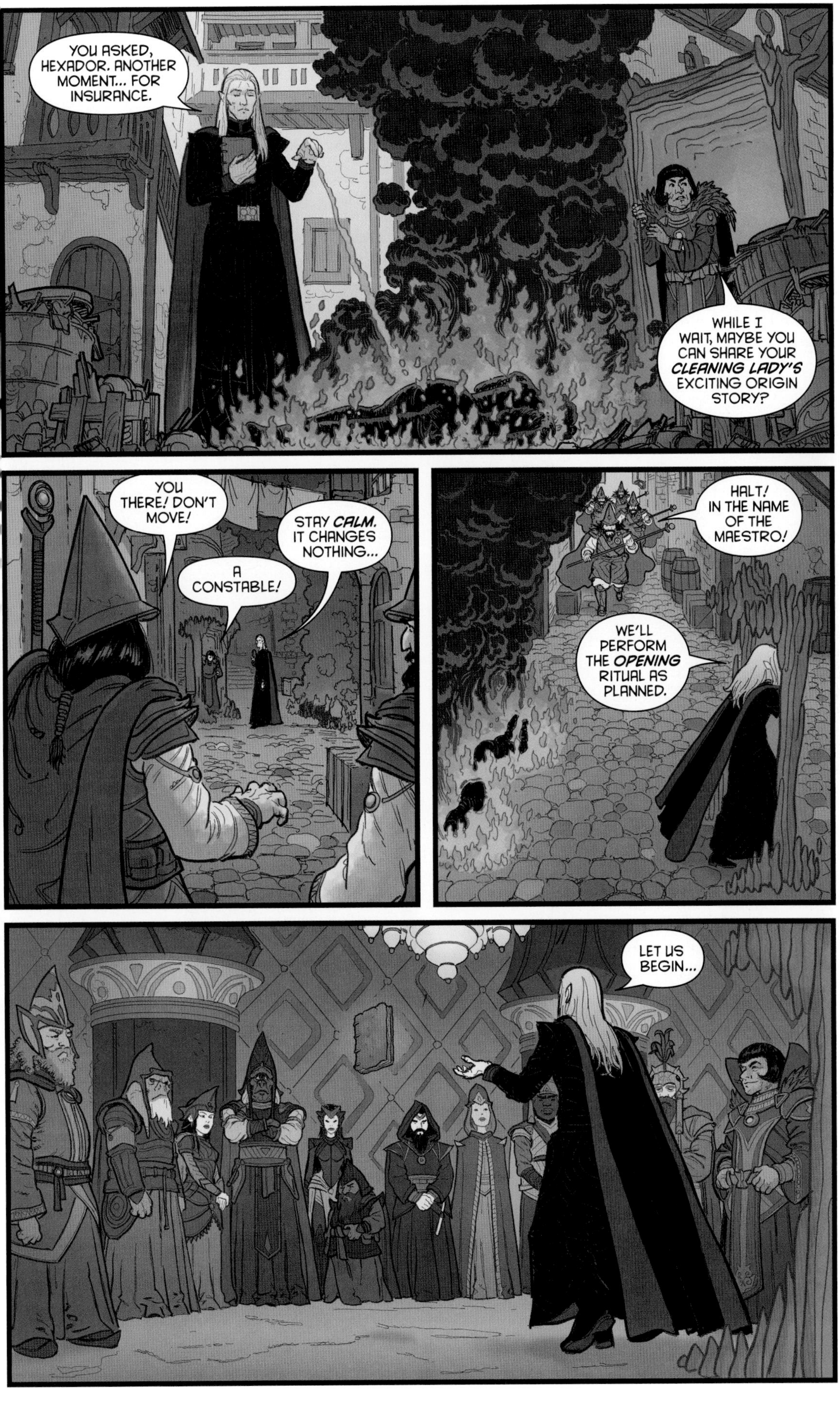
YOU ASKED, HEXADOR. ANOTHER MOMENT... FOR INSURANCE.
WHILE I WAIT, MAYBE YOU CAN SHARE YOUR *CLEANING LADY'S* EXCITING ORIGIN STORY?
YOU THERE! DON'T MOVE!
A CONSTABLE!
STAY *CALM.* IT CHANGES NOTHING...
HALT! IN THE NAME OF THE MAESTRO!
WE'LL PERFORM THE *OPENING* RITUAL AS PLANNED.
LET US BEGIN...

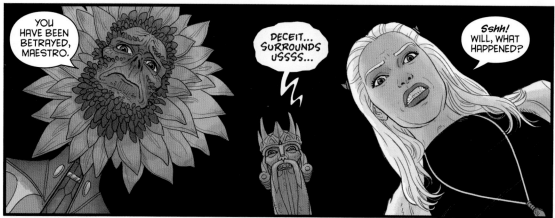

YOU HAVE BEEN BETRAYED, MAESTRO.

DECEIT... SURROUNDS USSSS...

Sshh! WILL, WHAT HAPPENED?

~Nngh~ RYGOL. HE DID SOMETHING TO WREN -- FUCKING MIND CONTROL SPELL... SHE STOLE THE BOOK.

MIND CONTROL. JESUS. THAT ARCANIST BASTARD.

DOESN'T LOOOK... GOOD...

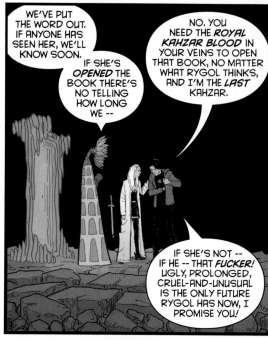

WE'VE PUT THE WORD OUT. IF ANYONE HAS SEEN HER, WE'LL KNOW SOON.

IF SHE'S OPENED THE BOOK THERE'S NO TELLING HOW LONG WE --

NO. YOU NEED THE ROYAL KAHZAR BLOOD IN YOUR VEINS TO OPEN THAT BOOK, NO MATTER WHAT RYGOL THINKS, AND I'M THE LAST KAHZAR.

IF SHE'S NOT -- IF HE -- THAT FUCKER! UGLY, PROLONGED, CRUEL-AND-UNUSUAL IS THE ONLY FUTURE RYGOL HAS NOW, I PROMISE YOU!

MY LOCATER ISN'T WORKING, I CAN'T FIND THE BOOK! HOW'S HE BLOCKING ME?

MAESTRO... THERE'S NEWS.

RYGOL HAS ESCAPED, YOUR GREATNESS, BUT WE'VE... FOUND THE GIRL.

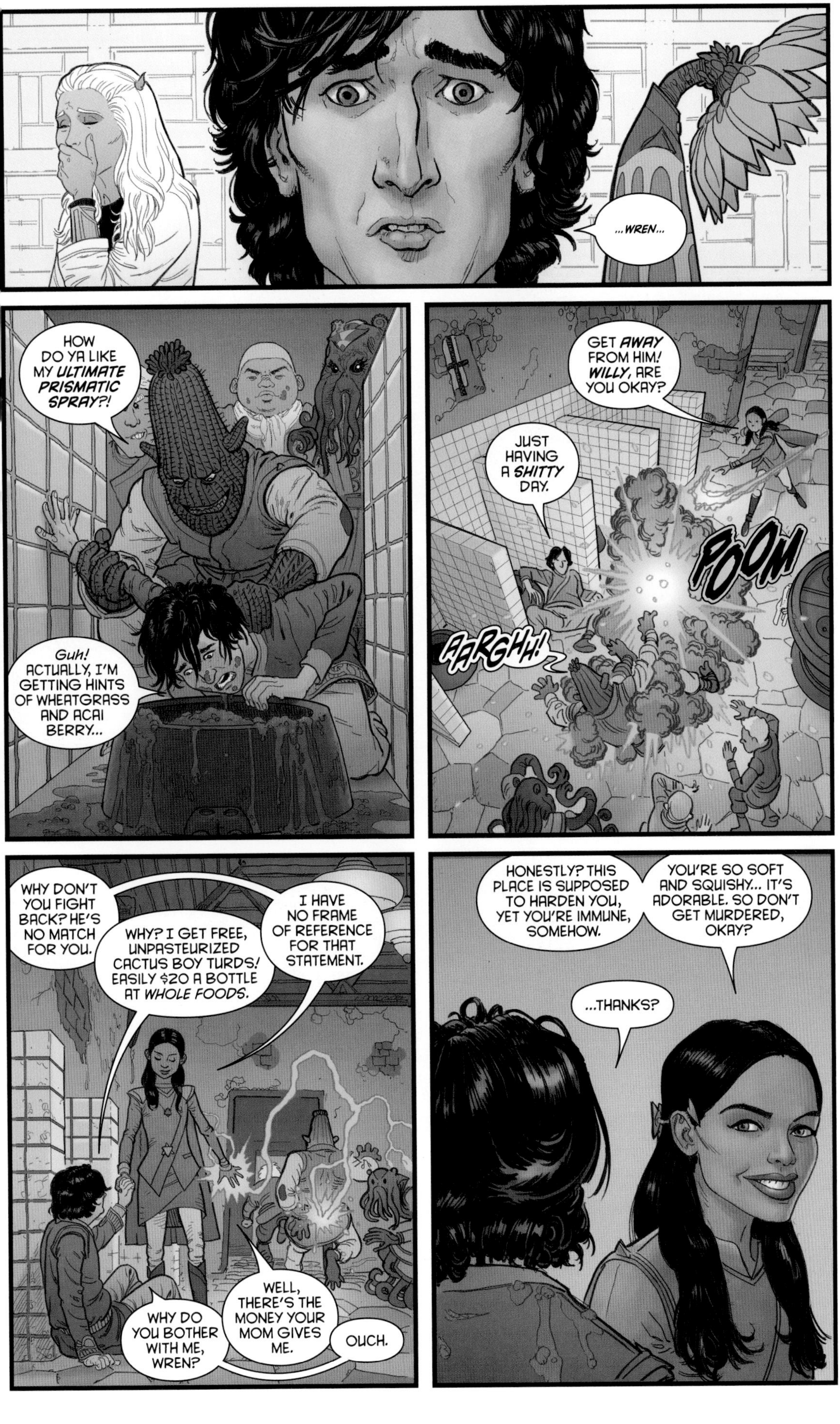
...WREN...
HOW DO YA LIKE MY *ULTIMATE PRISMATIC SPRAY*?!
Guh! ACTUALLY, I'M GETTING HINTS OF WHEATGRASS AND ACAI BERRY...
GET *AWAY* FROM HIM! *WILLY*, ARE YOU OKAY?
JUST HAVING A *SHITTY* DAY.
POOM
AARGHH!
WHY DON'T YOU FIGHT BACK? HE'S NO MATCH FOR YOU.
WHY? I GET FREE, UNPASTEURIZED CACTUS BOY TURDS! EASILY $20 A BOTTLE AT *WHOLE FOODS*.
I HAVE NO FRAME OF REFERENCE FOR THAT STATEMENT.
WHY DO YOU BOTHER WITH ME, WREN?
WELL, THERE'S THE MONEY YOUR MOM GIVES ME.
OUCH.
HONESTLY? THIS PLACE IS SUPPOSED TO HARDEN YOU, YET YOU'RE IMMUNE, SOMEHOW.
YOU'RE SO SOFT AND SQUISHY... IT'S ADORABLE. SO DON'T GET MURDERED, OKAY?
...THANKS?

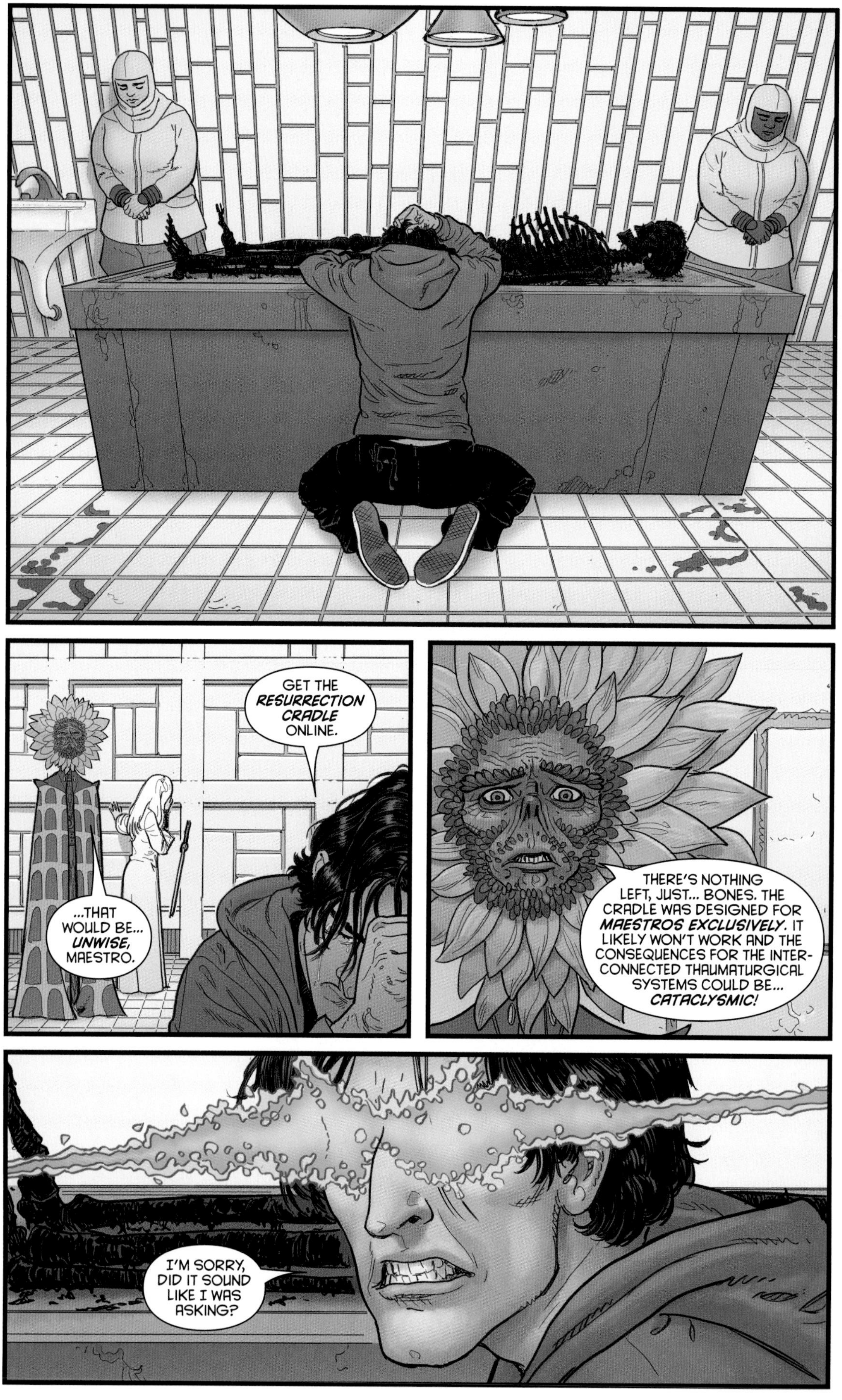
GET THE *RESURRECTION CRADLE* ONLINE.
...THAT WOULD BE... *UNWISE,* MAESTRO.
THERE'S NOTHING LEFT, JUST... BONES. THE CRADLE WAS DESIGNED FOR *MAESTROS EXCLUSIVELY.* IT LIKELY WON'T WORK AND THE CONSEQUENCES FOR THE INTER-CONNECTED THAUMATURGICAL SYSTEMS COULD BE... *CATACLYSMIC!*
I'M SORRY, DID IT SOUND LIKE I WAS ASKING?

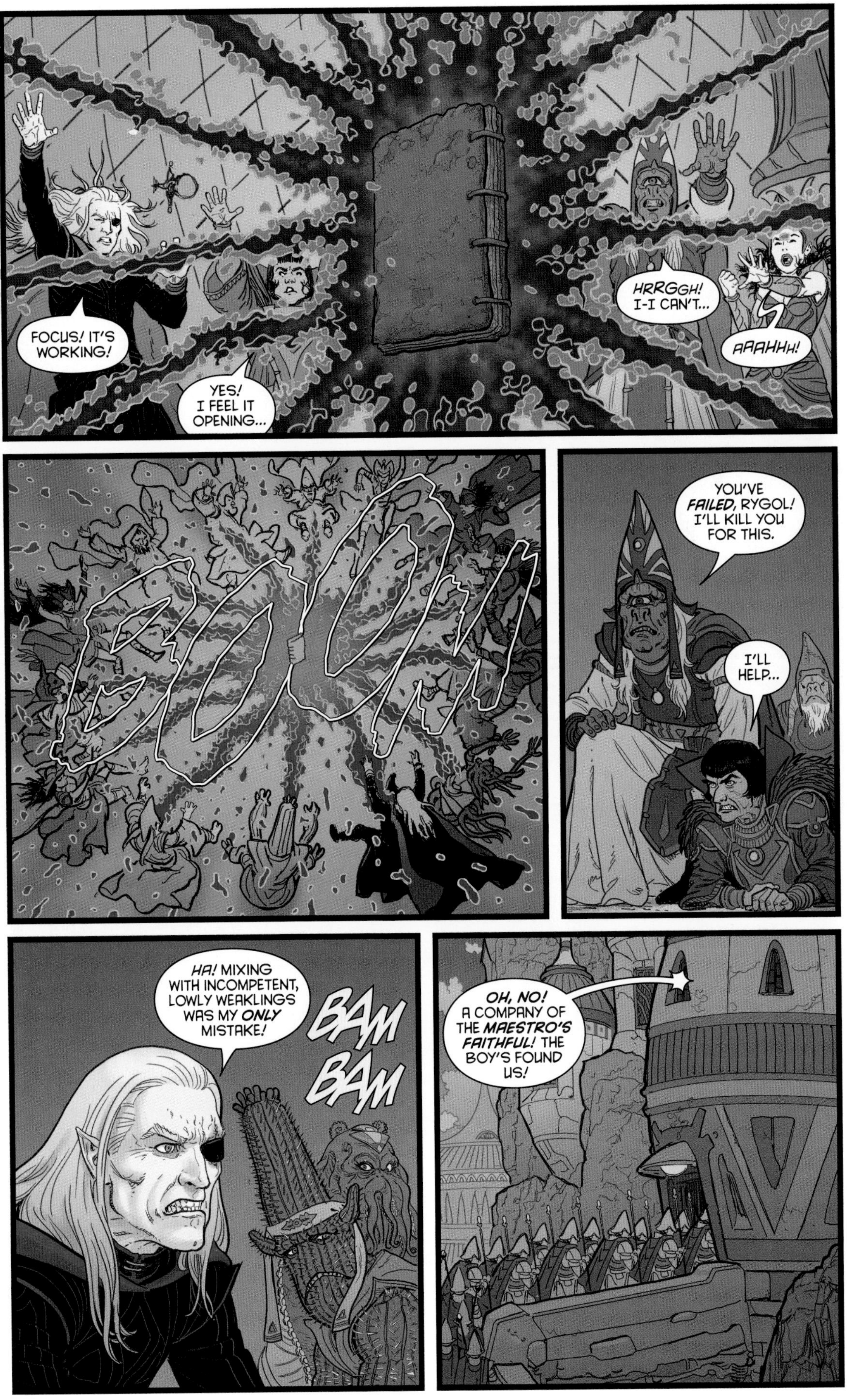
FOCUS! IT'S WORKING!
YES! I FEEL IT OPENING...
HRRGGH! I-I CAN'T...
AAAHHH!
BOOM
YOU'VE FAILED, RYGOL! I'LL KILL YOU FOR THIS.
I'LL HELP...
HA! MIXING WITH INCOMPETENT, LOWLY WEAKLINGS WAS MY ONLY MISTAKE!
BAM BAM
OH, NO! A COMPANY OF THE MAESTRO'S FAITHFUL! THE BOY'S FOUND US!

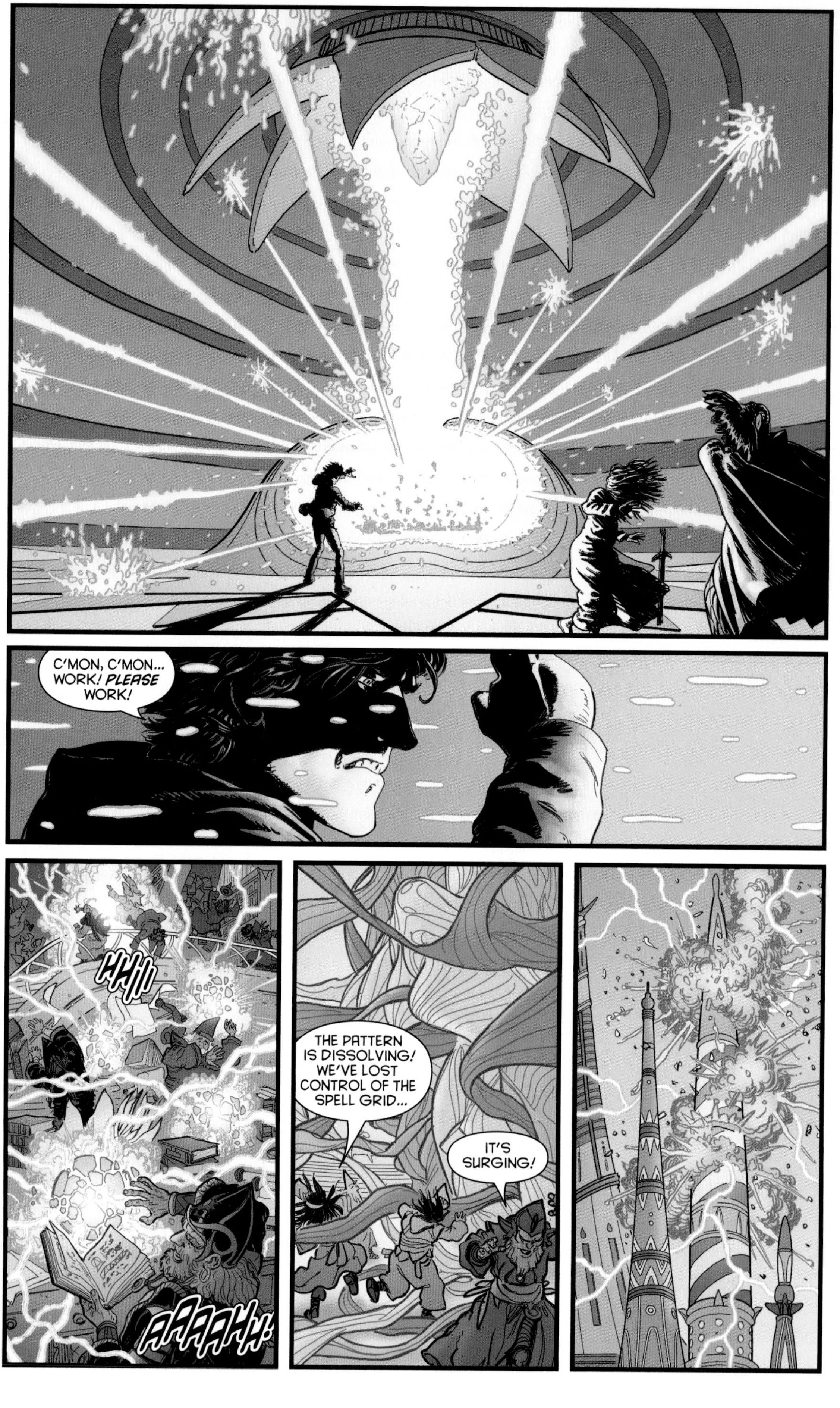
C'MON, C'MON...
WORK! *PLEASE* WORK!
HHH!!
AAAAAHH!
THE PATTERN IS DISSOLVING! WE'VE LOST CONTROL OF THE SPELL GRID...
IT'S SURGING!

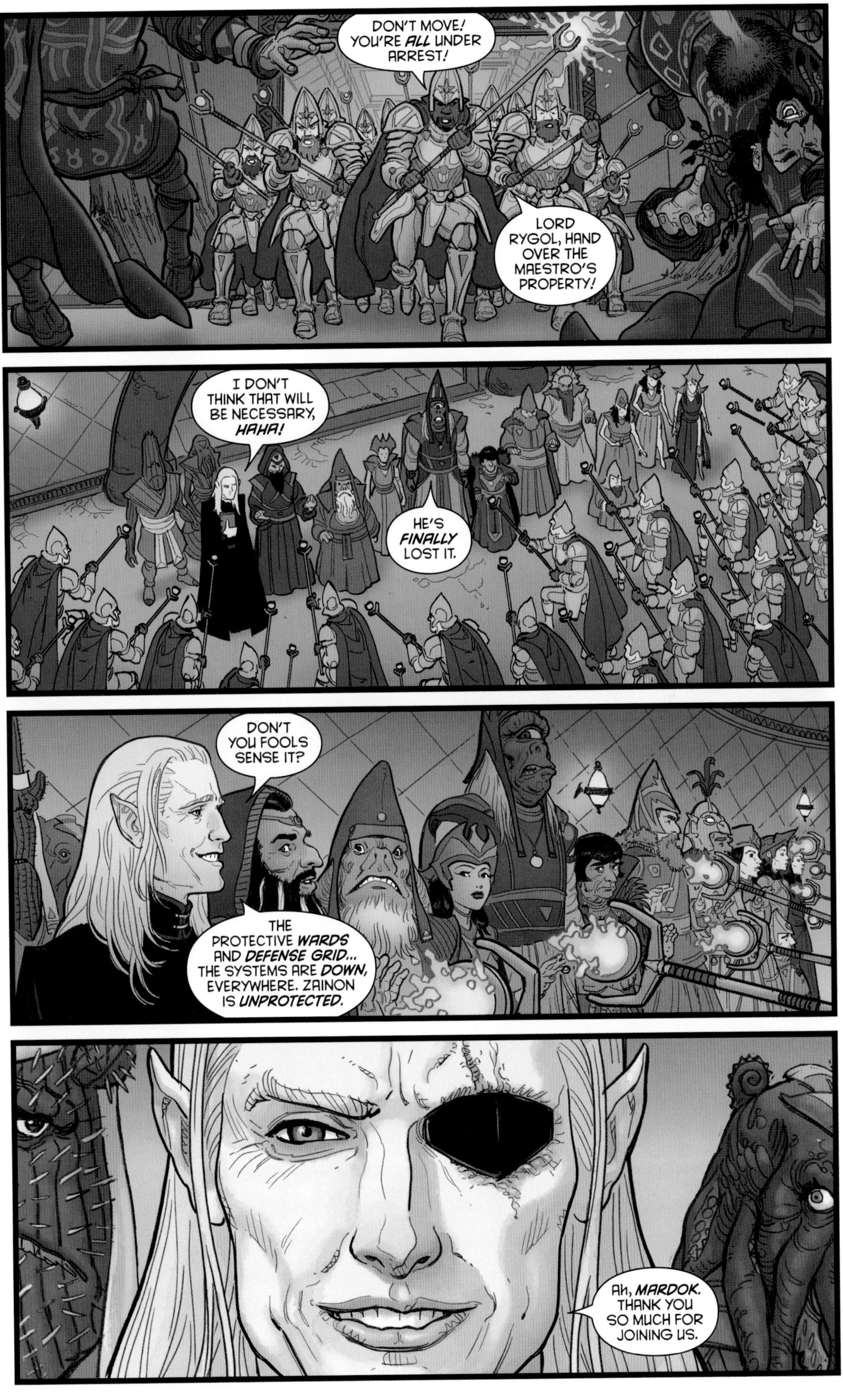
DON'T MOVE! YOU'RE ALL UNDER ARREST!
LORD RYGOL, HAND OVER THE MAESTRO'S PROPERTY!
I DON'T THINK THAT WILL BE NECESSARY, HAHA!
HE'S FINALLY LOST IT.
DON'T YOU FOOLS SENSE IT?
THE PROTECTIVE WARDS AND DEFENSE GRID... THE SYSTEMS ARE DOWN, EVERYWHERE. ZAINON IS UNPROTECTED.
Ah, MARDOK. THANK YOU SO MUCH FOR JOINING US.

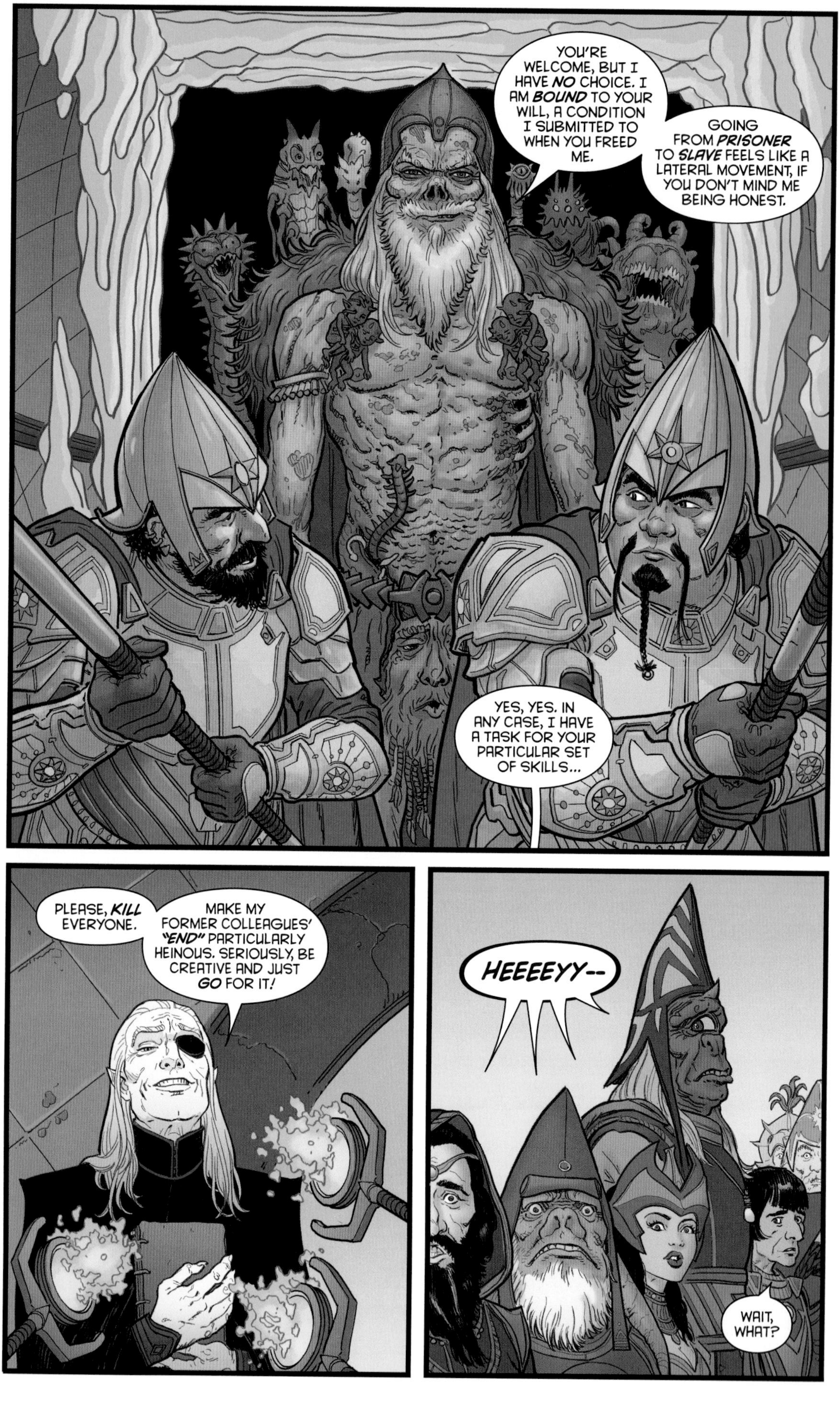
YOU'RE WELCOME, BUT I HAVE NO CHOICE. I AM BOUND TO YOUR WILL, A CONDITION I SUBMITTED TO WHEN YOU FREED ME.
GOING FROM PRISONER TO SLAVE FEELS LIKE A LATERAL MOVEMENT, IF YOU DON'T MIND ME BEING HONEST.
YES, YES. IN ANY CASE, I HAVE A TASK FOR YOUR PARTICULAR SET OF SKILLS...
PLEASE, KILL EVERYONE.
MAKE MY FORMER COLLEAGUES' "END" PARTICULARLY HEINOUS. SERIOUSLY, BE CREATIVE AND JUST GO FOR IT!
HEEEEYY--
WAIT, WHAT?

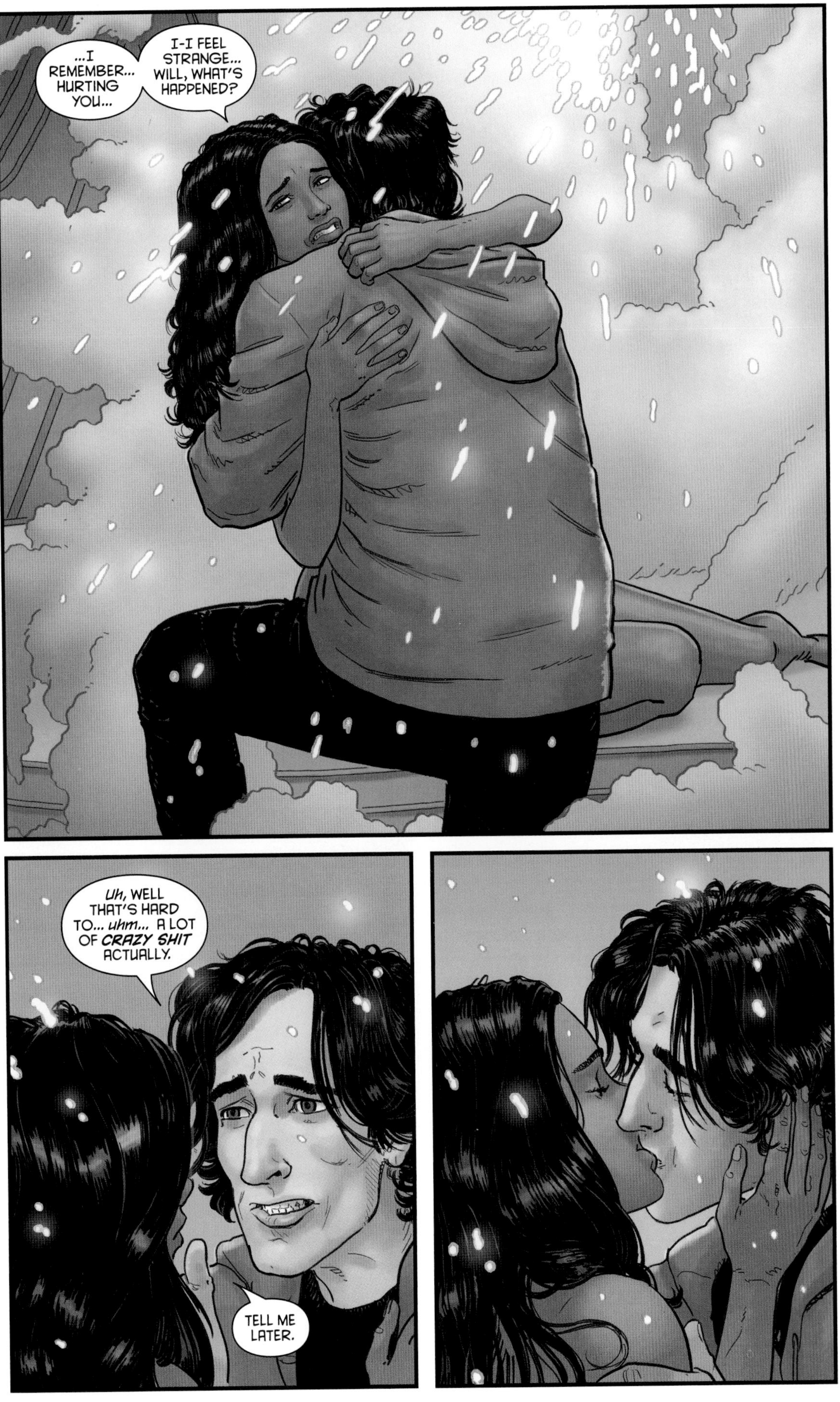
...I REMEMBER... HURTING YOU...
I-I FEEL STRANGE... WILL, WHAT'S HAPPENED?
Uh, WELL THAT'S HARD TO... *uhm...* A LOT OF ***CRAZY SHIT*** ACTUALLY.
TELL ME LATER.

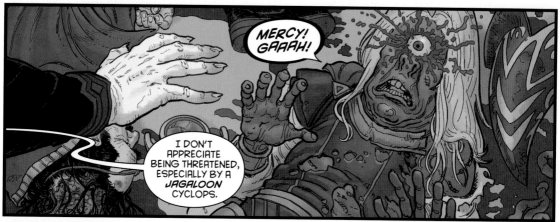

MERCY! GAAAH!

I DON'T APPRECIATE BEING THREATENED, ESPECIALLY BY A *JAGALOON* CYCLOPS.

THE NEXT *AGE* WILL NOT ABIDE INFERIOR BLOOD THAT DOESN'T KNOW ITS STATION.

-Tsk- YOU ARE A *PETTY* CREATURE, RYGOL. YOUR *REMAKING* WILL BE NOTHING NEW.

ANOTHER *AGE* BIRTHED FROM A JAUNDICED, POISONOUS EGO. IT'S JUST *MORE* OF THE SAME.

-HK-

GHL? PCP

WHAT DOES AN UNDEAD GHOUL *OBSESSED* WITH DESTROYING ALL LIFE KNOW OF TRUE VISION? ALL YOUR POWER AND I STILL FOUND YOU HELPLESS, UNDER A *ROCK*.

LEAVE THE THINKING TO ME.

-glig-

MY VISION IS CLEAR, ELF. IT'S SHAPED BY THE ONLY TRUTH THERE IS... *EMPTINESS.*

WHEN I'M FREE OF YOUR SHACKLES, I WILL *SHARE* ITS TRUTH WITH YOU, RYGOL.

IT'S A DATE.

THE *OPENING SPELL* HAS FAILED. I'LL NEED YOU TO DRAW THE BOY OUT.

WE'LL FORCE HIM TO OPEN THE BOOK FOR ME.

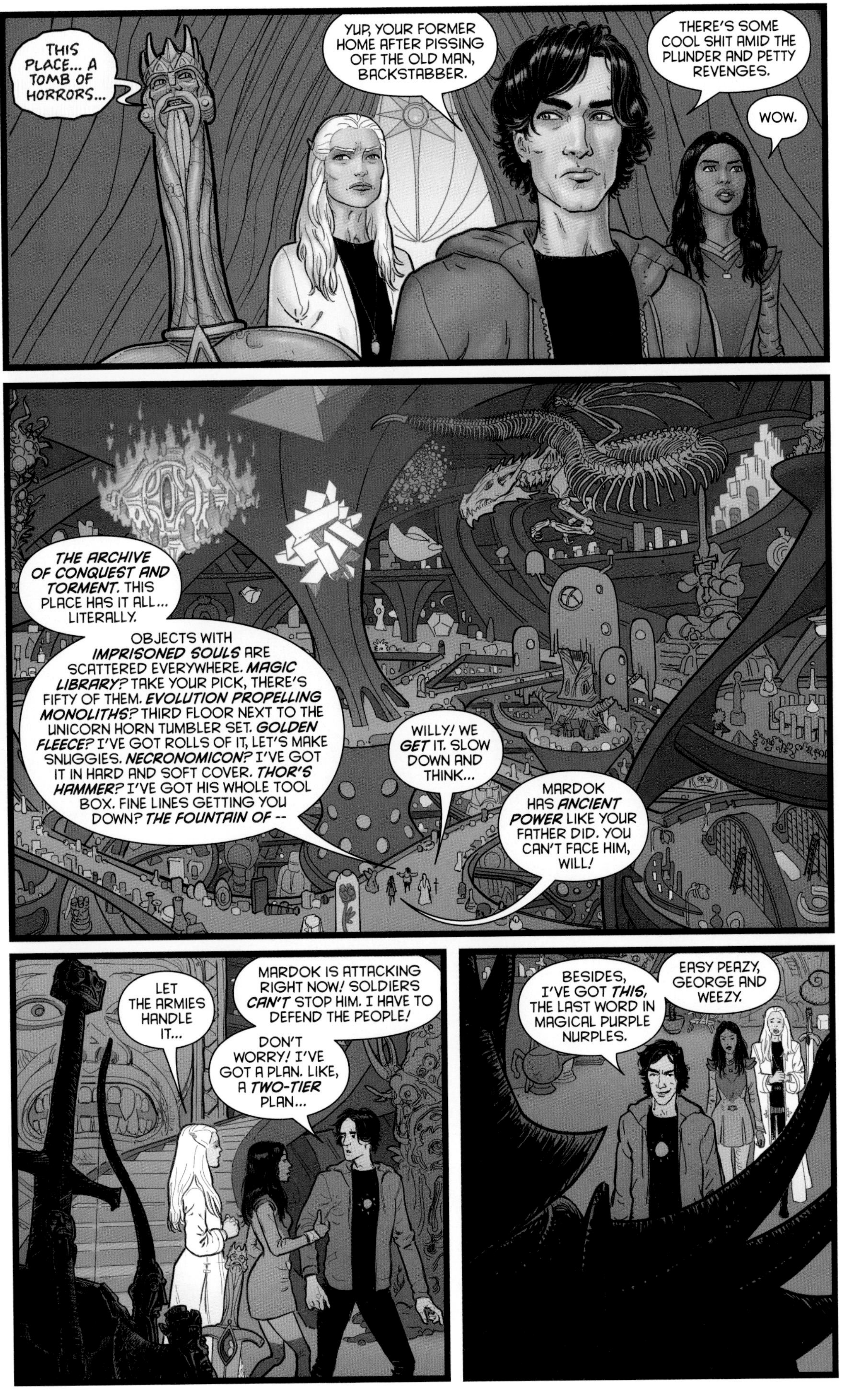

THIS PLACE... A TOMB OF HORRORS...
YUP, YOUR FORMER HOME AFTER PISSING OFF THE OLD MAN, BACKSTABBER.
THERE'S SOME COOL SHIT AMID THE PLUNDER AND PETTY REVENGES.
WOW.
THE ARCHIVE OF CONQUEST AND TORMENT. THIS PLACE HAS IT ALL... LITERALLY.
OBJECTS WITH IMPRISONED SOULS ARE SCATTERED EVERYWHERE. MAGIC LIBRARY? TAKE YOUR PICK, THERE'S FIFTY OF THEM. EVOLUTION PROPELLING MONOLITHS? THIRD FLOOR NEXT TO THE UNICORN HORN TUMBLER SET. GOLDEN FLEECE? I'VE GOT ROLLS OF IT, LET'S MAKE SNUGGIES. NECRONOMICON? I'VE GOT IT IN HARD AND SOFT COVER. THOR'S HAMMER? I'VE GOT HIS WHOLE TOOL BOX. FINE LINES GETTING YOU DOWN? THE FOUNTAIN OF --
WILLY! WE GET IT. SLOW DOWN AND THINK...
MARDOK HAS ANCIENT POWER LIKE YOUR FATHER DID. YOU CAN'T FACE HIM, WILL!
LET THE ARMIES HANDLE IT...
MARDOK IS ATTACKING RIGHT NOW! SOLDIERS CAN'T STOP HIM. I HAVE TO DEFEND THE PEOPLE!
DON'T WORRY! I'VE GOT A PLAN. LIKE, A TWO-TIER PLAN...
BESIDES, I'VE GOT THIS, THE LAST WORD IN MAGICAL PURPLE NURPLES.
EASY PEAZY, GEORGE AND WEEZY.

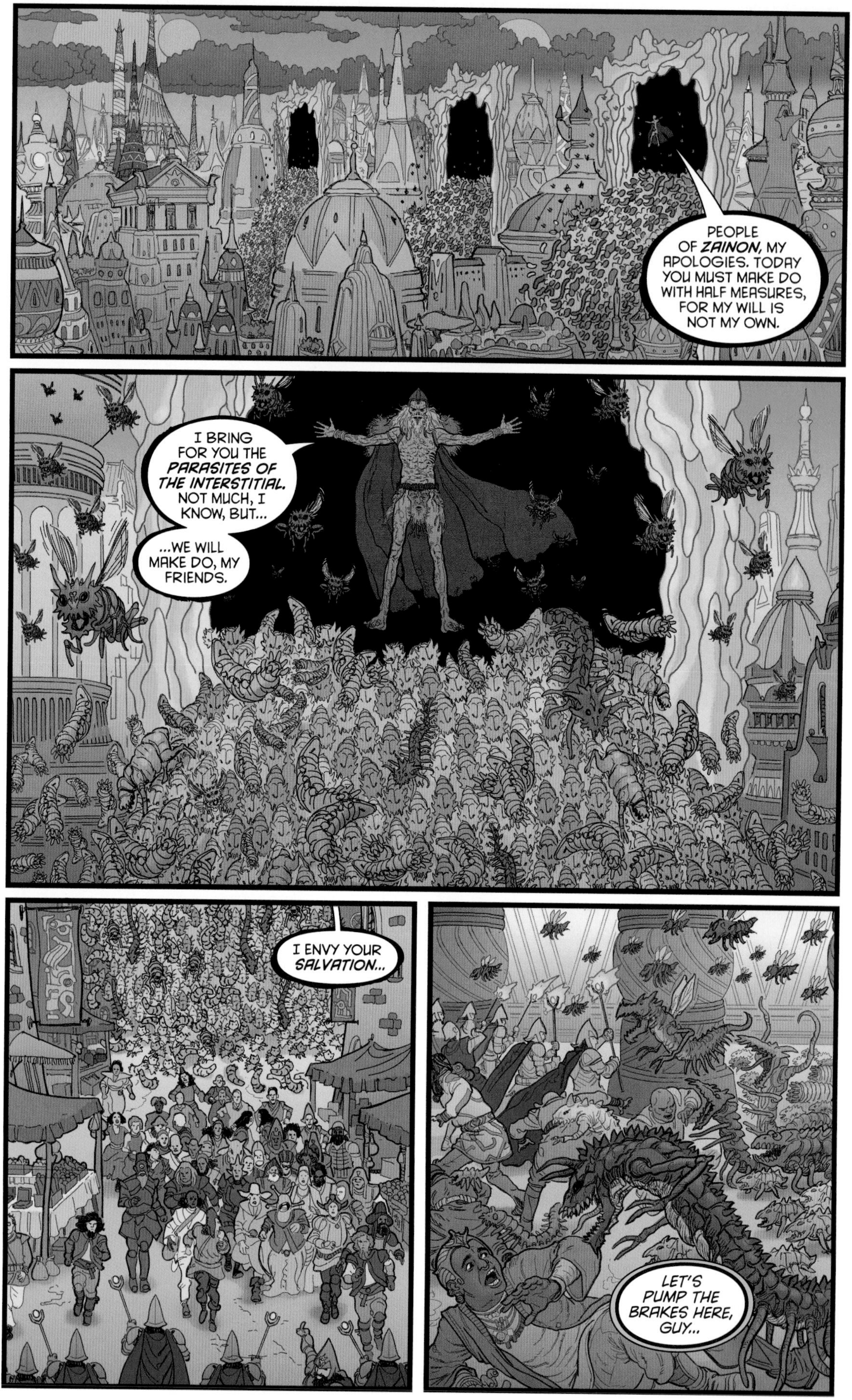
PEOPLE OF ZAINON, MY APOLOGIES. TODAY YOU MUST MAKE DO WITH HALF MEASURES, FOR MY WILL IS NOT MY OWN.
I BRING FOR YOU THE PARASITES OF THE INTERSTITIAL. NOT MUCH, I KNOW, BUT...
...WE WILL MAKE DO, MY FRIENDS.
I ENVY YOUR SALVATION...
LET'S PUMP THE BRAKES HERE, GUY...

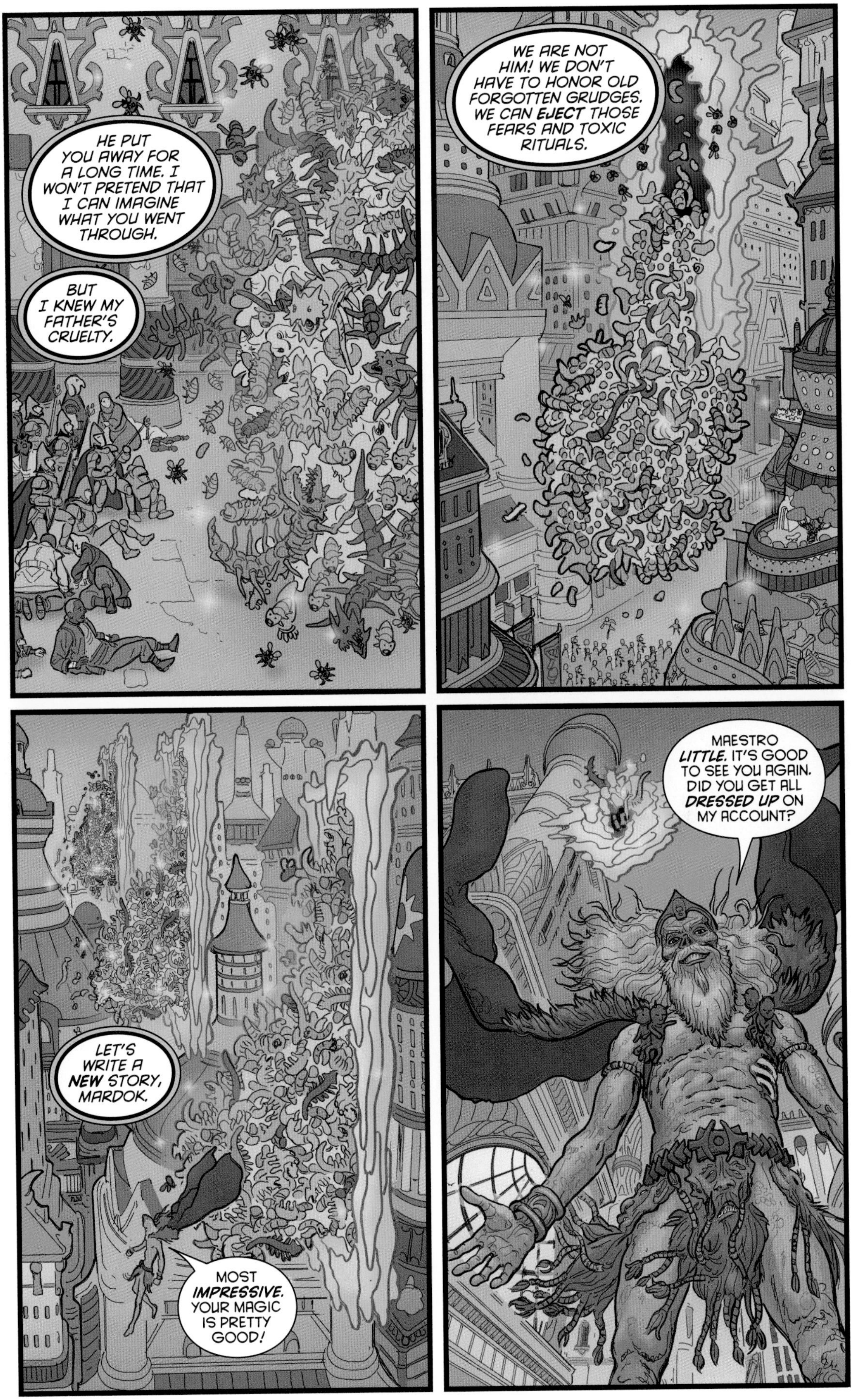
HE PUT YOU AWAY FOR A LONG TIME. I WON'T PRETEND THAT I CAN IMAGINE WHAT YOU WENT THROUGH.
BUT I KNEW MY FATHER'S CRUELTY.
WE ARE NOT HIM! WE DON'T HAVE TO HONOR OLD FORGOTTEN GRUDGES. WE CAN EJECT THOSE FEARS AND TOXIC RITUALS.
LET'S WRITE A NEW STORY, MARDOK.
MOST IMPRESSIVE. YOUR MAGIC IS PRETTY GOOD!
MAESTRO LITTLE. IT'S GOOD TO SEE YOU AGAIN. DID YOU GET ALL DRESSED UP ON MY ACCOUNT?

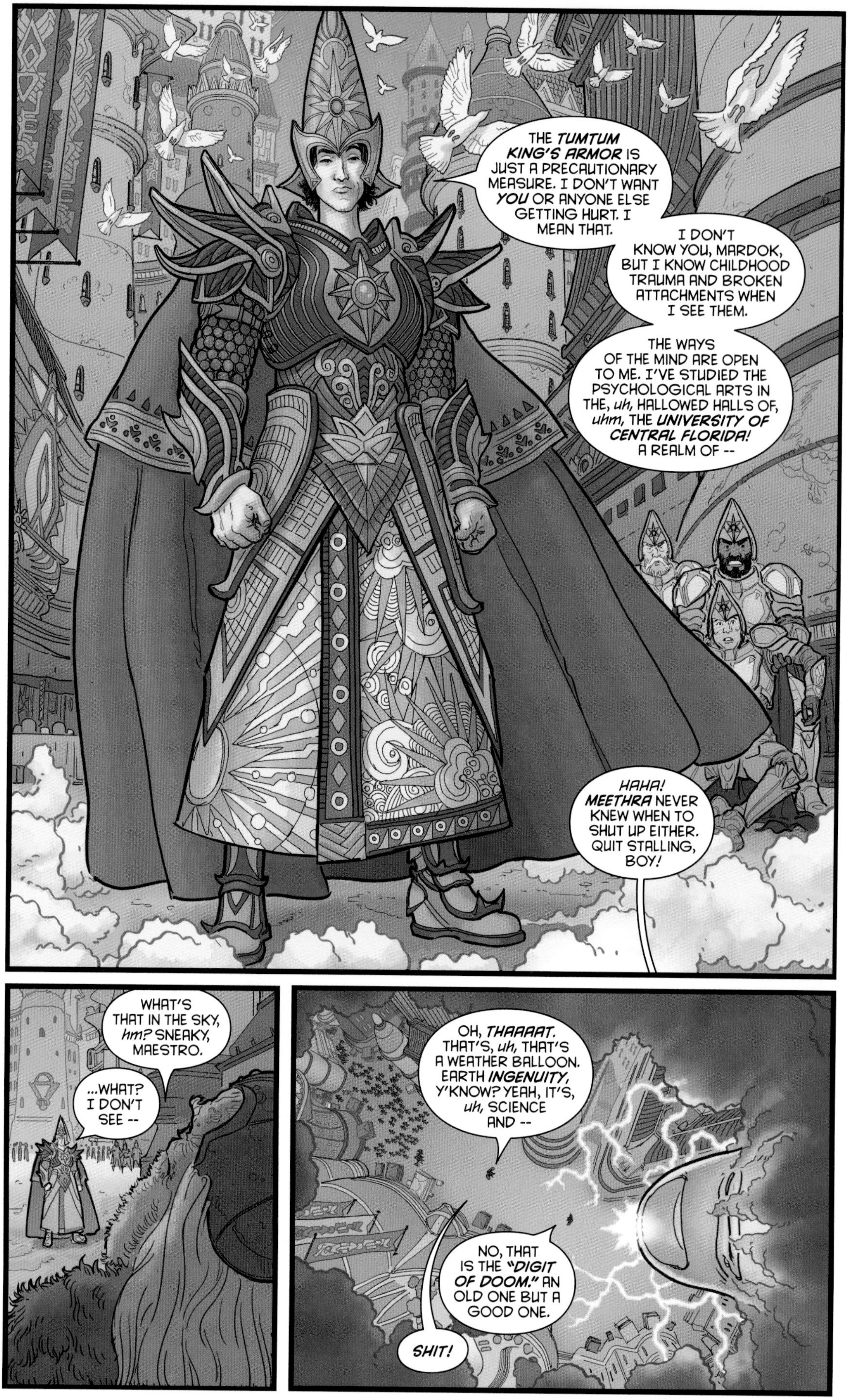
THE *TUMTUM KING'S ARMOR* IS JUST A PRECAUTIONARY MEASURE. I DON'T WANT *YOU* OR ANYONE ELSE GETTING HURT. I MEAN THAT.
I DON'T KNOW YOU, MARDOK, BUT I KNOW CHILDHOOD TRAUMA AND BROKEN ATTACHMENTS WHEN I SEE THEM.
THE WAYS OF THE MIND ARE OPEN TO ME. I'VE STUDIED THE PSYCHOLOGICAL ARTS IN THE, *uh,* HALLOWED HALLS OF, *uhm,* THE *UNIVERSITY OF CENTRAL FLORIDA!* A REALM OF --
HAHA! MEETHRA NEVER KNEW WHEN TO SHUT UP EITHER. QUIT STALLING, BOY!
WHAT'S THAT IN THE SKY, *hm?* SNEAKY, MAESTRO.
...WHAT? I DON'T SEE --
OH, *THAAAAT.* THAT'S, *uh,* THAT'S A WEATHER BALLOON. EARTH *INGENUITY,* Y'KNOW? YEAH, IT'S, *uh,* SCIENCE AND --
NO, THAT IS THE *"DIGIT OF DOOM."* AN OLD ONE BUT A GOOD ONE.
SHIT!

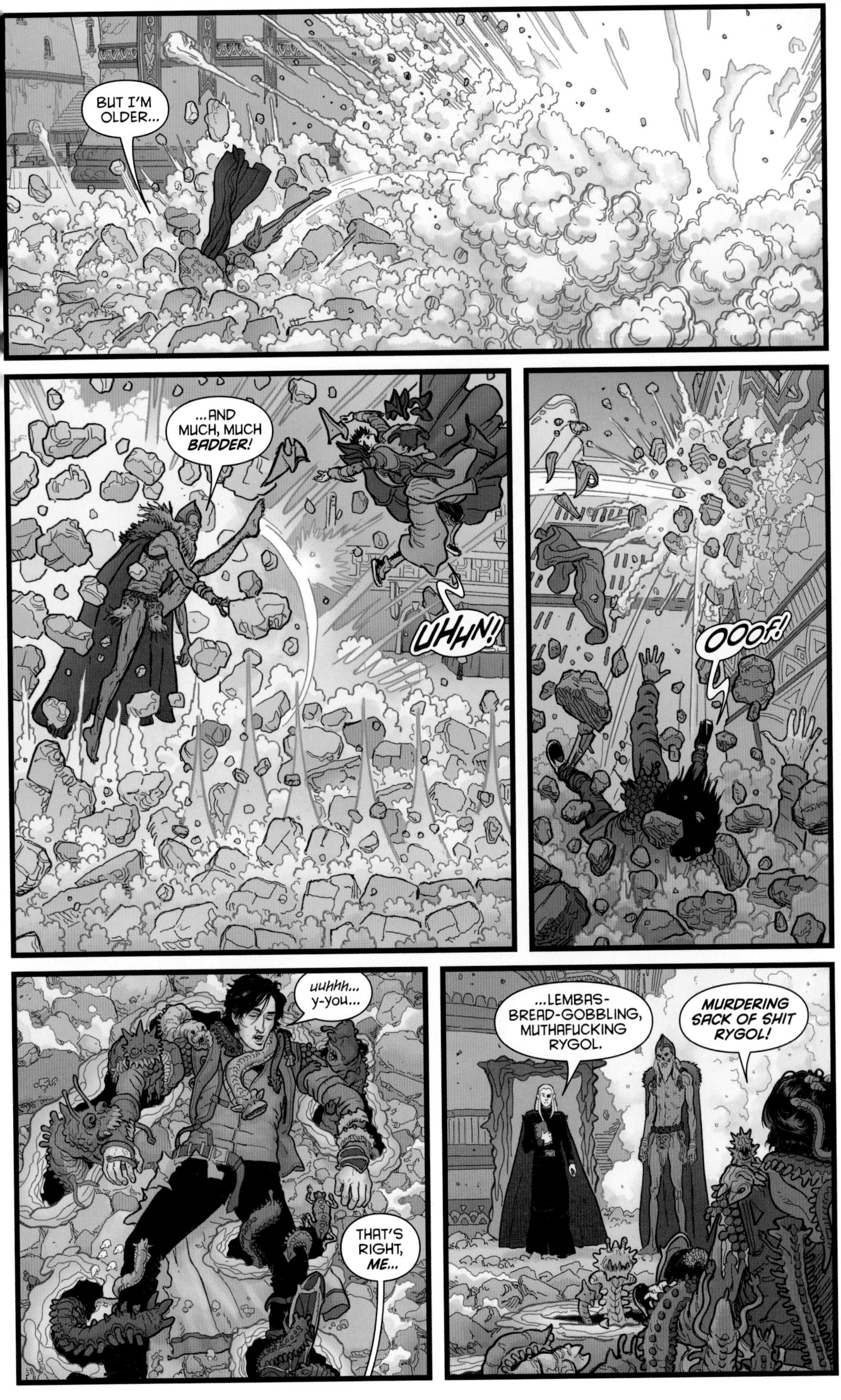
BUT I'M OLDER...
...AND MUCH, MUCH BADDER!
UHHN!
OOOF!
uuhhh... y-you...
THAT'S RIGHT, ME...
...LEMBAS-BREAD-GOBBLING, MUTHAFUCKING RYGOL.
MURDERING SACK OF SHIT RYGOL!

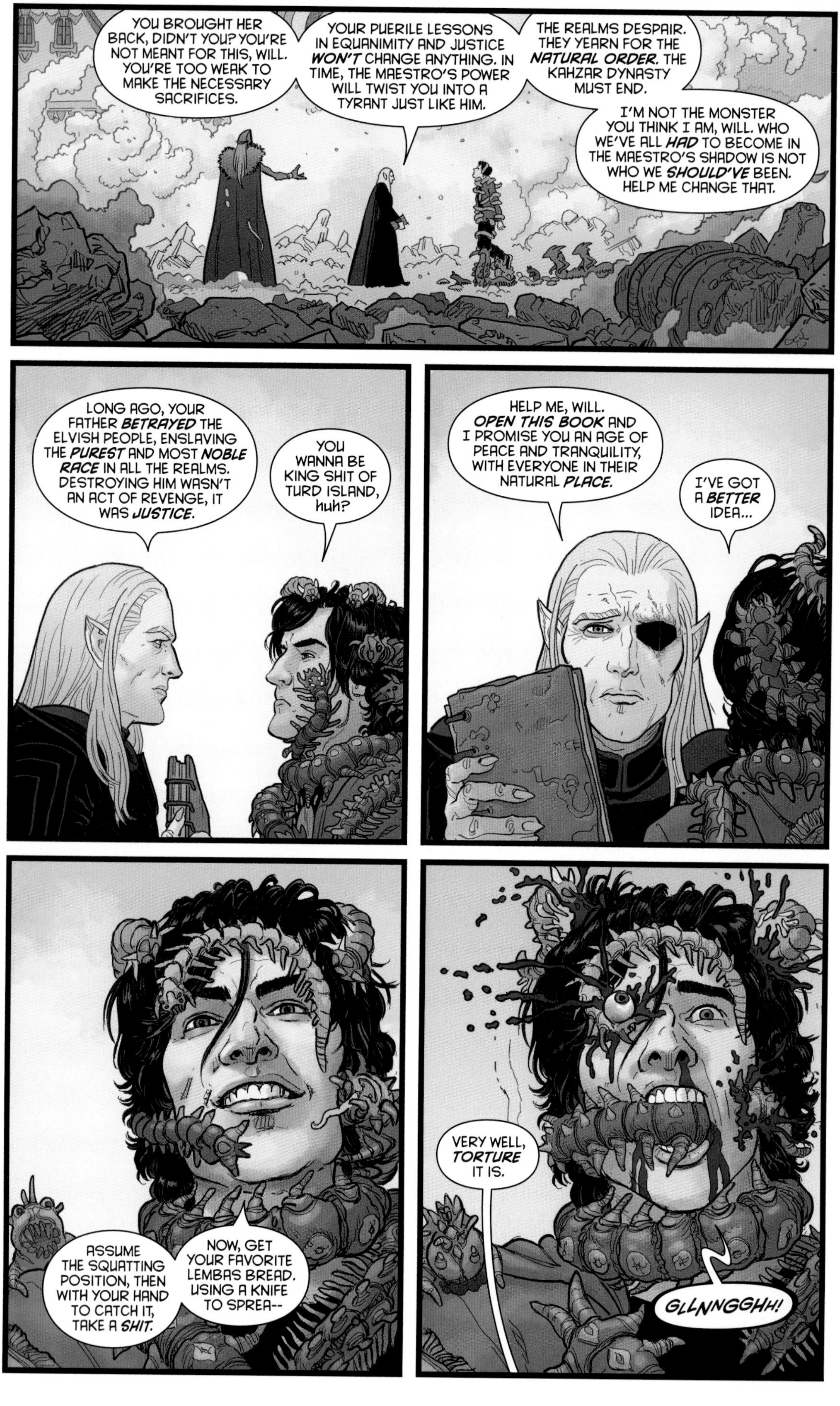
YOU BROUGHT HER BACK, DIDN'T YOU? YOU'RE NOT MEANT FOR THIS, WILL. YOU'RE TOO WEAK TO MAKE THE NECESSARY SACRIFICES.
YOUR PUERILE LESSONS IN EQUANIMITY AND JUSTICE WON'T CHANGE ANYTHING. IN TIME, THE MAESTRO'S POWER WILL TWIST YOU INTO A TYRANT JUST LIKE HIM.
THE REALMS DESPAIR. THEY YEARN FOR THE NATURAL ORDER. THE KAHZAR DYNASTY MUST END.
I'M NOT THE MONSTER YOU THINK I AM, WILL. WHO WE'VE ALL HAD TO BECOME IN THE MAESTRO'S SHADOW IS NOT WHO WE SHOULD'VE BEEN. HELP ME CHANGE THAT.
LONG AGO, YOUR FATHER BETRAYED THE ELVISH PEOPLE, ENSLAVING THE PUREST AND MOST NOBLE RACE IN ALL THE REALMS. DESTROYING HIM WASN'T AN ACT OF REVENGE, IT WAS JUSTICE.
YOU WANNA BE KING SHIT OF TURD ISLAND, huh?
HELP ME, WILL. OPEN THIS BOOK AND I PROMISE YOU AN AGE OF PEACE AND TRANQUILITY, WITH EVERYONE IN THEIR NATURAL PLACE.
I'VE GOT A BETTER IDEA...
ASSUME THE SQUATTING POSITION, THEN WITH YOUR HAND TO CATCH IT, TAKE A SHIT.
NOW, GET YOUR FAVORITE LEMBAS BREAD. USING A KNIFE TO SPREA--
VERY WELL, TORTURE IT IS.
GLLNNGGHH!

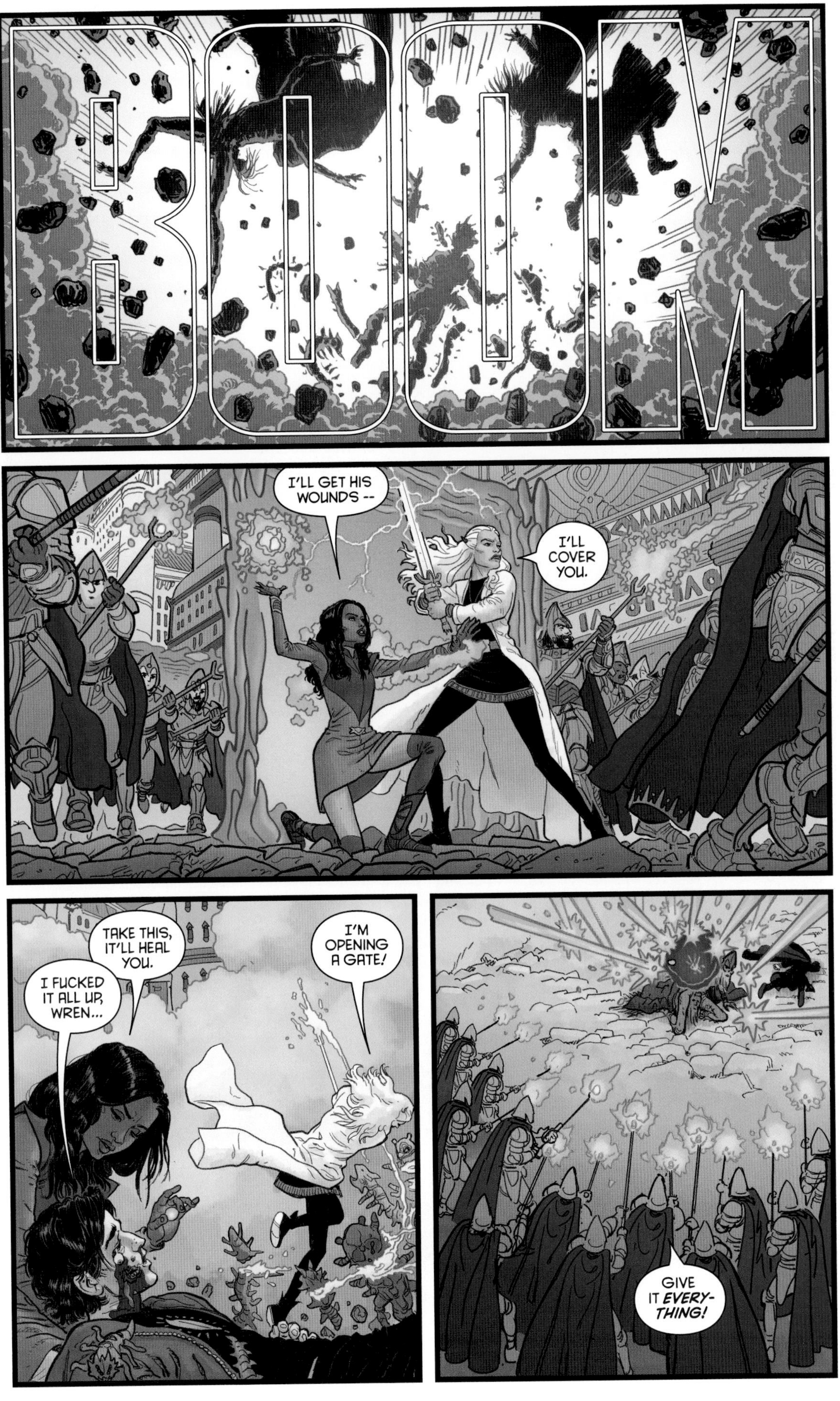
BOOM
I'LL GET HIS WOUNDS --
I'LL COVER YOU.
I FUCKED IT ALL UP, WREN...
TAKE THIS, IT'LL HEAL YOU.
I'M OPENING A GATE!
GIVE IT *EVERYTHING!*

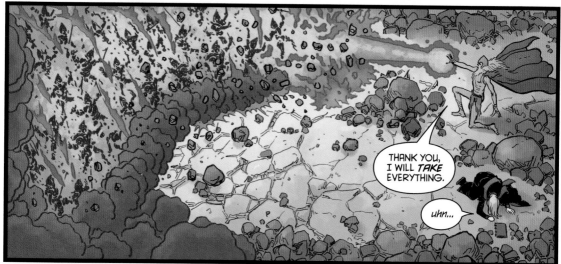

THANK YOU, I WILL *TAKE* EVERYTHING.

uhn...

MARDOK! THEY'RE ESCAPING!

TWO MORE STEPS, WILLY...

NOOOO!

IF IT'S ANY CONSOLATION, YOUR SCHEMES AND AMBITIONS ARE MEANINGLESS ANYWAY. *EMPTINESS* IS THE ONLY --

OH, SHUT UP! DO SOMETHING USEFUL AND TURN MEETHRA'S GAUDY CAPITAL INTO RUBBLE!

I THOUGHT YOU'D NEVER ASK.

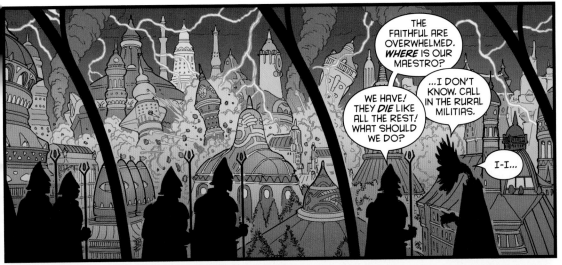

THE FAITHFUL ARE OVERWHELMED. *WHERE* IS OUR MAESTRO?

WE HAVE! THEY *DIE* LIKE ALL THE REST! WHAT SHOULD WE DO?

...I DON'T KNOW. CALL IN THE RURAL MILITIAS.

I-I...

AAAHH!

YOUR *LIBERATION* IS AT HAND!

...uhhhhngh...

WAKE UP, VIZIER, AND LOOK UPON THE FACE OF YOUR SALVATION...

...AND *REJOICE.*

EYAAARRGGH!

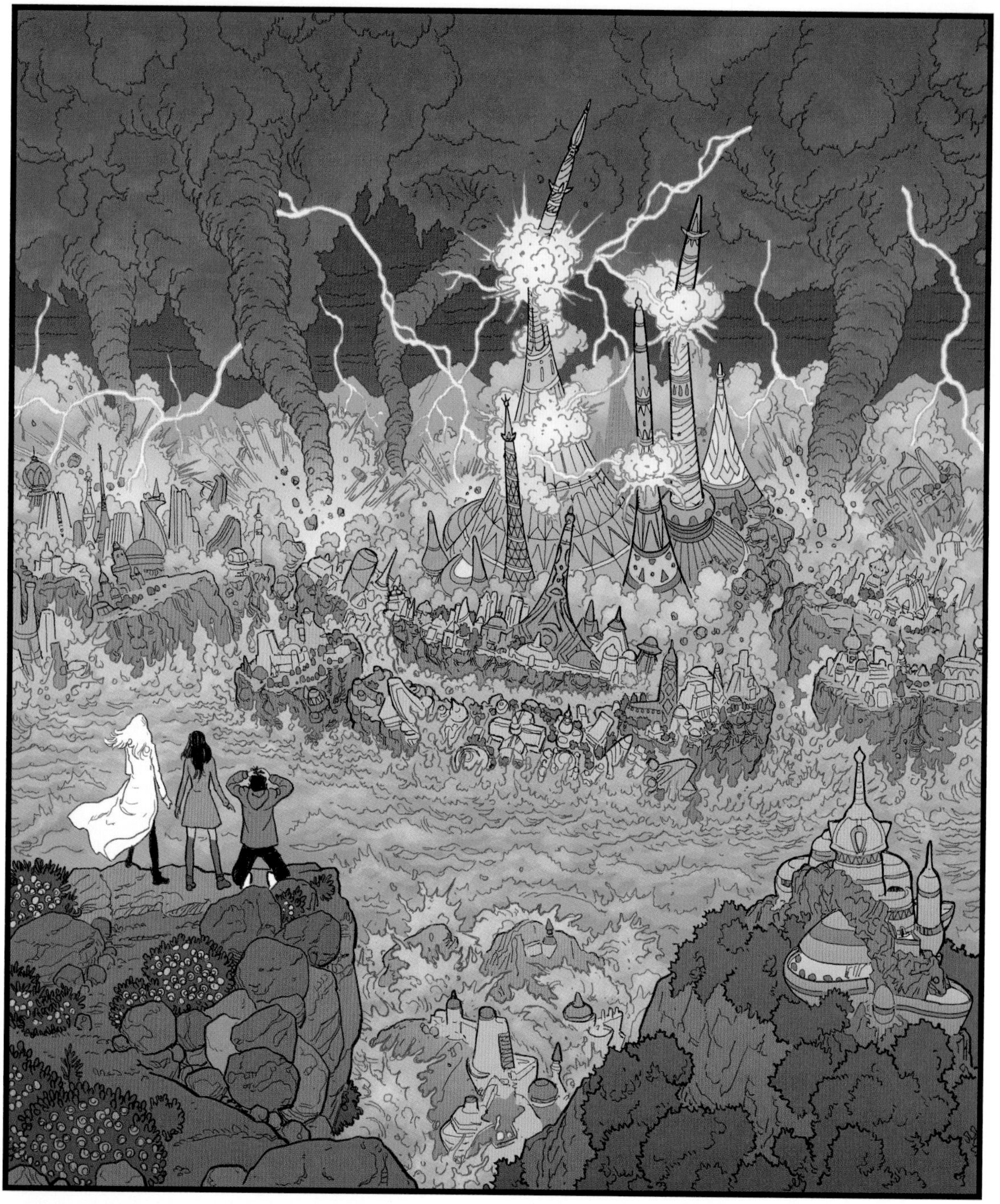

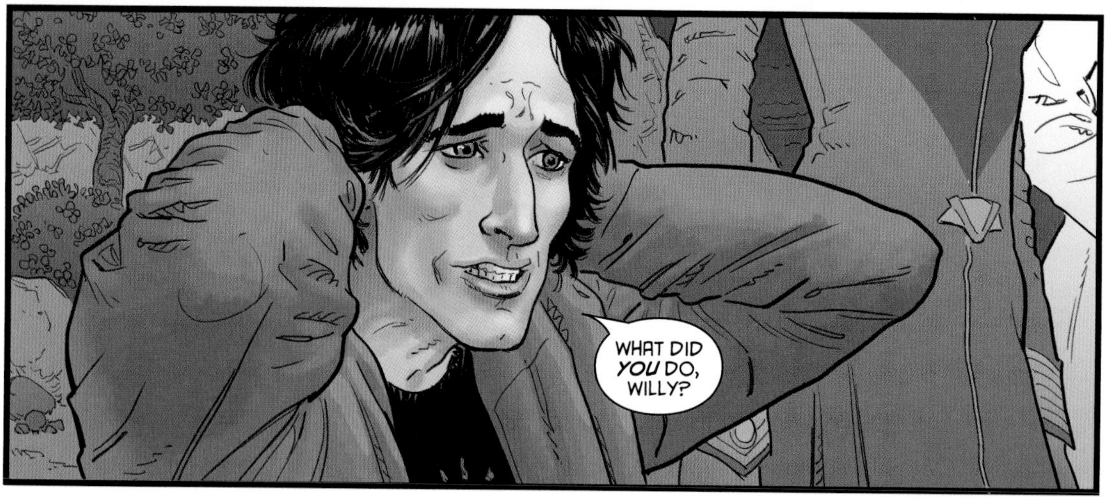
WHAT DID YOU DO, WILLY?

CHAPTER FOUR

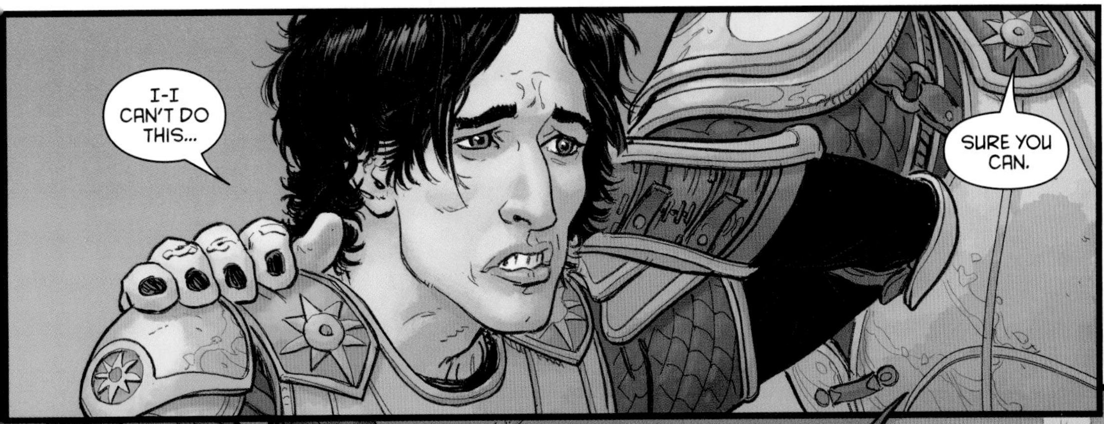
I-I CAN'T DO THIS...
SURE YOU CAN.

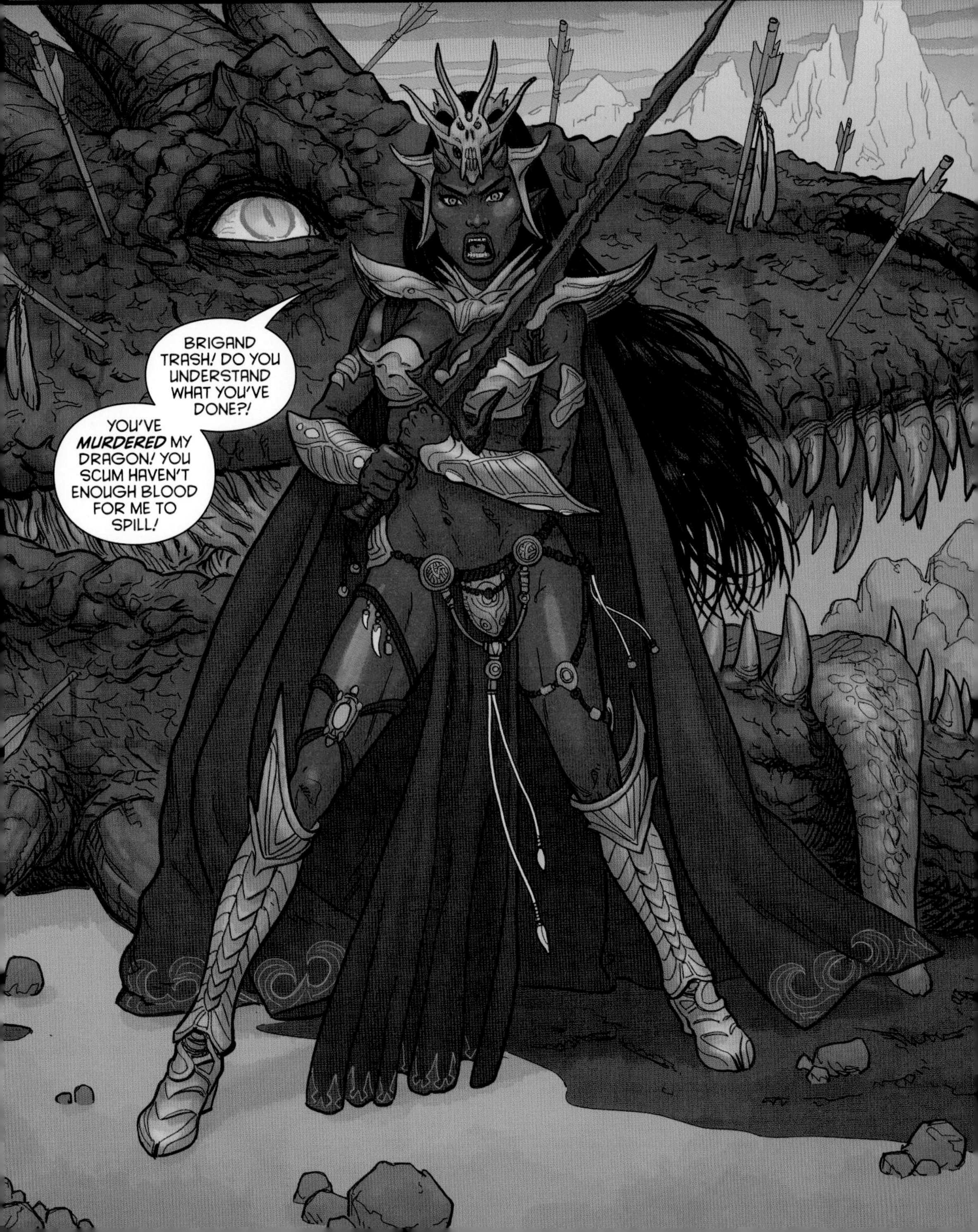
BRIGAND TRASH! DO YOU UNDERSTAND WHAT YOU'VE DONE?!
YOU'VE ***MURDERED*** MY DRAGON! YOU SCUM HAVEN'T ENOUGH BLOOD FOR ME TO SPILL!

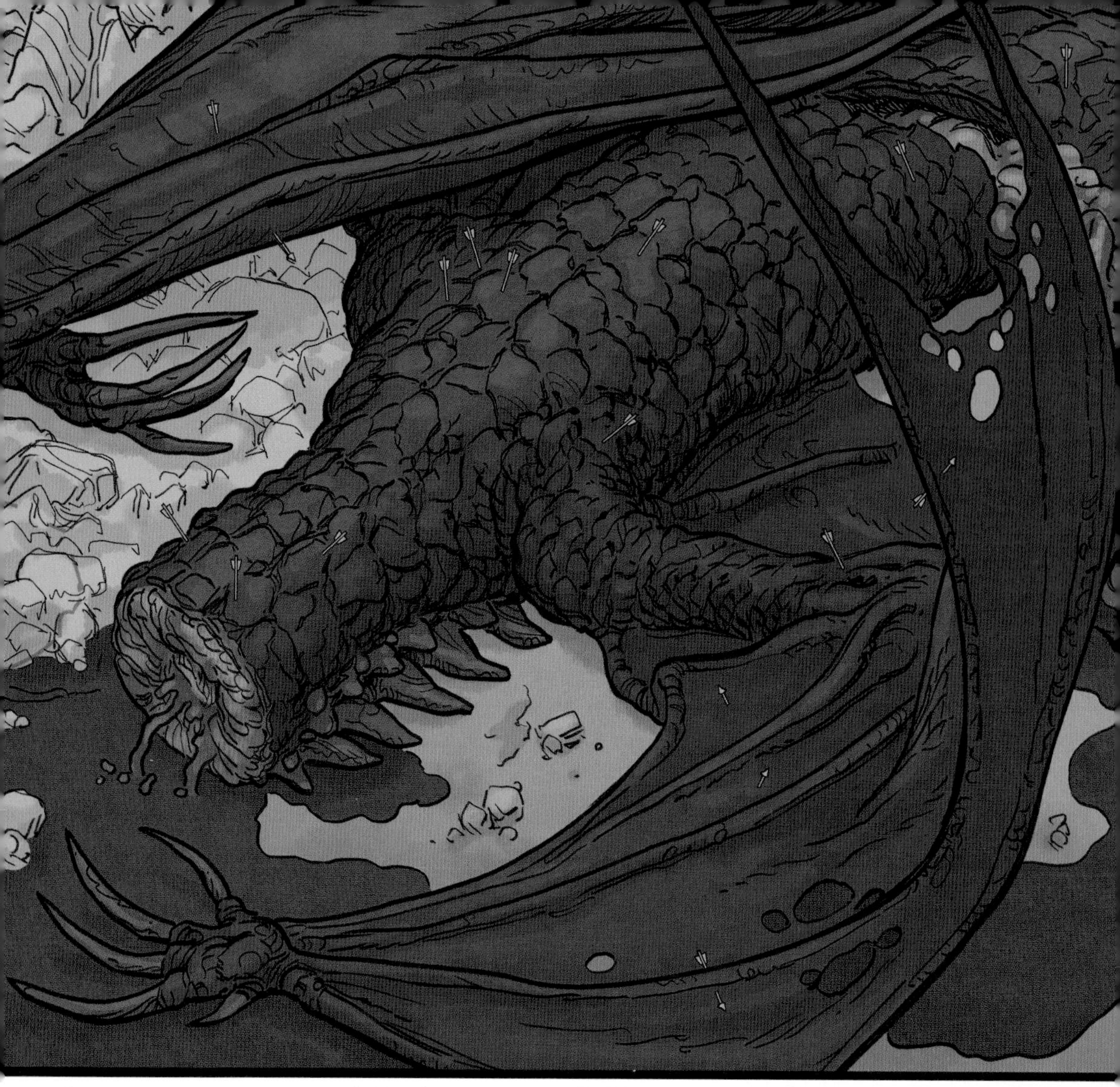

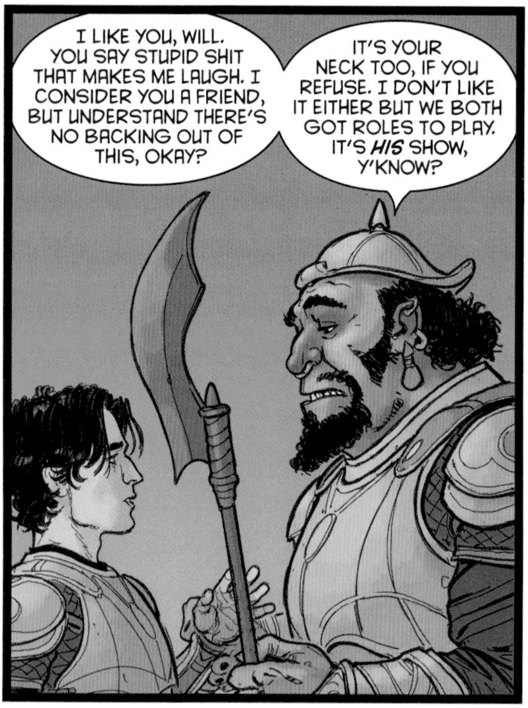

I LIKE YOU, WILL. YOU SAY STUPID SHIT THAT MAKES ME LAUGH. I CONSIDER YOU A FRIEND, BUT UNDERSTAND THERE'S NO BACKING OUT OF THIS, OKAY?
IT'S YOUR NECK TOO, IF YOU REFUSE. I DON'T LIKE IT EITHER BUT WE BOTH GOT ROLES TO PLAY. IT'S ***HIS*** SHOW, Y'KNOW?

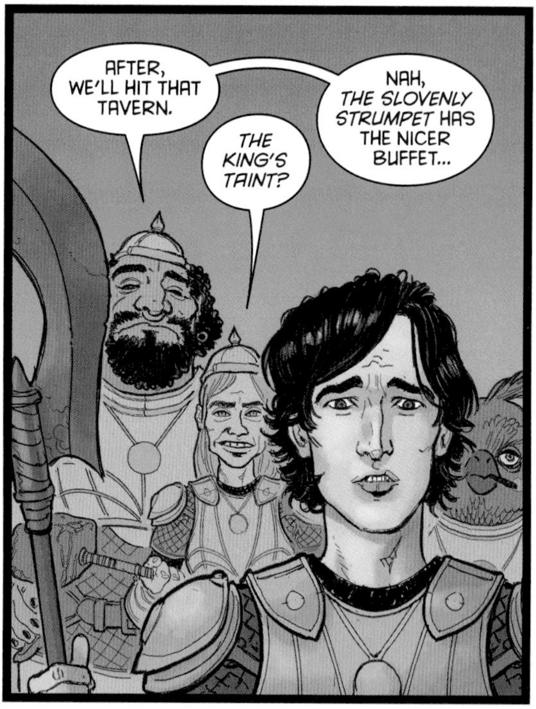

AFTER, WE'LL HIT THAT TAVERN.
THE KING'S TAINT?
NAH, *THE SLOVENLY STRUMPET* HAS THE NICER BUFFET...

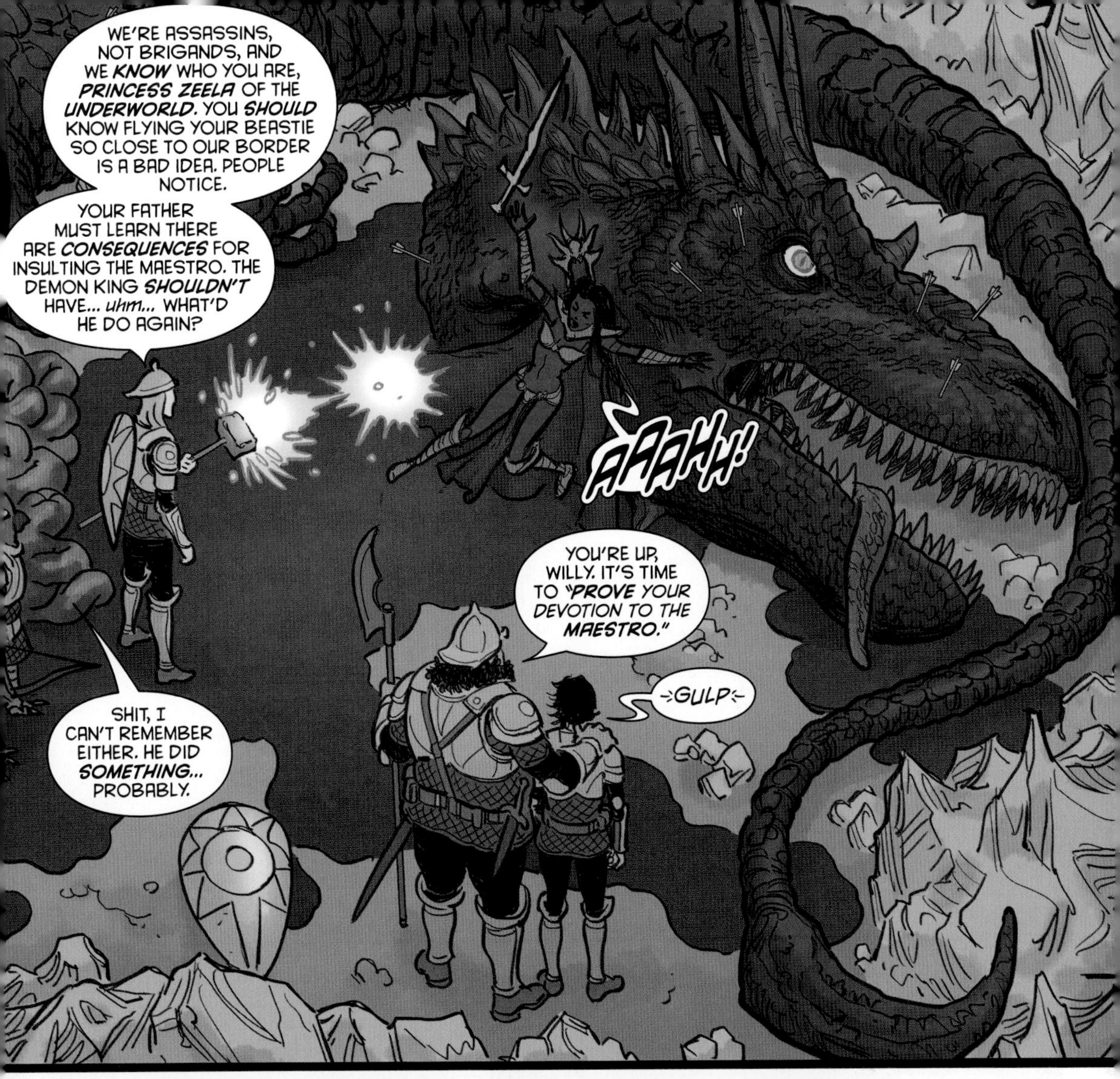
WE'RE ASSASSINS, NOT BRIGANDS, AND WE KNOW WHO YOU ARE, PRINCESS ZEELA OF THE UNDERWORLD. YOU SHOULD KNOW FLYING YOUR BEASTIE SO CLOSE TO OUR BORDER IS A BAD IDEA. PEOPLE NOTICE.
YOUR FATHER MUST LEARN THERE ARE CONSEQUENCES FOR INSULTING THE MAESTRO. THE DEMON KING SHOULDN'T HAVE... uhm... WHAT'D HE DO AGAIN?
AAAHH!
SHIT, I CAN'T REMEMBER EITHER. HE DID SOMETHING... PROBABLY.
YOU'RE UP, WILLY. IT'S TIME TO "PROVE YOUR DEVOTION TO THE MAESTRO."
GULP

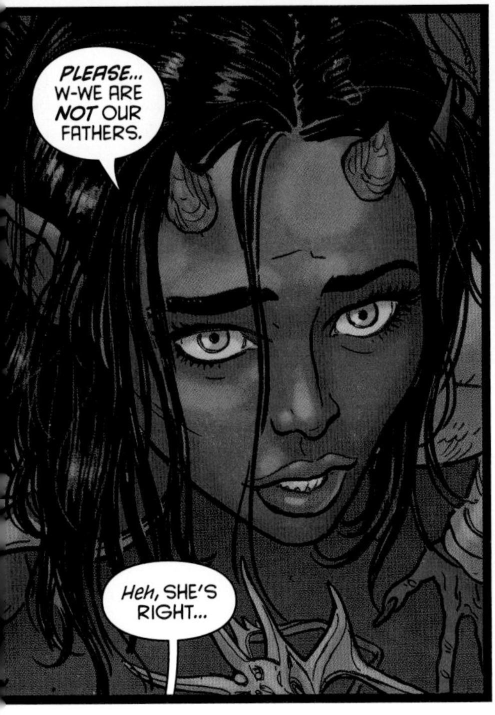
PLEASE... W-WE ARE NOT OUR FATHERS.
Heh, SHE'S RIGHT...

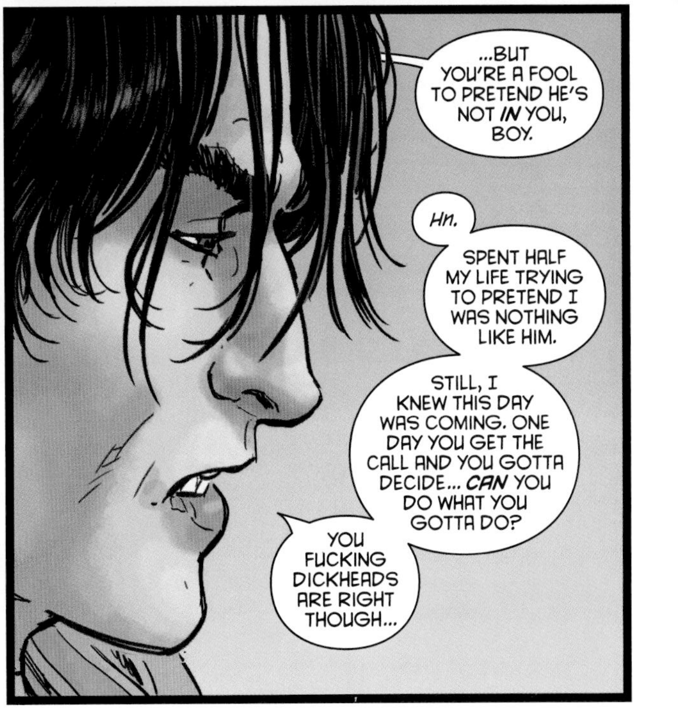
...BUT YOU'RE A FOOL TO PRETEND HE'S NOT IN YOU, BOY.
Hn.
SPENT HALF MY LIFE TRYING TO PRETEND I WAS NOTHING LIKE HIM.
STILL, I KNEW THIS DAY WAS COMING. ONE DAY YOU GET THE CALL AND YOU GOTTA DECIDE... CAN YOU DO WHAT YOU GOTTA DO?
YOU FUCKING DICKHEADS ARE RIGHT THOUGH...

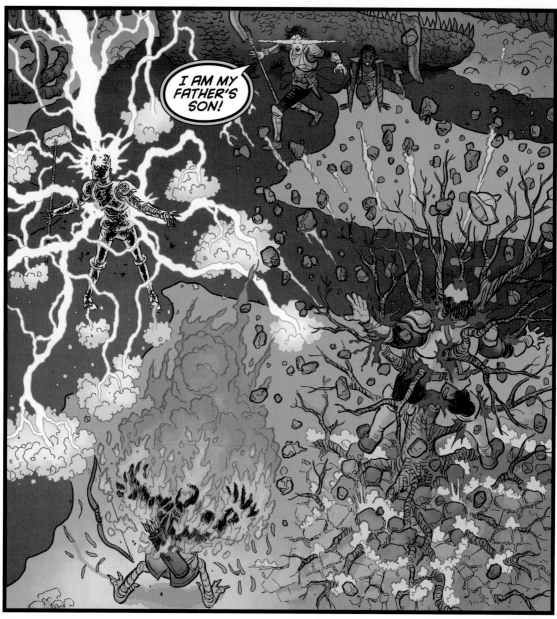

I AM MY FATHER'S SON!

INCREDIBLE! YOU DESTROYED THEM LIKE THEY WERE NOTHING!

OH JESUS, ADRENALINE'S WEARING OFF. OH SHIT, OH SHIT, I AM FUCKED!

WHAT WAS I THINKING?

FEAR NOT, BRAVE PRINCE. MY FATHER WILL GRANT YOU *SANCTUARY*. THE MAESTRO CANNOT REACH YOU IN THE UNDERWORLD. YOU'LL BE SAFE. WE ARE NOT THE MONSTERS YOU ARE LED TO BELIEVE.

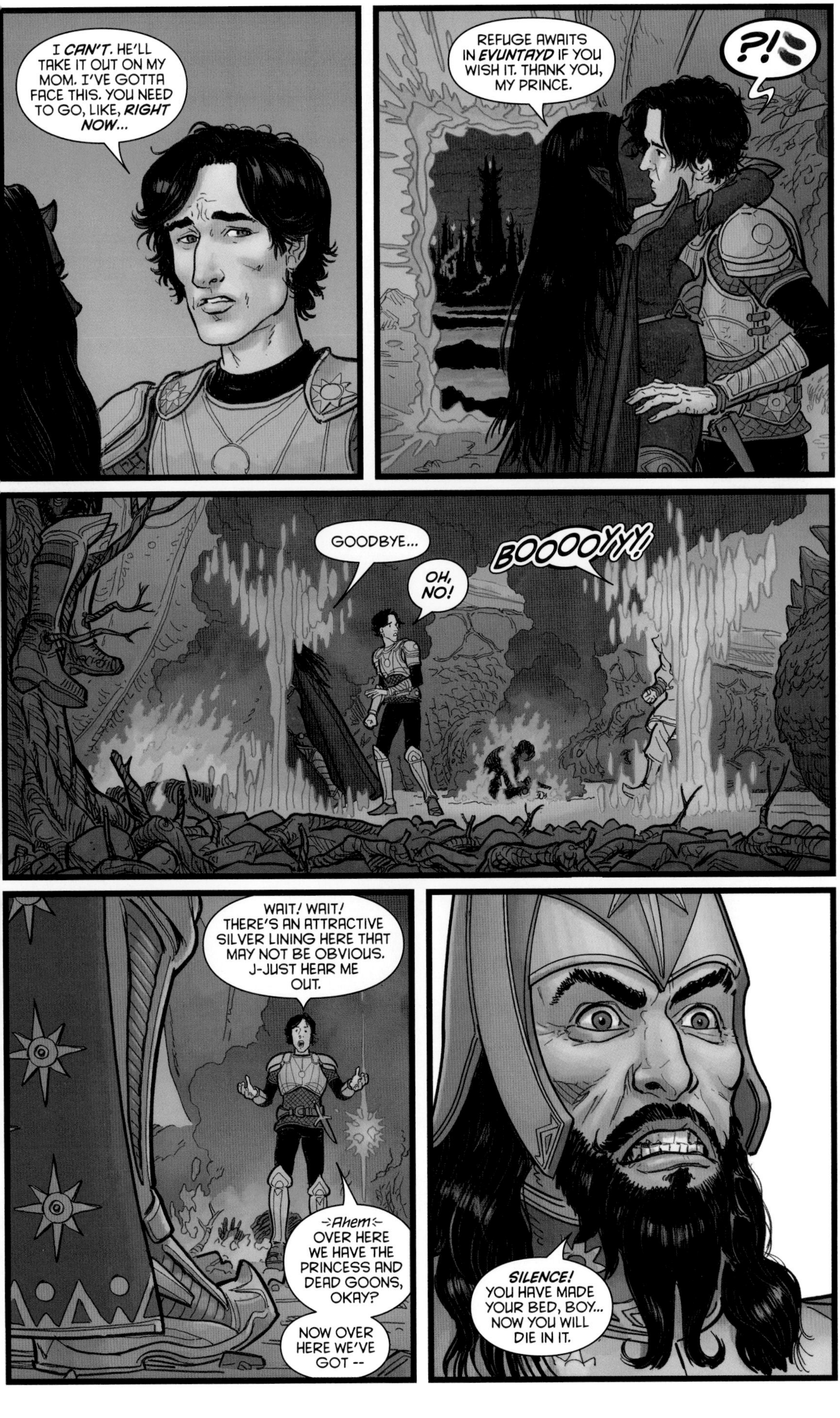
I CAN'T. HE'LL TAKE IT OUT ON MY MOM. I'VE GOTTA FACE THIS. YOU NEED TO GO, LIKE, RIGHT NOW...
REFUGE AWAITS IN EVUNTAYD IF YOU WISH IT. THANK YOU, MY PRINCE.
?!
GOODBYE...
OH, NO!
BOOOOYYY!
WAIT! WAIT! THERE'S AN ATTRACTIVE SILVER LINING HERE THAT MAY NOT BE OBVIOUS. J-JUST HEAR ME OUT.
Ahem OVER HERE WE HAVE THE PRINCESS AND DEAD GOONS, OKAY?
NOW OVER HERE WE'VE GOT --
SILENCE! YOU HAVE MADE YOUR BED, BOY... NOW YOU WILL DIE IN IT.

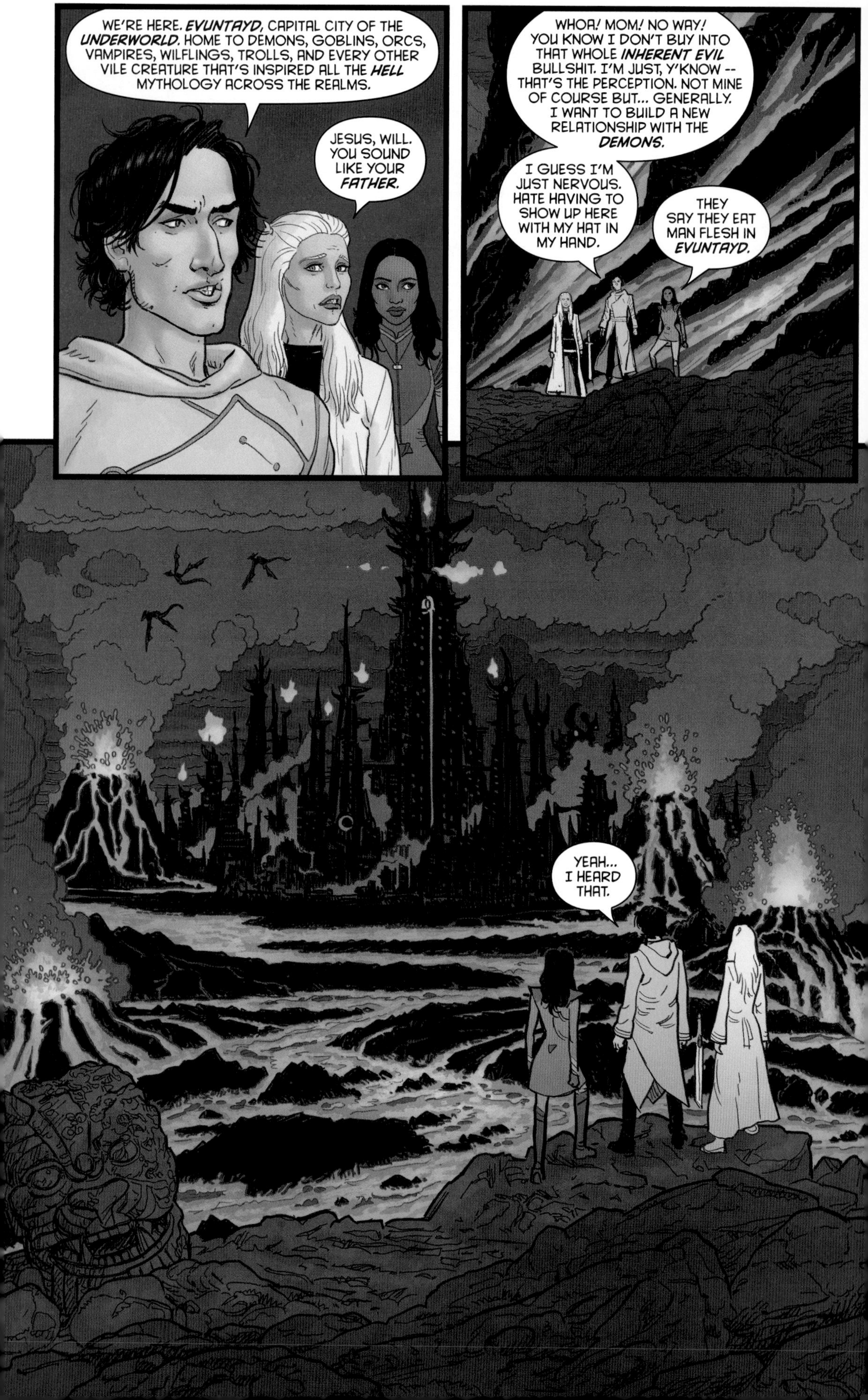
WE'RE HERE. EVUNTAYD, CAPITAL CITY OF THE UNDERWORLD. HOME TO DEMONS, GOBLINS, ORCS, VAMPIRES, WILFLINGS, TROLLS, AND EVERY OTHER VILE CREATURE THAT'S INSPIRED ALL THE HELL MYTHOLOGY ACROSS THE REALMS.
JESUS, WILL. YOU SOUND LIKE YOUR FATHER.
WHOA! MOM! NO WAY! YOU KNOW I DON'T BUY INTO THAT WHOLE INHERENT EVIL BULLSHIT. I'M JUST, Y'KNOW -- THAT'S THE PERCEPTION. NOT MINE OF COURSE BUT... GENERALLY. I WANT TO BUILD A NEW RELATIONSHIP WITH THE DEMONS.
I GUESS I'M JUST NERVOUS. HATE HAVING TO SHOW UP HERE WITH MY HAT IN MY HAND.
THEY SAY THEY EAT MAN FLESH IN EVUNTAYD.
YEAH... I HEARD THAT.

I HATE THIS, I SHOULD BE GOING WITH YOU. IT'S ALL MY FAULT, WILL. I SHOULD'VE KNOWN RYGOL WOULD USE ME, WOULD DO ANYTHING TO GET WHAT HE WANTED.

DON'T TALK CRAZY. YOU CAN'T PREDICT THAT BASTARD. HE'S PROBABLY BEEN PLANNING TO STEAL THE *BOOK OF REMAKING* FOR A THOUSAND YEARS.

I'D LET IT ALL BURN DOWN AGAIN TO *SAVE YOU*, WREN. IF IT'S ANYONE'S FAULT, IT'S MY ARROGANT ASS. I SHOULD'VE LOCKED HIM UP WHEN I HAD THE CHANCE. I GUESS I AM A SHITTY MAESTRO.

THE PRINCESS WILL HELP *BUT* IF THINGS GO BAD, I CAN'T CHANCE THEM HOSTAGE-ING YOU TWO AGAINST ME. STICK TO THE PLAN. I'LL MEET YOU BOTH BACK IN ORLANDO. DON'T WORRY, I'VE GOT SOMETHING THE KING *WANTS*.

MAESTROS DIDN'T MAKE THE UNDERWORLD, SO NO PORTAL-ING AROUND. YOUR MAGIC'S STILL STRONG, WILL. REMEMBER THAT.

I WILL, AND DON'T FORGET TO DO A *PRICELO* RUN -- WHEN THIS IS OVER I'M STUFFING MYSELF WITH PROCESSED FOOD. ALSO, I LOVE YOU BOTH.

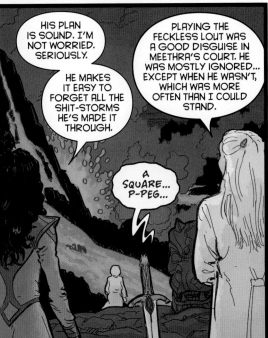

HIS PLAN IS SOUND. I'M NOT WORRIED. SERIOUSLY.

HE MAKES IT EASY TO FORGET ALL THE SHIT-STORMS HE'S MADE IT THROUGH.

PLAYING THE FECKLESS LOUT WAS A GOOD DISGUISE IN MEETHRA'S COURT. HE WAS MOSTLY IGNORED... EXCEPT WHEN HE WASN'T, WHICH WAS MORE OFTEN THAN I COULD STAND.

A SQUARE... P-PEG...

FOR A LONG TIME, ALL I WISHED FOR WAS THAT HE'D FIND A WAY TO FIT INTO HIS FATHER'S SICK WORLD JUST SO HE COULD BE LEFT ALONE.

HE TRIED. HE REALLY, REALLY DID, BUT HE NEVER GOT THE HANG OF IT AND I'VE NEVER BEEN MORE GRATEFUL FOR ANYTHING IN MY ENTIRE LIFE.

YOU WERE A SQUARE PEG TOO... ÷HNN÷

FOR THAT... I AM ALSO GRATEFUL, BUT...

...SAD...

FOR THE PRICE YOU PAID...

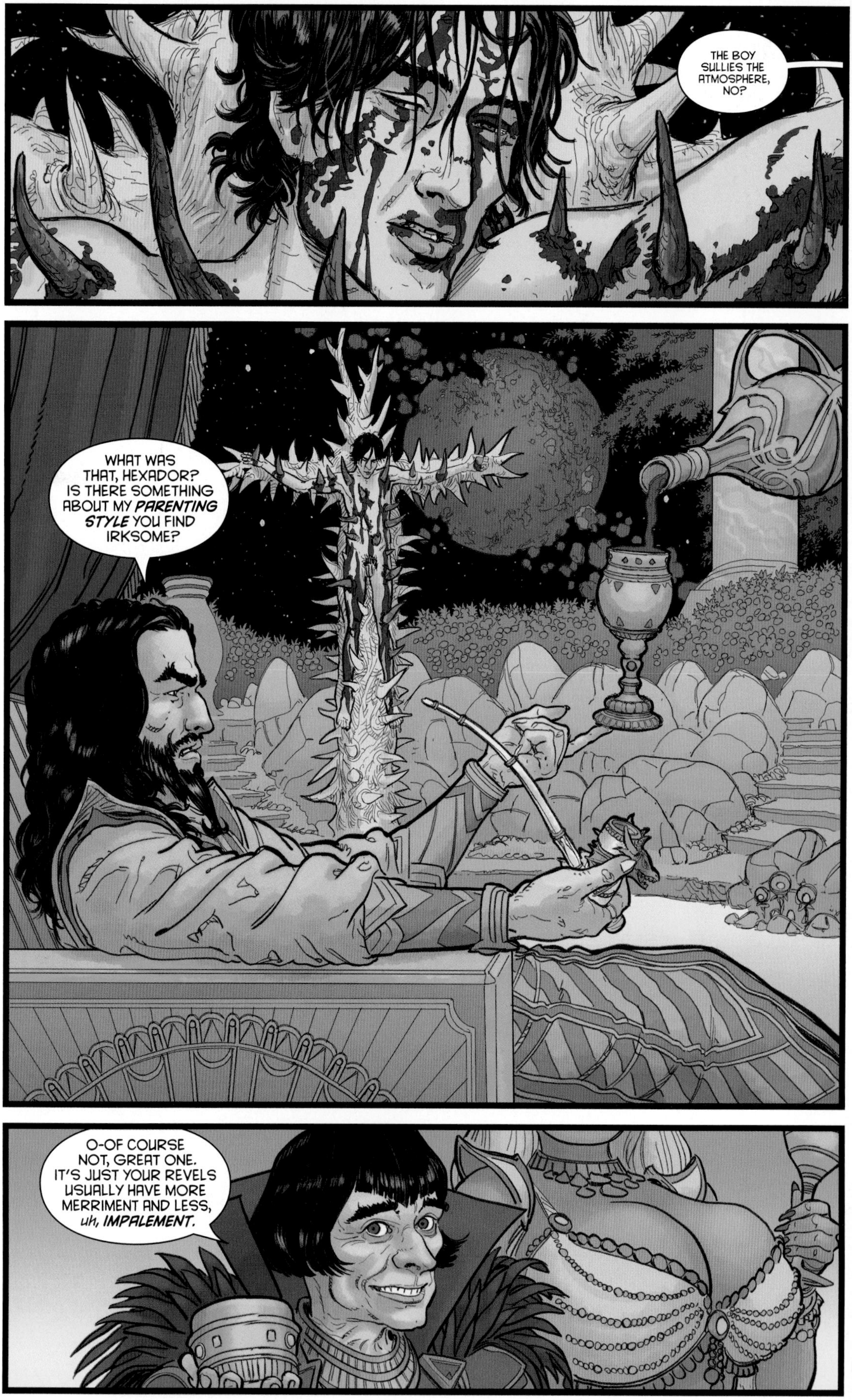
THE BOY SULLIES THE ATMOSPHERE, NO?
WHAT WAS THAT, HEXADOR? IS THERE SOMETHING ABOUT MY *PARENTING STYLE* YOU FIND IRKSOME?
O-OF COURSE NOT, GREAT ONE. IT'S JUST YOUR REVELS USUALLY HAVE MORE MERRIMENT AND LESS, *uh,* ***IMPALEMENT.***

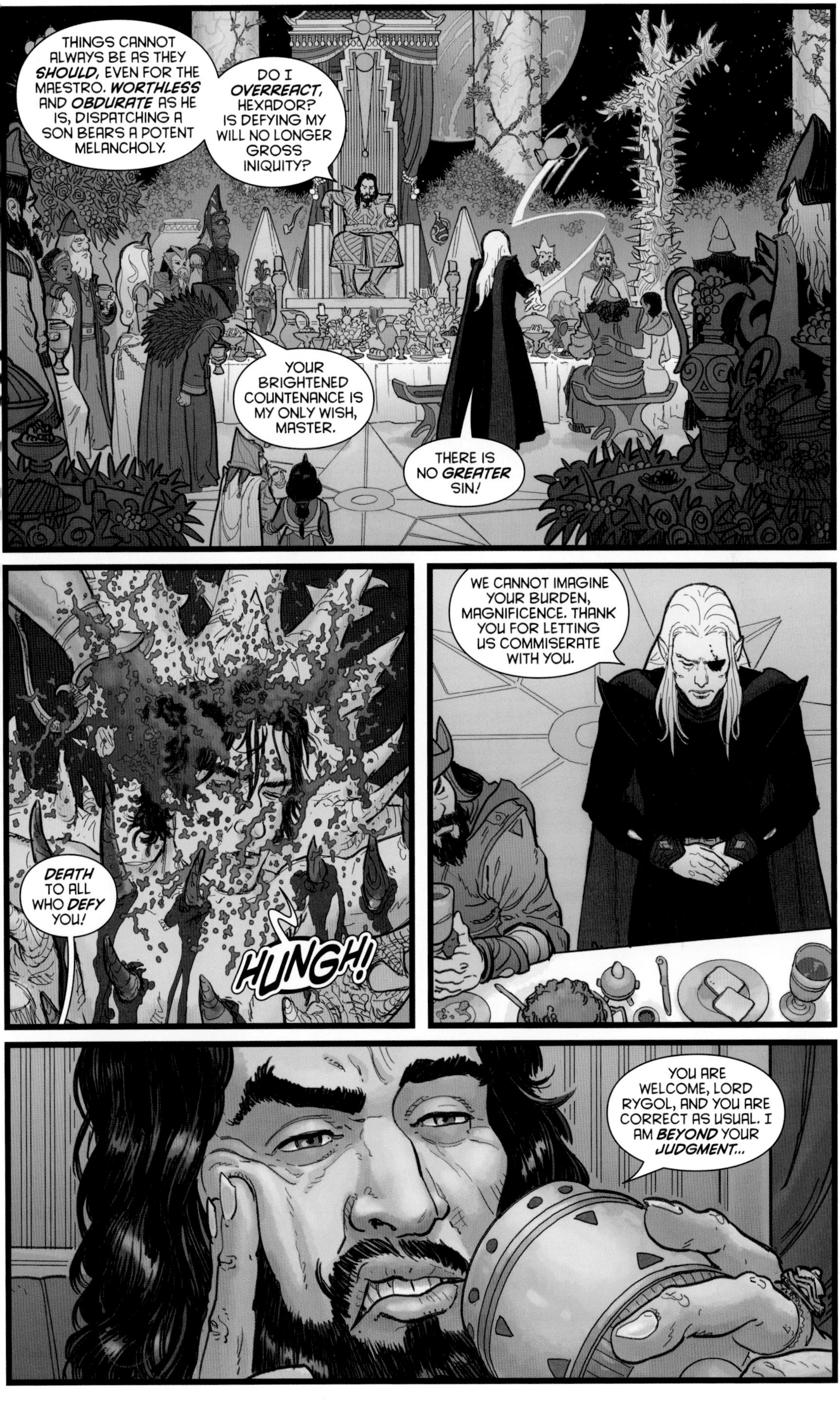
THINGS CANNOT ALWAYS BE AS THEY SHOULD, EVEN FOR THE MAESTRO. WORTHLESS AND OBDURATE AS HE IS, DISPATCHING A SON BEARS A POTENT MELANCHOLY.
DO I OVERREACT, HEXADOR? IS DEFYING MY WILL NO LONGER GROSS INIQUITY?
YOUR BRIGHTENED COUNTENANCE IS MY ONLY WISH, MASTER.
THERE IS NO GREATER SIN!
DEATH TO ALL WHO DEFY YOU!
HUNGH!
WE CANNOT IMAGINE YOUR BURDEN, MAGNIFICENCE. THANK YOU FOR LETTING US COMMISERATE WITH YOU.
YOU ARE WELCOME, LORD RYGOL, AND YOU ARE CORRECT AS USUAL. I AM BEYOND YOUR JUDGMENT...

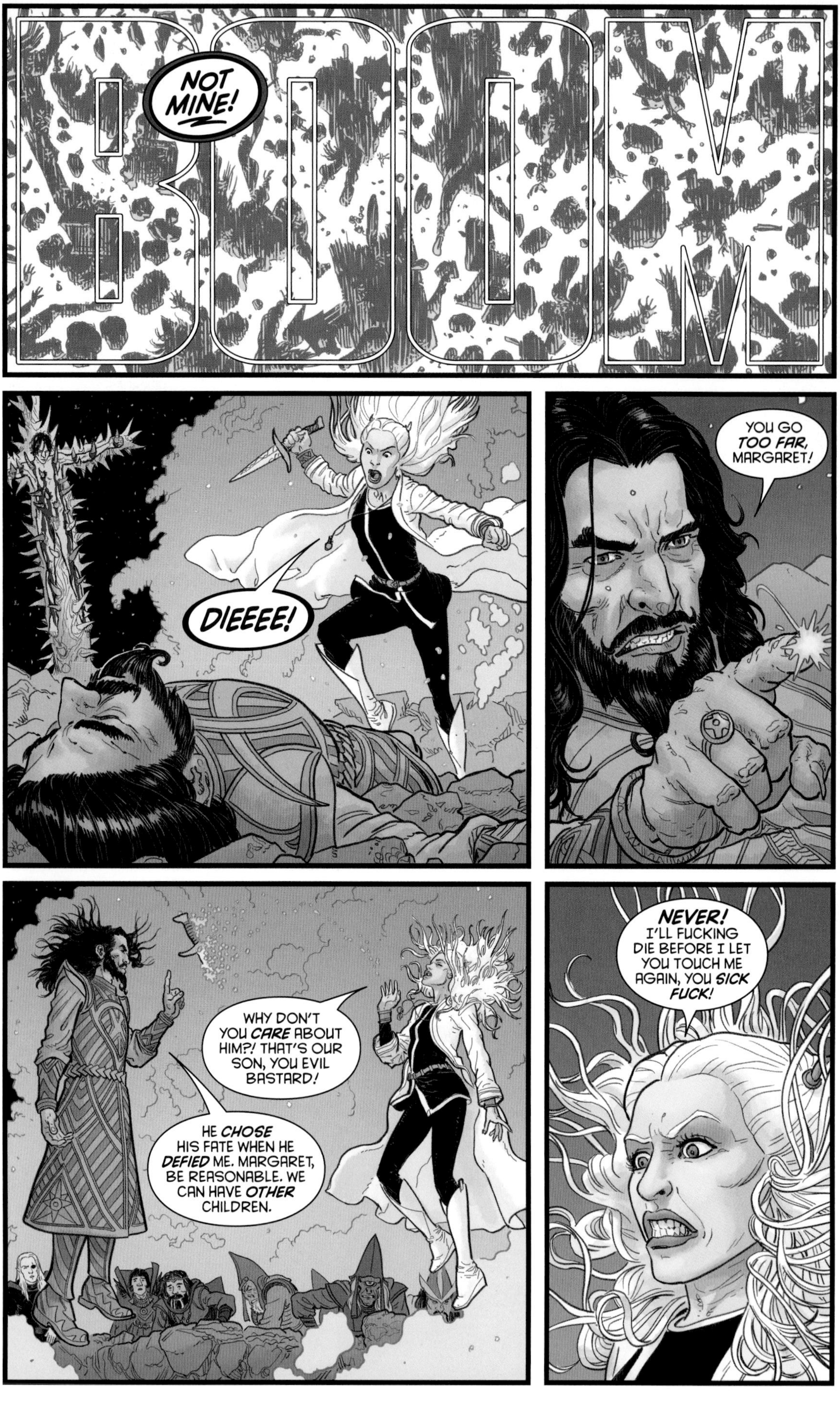
NOT MINE!
BOOM
DIEEEE!
YOU GO TOO FAR, MARGARET!
WHY DON'T YOU CARE ABOUT HIM?! THAT'S OUR SON, YOU EVIL BASTARD!
HE CHOSE HIS FATE WHEN HE DEFIED ME. MARGARET, BE REASONABLE. WE CAN HAVE OTHER CHILDREN.
NEVER! I'LL FUCKING DIE BEFORE I LET YOU TOUCH ME AGAIN, YOU SICK FUCK!

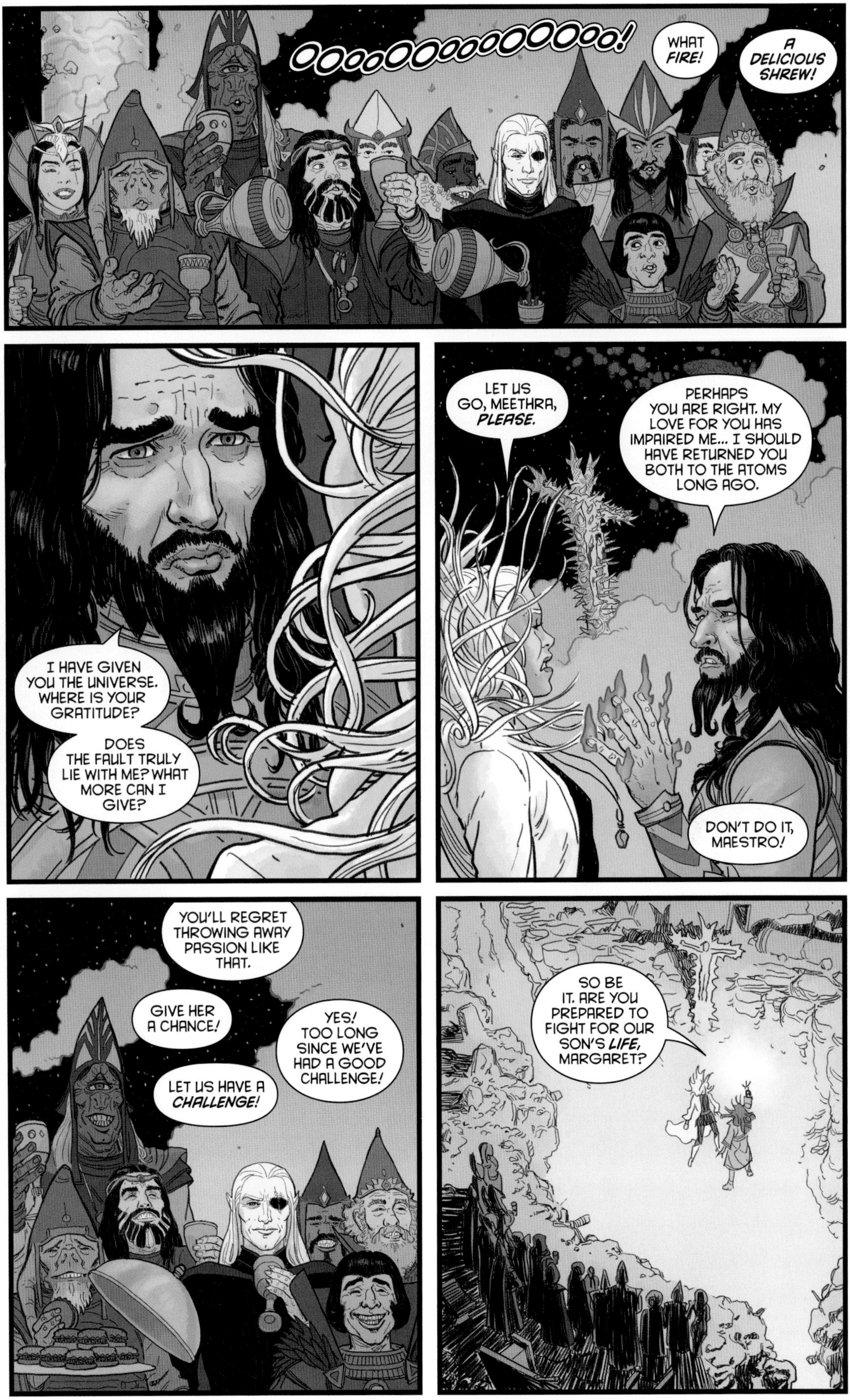
OOOoOOOooOOOOoo!
WHAT FIRE!
A DELICIOUS SHREW!
I HAVE GIVEN YOU THE UNIVERSE. WHERE IS YOUR GRATITUDE?
DOES THE FAULT TRULY LIE WITH ME? WHAT MORE CAN I GIVE?
LET US GO, MEETHRA, PLEASE.
PERHAPS YOU ARE RIGHT. MY LOVE FOR YOU HAS IMPAIRED ME... I SHOULD HAVE RETURNED YOU BOTH TO THE ATOMS LONG AGO.
DON'T DO IT, MAESTRO!
YOU'LL REGRET THROWING AWAY PASSION LIKE THAT.
GIVE HER A CHANCE!
YES! TOO LONG SINCE WE'VE HAD A GOOD CHALLENGE!
LET US HAVE A CHALLENGE!
SO BE IT. ARE YOU PREPARED TO FIGHT FOR OUR SON'S LIFE, MARGARET?

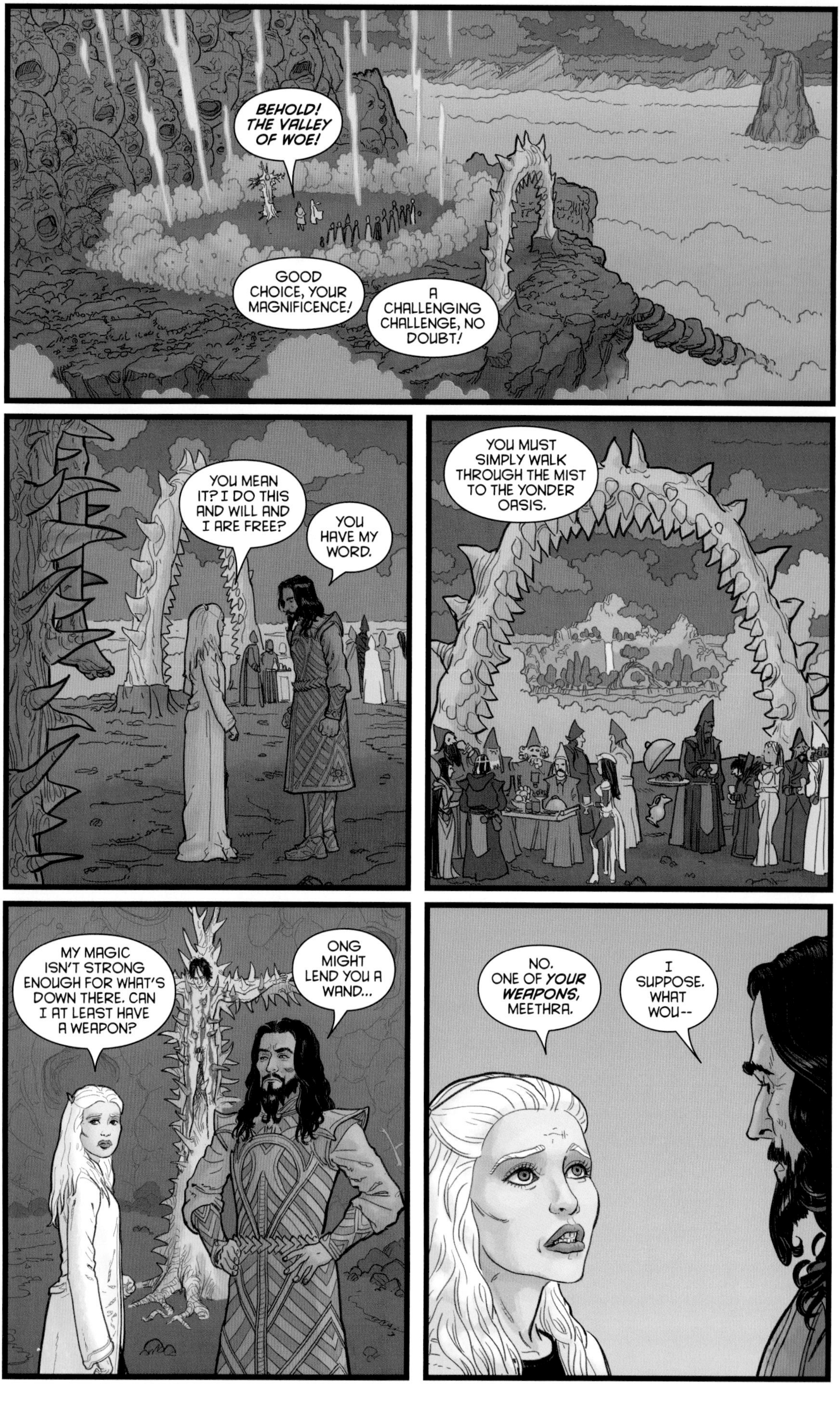
BEHOLD! THE VALLEY OF WOE!
GOOD CHOICE, YOUR MAGNIFICENCE!
A CHALLENGING CHALLENGE, NO DOUBT!
YOU MEAN IT? I DO THIS AND WILL AND I ARE FREE?
YOU HAVE MY WORD.
YOU MUST SIMPLY WALK THROUGH THE MIST TO THE YONDER OASIS.
MY MAGIC ISN'T STRONG ENOUGH FOR WHAT'S DOWN THERE. CAN I AT LEAST HAVE A WEAPON?
ONG MIGHT LEND YOU A WAND...
I SUPPOSE. WHAT WOU--
NO. ONE OF YOUR WEAPONS, MEETHRA.

WITH *HIS* PERMISSION, LET THESE WORDS BE HEARD IN THE *HALLS* OF CONQUEST AND TORMENT!

WHO AMONG YOU KNOWS HIS *MALICE* AND *CRUELTY* BEST?

NNNNNGHHHHUUUU...

I CALL ON THE *STRONGEST* STEEL WITH THE *SHARPEST* EDGE AND THE MOST *BETRAYED* SOUL WITHIN!

JUUUNNNGGGRR...

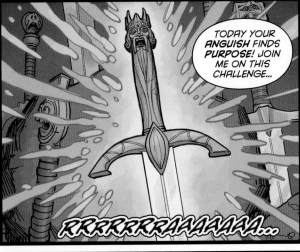

TODAY YOUR *ANGUISH* FINDS *PURPOSE!* JOIN ME ON THIS CHALLENGE...

RRRRRRRRAAAAAAAA...

AND TOGETHER WE MAY HAVE THE *MAESTRO'S* CHAGRIN!

AAARRRRRGGGHHH!

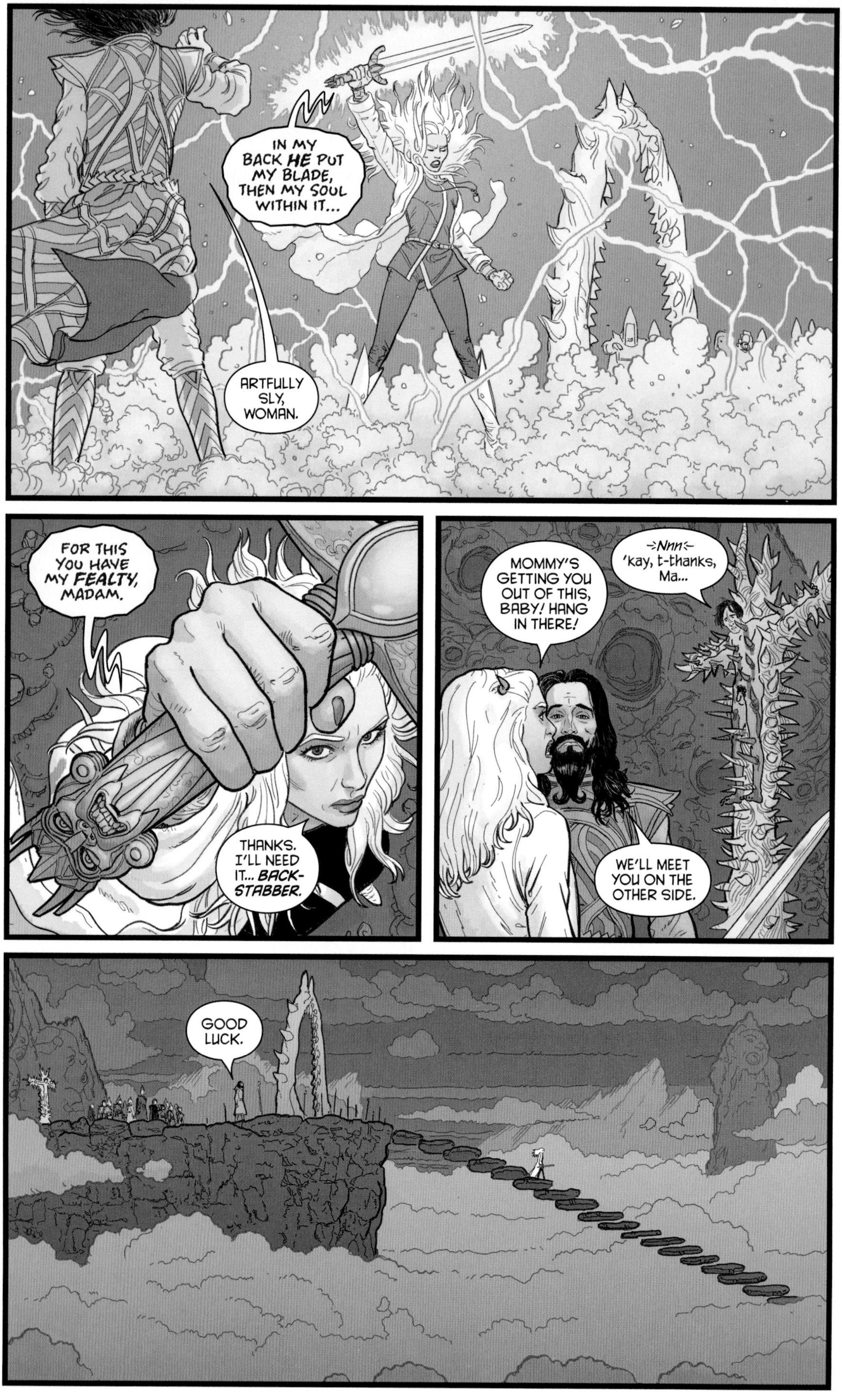
IN MY BACK HE PUT MY BLADE, THEN MY SOUL WITHIN IT...
ARTFULLY SLY, WOMAN.
FOR THIS YOU HAVE MY FEALTY, MADAM.
THANKS. I'LL NEED IT... BACK-STABBER.
MOMMY'S GETTING YOU OUT OF THIS, BABY! HANG IN THERE!
Nnn
'kay, t-thanks, Ma...
WE'LL MEET YOU ON THE OTHER SIDE.
GOOD LUCK.

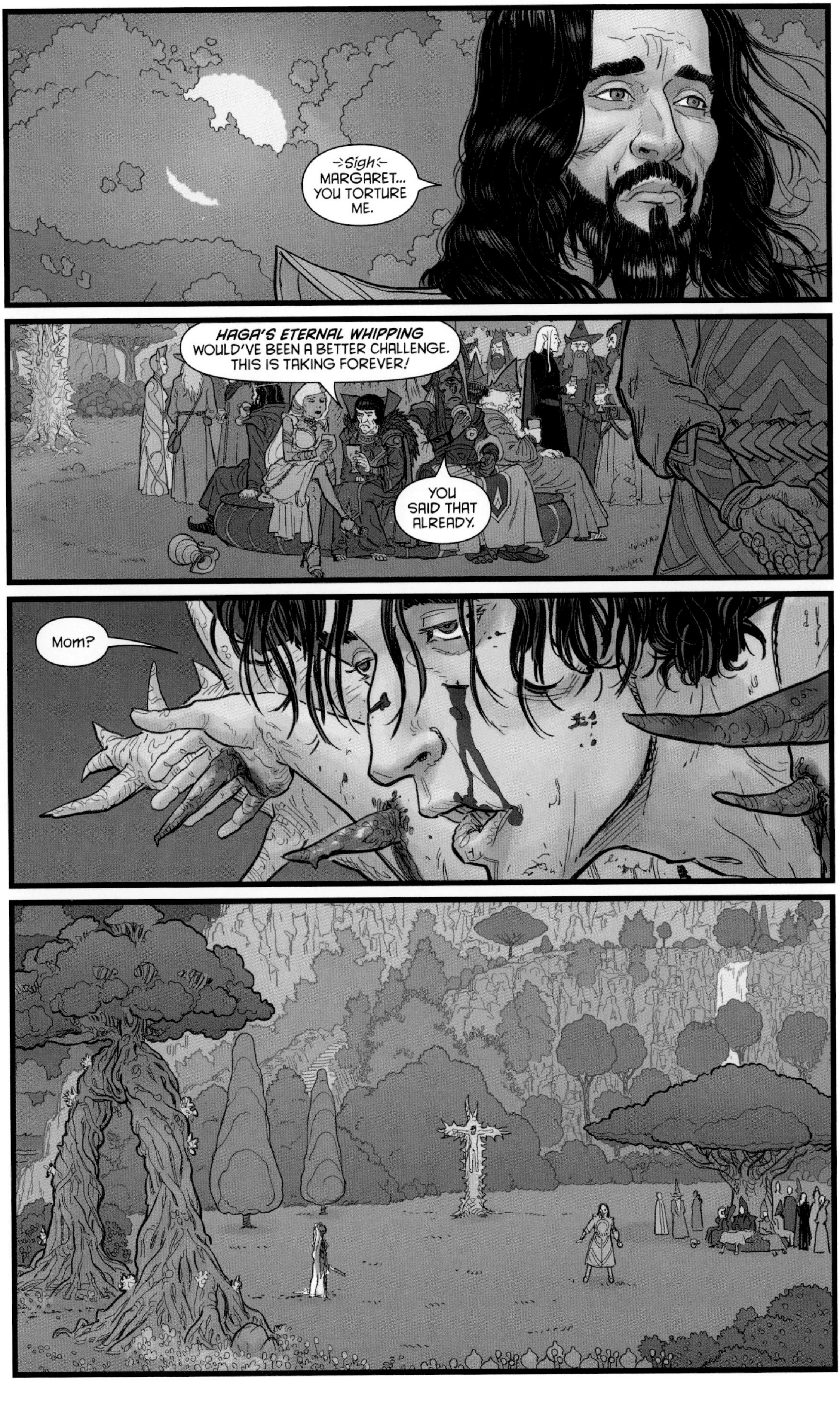

Sigh
MARGARET... YOU TORTURE ME.
HAGA'S ETERNAL WHIPPING WOULD'VE BEEN A BETTER CHALLENGE. THIS IS TAKING FOREVER!
YOU SAID THAT ALREADY.
Mom?

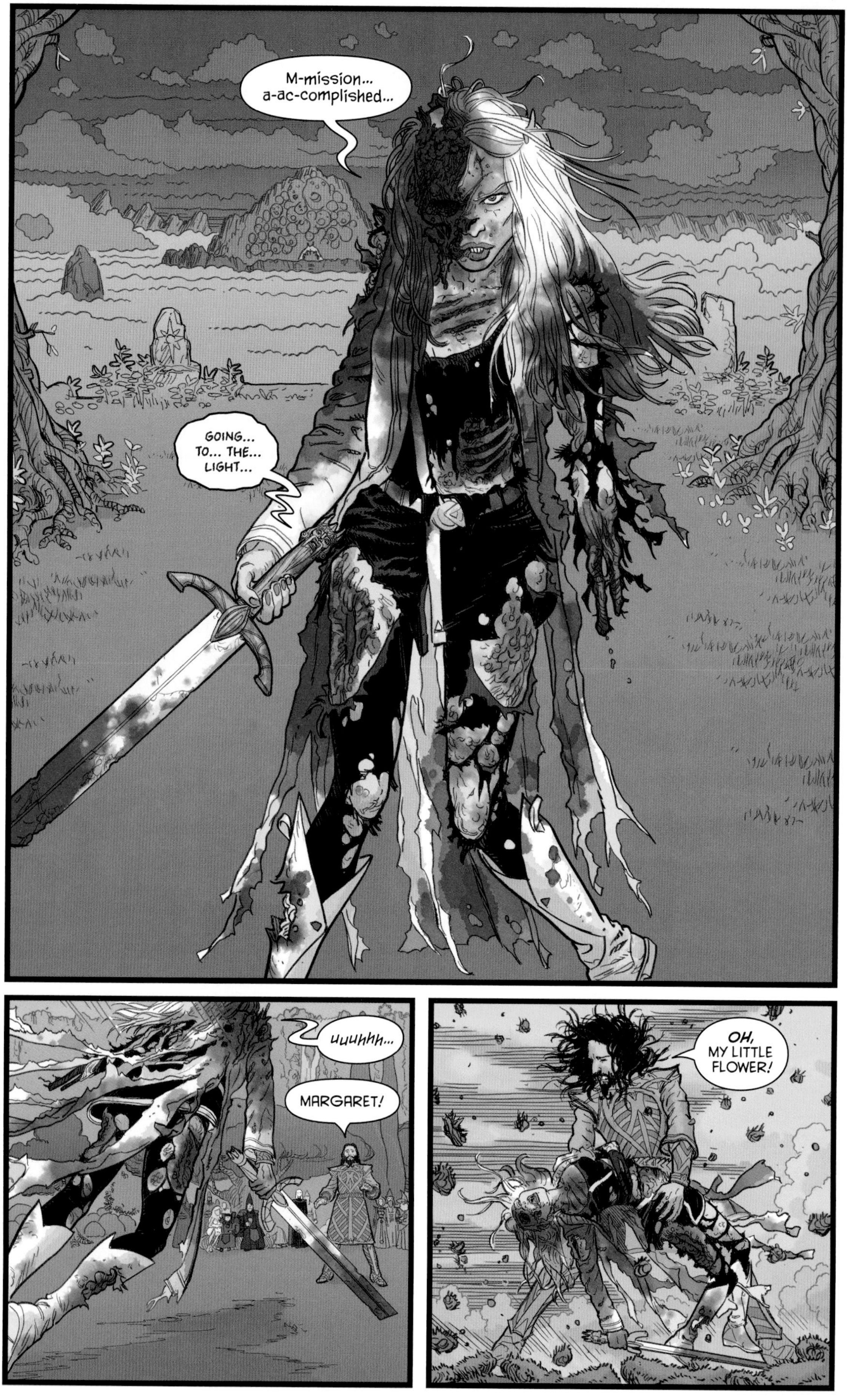
M-mission... a-ac-complished...
GOING... TO... THE... LIGHT...
uuuhhh...
MARGARET!
OH, MY LITTLE FLOWER!

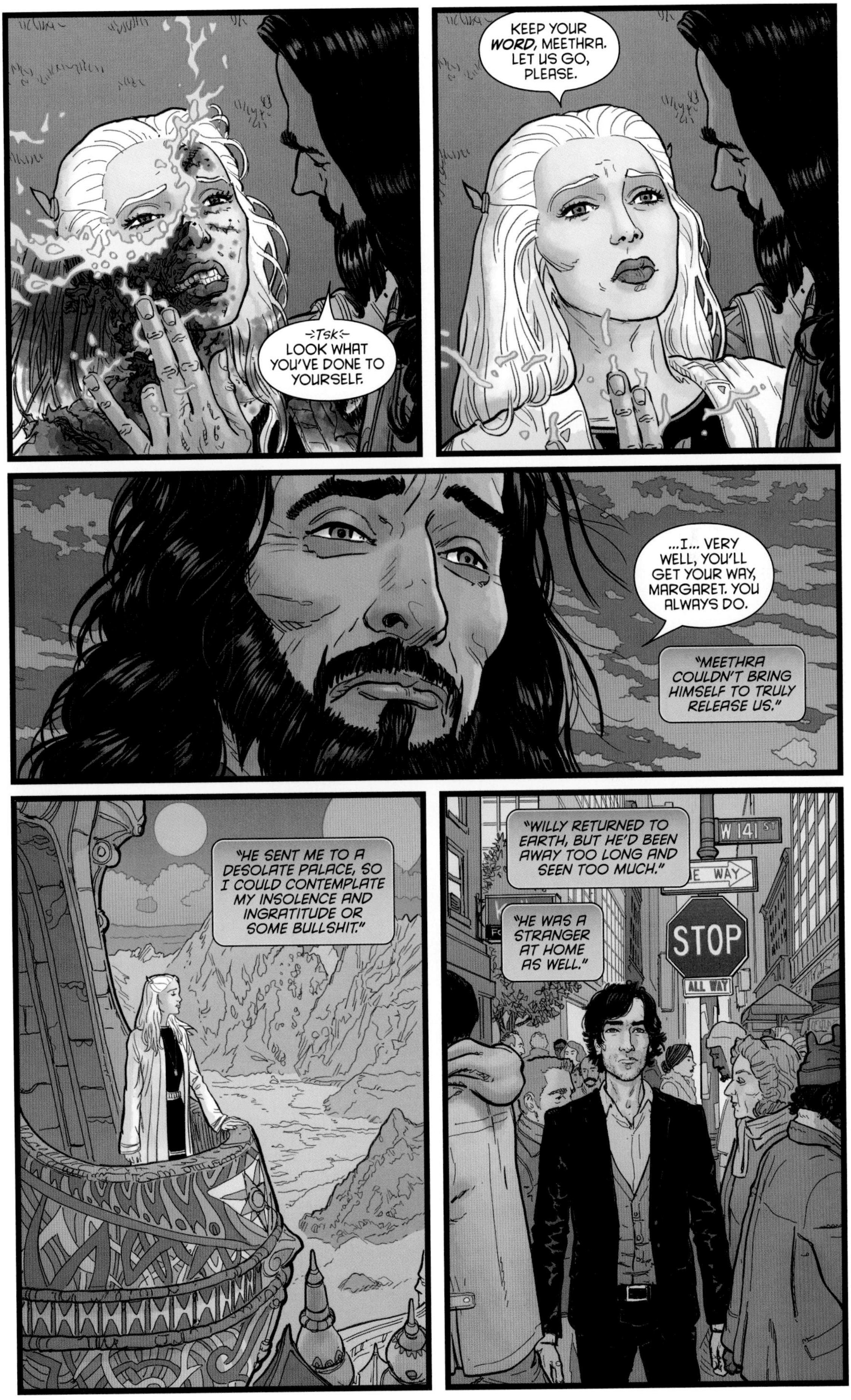
-Tsk-
LOOK WHAT YOU'VE DONE TO YOURSELF.
KEEP YOUR WORD, MEETHRA. LET US GO, PLEASE.
...I... VERY WELL, YOU'LL GET YOUR WAY, MARGARET. YOU ALWAYS DO.
"MEETHRA COULDN'T BRING HIMSELF TO TRULY RELEASE US."
"HE SENT ME TO A DESOLATE PALACE, SO I COULD CONTEMPLATE MY INSOLENCE AND INGRATITUDE OR SOME BULLSHIT."
"WILLY RETURNED TO EARTH, BUT HE'D BEEN AWAY TOO LONG AND SEEN TOO MUCH."
W 141 ST
E WAY
STOP
ALL WAY
"HE WAS A STRANGER AT HOME AS WELL."

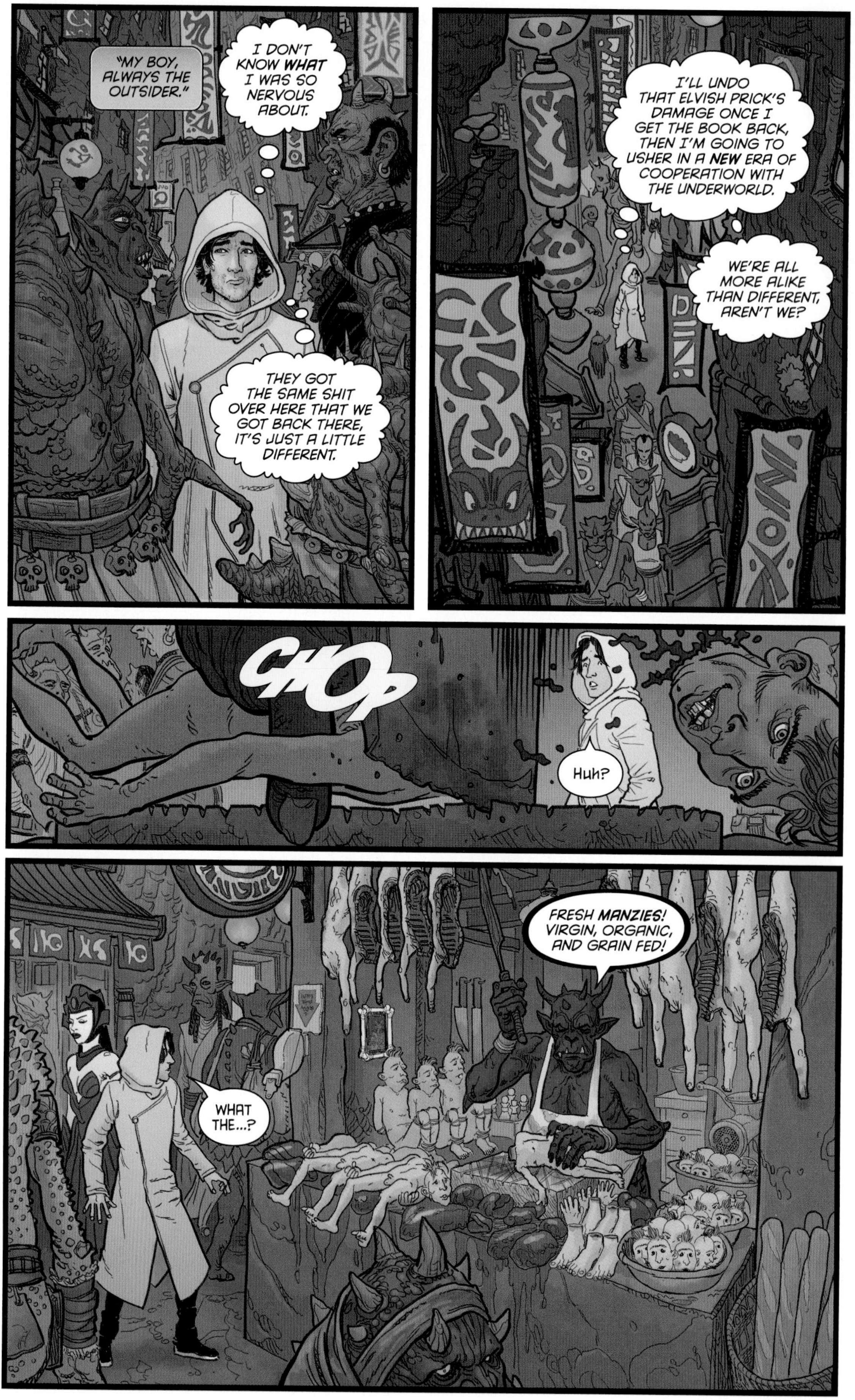
"MY BOY, ALWAYS THE OUTSIDER."
I DON'T KNOW **WHAT** I WAS SO NERVOUS ABOUT.
THEY GOT THE SAME SHIT OVER HERE THAT WE GOT BACK THERE, IT'S JUST A LITTLE DIFFERENT.
I'LL UNDO THAT ELVISH PRICK'S DAMAGE ONCE I GET THE BOOK BACK, THEN I'M GOING TO USHER IN A **NEW** ERA OF COOPERATION WITH THE UNDERWORLD.
WE'RE ALL MORE ALIKE THAN DIFFERENT, AREN'T WE?
CHOP
Huh?
FRESH **MANZIES!** VIRGIN, ORGANIC, AND GRAIN FED!
WHAT THE...?

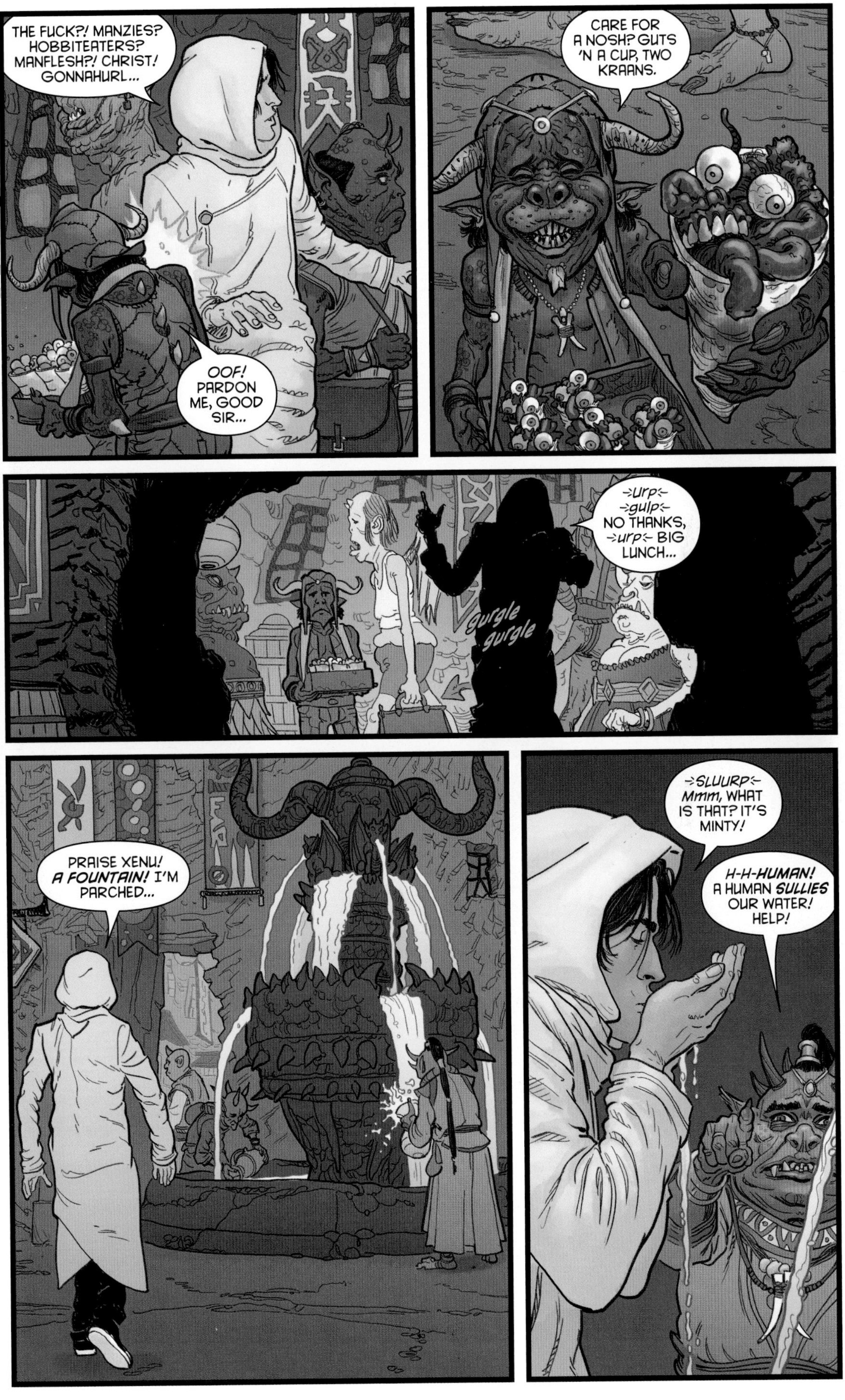
THE FUCK?! MANZIES? HOBBITEATERS? MANFLESH?! CHRIST! GONNAHURL...
OOF! PARDON ME, GOOD SIR...
CARE FOR A NOSH? GUTS 'N A CUP, TWO KRAANS.
urp gulp NO THANKS, urp BIG LUNCH...
gurgle gurgle
PRAISE XENU! A FOUNTAIN! I'M PARCHED...
SLUURP Mmm, WHAT IS THAT? IT'S MINTY!
H-H-HUMAN! A HUMAN SULLIES OUR WATER! HELP!

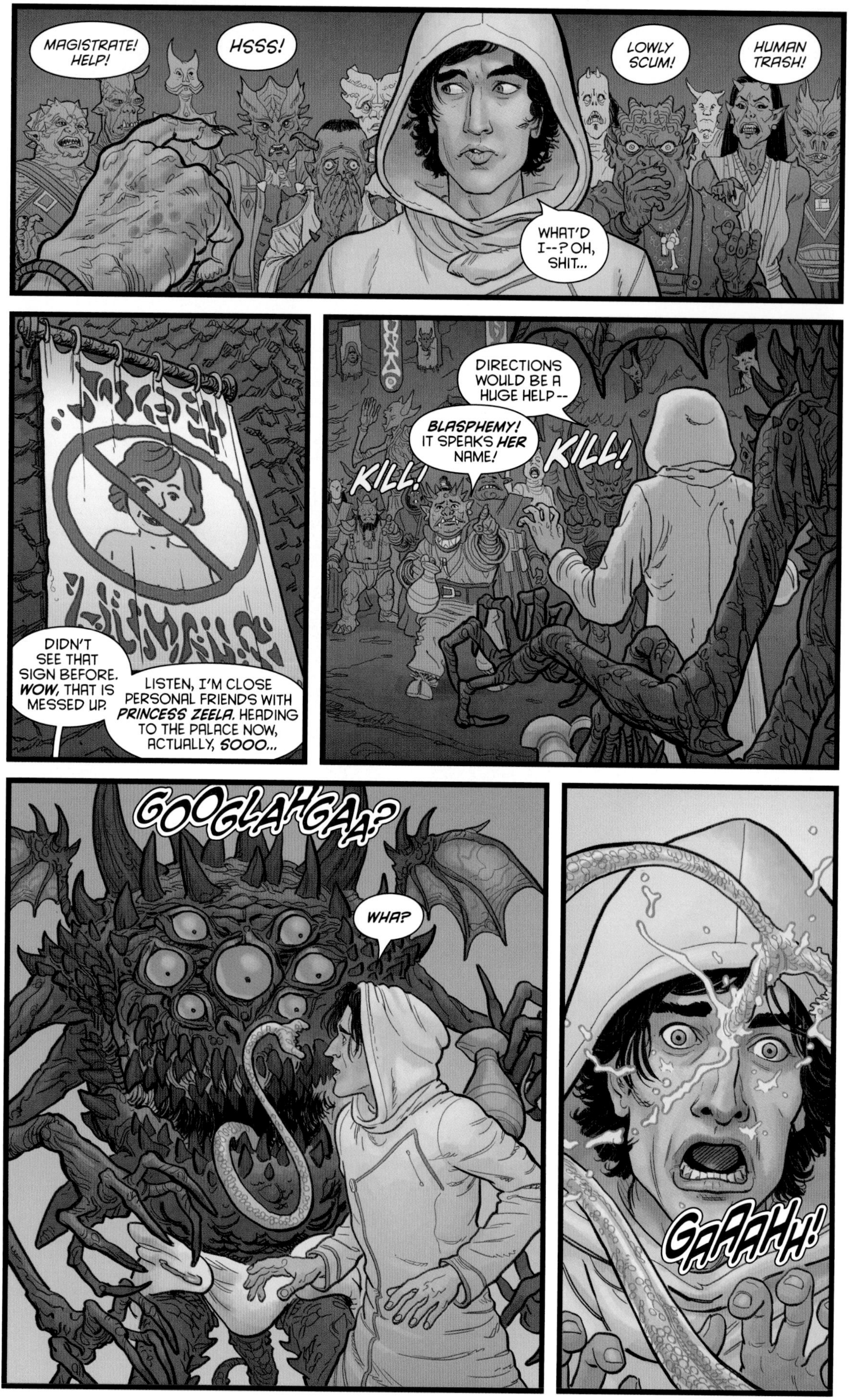
MAGISTRATE! HELP!
HSSS!
LOWLY SCUM!
HUMAN TRASH!
WHAT'D I--? OH, SHIT...
DIDN'T SEE THAT SIGN BEFORE. WOW, THAT IS MESSED UP.
LISTEN, I'M CLOSE PERSONAL FRIENDS WITH PRINCESS ZEELA. HEADING TO THE PALACE NOW, ACTUALLY, SOOO...
DIRECTIONS WOULD BE A HUGE HELP--
BLASPHEMY! IT SPEAKS HER NAME!
KILL!
KILL!
GOOGLAH'GAA?
WHA?
GAAAHH!

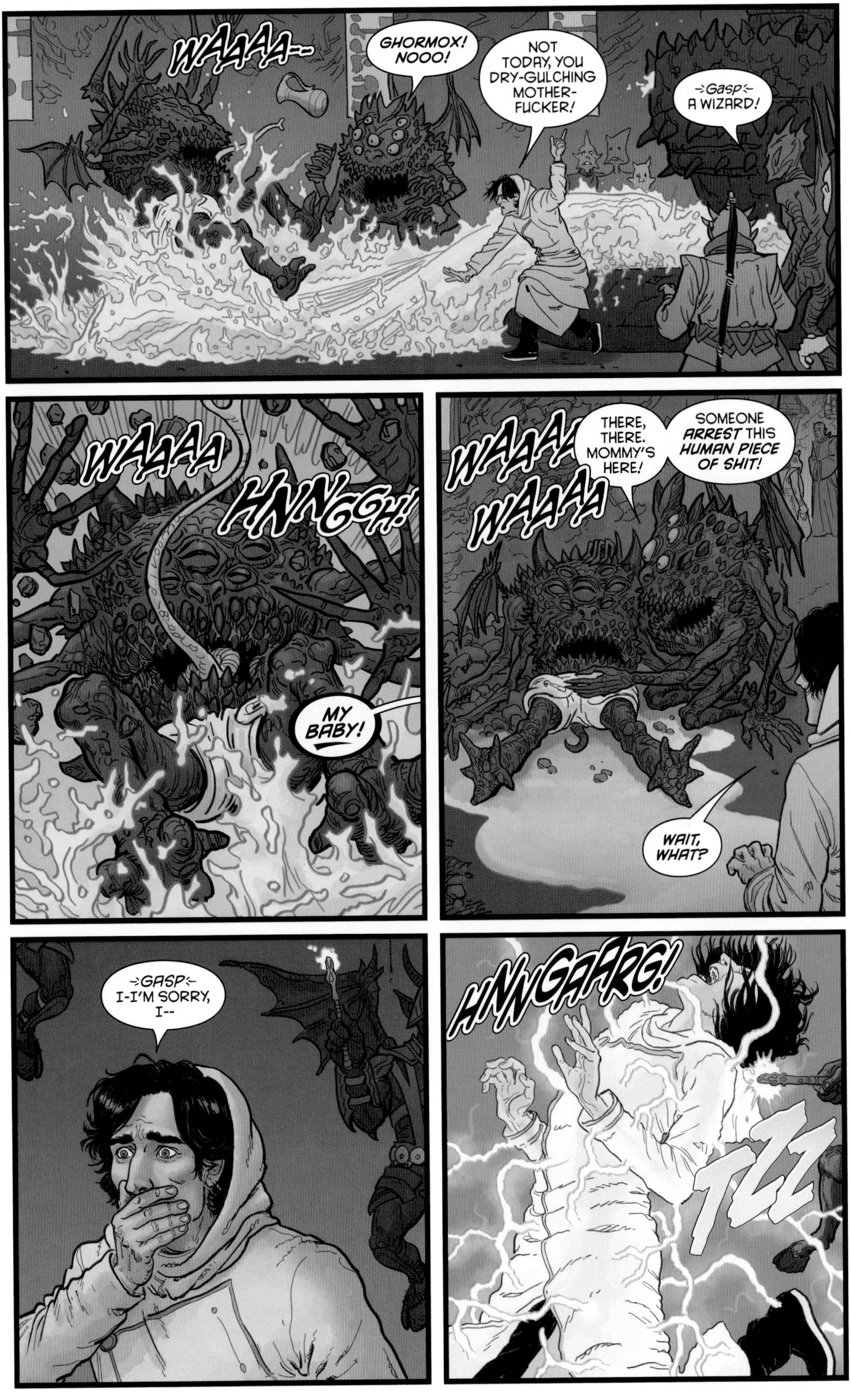
WAAAAA--
GHORMOX! NOOO!
NOT TODAY, YOU DRY-GULCHING MOTHER-FUCKER!
-Gasp- A WIZARD!
WAAAA
HNNGGH!
MY BABY!
WAAAA
WAAAA
THERE, THERE. MOMMY'S HERE!
SOMEONE ARREST THIS HUMAN PIECE OF SHIT!
WAIT, WHAT?
-GASP- I-I'M SORRY, I--
HNNGAARG!
TZZ

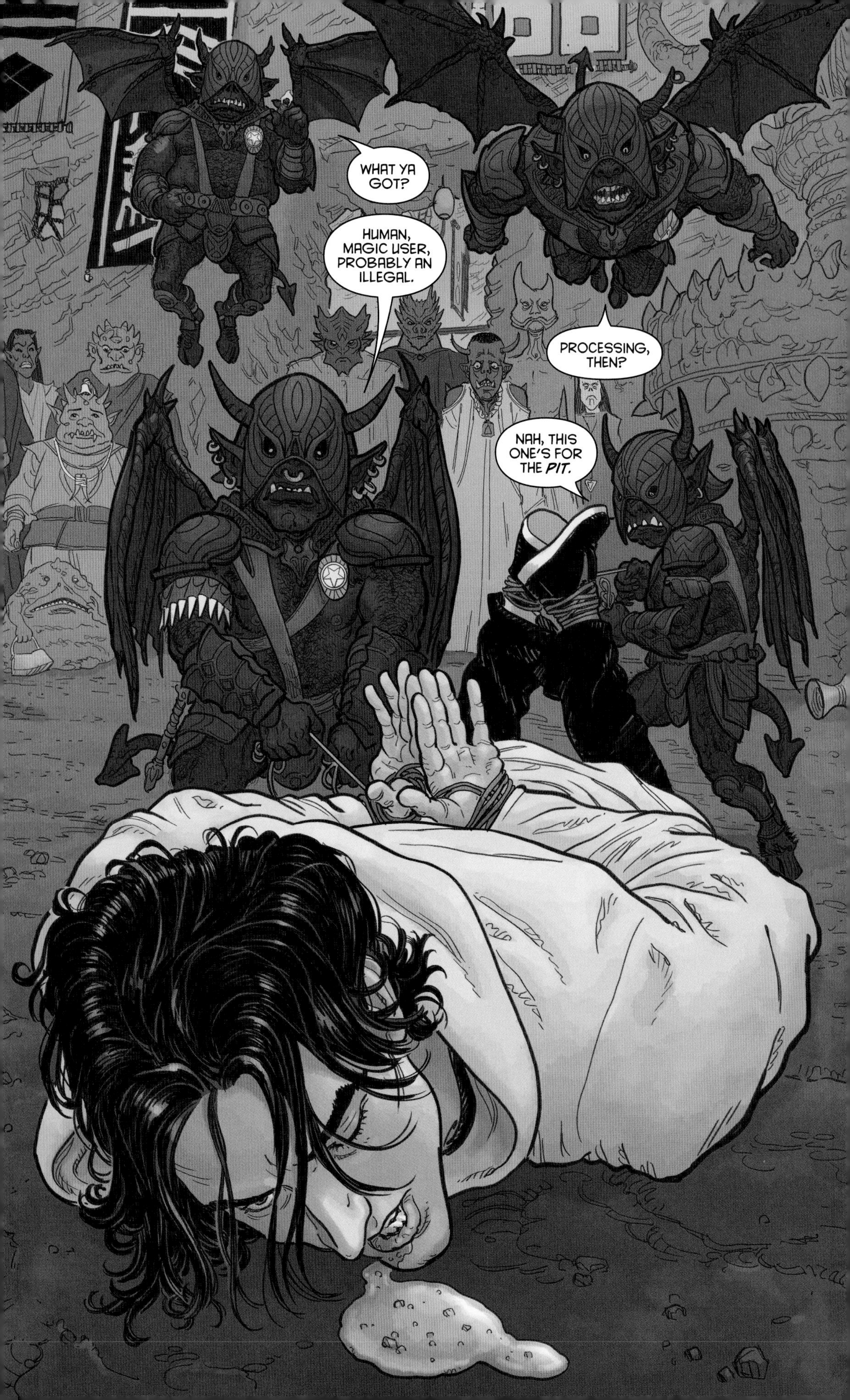
WHAT YA GOT?
HUMAN, MAGIC USER, PROBABLY AN ILLEGAL.
PROCESSING, THEN?
NAH, THIS ONE'S FOR THE *PIT*.

CHAPTER FIVE

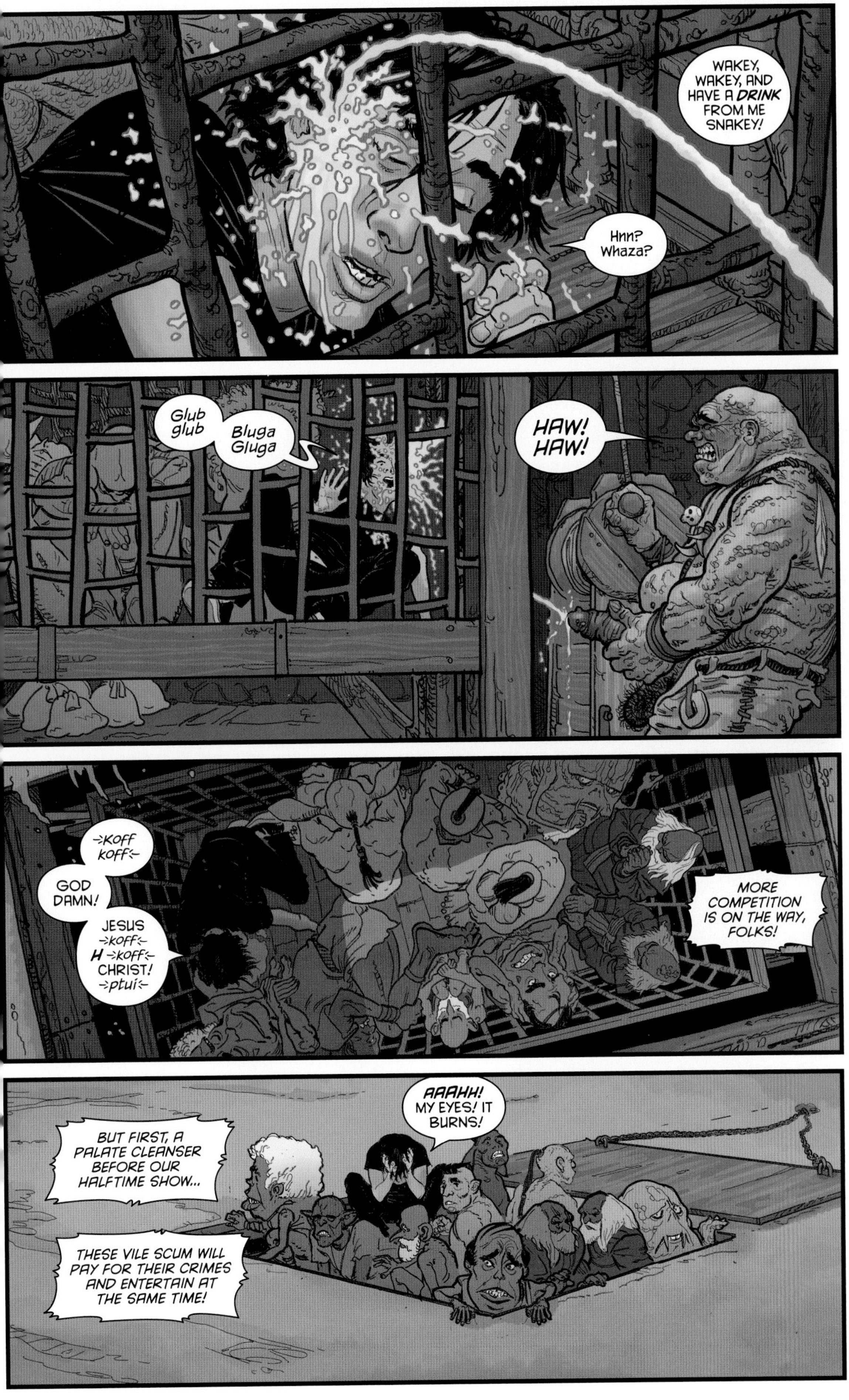
WAKEY, WAKEY, AND HAVE A DRINK FROM ME SNAKEY!
Hnn? Whaza?
Glub glub
Bluga Gluga
HAW! HAW!
-KOFF KOFF-
GOD DAMN!
JESUS -KOFF- H -KOFF- CHRIST! -PTUI-
MORE COMPETITION IS ON THE WAY, FOLKS!
BUT FIRST, A PALATE CLEANSER BEFORE OUR HALFTIME SHOW...
AAAHH! MY EYES! IT BURNS!
THESE VILE SCUM WILL PAY FOR THEIR CRIMES AND ENTERTAIN AT THE SAME TIME!

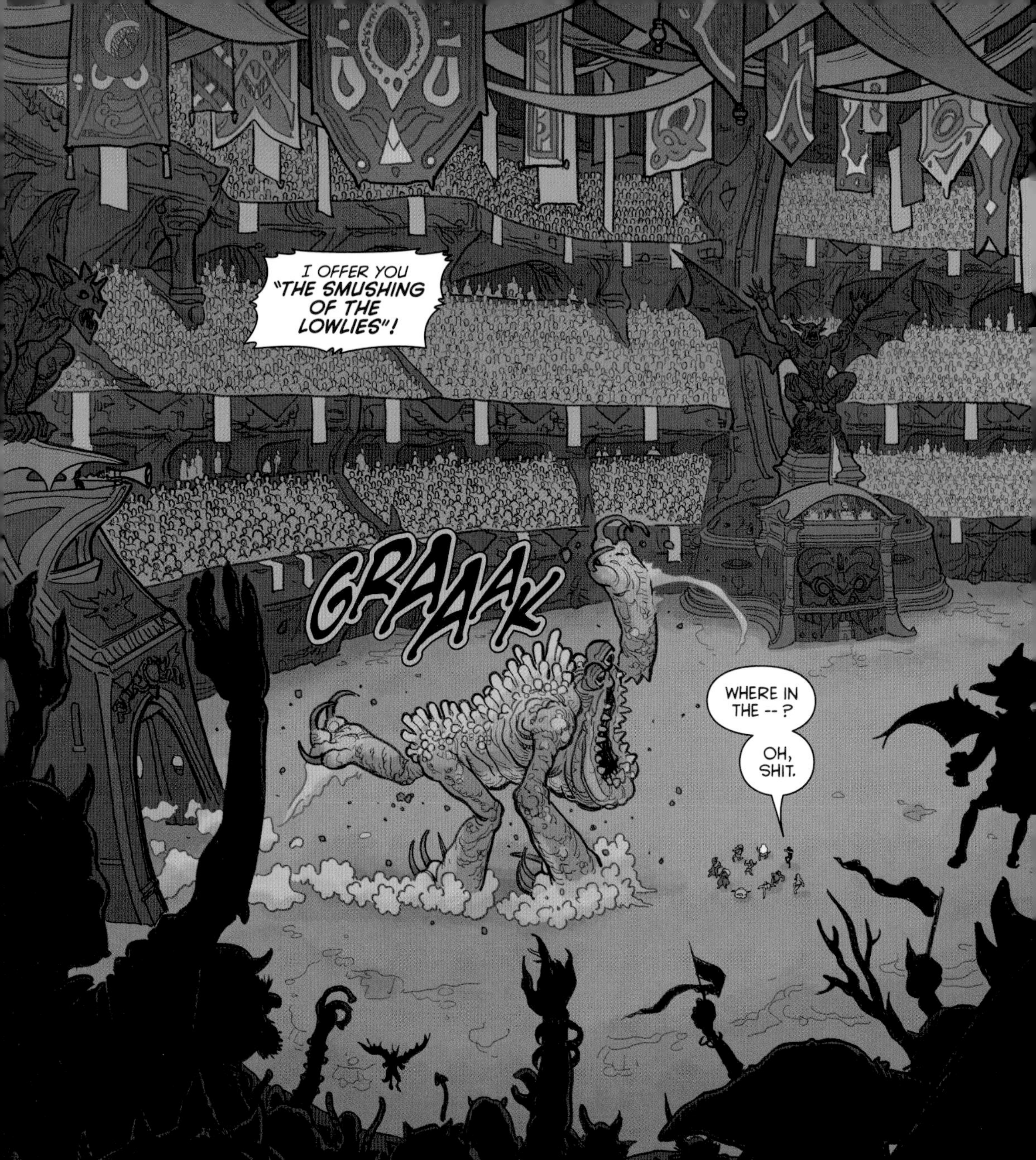
I OFFER YOU "THE SMUSHING OF THE LOWLIES"!
GRAAAK
WHERE IN THE -- ?
OH, SHIT.
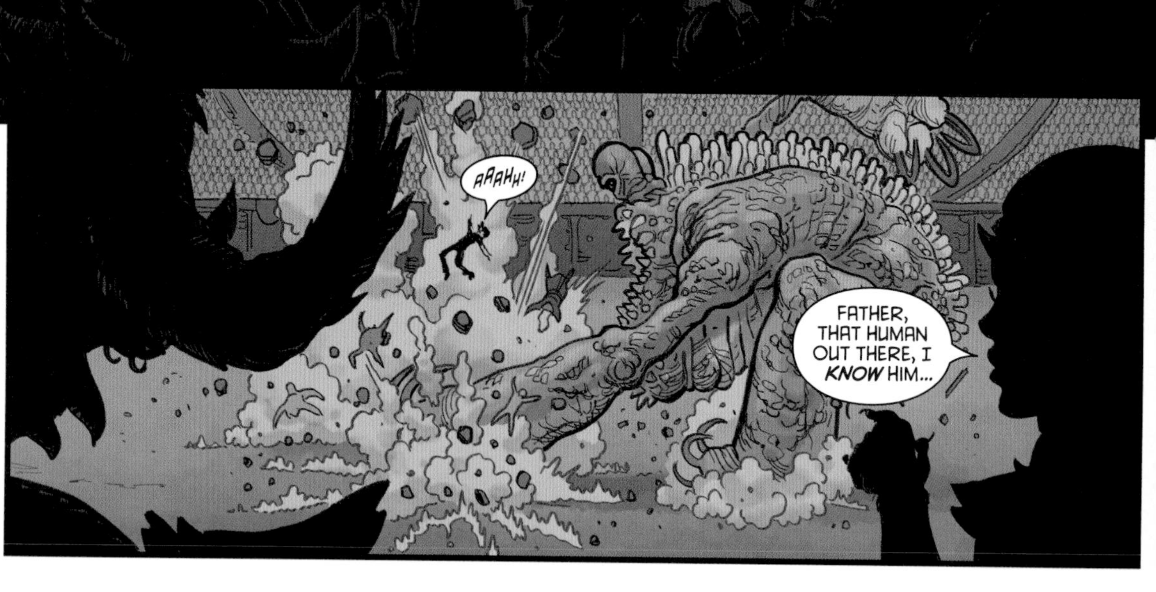
AAAHH!
FATHER, THAT HUMAN OUT THERE, I KNOW HIM...

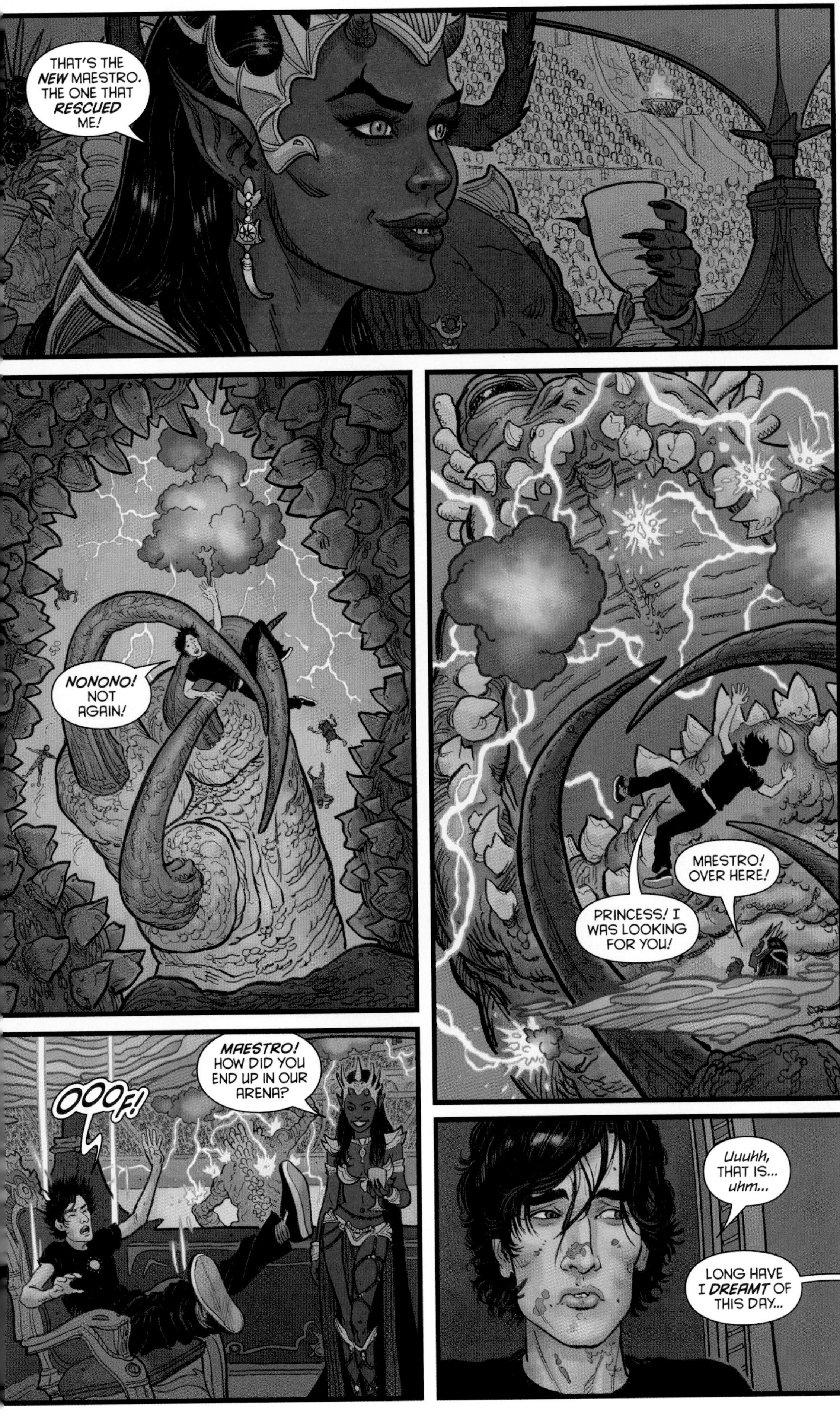
THAT'S THE NEW MAESTRO. THE ONE THAT RESCUED ME!
NONONO! NOT AGAIN!
MAESTRO! OVER HERE!
PRINCESS! I WAS LOOKING FOR YOU!
OOOF!
MAESTRO! HOW DID YOU END UP IN OUR ARENA?
Uuuhh, THAT IS... uhm...
LONG HAVE I DREAMT OF THIS DAY...

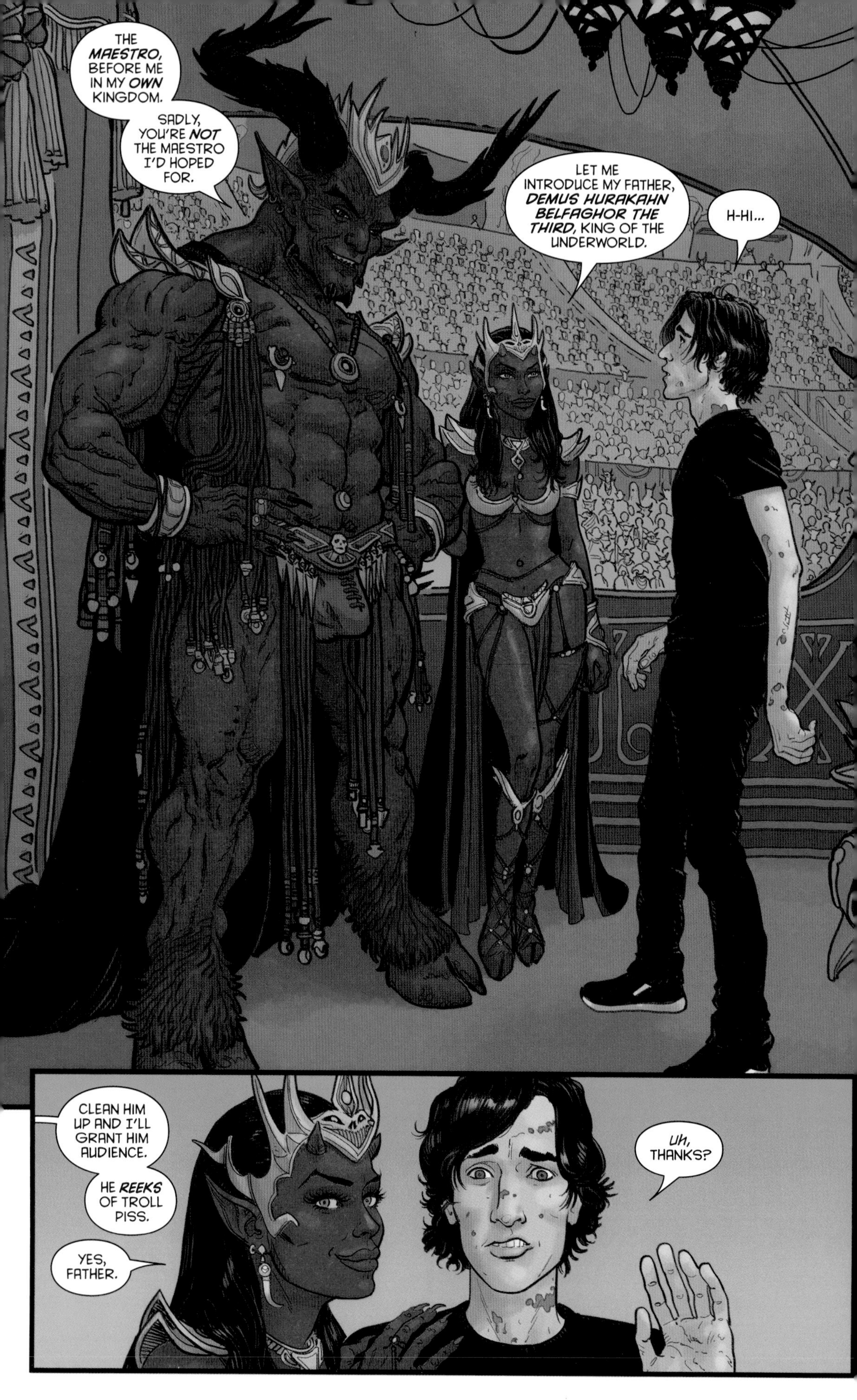
THE *MAESTRO*, BEFORE ME IN MY *OWN* KINGDOM.
SADLY, YOU'RE *NOT* THE MAESTRO I'D HOPED FOR.
LET ME INTRODUCE MY FATHER, *DEMUS HURAKAHN BELFAGHOR THE THIRD*, KING OF THE UNDERWORLD.
H-HI...
CLEAN HIM UP AND I'LL GRANT HIM AUDIENCE.
HE *REEKS* OF TROLL PISS.
YES, FATHER.
UH, THANKS?

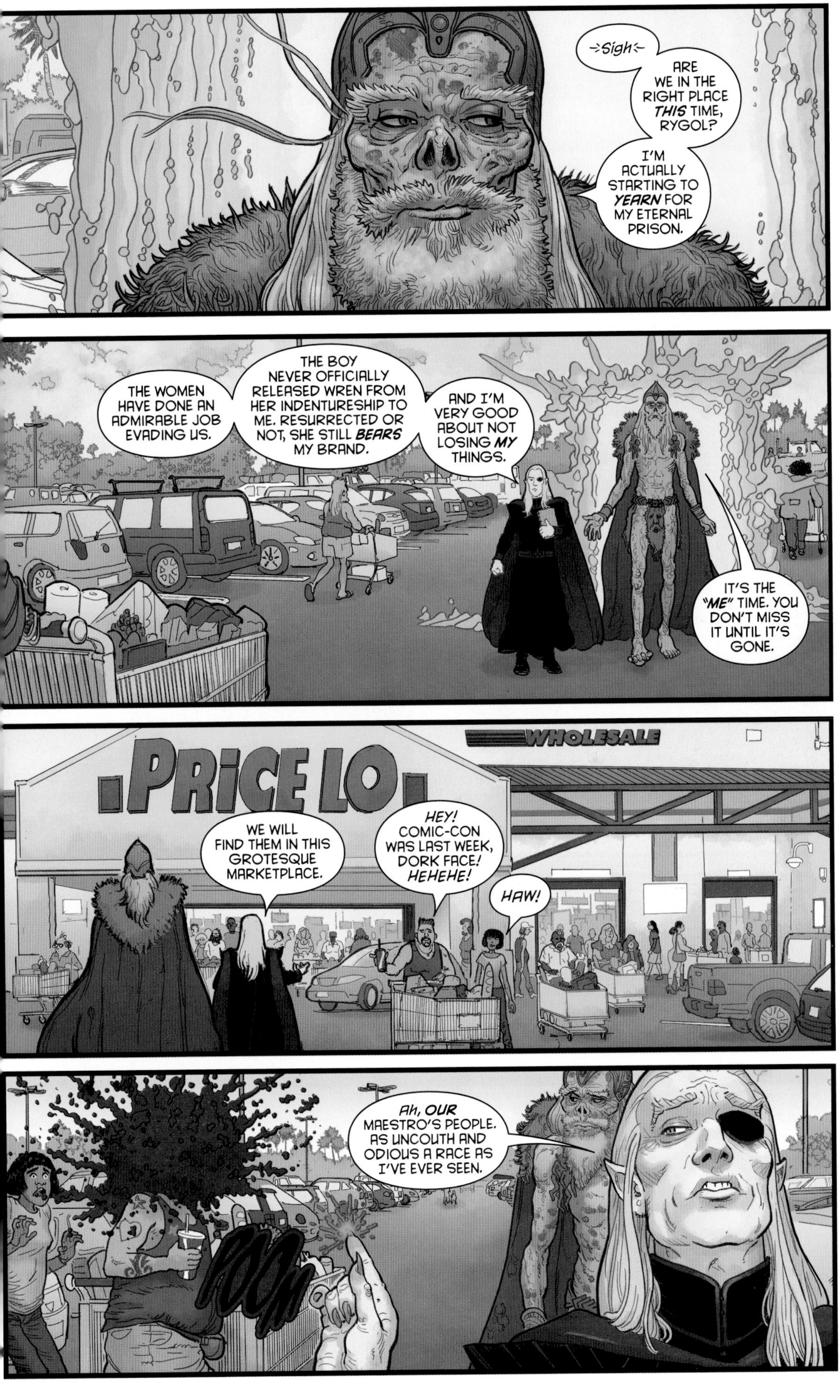

-Sigh-
ARE WE IN THE RIGHT PLACE *THIS* TIME, RYGOL?
I'M ACTUALLY STARTING TO *YEARN* FOR MY ETERNAL PRISON.
THE WOMEN HAVE DONE AN ADMIRABLE JOB EVADING US.
THE BOY NEVER OFFICIALLY RELEASED WREN FROM HER INDENTURESHIP TO ME. RESURRECTED OR NOT, SHE STILL *BEARS* MY BRAND.
AND I'M VERY GOOD ABOUT NOT LOSING *MY* THINGS.
IT'S THE *"ME"* TIME. YOU DON'T MISS IT UNTIL IT'S GONE.
PRICE LO
WHOLESALE
WE WILL FIND THEM IN THIS GROTESQUE MARKETPLACE.
HEY! COMIC-CON WAS LAST WEEK, DORK FACE! *HEHEHE!*
HAW!
Ah, *OUR* MAESTRO'S PEOPLE. AS UNCOUTH AND ODIOUS A RACE AS I'VE EVER SEEN.

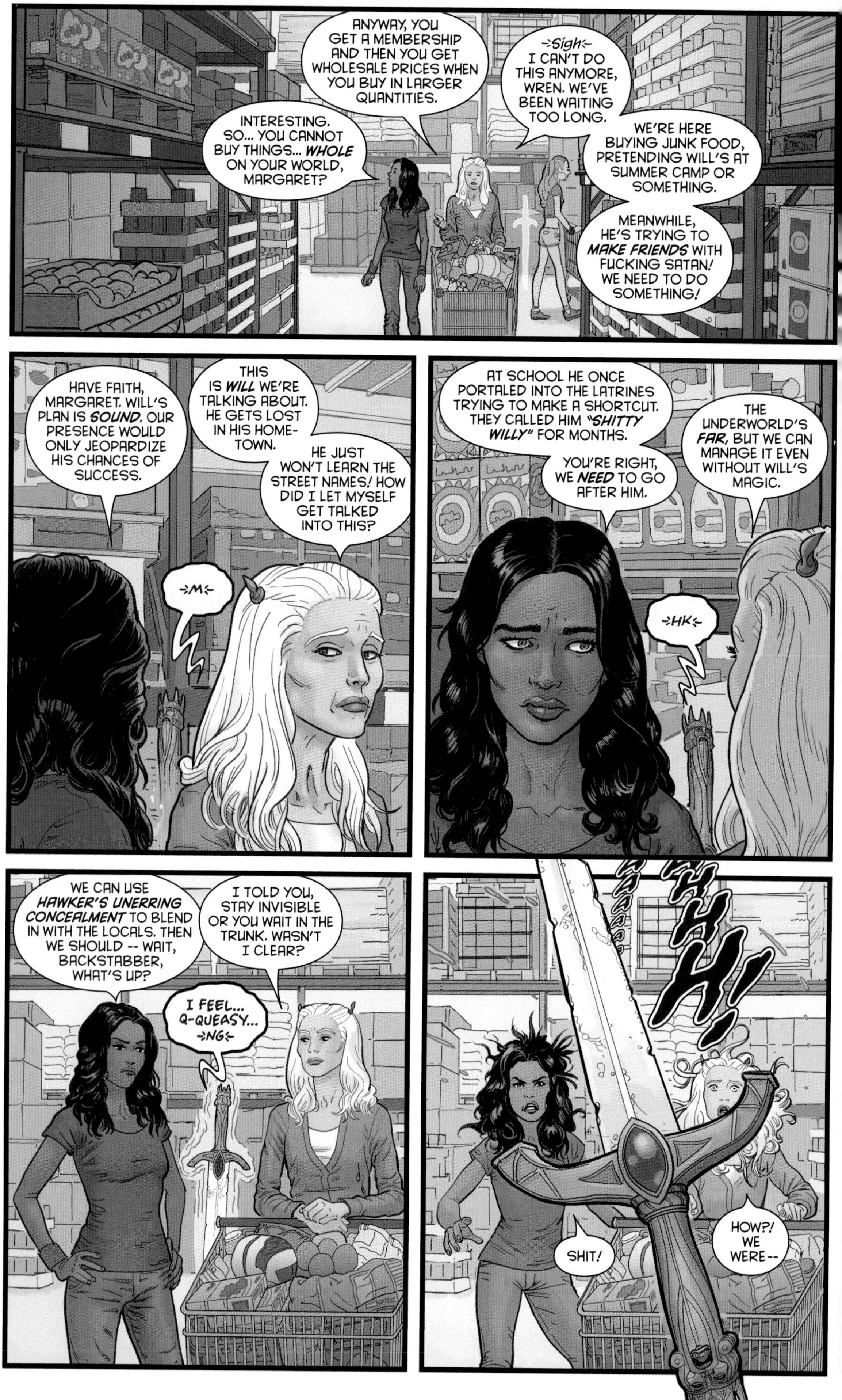

ANYWAY, YOU GET A MEMBERSHIP AND THEN YOU GET WHOLESALE PRICES WHEN YOU BUY IN LARGER QUANTITIES.
INTERESTING. SO... YOU CANNOT BUY THINGS... *WHOLE* ON YOUR WORLD, MARGARET?
Sigh
I CAN'T DO THIS ANYMORE, WREN. WE'VE BEEN WAITING TOO LONG.
WE'RE HERE BUYING JUNK FOOD, PRETENDING WILL'S AT SUMMER CAMP OR SOMETHING.
MEANWHILE, HE'S TRYING TO *MAKE FRIENDS* WITH FUCKING SATAN! WE NEED TO DO SOMETHING!
HAVE FAITH, MARGARET. WILL'S PLAN IS *SOUND*. OUR PRESENCE WOULD ONLY JEOPARDIZE HIS CHANCES OF SUCCESS.
THIS IS *WILL* WE'RE TALKING ABOUT. HE GETS LOST IN HIS HOME-TOWN.
HE JUST WON'T LEARN THE STREET NAMES! HOW DID I LET MYSELF GET TALKED INTO THIS?
M
AT SCHOOL HE ONCE PORTALED INTO THE LATRINES TRYING TO MAKE A SHORTCUT. THEY CALLED HIM *"SHITTY WILLY"* FOR MONTHS.
YOU'RE RIGHT, WE *NEED* TO GO AFTER HIM.
THE UNDERWORLD'S *FAR*, BUT WE CAN MANAGE IT EVEN WITHOUT WILL'S MAGIC.
HK
WE CAN USE *HAWKER'S UNERRING CONCEALMENT* TO BLEND IN WITH THE LOCALS. THEN WE SHOULD -- WAIT, BACKSTABBER, WHAT'S UP?
I TOLD YOU, STAY INVISIBLE OR YOU WAIT IN THE TRUNK. WASN'T I CLEAR?
I FEEL... Q-QUEASY... NG
SHIT!
HOW?! WE WERE--

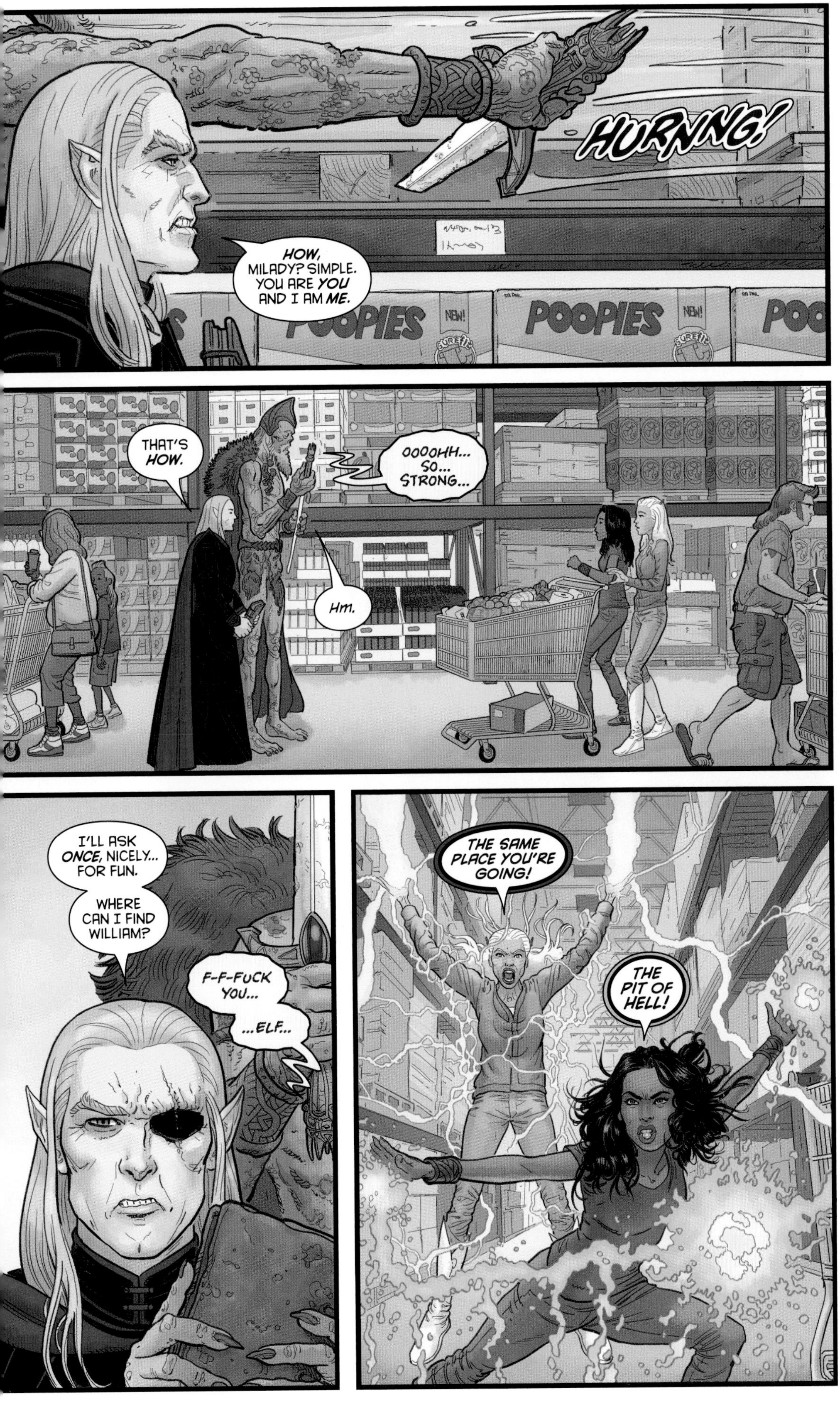
HURNNG!
HOW, MILADY? SIMPLE. YOU ARE YOU AND I AM ME.
POOPIES
NEW!
POOPIES
NEW!
THAT'S HOW.
OOOOHH... SO... STRONG...
Hm.
I'LL ASK ONCE, NICELY... FOR FUN.
WHERE CAN I FIND WILLIAM?
F-F-FUCK YOU...
...ELF...
THE SAME PLACE YOU'RE GOING!
THE PIT OF HELL!

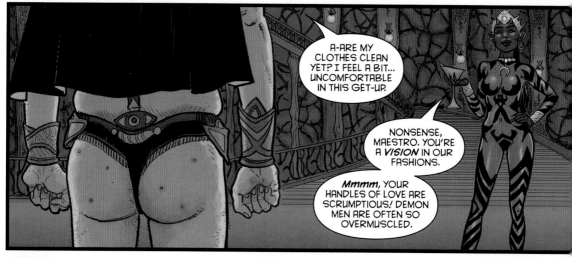

A-ARE MY CLOTHES CLEAN YET? I FEEL A BIT... UNCOMFORTABLE IN THIS GET-UP.

NONSENSE, MAESTRO. YOU'RE A *VISION* IN OUR FASHIONS.

Mmmm, YOUR HANDLES OF LOVE ARE SCRUMPTIOUS! DEMON MEN ARE OFTEN SO OVERMUSCLED.

Heh, A HOLDOVER FROM MY CHUNKY YEARS.

NOW, DON'T WORRY. THERE'S A *GOOD* CHANCE FATHER WILL GRANT YOU SANCTUARY. HE *OWES* YOU FOR SAVING ME.

I THOUGHT *YOU* GAVE ME THAT ALREADY?

⇥*Tch*⇤ MY LIFE WAS IN DANGER, YOU RESCUED ME --

-- I WANTED TO RECIPROCATE.

TRUTHFULLY, ONLY THE *KING* CAN GRANT SANCTUARY.

FUCK! I NEED HIS ARMY TO HELP GET MY THRONE BACK.

OOF. THAT'S A *REACH.* THE REAL WORRY IS THAT HE'S TOYING WITH YOU.

HUH?

HE *SO* HATED YOUR FATHER.

EVERYTHING WILL BE FINE. REMEMBER, YOU HAVE MY *FULL* SUPPORT.

⇥*Sigh*⇤ SUPER.

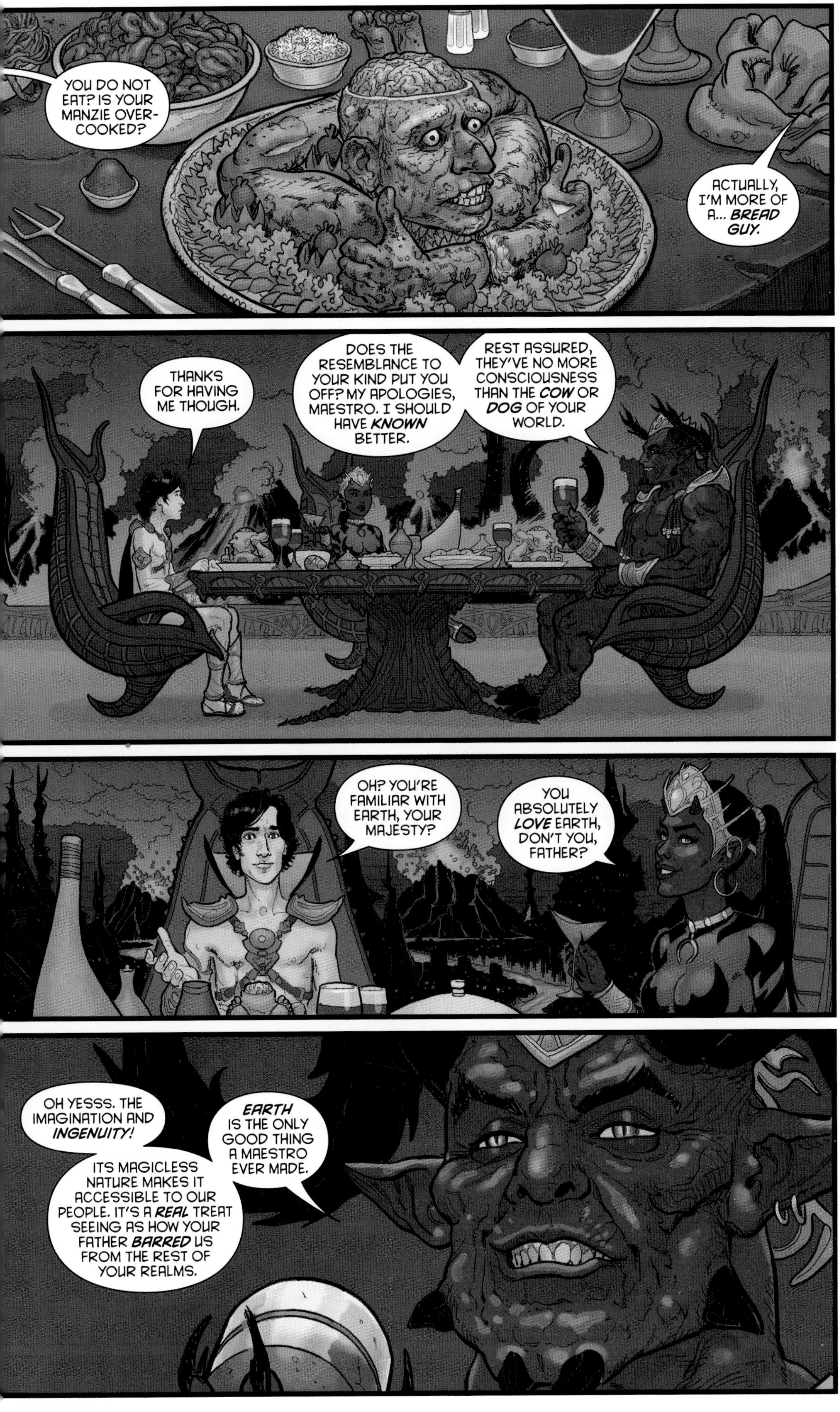
YOU DO NOT EAT? IS YOUR MANZIE OVER-COOKED?
ACTUALLY, I'M MORE OF A... BREAD GUY.
THANKS FOR HAVING ME THOUGH.
DOES THE RESEMBLANCE TO YOUR KIND PUT YOU OFF? MY APOLOGIES, MAESTRO. I SHOULD HAVE KNOWN BETTER.
REST ASSURED, THEY'VE NO MORE CONSCIOUSNESS THAN THE COW OR DOG OF YOUR WORLD.
OH? YOU'RE FAMILIAR WITH EARTH, YOUR MAJESTY?
YOU ABSOLUTELY LOVE EARTH, DON'T YOU, FATHER?
OH YESSS. THE IMAGINATION AND INGENUITY!
EARTH IS THE ONLY GOOD THING A MAESTRO EVER MADE.
ITS MAGICLESS NATURE MAKES IT ACCESSIBLE TO OUR PEOPLE. IT'S A REAL TREAT SEEING AS HOW YOUR FATHER BARRED US FROM THE REST OF YOUR REALMS.

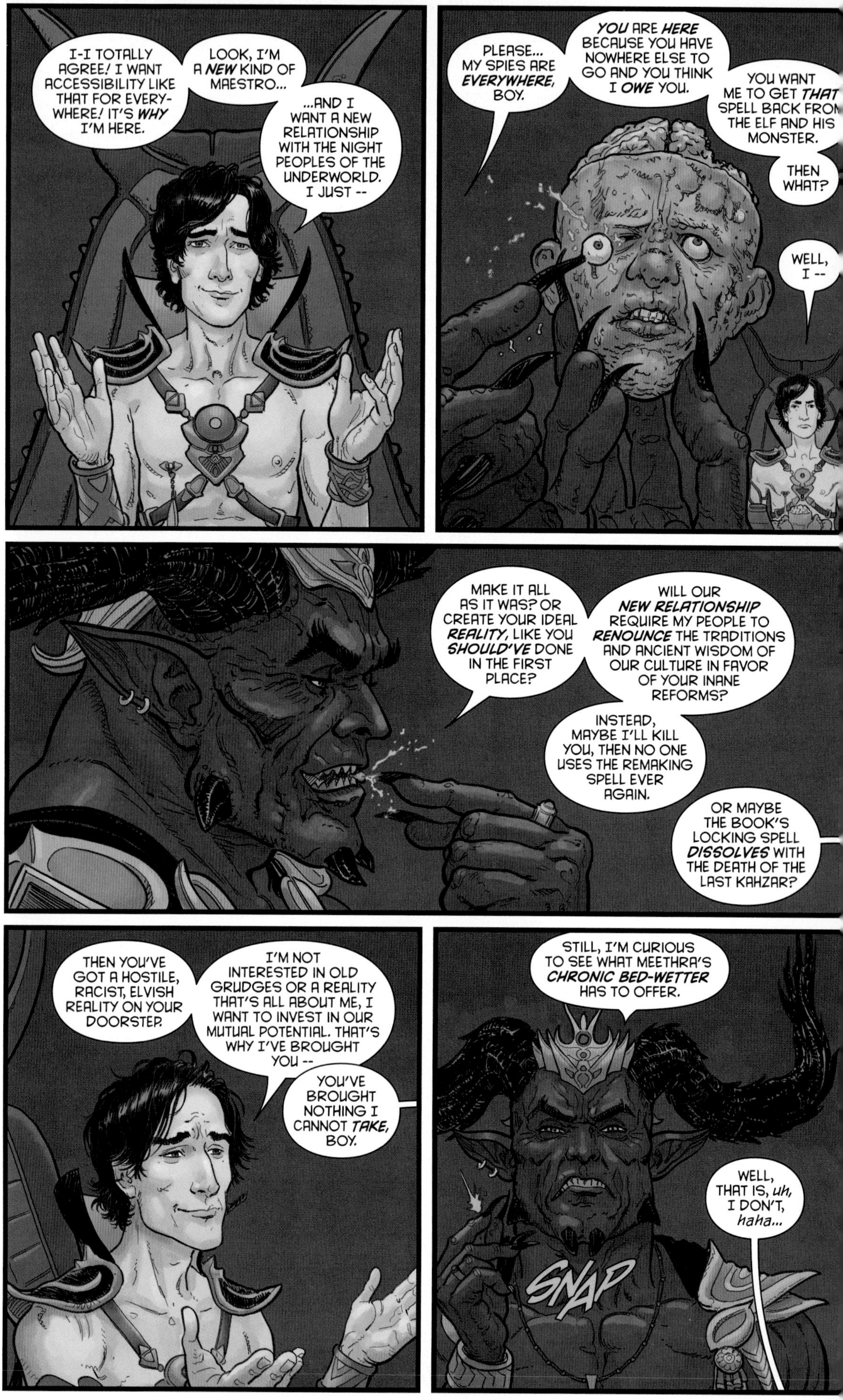
I-I TOTALLY AGREE! I WANT ACCESSIBILITY LIKE THAT FOR EVERY-WHERE! IT'S *WHY* I'M HERE.
LOOK, I'M A *NEW* KIND OF MAESTRO...
...AND I WANT A NEW RELATIONSHIP WITH THE NIGHT PEOPLES OF THE UNDERWORLD. I JUST --
PLEASE... MY SPIES ARE *EVERYWHERE,* BOY.
YOU ARE *HERE* BECAUSE YOU HAVE NOWHERE ELSE TO GO AND YOU THINK I *OWE* YOU.
YOU WANT ME TO GET *THAT* SPELL BACK FROM THE ELF AND HIS MONSTER.
THEN WHAT?
WELL, I --
MAKE IT ALL AS IT WAS? OR CREATE YOUR IDEAL *REALITY,* LIKE YOU *SHOULD'VE* DONE IN THE FIRST PLACE?
WILL OUR *NEW RELATIONSHIP* REQUIRE MY PEOPLE TO *RENOUNCE* THE TRADITIONS AND ANCIENT WISDOM OF OUR CULTURE IN FAVOR OF YOUR INANE REFORMS?
INSTEAD, MAYBE I'LL KILL YOU, THEN NO ONE USES THE REMAKING SPELL EVER AGAIN.
OR MAYBE THE BOOK'S LOCKING SPELL *DISSOLVES* WITH THE DEATH OF THE LAST KAHZAR?
THEN YOU'VE GOT A HOSTILE, RACIST, ELVISH REALITY ON YOUR DOORSTEP.
I'M NOT INTERESTED IN OLD GRUDGES OR A REALITY THAT'S ALL ABOUT ME, I WANT TO INVEST IN OUR MUTUAL POTENTIAL. THAT'S WHY I'VE BROUGHT YOU --
YOU'VE BROUGHT NOTHING I CANNOT *TAKE,* BOY.
STILL, I'M CURIOUS TO SEE WHAT MEETHRA'S *CHRONIC BED-WETTER* HAS TO OFFER.
SNAP
WELL, THAT IS, *uh,* I DON'T, *haha...*

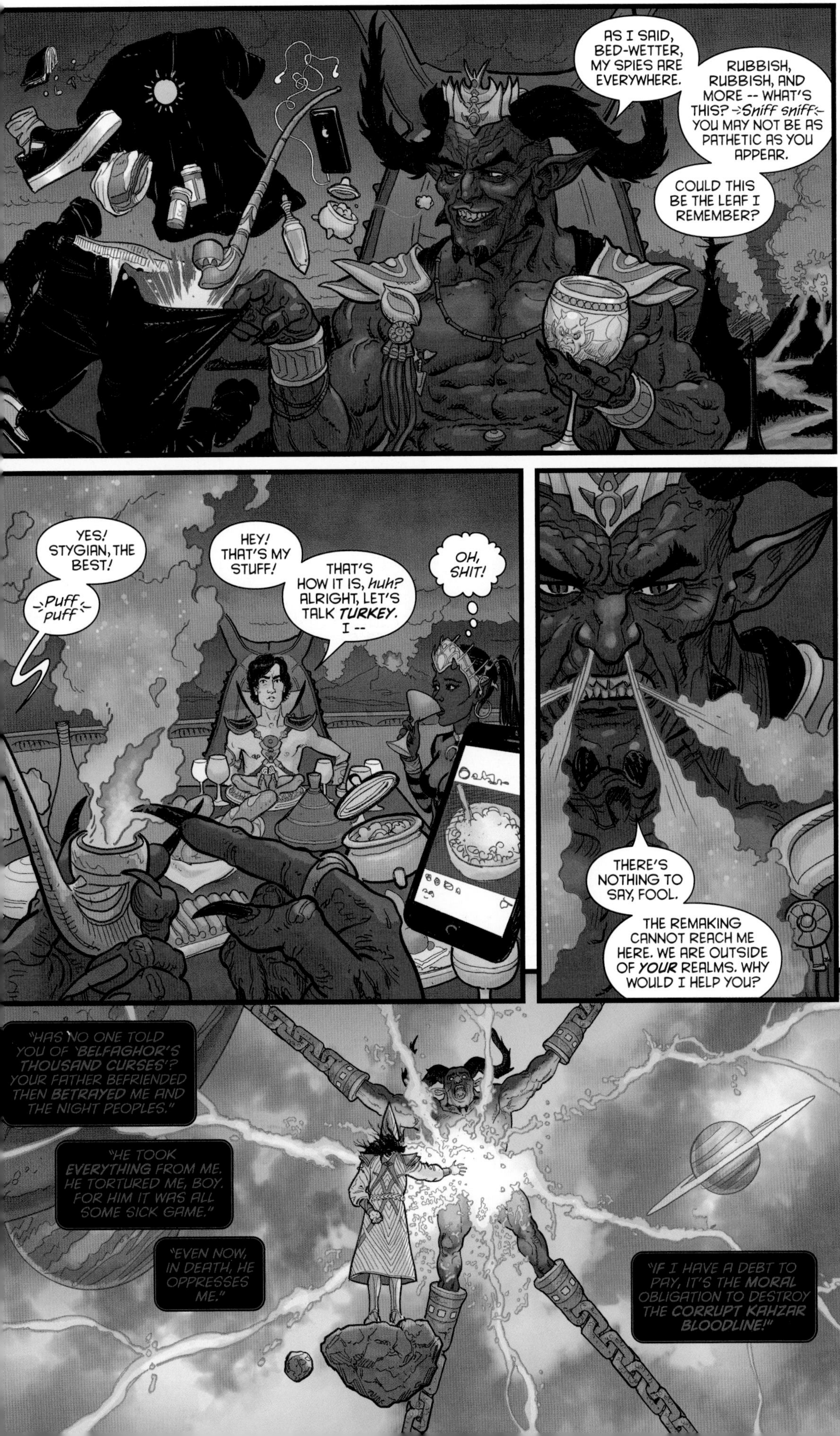
AS I SAID, BED-WETTER, MY SPIES ARE EVERYWHERE.
RUBBISH, RUBBISH, AND MORE -- WHAT'S THIS? Sniff sniff YOU MAY NOT BE AS PATHETIC AS YOU APPEAR.
COULD THIS BE THE LEAF I REMEMBER?
YES! STYGIAN, THE BEST!
Puff puff
HEY! THAT'S MY STUFF!
THAT'S HOW IT IS, huh? ALRIGHT, LET'S TALK TURKEY. I --
OH, SHIT!
THERE'S NOTHING TO SAY, FOOL.
THE REMAKING CANNOT REACH ME HERE. WE ARE OUTSIDE OF YOUR REALMS. WHY WOULD I HELP YOU?
"HAS NO ONE TOLD YOU OF 'BELFAGHOR'S THOUSAND CURSES'? YOUR FATHER BEFRIENDED THEN BETRAYED ME AND THE NIGHT PEOPLES."
"HE TOOK EVERYTHING FROM ME. HE TORTURED ME, BOY. FOR HIM IT WAS ALL SOME SICK GAME."
"EVEN NOW, IN DEATH, HE OPPRESSES ME."
"IF I HAVE A DEBT TO PAY, IT'S THE MORAL OBLIGATION TO DESTROY THE CORRUPT KAHZAR BLOODLINE!"

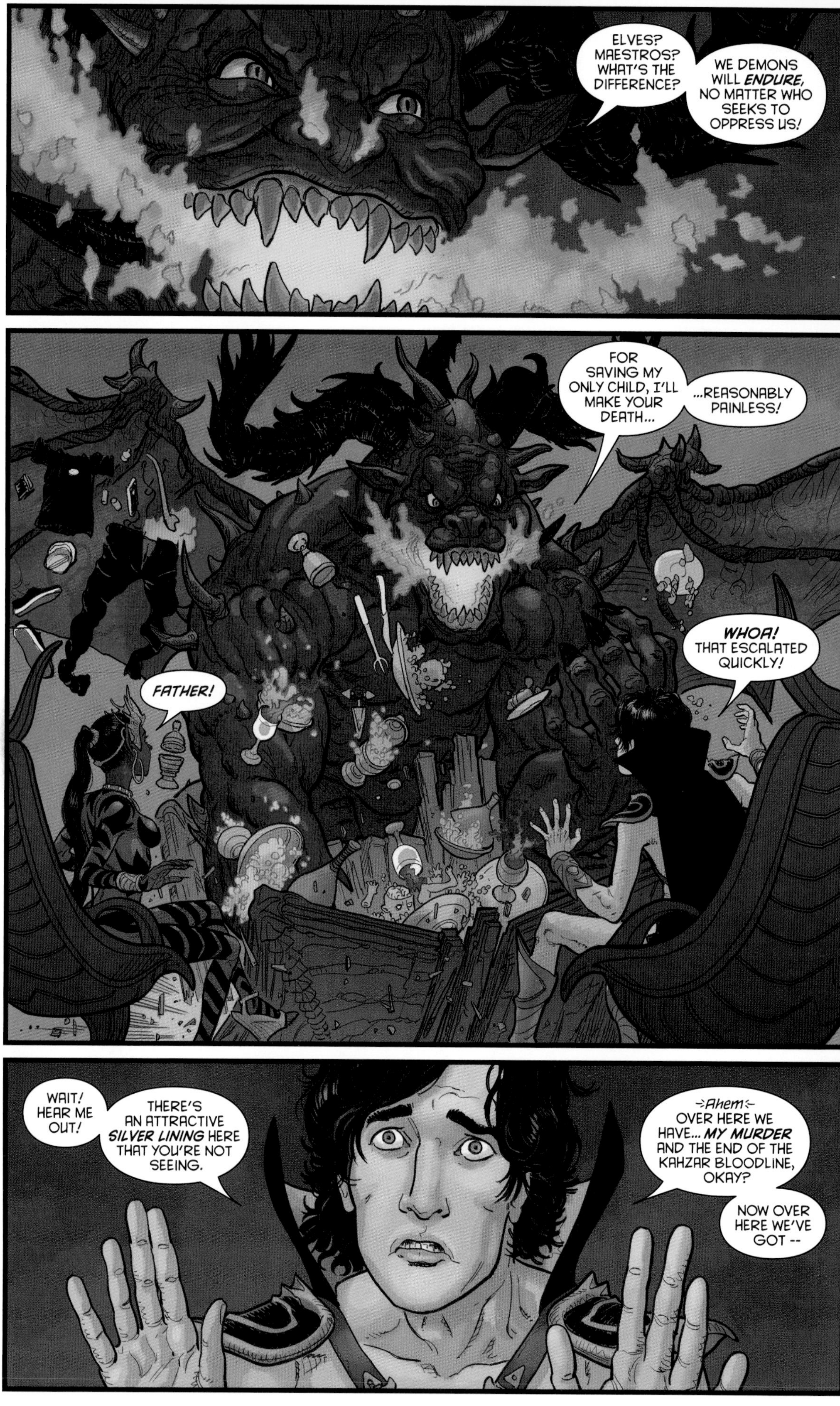
ELVES? MAESTROS? WHAT'S THE DIFFERENCE?
WE DEMONS WILL ***ENDURE,*** NO MATTER WHO SEEKS TO OPPRESS US!
FOR SAVING MY ONLY CHILD, I'LL MAKE YOUR DEATH...
...REASONABLY PAINLESS!
FATHER!
WHOA! THAT ESCALATED QUICKLY!
WAIT! HEAR ME OUT!
THERE'S AN ATTRACTIVE ***SILVER LINING*** HERE THAT YOU'RE NOT SEEING.
Ahem
OVER HERE WE HAVE... ***MY MURDER*** AND THE END OF THE KAHZAR BLOODLINE, OKAY?
NOW OVER HERE WE'VE GOT --

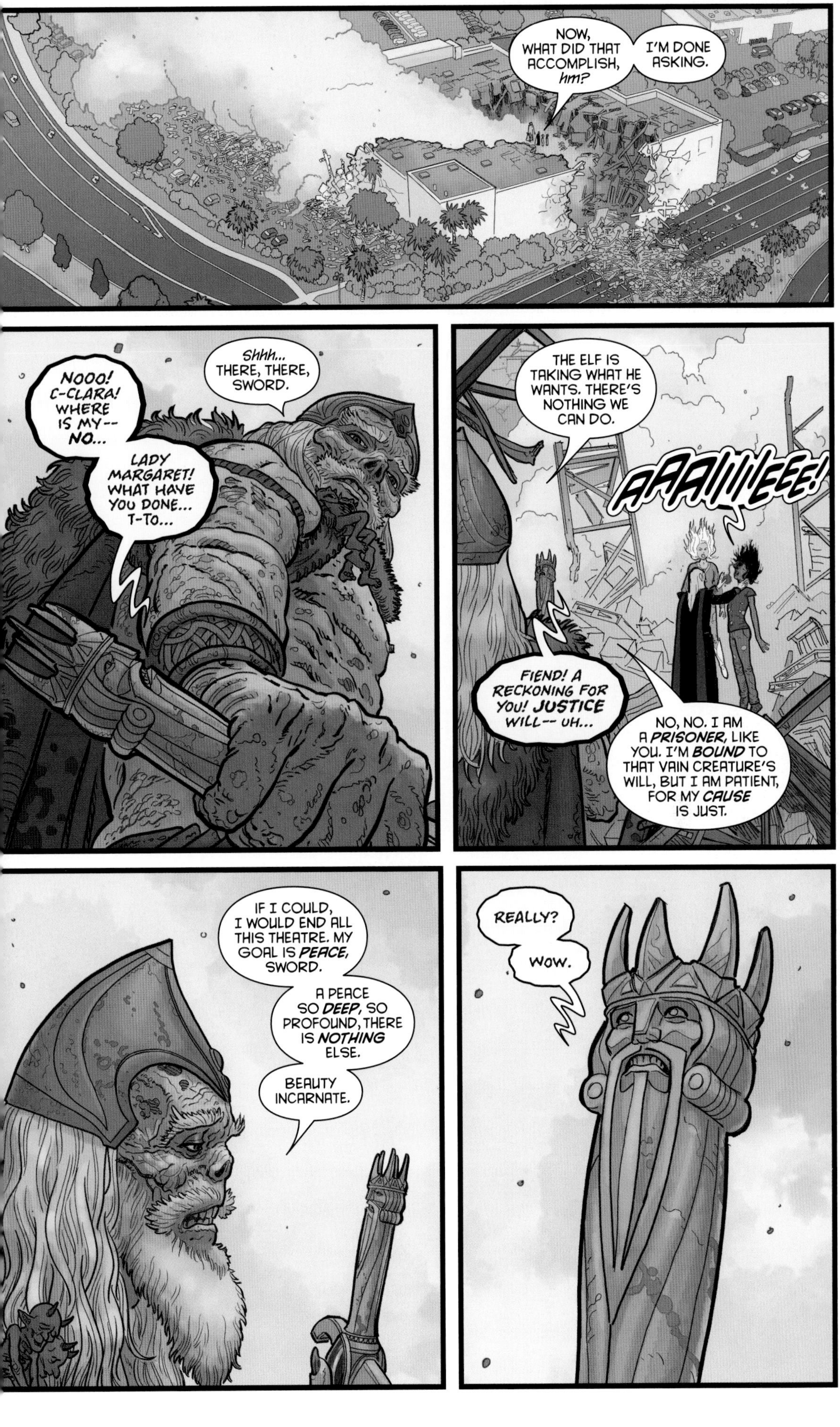
NOW, WHAT DID THAT ACCOMPLISH, hm?
I'M DONE ASKING.
NOOO! C-CLARA! WHERE IS MY-- NO...
LADY MARGARET! WHAT HAVE YOU DONE... T-TO...
Shhh... THERE, THERE, SWORD.
THE ELF IS TAKING WHAT HE WANTS. THERE'S NOTHING WE CAN DO.
AAAIIIIEEE!
FIEND! A RECKONING FOR YOU! JUSTICE WILL-- UH...
NO, NO. I AM A PRISONER, LIKE YOU. I'M BOUND TO THAT VAIN CREATURE'S WILL, BUT I AM PATIENT, FOR MY CAUSE IS JUST.
IF I COULD, I WOULD END ALL THIS THEATRE. MY GOAL IS PEACE, SWORD.
A PEACE SO DEEP, SO PROFOUND, THERE IS NOTHING ELSE.
BEAUTY INCARNATE.
REALLY?
WOW.

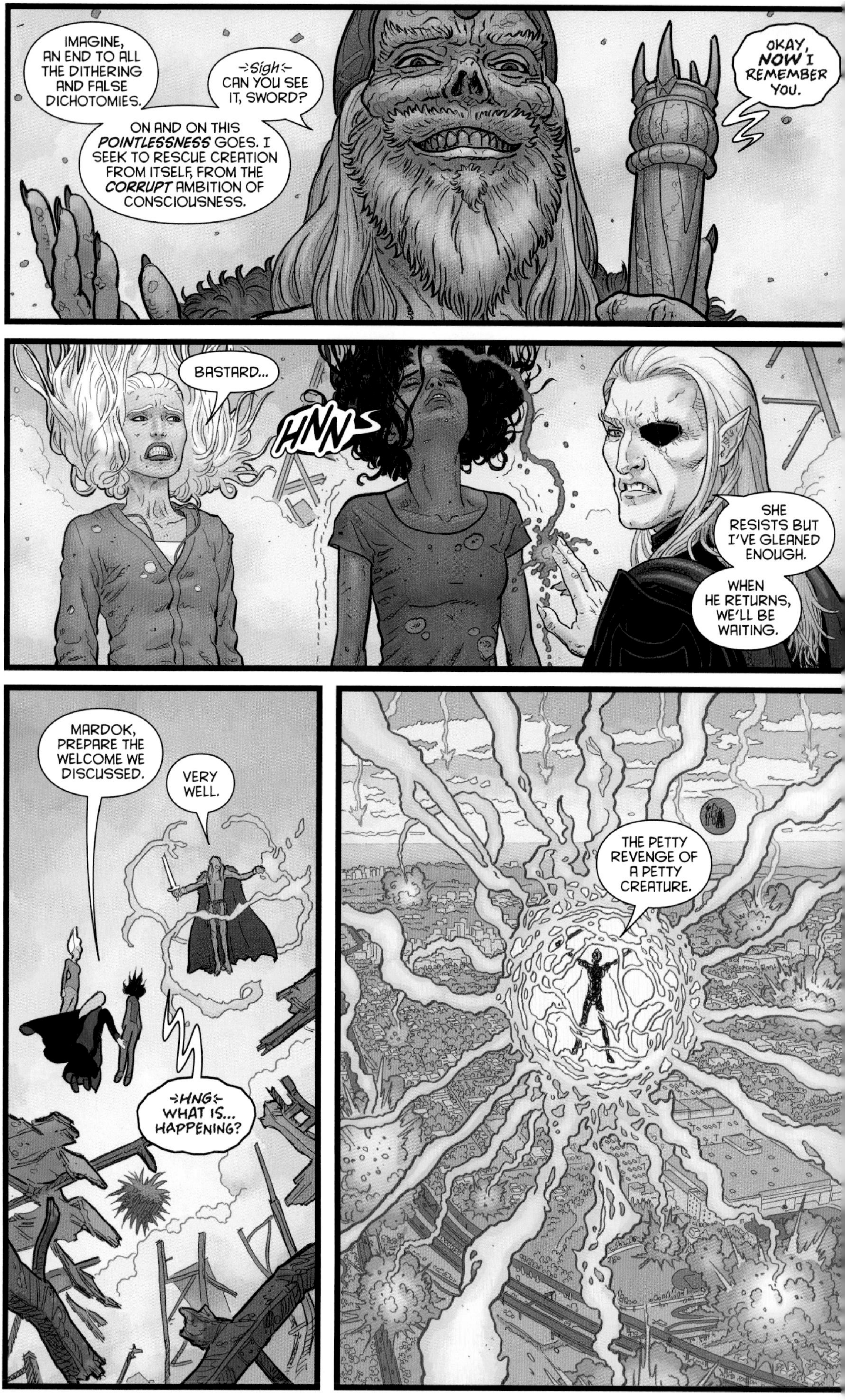

IMAGINE, AN END TO ALL THE DITHERING AND FALSE DICHOTOMIES.
ON AND ON THIS POINTLESSNESS GOES. I SEEK TO RESCUE CREATION FROM ITSELF, FROM THE CORRUPT AMBITION OF CONSCIOUSNESS.
SIGH
CAN YOU SEE IT, SWORD?
OKAY, NOW I REMEMBER YOU.
BASTARD...
HNN
SHE RESISTS BUT I'VE GLEANED ENOUGH.
WHEN HE RETURNS, WE'LL BE WAITING.
MARDOK, PREPARE THE WELCOME WE DISCUSSED.
VERY WELL.
HNG
WHAT IS... HAPPENING?
THE PETTY REVENGE OF A PETTY CREATURE.

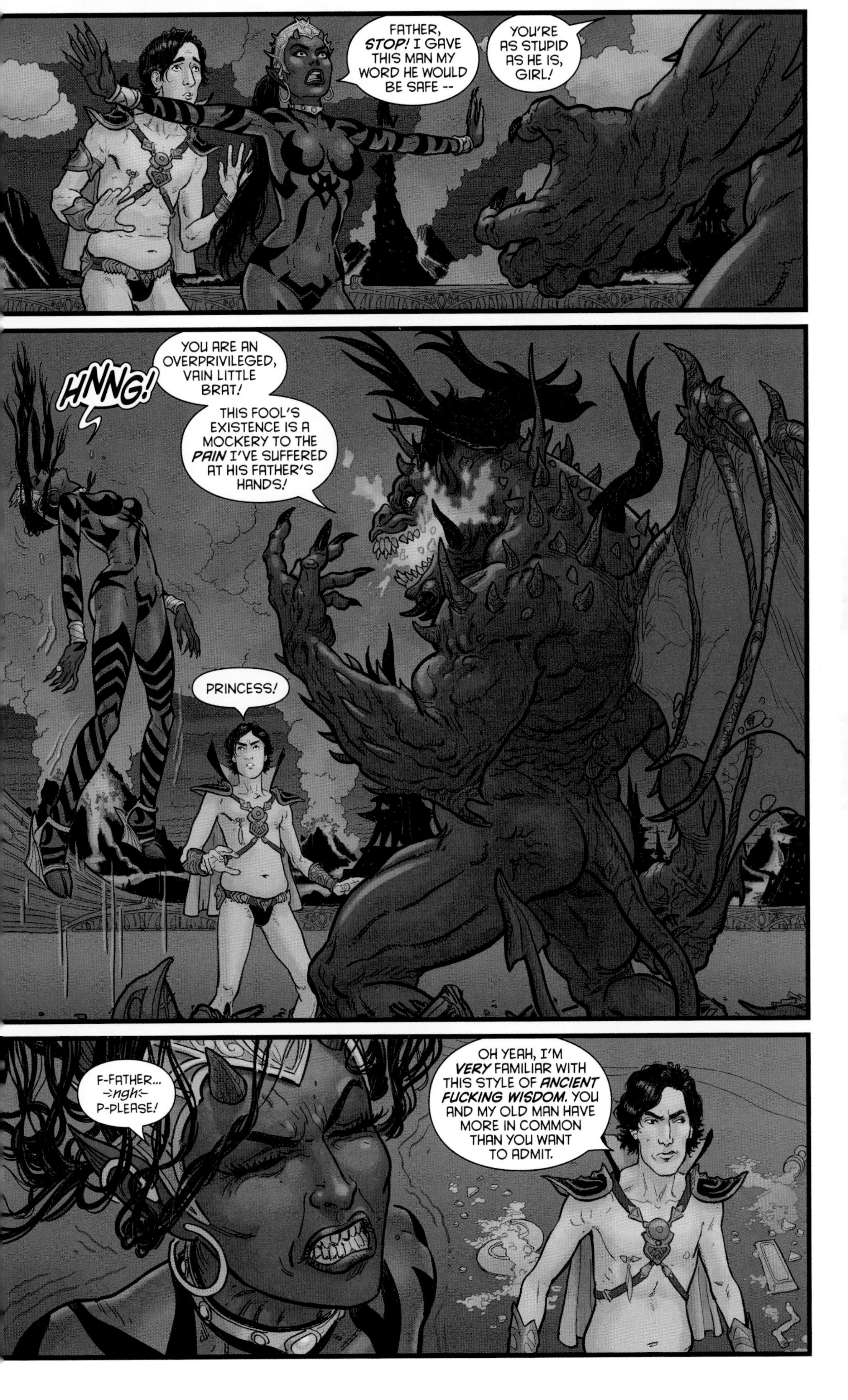
FATHER, STOP! I GAVE THIS MAN MY WORD HE WOULD BE SAFE --
YOU'RE AS STUPID AS HE IS, GIRL!
HNNG!
YOU ARE AN OVERPRIVILEGED, VAIN LITTLE BRAT!
THIS FOOL'S EXISTENCE IS A MOCKERY TO THE PAIN I'VE SUFFERED AT HIS FATHER'S HANDS!
PRINCESS!
F-FATHER... ngh P-PLEASE!
OH YEAH, I'M VERY FAMILIAR WITH THIS STYLE OF ANCIENT FUCKING WISDOM. YOU AND MY OLD MAN HAVE MORE IN COMMON THAN YOU WANT TO ADMIT.

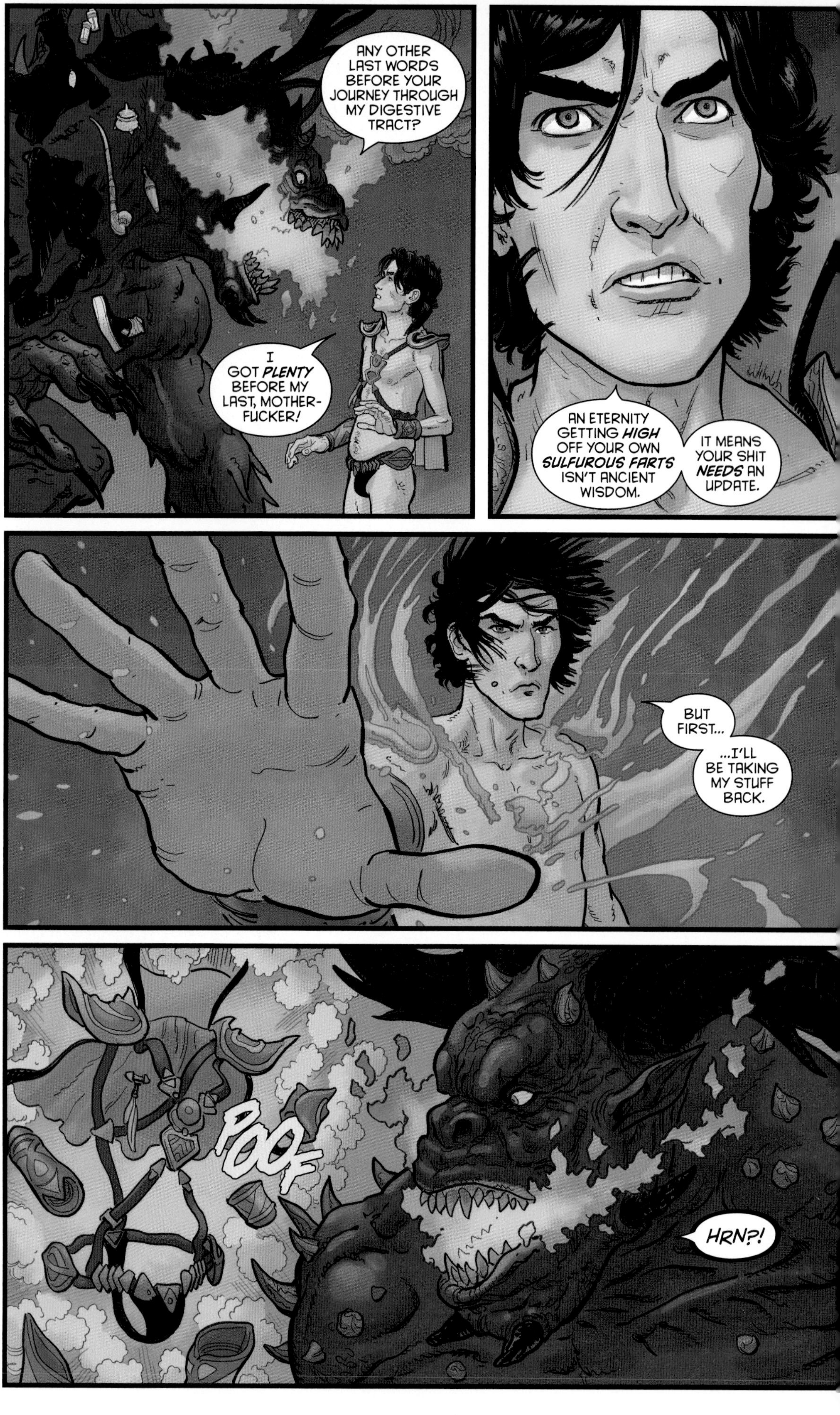
ANY OTHER LAST WORDS BEFORE YOUR JOURNEY THROUGH MY DIGESTIVE TRACT?
I GOT PLENTY BEFORE MY LAST, MOTHER-FUCKER!
AN ETERNITY GETTING HIGH OFF YOUR OWN SULFUROUS FARTS ISN'T ANCIENT WISDOM.
IT MEANS YOUR SHIT NEEDS AN UPDATE.
BUT FIRST...
...I'LL BE TAKING MY STUFF BACK.
POOF
HRN?!

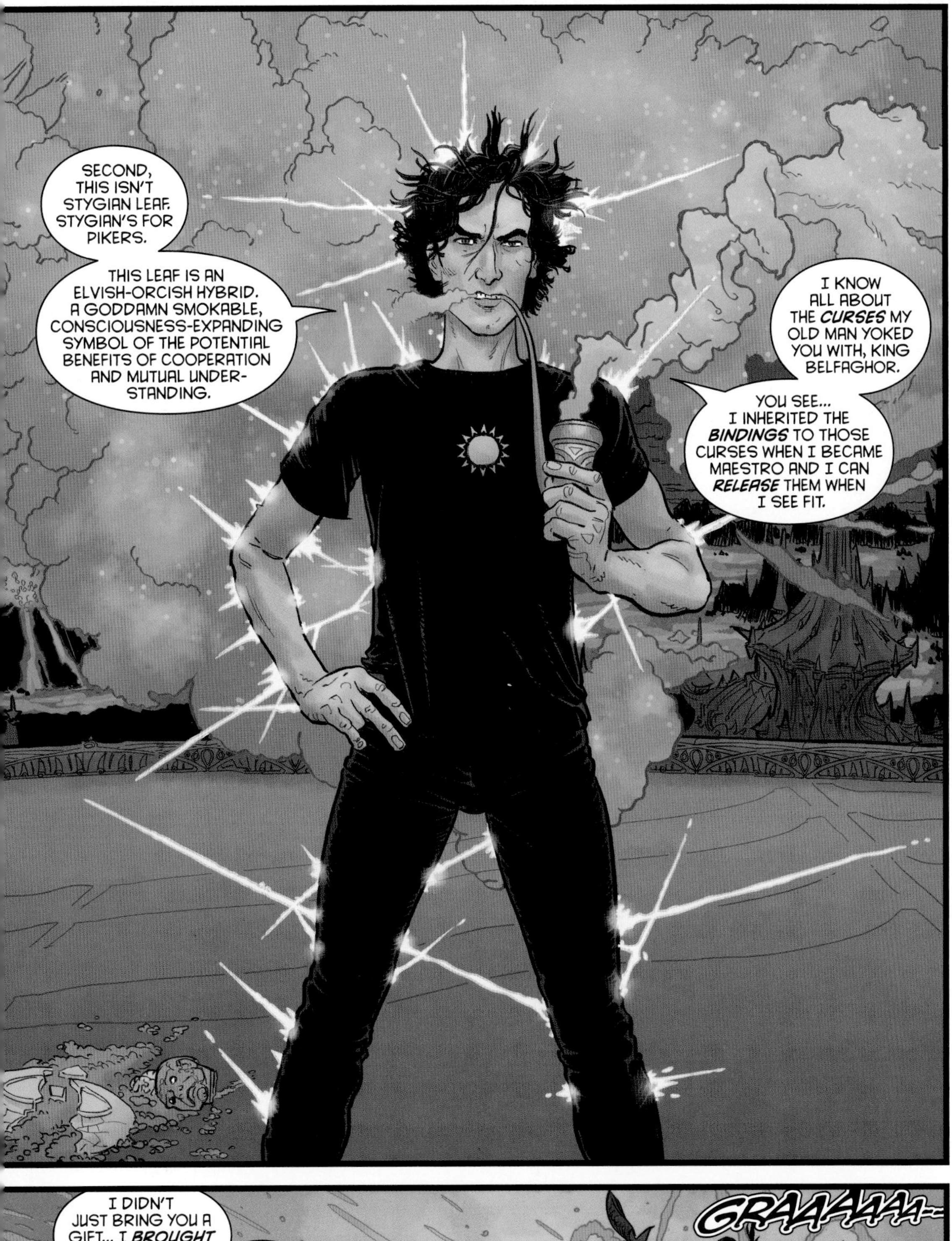
SECOND, THIS ISN'T STYGIAN LEAF. STYGIAN'S FOR PIKERS.
THIS LEAF IS AN ELVISH-ORCISH HYBRID. A GODDAMN SMOKABLE, CONSCIOUSNESS-EXPANDING SYMBOL OF THE POTENTIAL BENEFITS OF COOPERATION AND MUTUAL UNDER-STANDING.
I KNOW ALL ABOUT THE *CURSES* MY OLD MAN YOKED YOU WITH, KING BELFAGHOR.
YOU SEE... I INHERITED THE *BINDINGS* TO THOSE CURSES WHEN I BECAME MAESTRO AND I CAN *RELEASE* THEM WHEN I SEE FIT.

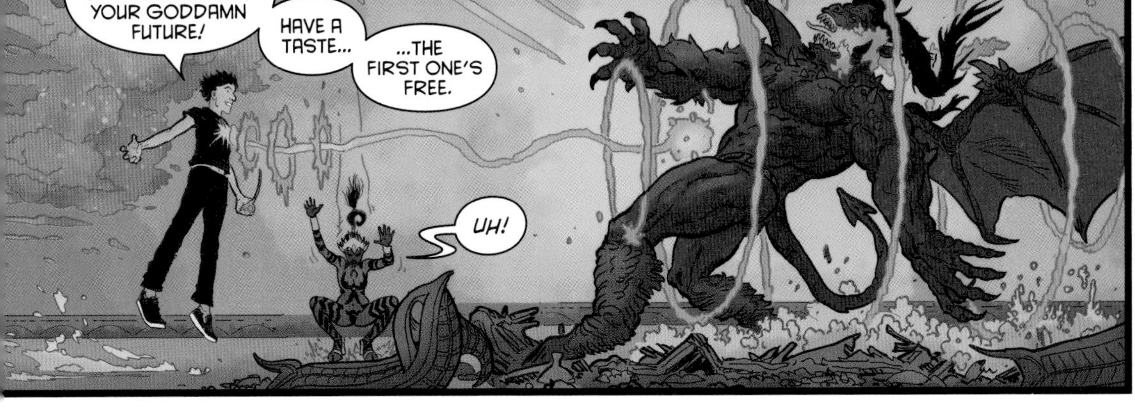
I DIDN'T JUST BRING YOU A GIFT... I *BROUGHT* YOUR GODDAMN FUTURE!
HAVE A TASTE...
...THE FIRST ONE'S FREE.
GRAAAAAA--
UH!

HELP ME GET THE BOOK OF REMAKING BACK AND WE CAN SEE ABOUT UNDOING *ALL* OF MY FATHER'S CURSES.

Uh!

W-WHAT HAVE YOU DONE?

I-I FEEL... *STRANGE.*

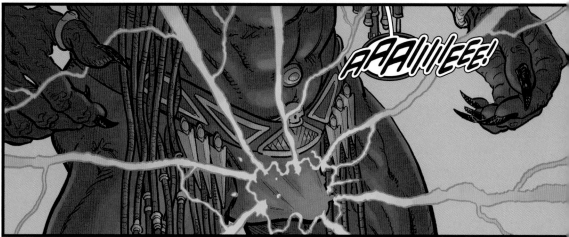

AAAIIIEEE!

~GASP~ FATHER! I CAN'T WATCH!

BLECH!

THAT'S THE MOST *NORMAL* THING THAT'S HAPPENED TO ME ALL WEEK.

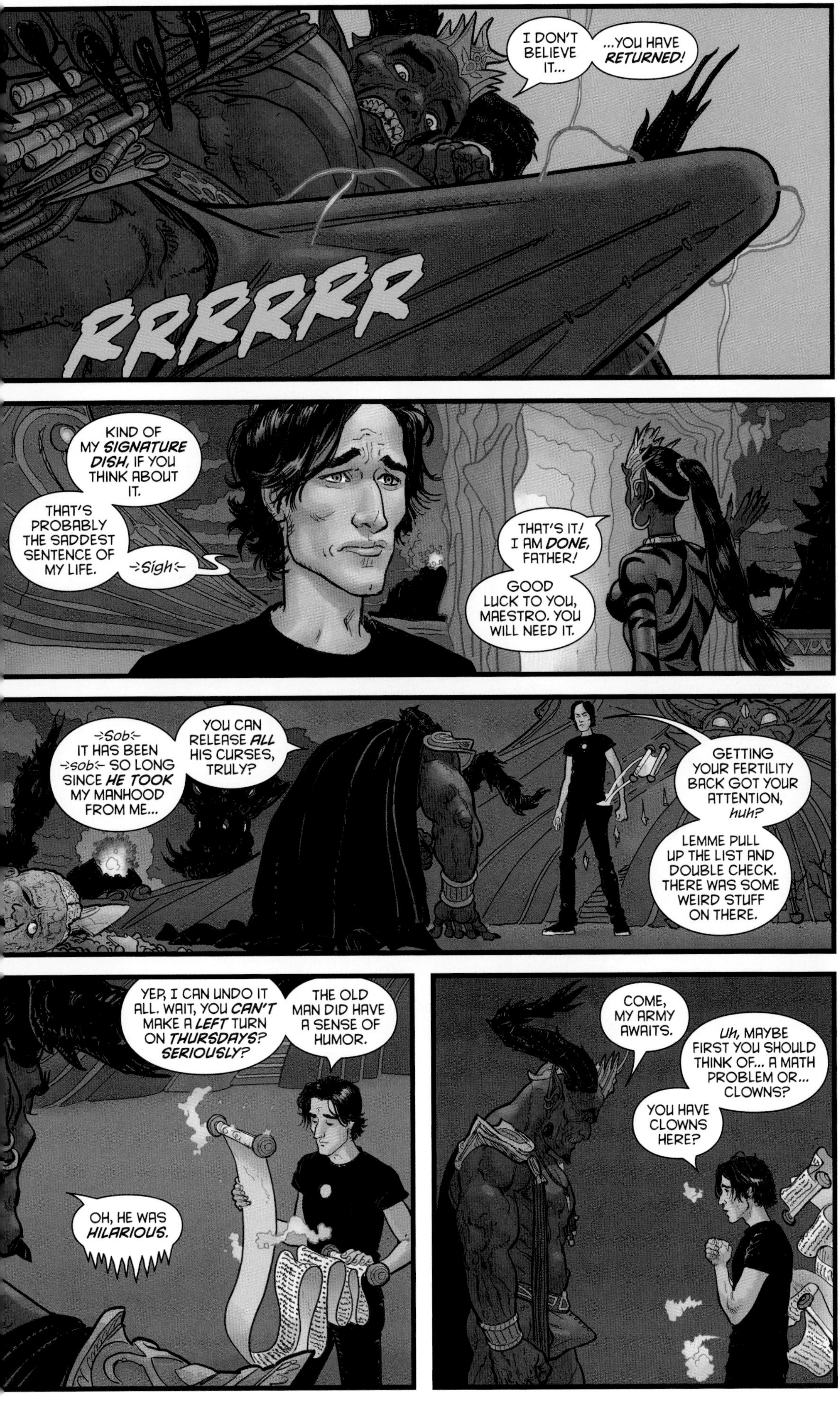
I DON'T BELIEVE IT...
...YOU HAVE RETURNED!
RRRRRR
KIND OF MY SIGNATURE DISH, IF YOU THINK ABOUT IT.
THAT'S PROBABLY THE SADDEST SENTENCE OF MY LIFE.
Sigh
THAT'S IT! I AM DONE, FATHER!
GOOD LUCK TO YOU, MAESTRO. YOU WILL NEED IT.
Sob
IT HAS BEEN
sob
SO LONG SINCE HE TOOK MY MANHOOD FROM ME...
YOU CAN RELEASE ALL HIS CURSES, TRULY?
GETTING YOUR FERTILITY BACK GOT YOUR ATTENTION, huh?
LEMME PULL UP THE LIST AND DOUBLE CHECK. THERE WAS SOME WEIRD STUFF ON THERE.
YEP, I CAN UNDO IT ALL. WAIT, YOU CAN'T MAKE A LEFT TURN ON THURSDAYS? SERIOUSLY?
THE OLD MAN DID HAVE A SENSE OF HUMOR.
OH, HE WAS HILARIOUS.
COME, MY ARMY AWAITS.
Uh, MAYBE FIRST YOU SHOULD THINK OF... A MATH PROBLEM OR... CLOWNS?
YOU HAVE CLOWNS HERE?

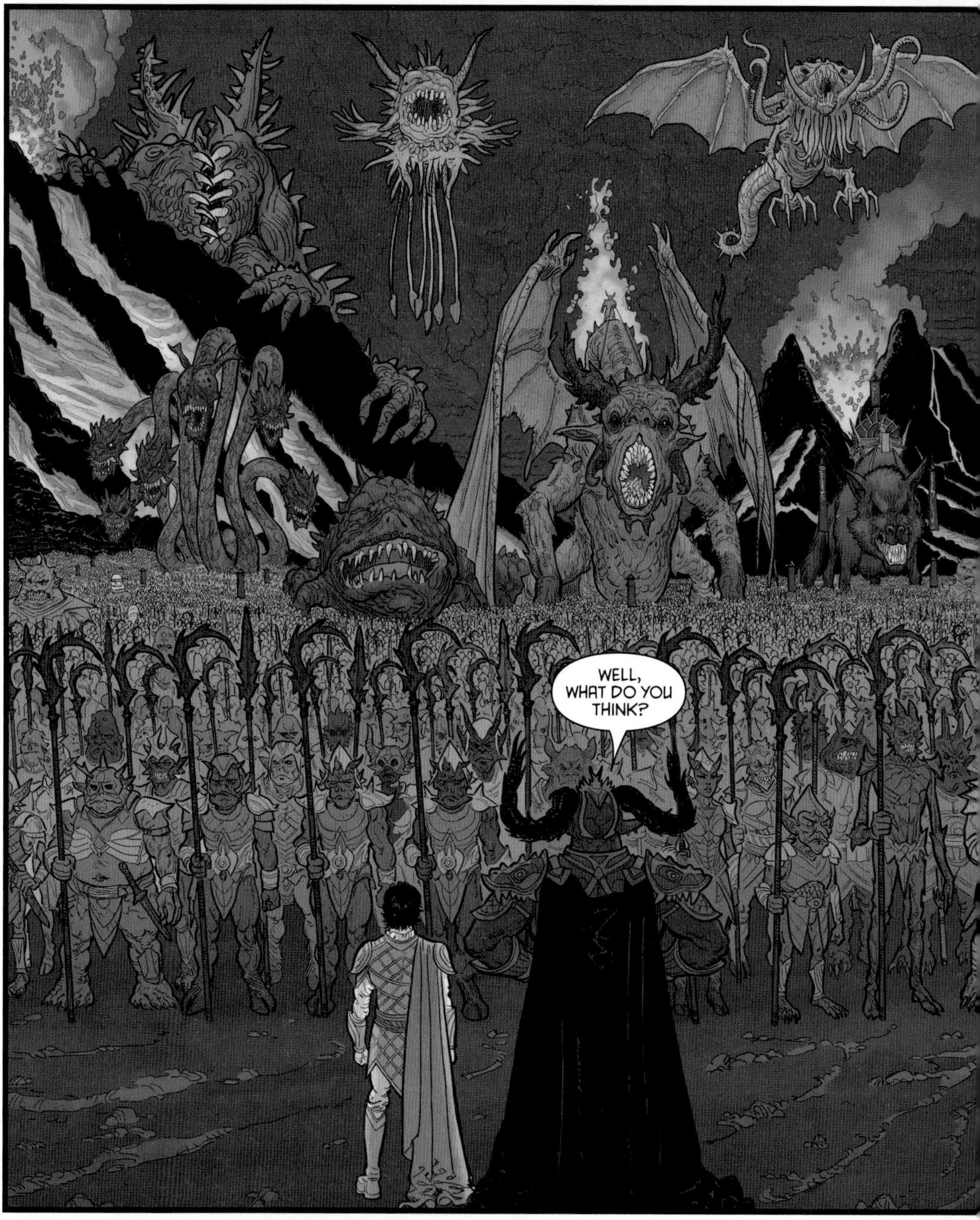
WELL, WHAT DO YOU THINK?

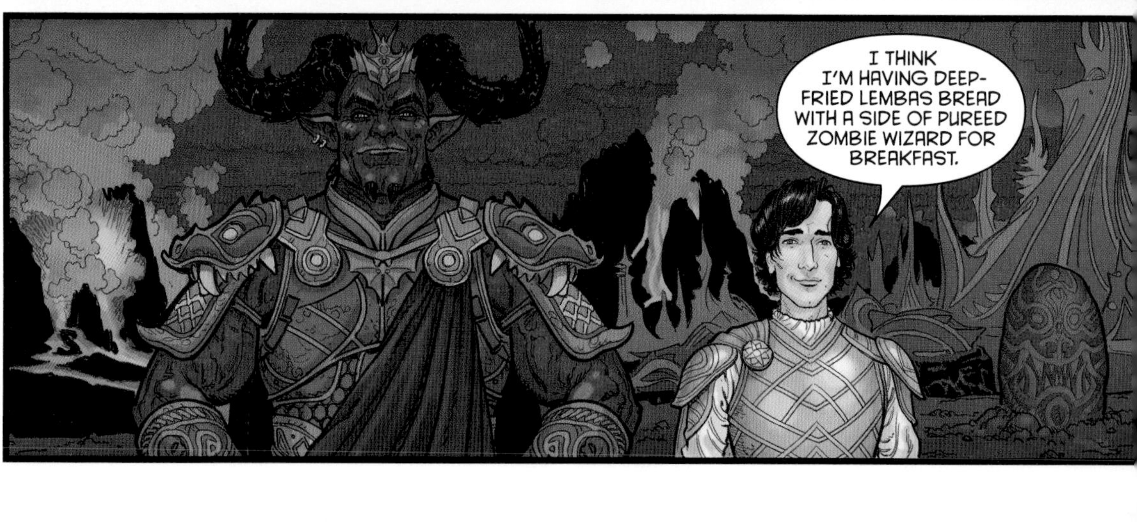
I THINK I'M HAVING DEEP-FRIED LEMBAS BREAD WITH A SIDE OF PUREED ZOMBIE WIZARD FOR BREAKFAST.

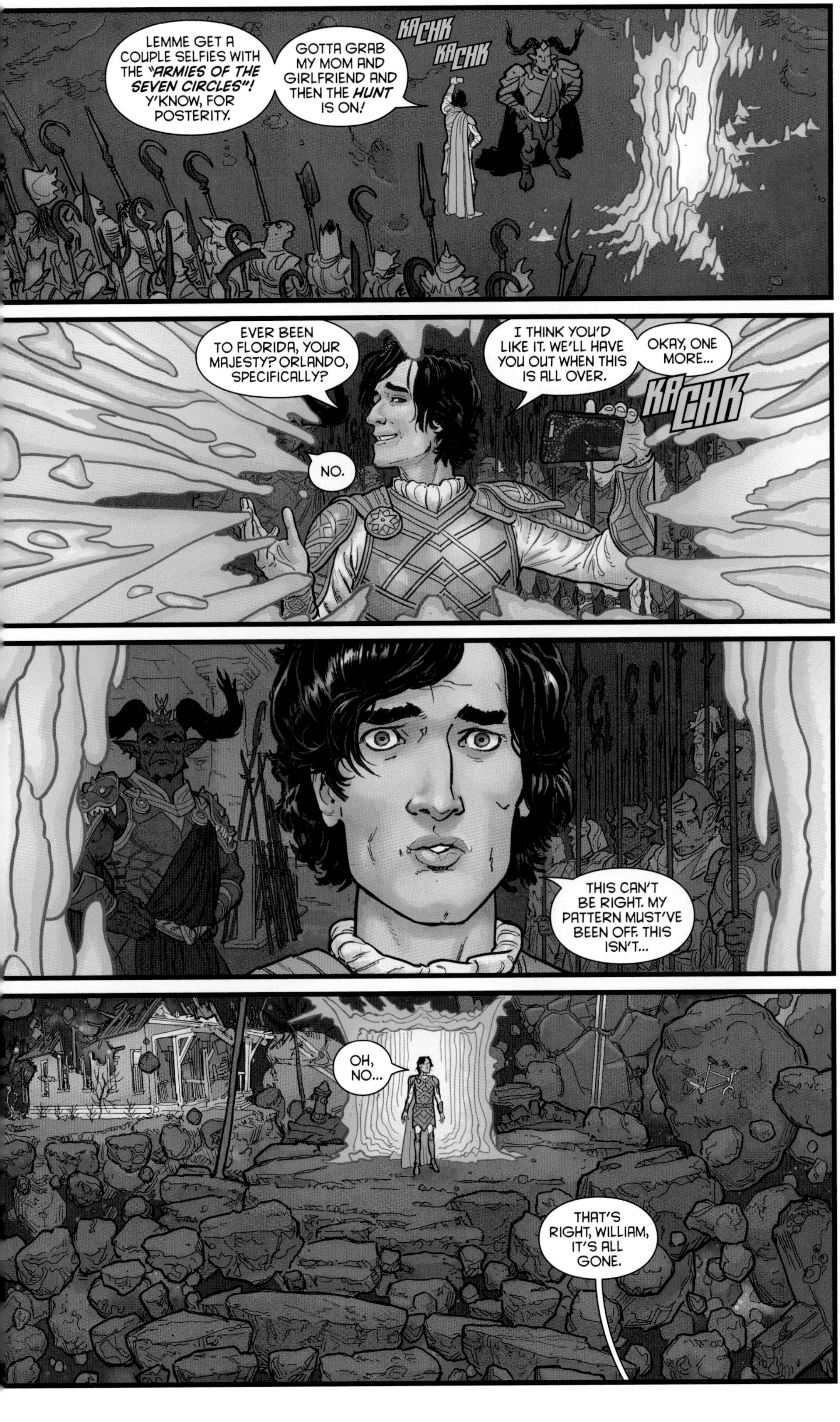
LEMME GET A COUPLE SELFIES WITH THE "ARMIES OF THE SEVEN CIRCLES"! Y'KNOW, FOR POSTERITY.
GOTTA GRAB MY MOM AND GIRLFRIEND AND THEN THE HUNT IS ON!
KACHK
KACHK
EVER BEEN TO FLORIDA, YOUR MAJESTY? ORLANDO, SPECIFICALLY?
NO.
I THINK YOU'D LIKE IT. WE'LL HAVE YOU OUT WHEN THIS IS ALL OVER.
OKAY, ONE MORE...
KACHK
THIS CAN'T BE RIGHT. MY PATTERN MUST'VE BEEN OFF. THIS ISN'T...
OH, NO...
THAT'S RIGHT, WILLIAM, IT'S ALL GONE.

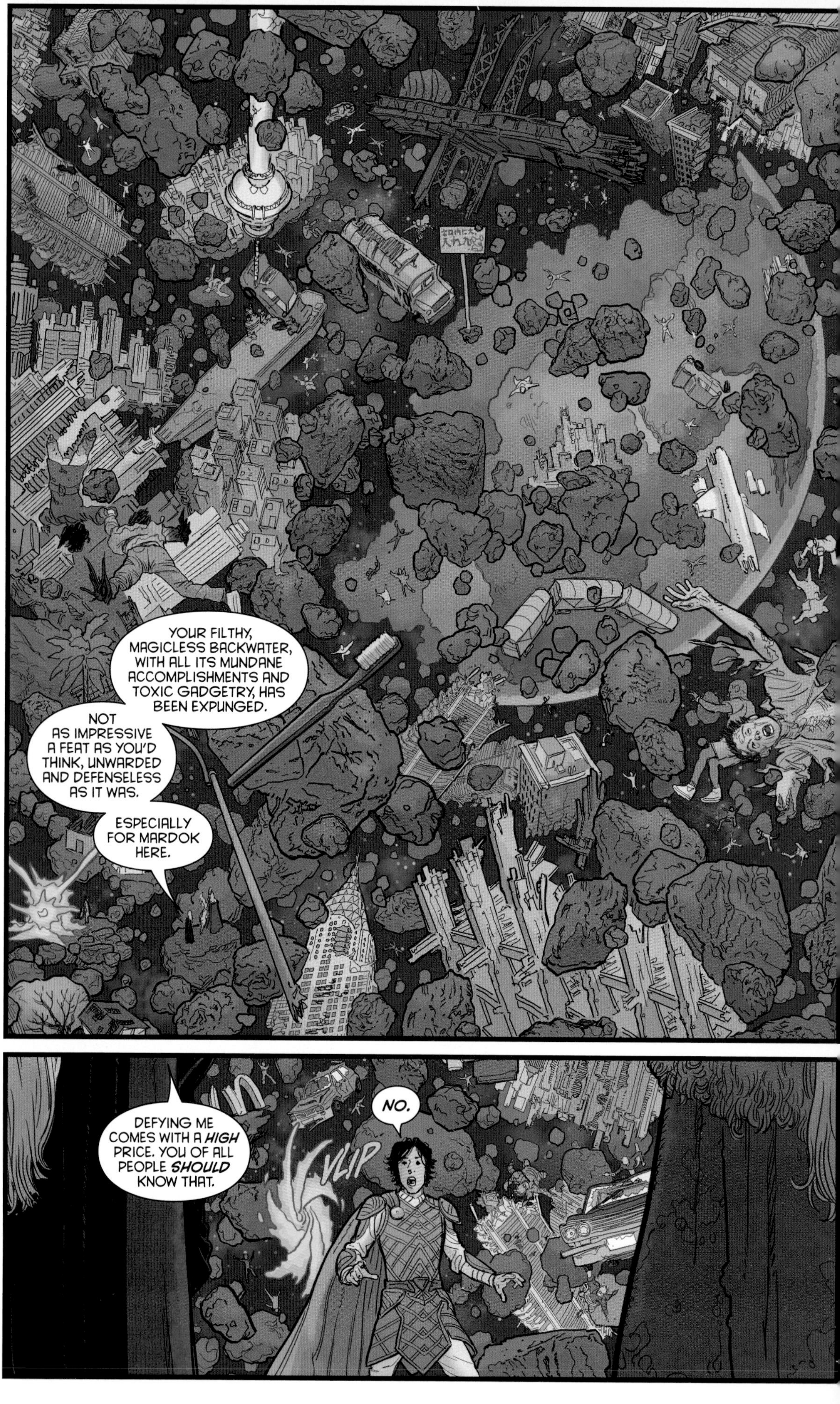

YOUR FILTHY, MAGICLESS BACKWATER, WITH ALL ITS MUNDANE ACCOMPLISHMENTS AND TOXIC GADGETRY, HAS BEEN EXPUNGED.
NOT AS IMPRESSIVE A FEAT AS YOU'D THINK, UNWARDED AND DEFENSELESS AS IT WAS.
ESPECIALLY FOR MARDOK HERE.
DEFYING ME COMES WITH A *HIGH* PRICE. YOU OF ALL PEOPLE *SHOULD* KNOW THAT.
NO.
VLIP

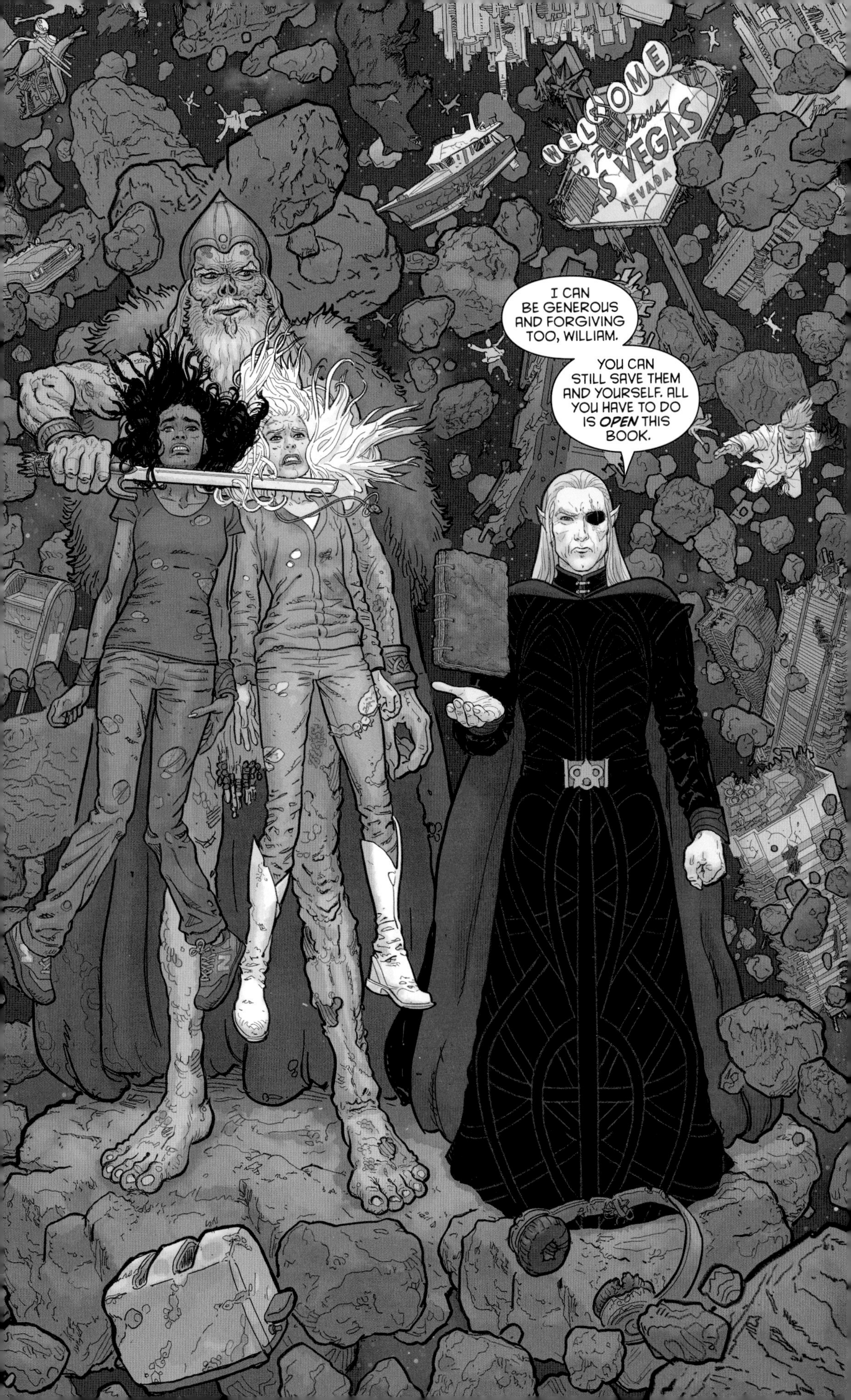
I CAN BE GENEROUS AND FORGIVING TOO, WILLIAM.
YOU CAN STILL SAVE THEM AND YOURSELF. ALL YOU HAVE TO DO IS *OPEN* THIS BOOK.
WELCOME to Fabulous LAS VEGAS NEVADA

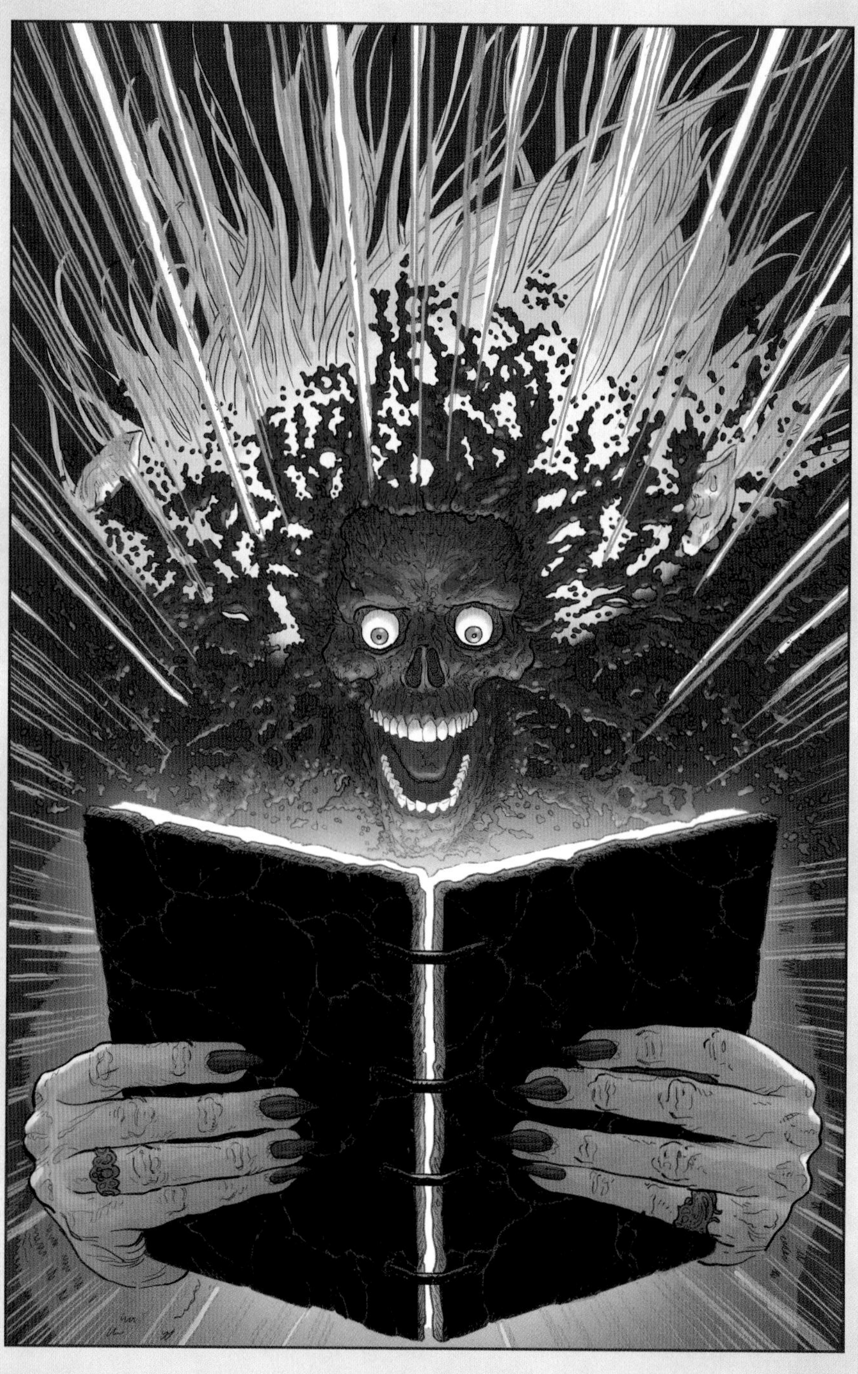

CHAPTER SIX

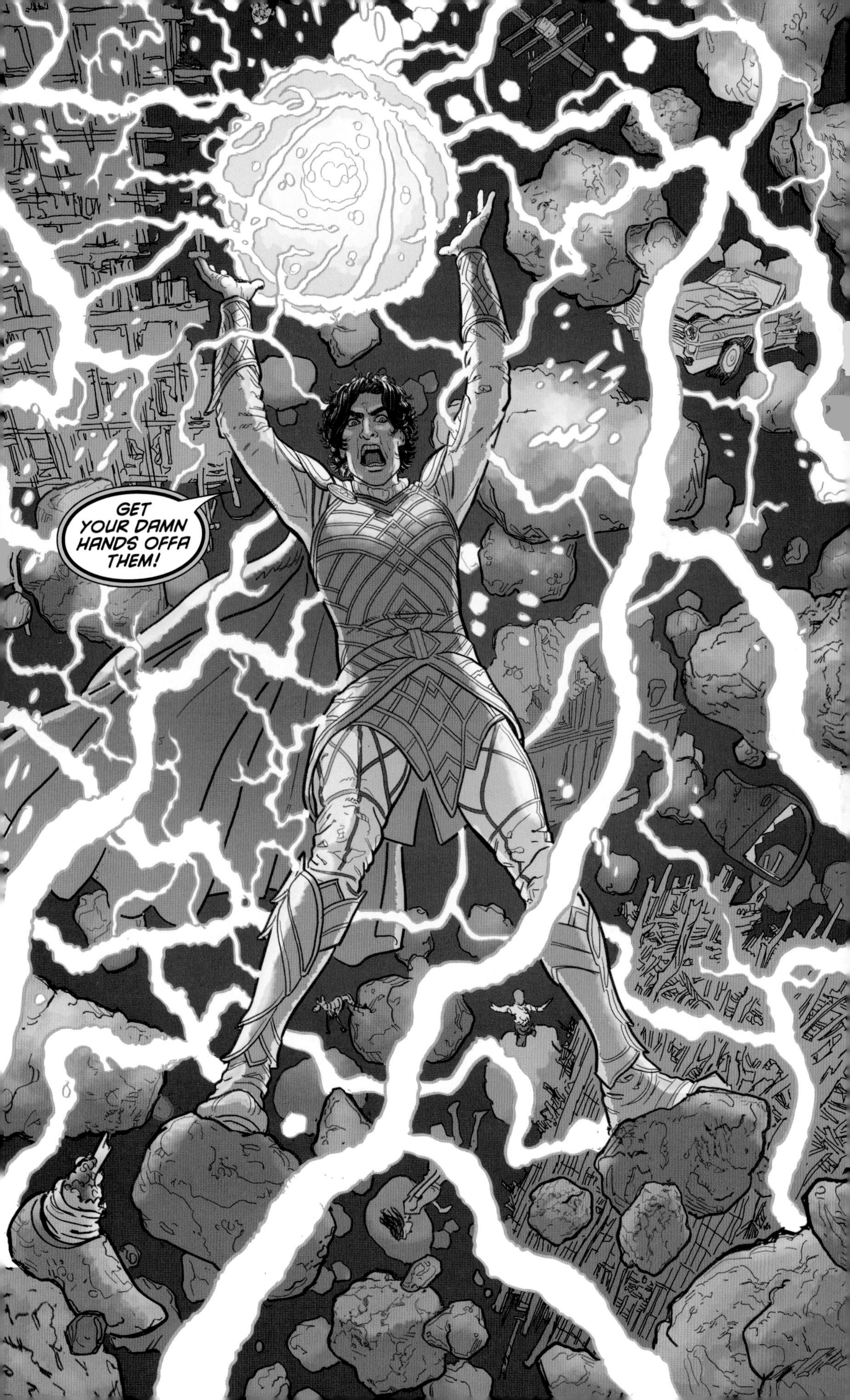
GET YOUR DAMN HANDS OFFA THEM!

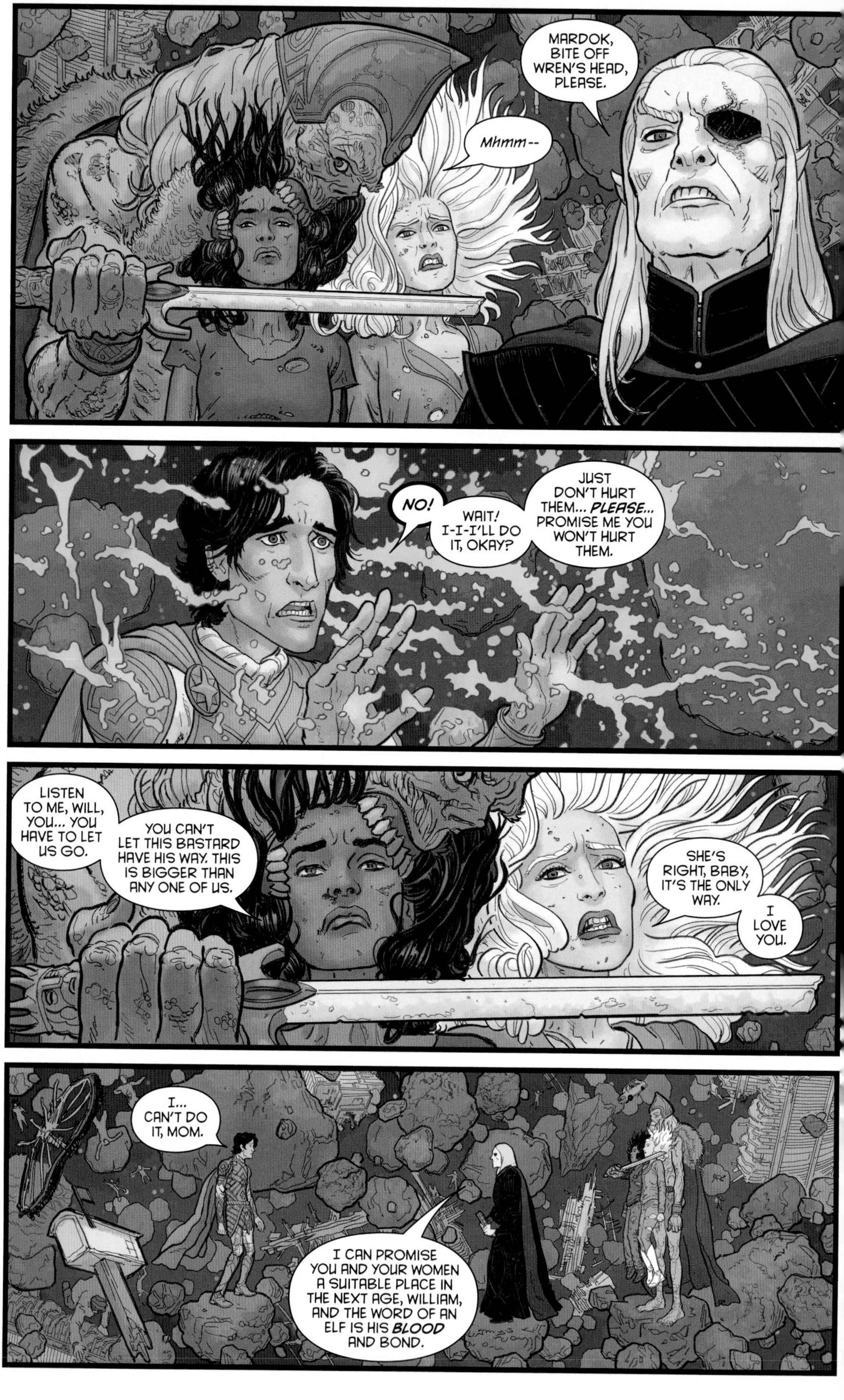
MARDOK, BITE OFF WREN'S HEAD, PLEASE.
Mhmm--
NO!
WAIT! I-I-I'LL DO IT, OKAY?
JUST DON'T HURT THEM... PLEASE... PROMISE ME YOU WON'T HURT THEM.
LISTEN TO ME, WILL, YOU... YOU HAVE TO LET US GO.
YOU CAN'T LET THIS BASTARD HAVE HIS WAY. THIS IS BIGGER THAN ANY ONE OF US.
SHE'S RIGHT, BABY, IT'S THE ONLY WAY.
I LOVE YOU.
I... CAN'T DO IT, MOM.
I CAN PROMISE YOU AND YOUR WOMEN A SUITABLE PLACE IN THE NEXT AGE, WILLIAM, AND THE WORD OF AN ELF IS HIS BLOOD AND BOND.

OPEN THE BOOK WITH ITS PAGES *FACING* ME.

THAT'S IT, BOY.

YOU CAN DO IT.

NOOO! YOU CAN'T TRUST HIM, WILL!

HE'LL ENSLAVE EVERYONE!

≈GULP≈

YES! YES!

THAT'S IT!

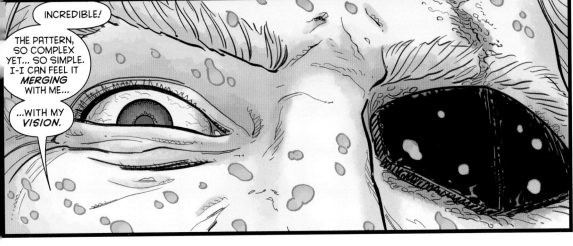

INCREDIBLE!

THE PATTERN, SO COMPLEX YET... SO SIMPLE. I-I CAN FEEL IT *MERGING* WITH ME...

...WITH MY *VISION.*

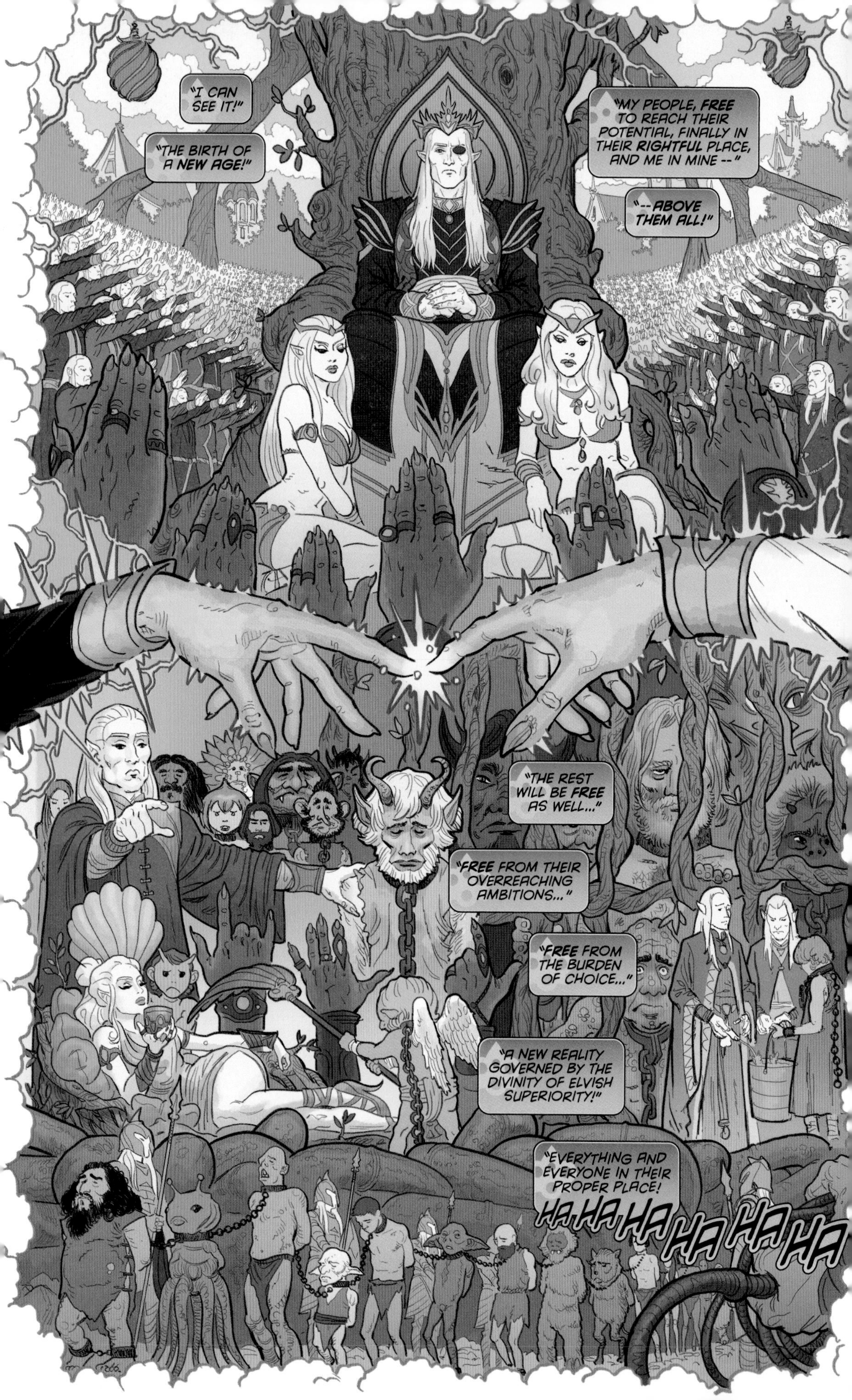
"I CAN SEE IT!"
"THE BIRTH OF A NEW AGE!"
"MY PEOPLE, FREE TO REACH THEIR POTENTIAL, FINALLY IN THEIR RIGHTFUL PLACE, AND ME IN MINE --"
"-- ABOVE THEM ALL!"
"THE REST WILL BE FREE AS WELL..."
"FREE FROM THEIR OVERREACHING AMBITIONS..."
"FREE FROM THE BURDEN OF CHOICE..."
"A NEW REALITY GOVERNED BY THE DIVINITY OF ELVISH SUPERIORITY!"
"EVERYTHING AND EVERYONE IN THEIR PROPER PLACE!
HA HA HA HA HA HA HA

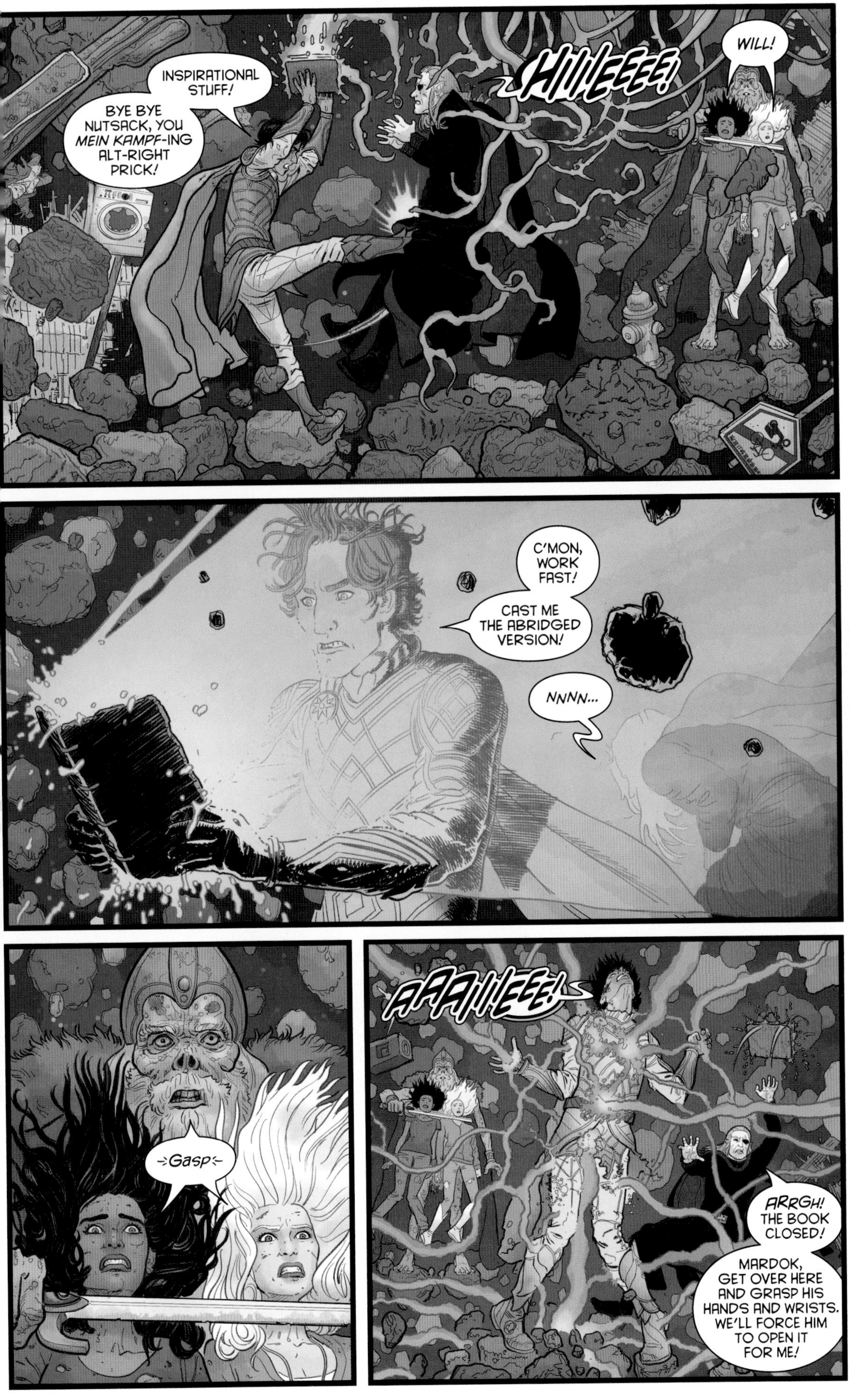
INSPIRATIONAL STUFF!
BYE BYE NUTSACK, YOU *MEIN KAMPF*-ING ALT-RIGHT PRICK!
HIIIEEEE!
WILL!
C'MON, WORK FAST!
CAST ME THE ABRIDGED VERSION!
NNNN...
-Gasp-
AAAIIEEE!
ARRGH! THE BOOK CLOSED!
MARDOK, GET OVER HERE AND GRASP HIS HANDS AND WRISTS. WE'LL FORCE HIM TO OPEN IT FOR ME!

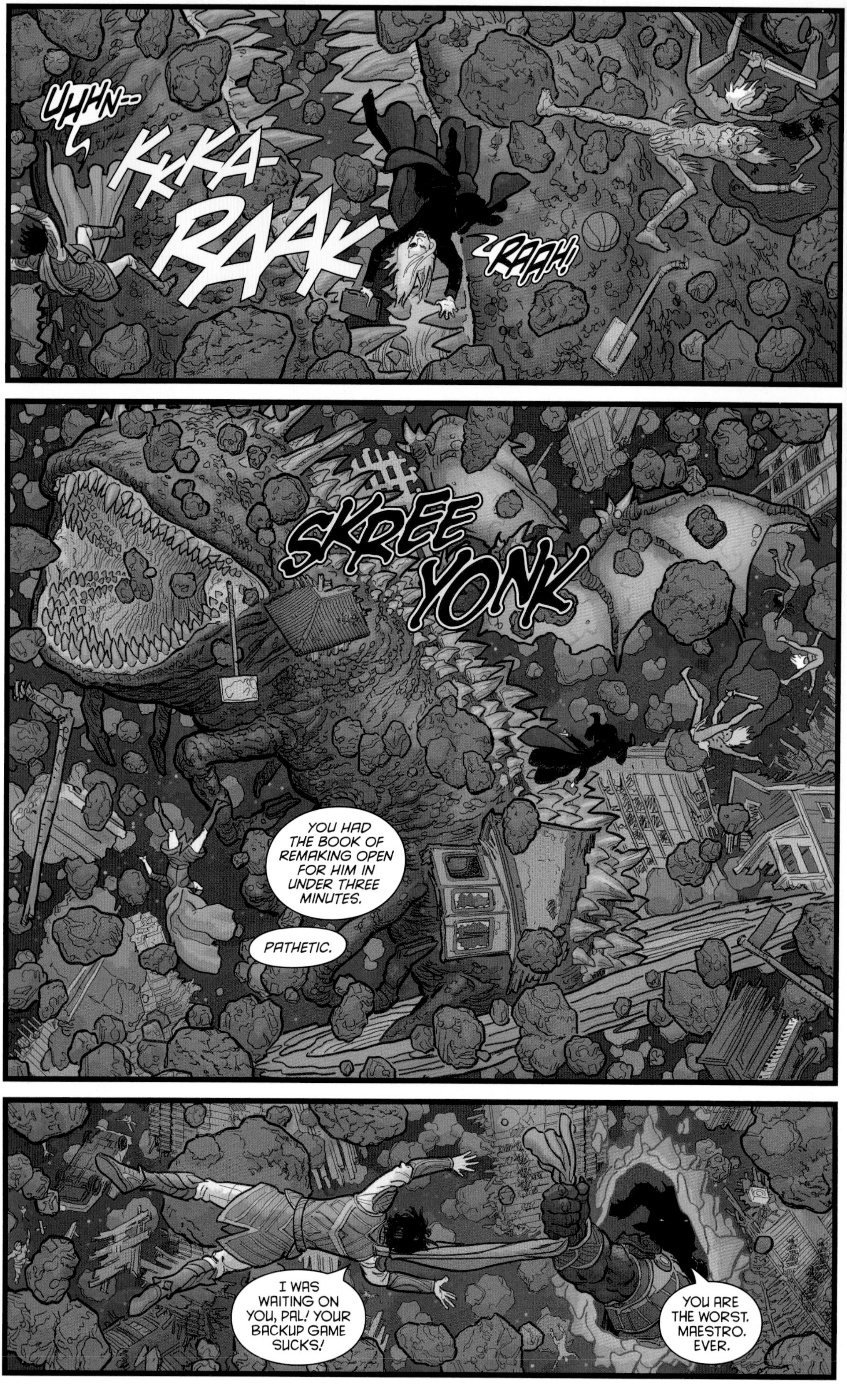
UHHN--
KKKA-RAAK
RAAH!
SKREE YONK
YOU HAD THE BOOK OF REMAKING OPEN FOR HIM IN UNDER THREE MINUTES.
PATHETIC.
I WAS WAITING ON YOU, PAL! YOUR BACKUP GAME SUCKS!
YOU ARE THE WORST. MAESTRO. EVER.

HNK--

DON'T LOOK SO SAD. THIS WAS ALWAYS THE ONLY OUTCOME, BOY. I NEEDED YOU TO LEAD ME TO THAT BOOK...

...SO I CAN *DESTROY* IT!

IT'S TOO MUCH POWER FOR ANYONE.

GRKK

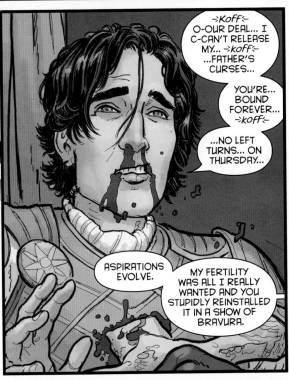

→Koff← O-OUR DEAL... I C-CAN'T RELEASE MY... →koff← ...FATHER'S CURSES...

YOU'RE... BOUND FOREVER... →koff←

...NO LEFT TURNS... ON THURSDAY...

ASPIRATIONS EVOLVE.

MY FERTILITY WAS ALL I REALLY WANTED AND YOU STUPIDLY REINSTALLED IT IN A SHOW OF BRAVURA.

CURSES LIMITING MY POWER AND MY PEOPLE'S RIGHT TO EXPANSION MEANT SOMETHING TO ME ONCE BUT FAMILY IS THE ONLY FUTURE I CARE ABOUT NOW.

ALSO, I STAY IN ON THURSDAYS AND READ.

THE ONLY MEANINGFUL CONQUEST IS ONE'S SELF, BOY.

SADLY, YOU'LL NEVER KNOW THIS. YOUR JOURNEY ENDS HERE IN THE FIERY RIVERS OF ACHERON.

GOODBYE, LITTLE MAESTRO.

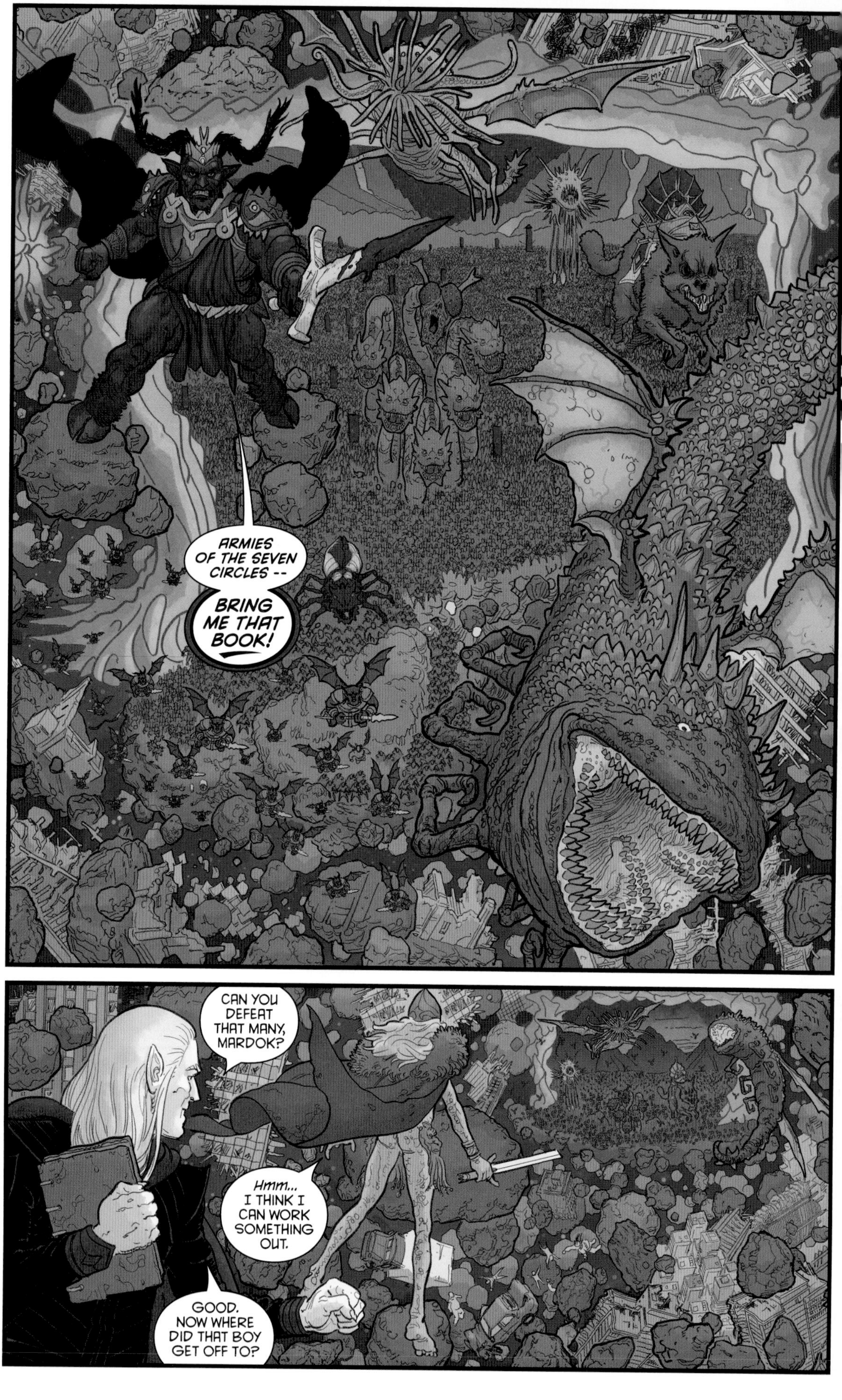
ARMIES OF THE SEVEN CIRCLES --
BRING ME THAT BOOK!
CAN YOU DEFEAT THAT MANY, MARDOK?
Hmm... I THINK I CAN WORK SOMETHING OUT.
GOOD. NOW WHERE DID THAT BOY GET OFF TO?

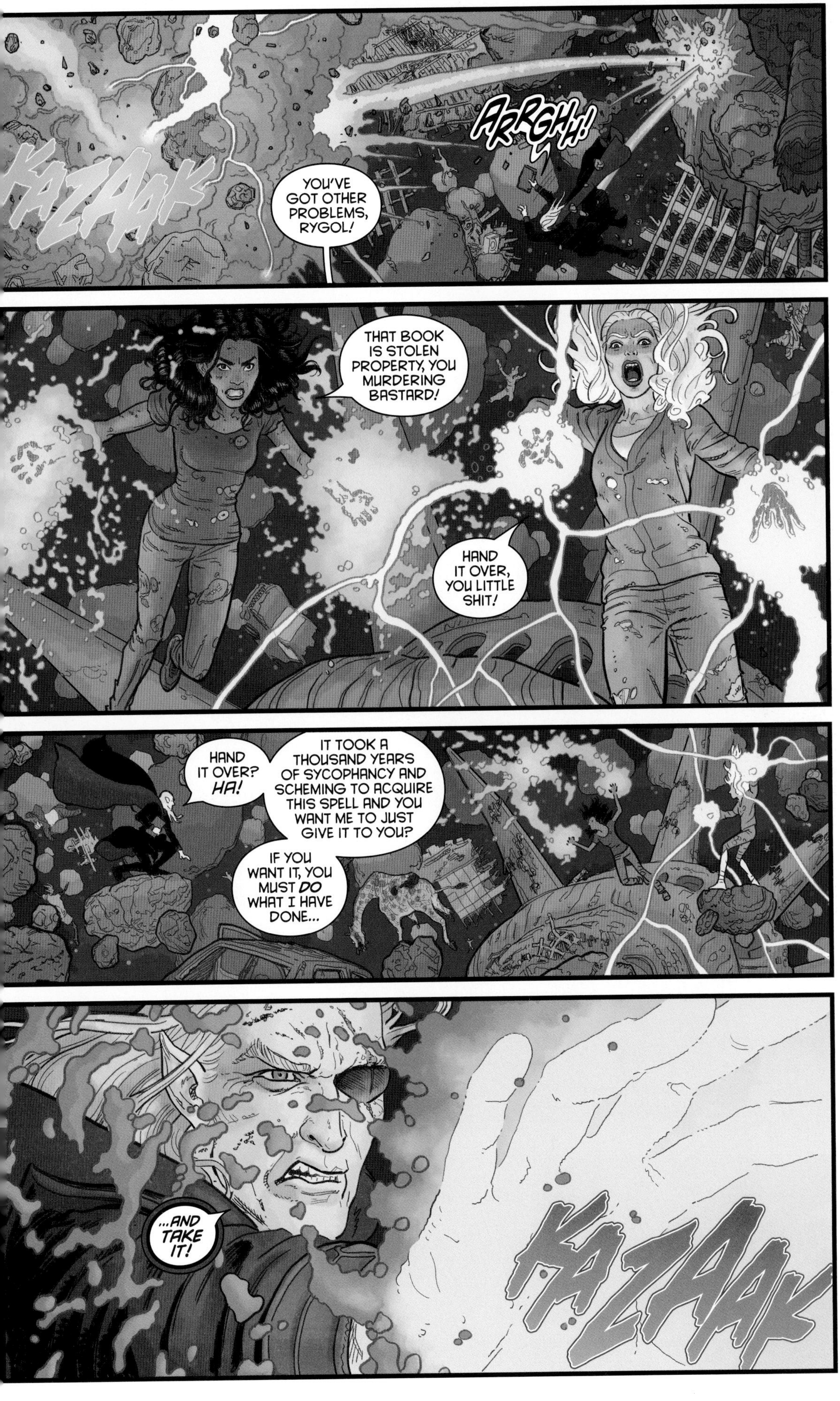
KAZAAK
ARRGHH!
YOU'VE GOT OTHER PROBLEMS, RYGOL!
THAT BOOK IS STOLEN PROPERTY, YOU MURDERING BASTARD!
HAND IT OVER, YOU LITTLE SHIT!
HAND IT OVER? HA!
IT TOOK A THOUSAND YEARS OF SYCOPHANCY AND SCHEMING TO ACQUIRE THIS SPELL AND YOU WANT ME TO JUST GIVE IT TO YOU?
IF YOU WANT IT, YOU MUST DO WHAT I HAVE DONE...
...AND TAKE IT!
KAZAAK

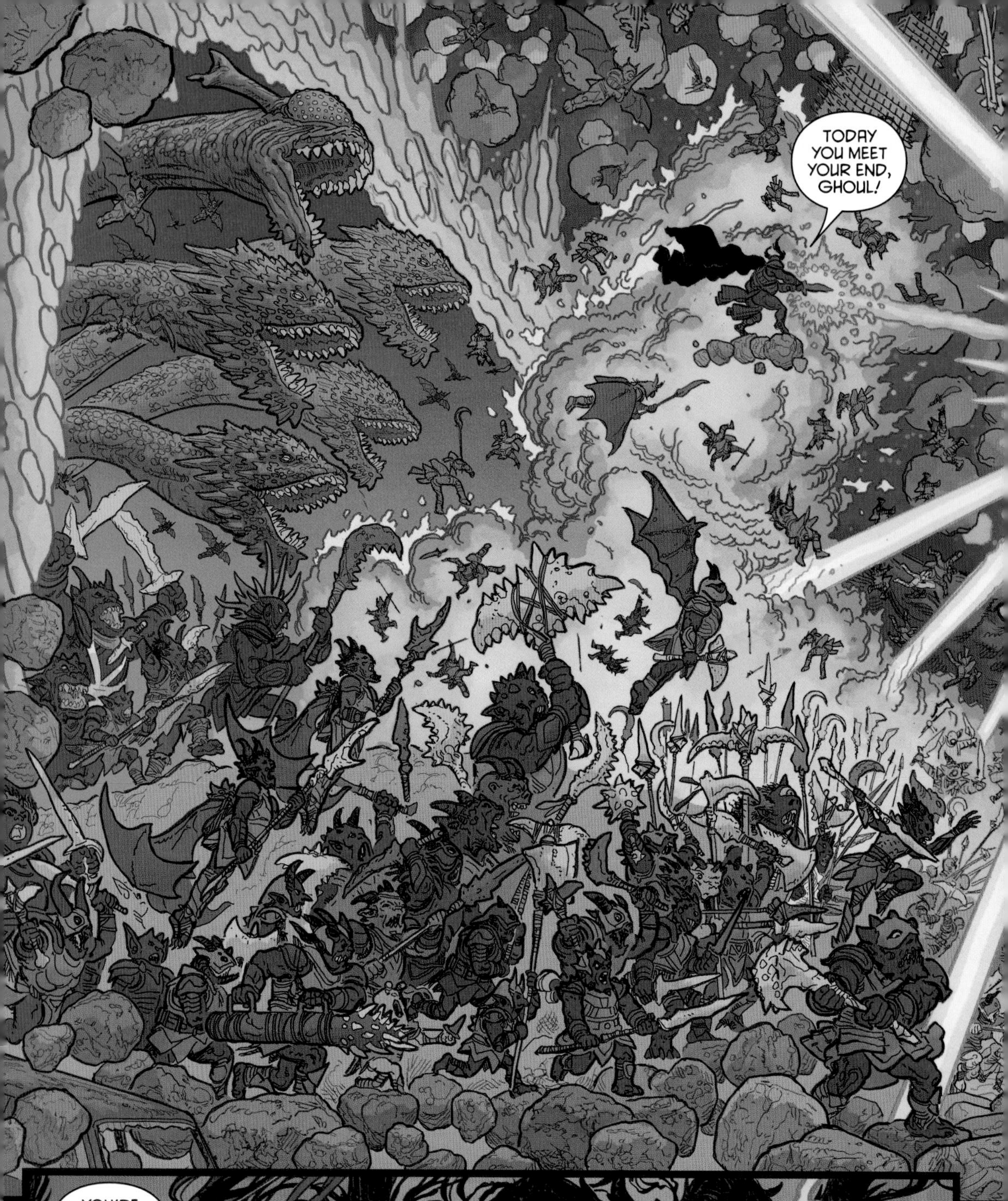
TODAY YOU MEET YOUR END, GHOUL!

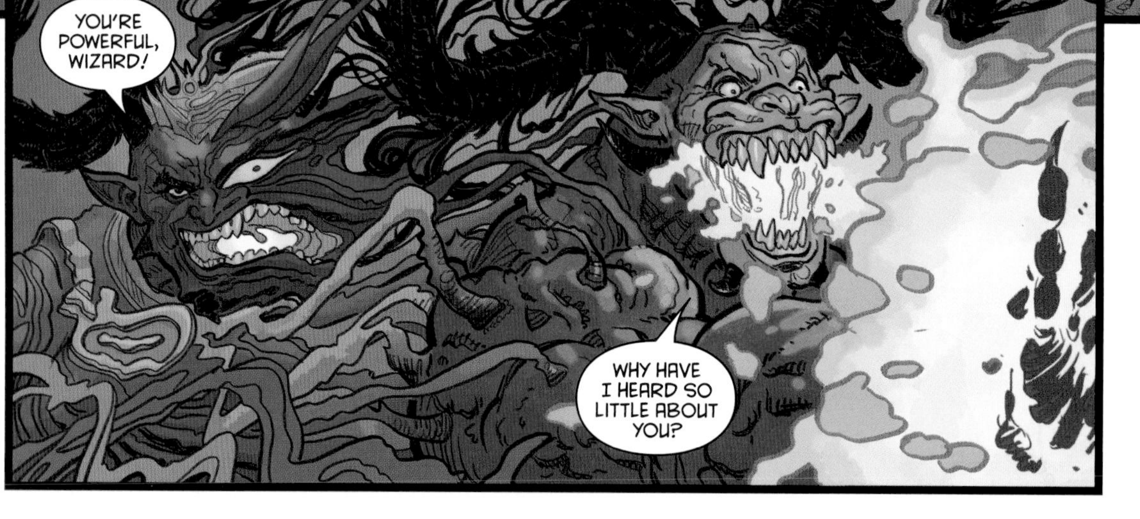
YOU'RE POWERFUL, WIZARD!
WHY HAVE I HEARD SO LITTLE ABOUT YOU?

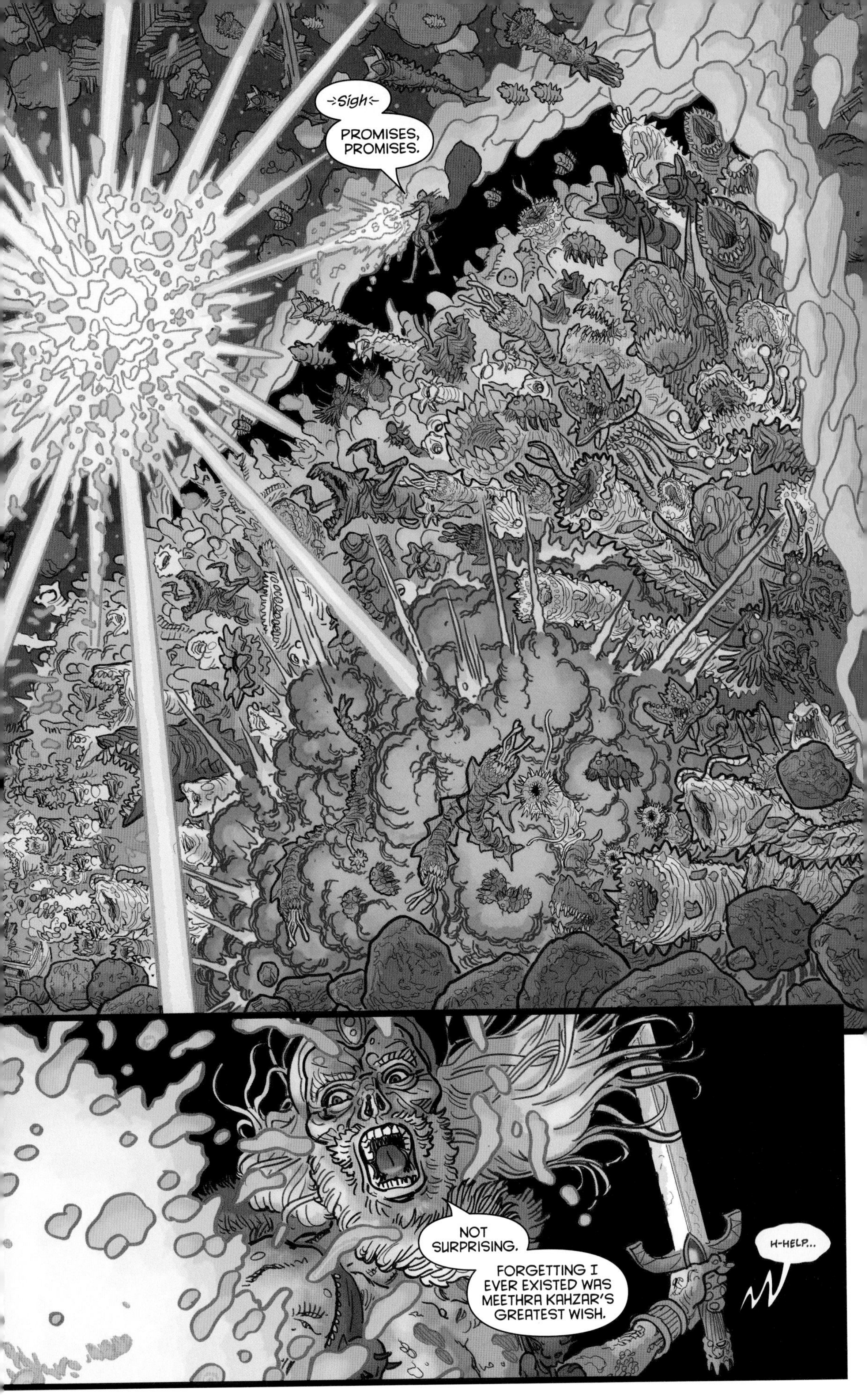

-Sigh-
PROMISES, PROMISES.
NOT SURPRISING.
FORGETTING I EVER EXISTED WAS MEETHRA KAHZAR'S GREATEST WISH.
H-HELP...

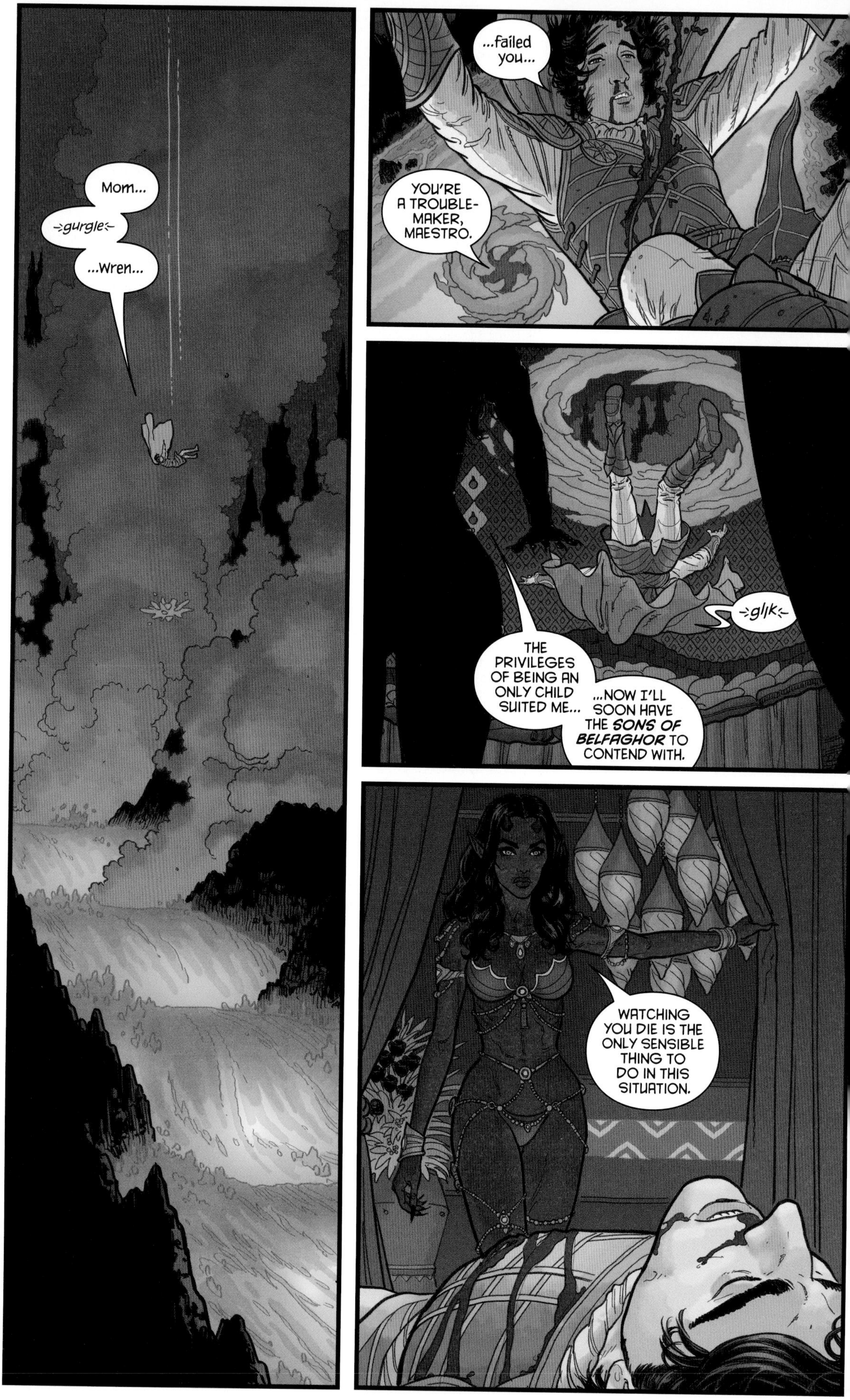
Mom...
-gurgle-
...Wren...
...failed you...
YOU'RE A TROUBLE-MAKER, MAESTRO.
-glik-
THE PRIVILEGES OF BEING AN ONLY CHILD SUITED ME...
...NOW I'LL SOON HAVE THE SONS OF BELFAGHOR TO CONTEND WITH.
WATCHING YOU DIE IS THE ONLY SENSIBLE THING TO DO IN THIS SITUATION.

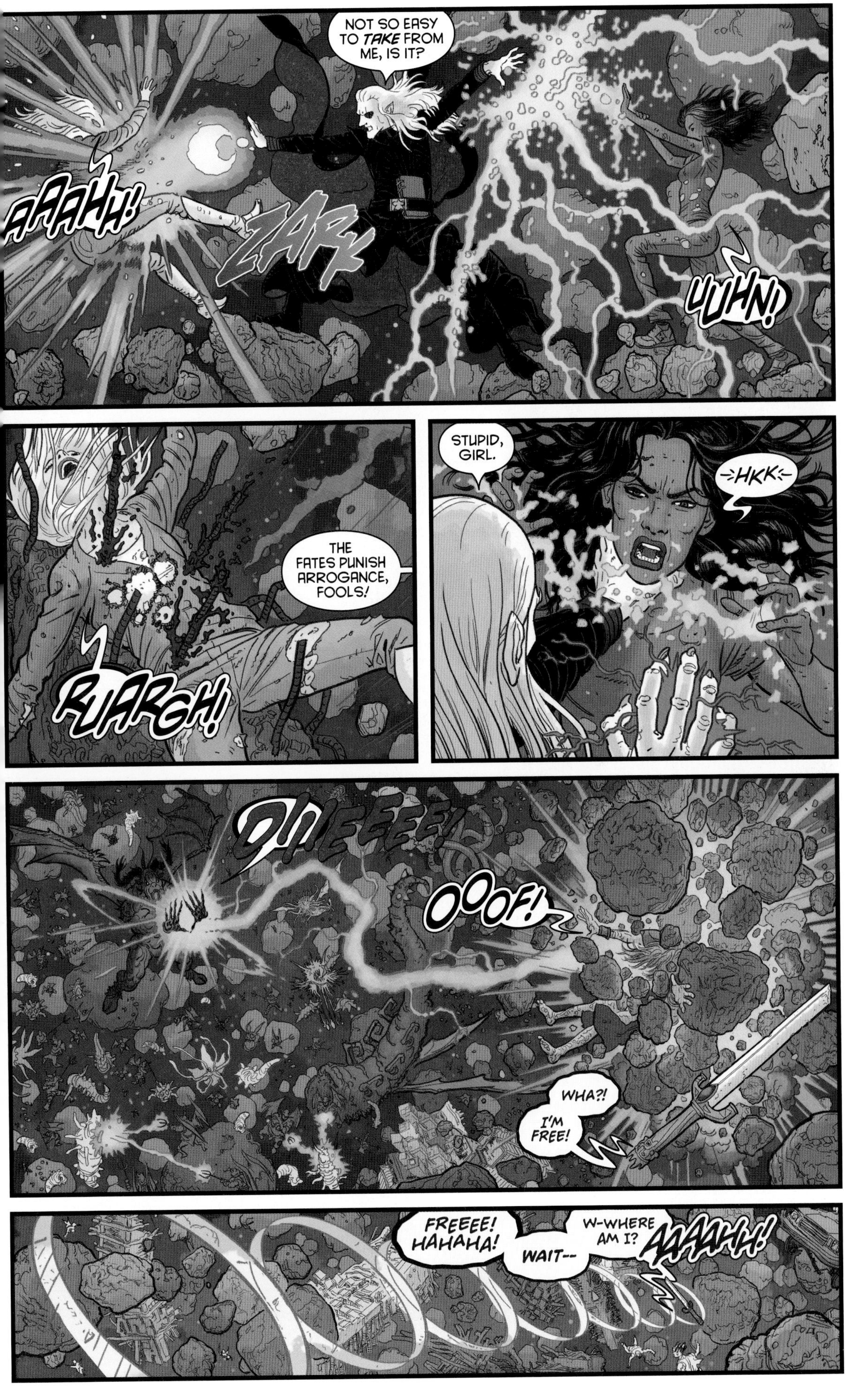
NOT SO EASY TO TAKE FROM ME, IS IT?
AAAHH!
ZARK
UUHN!
THE FATES PUNISH ARROGANCE, FOOLS!
RUARGH!
STUPID, GIRL.
HKK
DWEEEEE!
OOOF!
WHA?!
I'M FREE!
FREEEE! HAHAHA!
WAIT--
W-WHERE AM I?
AAAAHH!

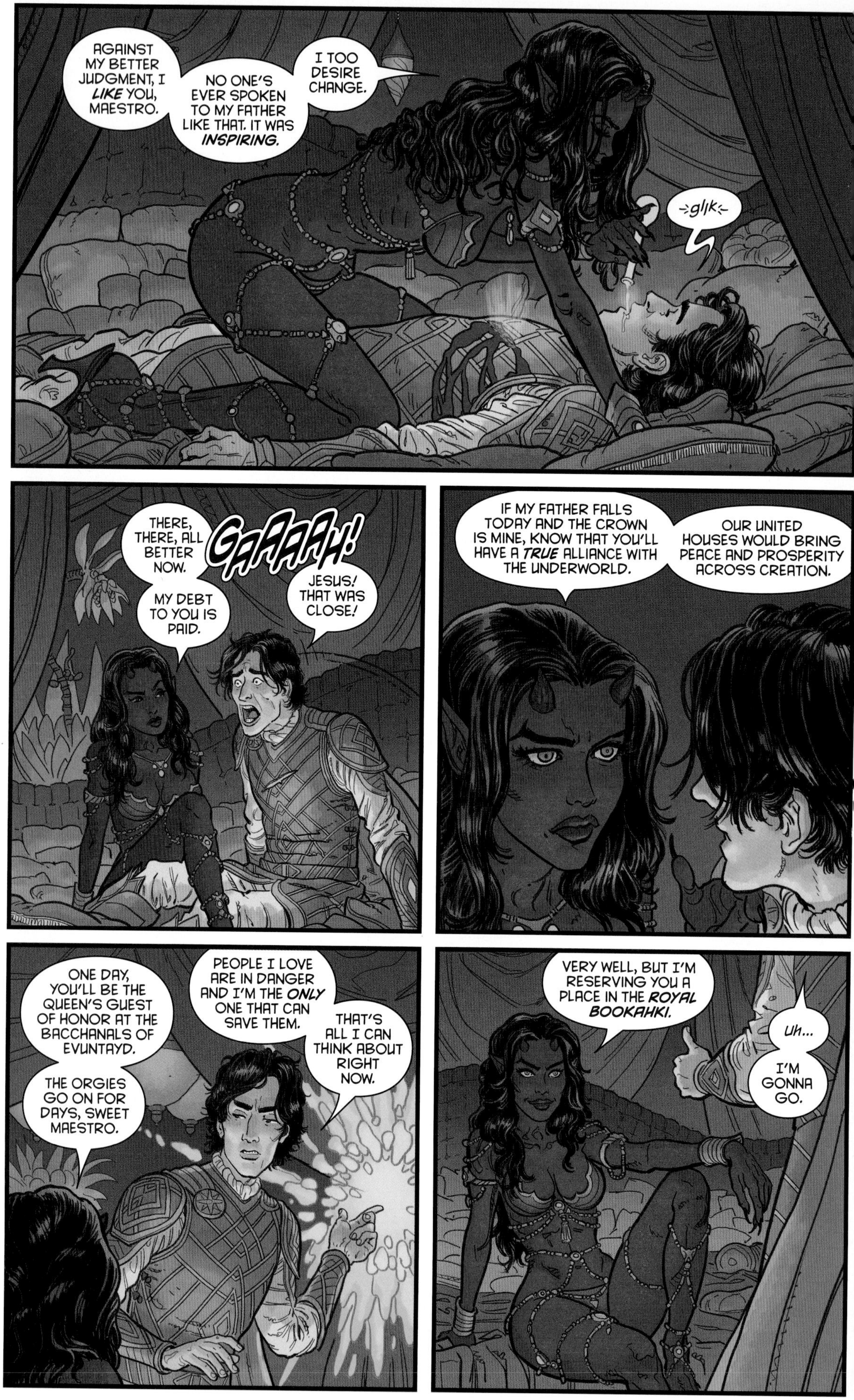
AGAINST MY BETTER JUDGMENT, I *LIKE* YOU, MAESTRO.
NO ONE'S EVER SPOKEN TO MY FATHER LIKE THAT. IT WAS *INSPIRING.*
I TOO DESIRE CHANGE.
-glik-
THERE, THERE, ALL BETTER NOW.
GAAAAAH!
MY DEBT TO YOU IS PAID.
JESUS! THAT WAS CLOSE!
IF MY FATHER FALLS TODAY AND THE CROWN IS MINE, KNOW THAT YOU'LL HAVE A *TRUE* ALLIANCE WITH THE UNDERWORLD.
OUR UNITED HOUSES WOULD BRING PEACE AND PROSPERITY ACROSS CREATION.
ONE DAY, YOU'LL BE THE QUEEN'S GUEST OF HONOR AT THE BACCHANALS OF EVUNTAYD.
THE ORGIES GO ON FOR DAYS, SWEET MAESTRO.
PEOPLE I LOVE ARE IN DANGER AND I'M THE *ONLY* ONE THAT CAN SAVE THEM.
THAT'S ALL I CAN THINK ABOUT RIGHT NOW.
VERY WELL, BUT I'M RESERVING YOU A PLACE IN THE *ROYAL BOOKAHKI.*
Uh...
I'M GONNA GO.

→Gasp← HEAR ME...
→choke← LOYAL BACKSTABBER,
→gasp← I... NEED YOU.

MILADY...? I-I HEAR YOU! I...

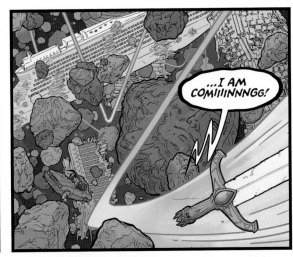

...I AM COMIIIINNNGG!

HEEELP IIIS HEEERE!

→Gasp← HELP...

...HER... →Gasp←

YOU LEMBAS BREAD—

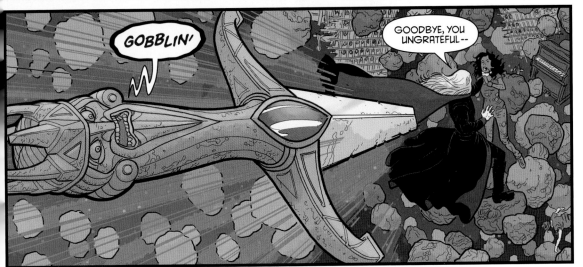

GOBBLIN'

GOODBYE, YOU UNGRATEFUL--

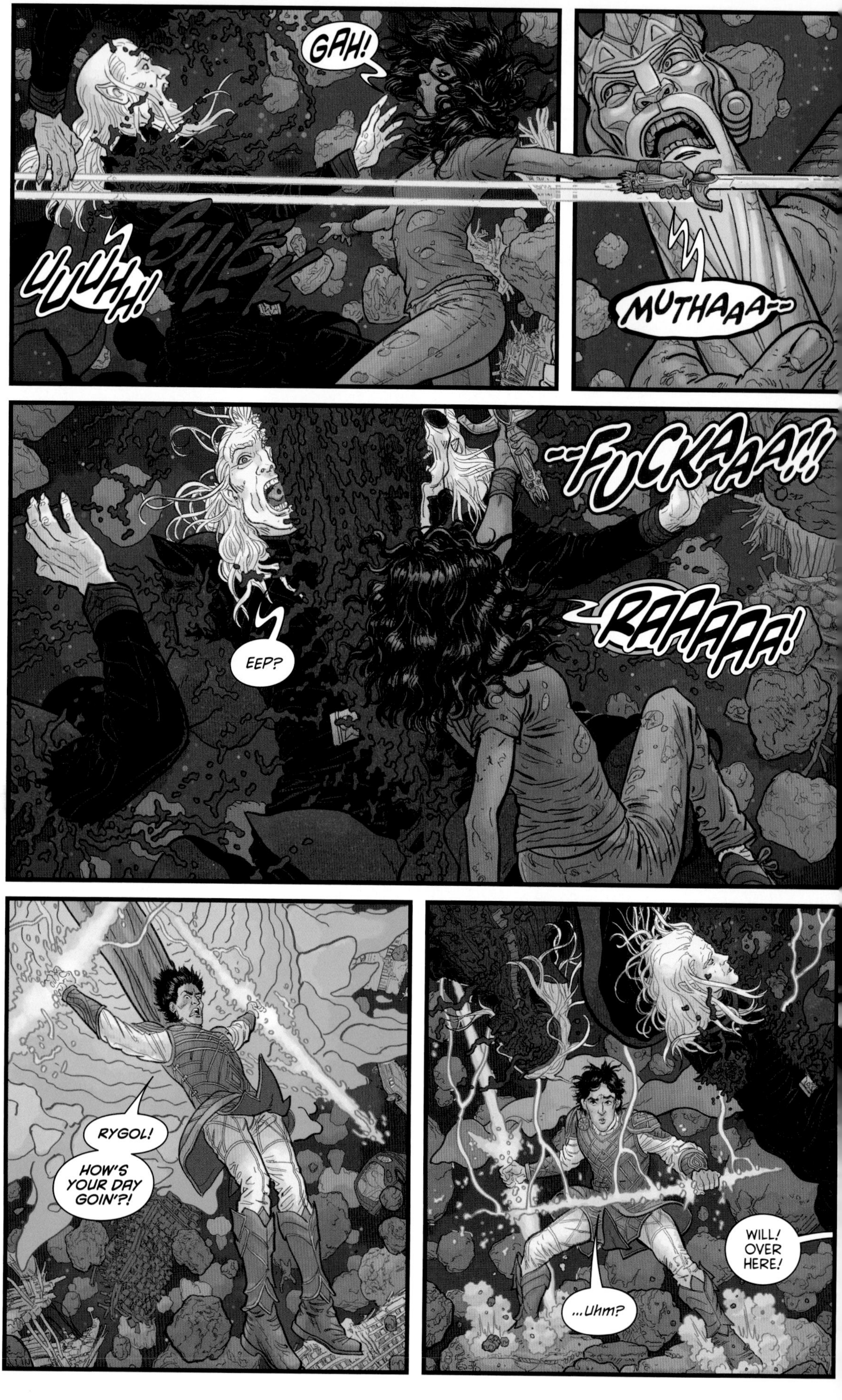
GAH!
UUUHH!
MUTHAAA--
--FUCKAAA!!
EEP?
RAAAAAA!
RYGOL!
HOW'S YOUR DAY GOIN'?!
WILL! OVER HERE!
...UHM?

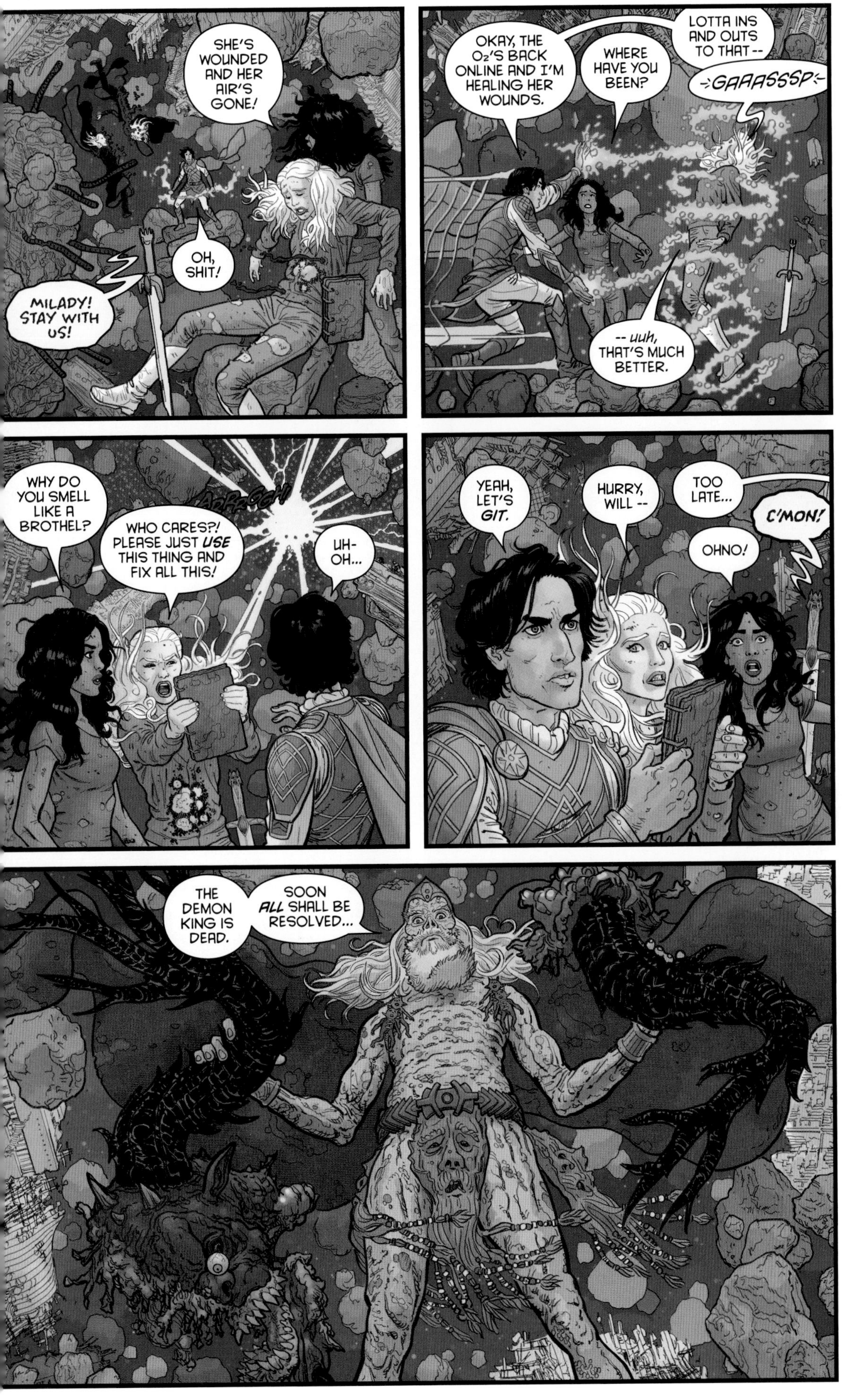

SHE'S WOUNDED AND HER AIR'S GONE!
OH, SHIT!
MILADY! STAY WITH US!
OKAY, THE O₂'S BACK ONLINE AND I'M HEALING HER WOUNDS.
WHERE HAVE YOU BEEN?
LOTTA INS AND OUTS TO THAT --
GAAASSSP
-- uuh, THAT'S MUCH BETTER.
WHY DO YOU SMELL LIKE A BROTHEL?
WHO CARES?! PLEASE JUST USE THIS THING AND FIX ALL THIS!
AARRGGH!
UH-OH...
YEAH, LET'S GIT.
HURRY, WILL --
TOO LATE...
C'MON!
OHNO!
THE DEMON KING IS DEAD.
SOON ALL SHALL BE RESOLVED...

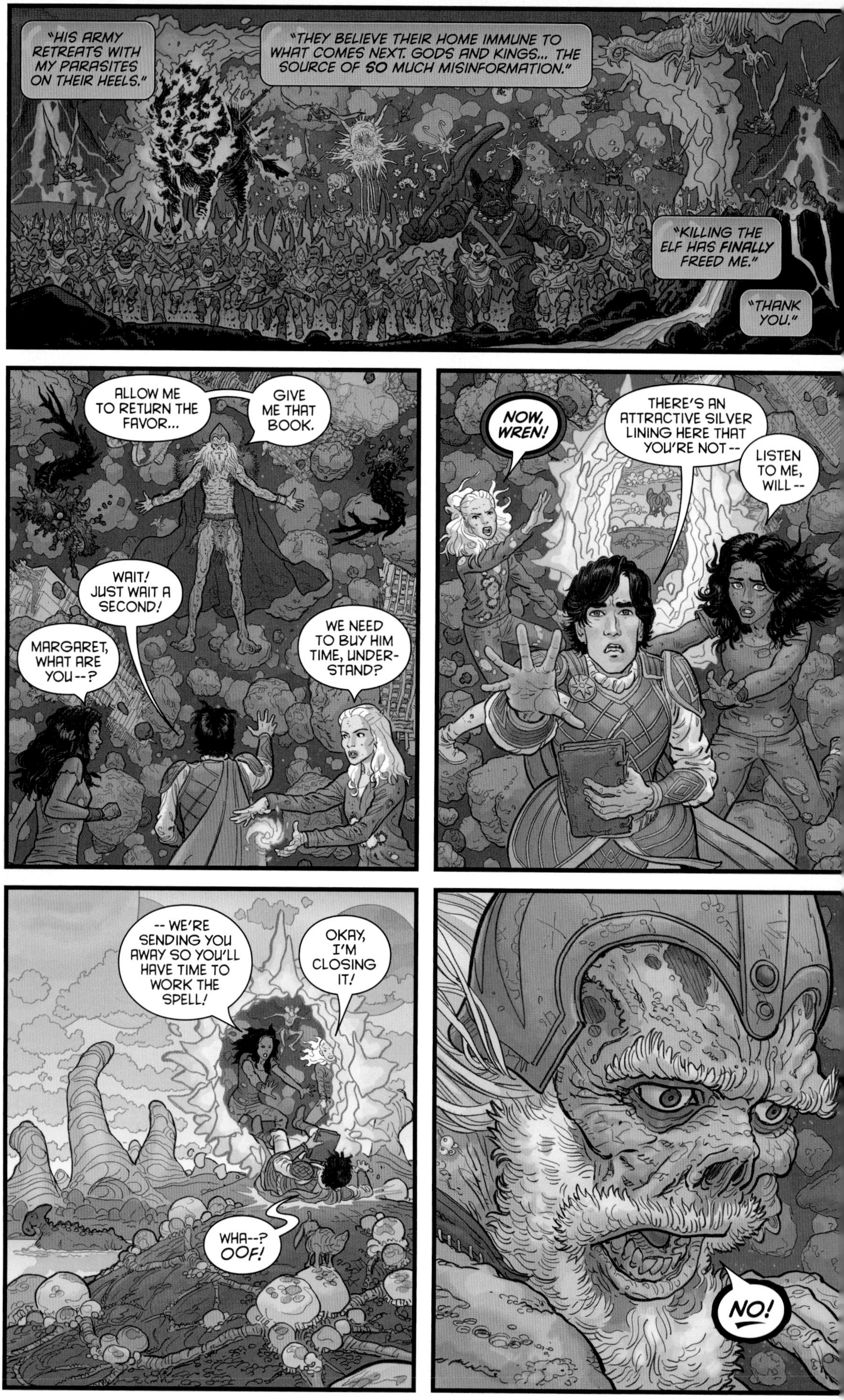
"HIS ARMY RETREATS WITH MY PARASITES ON THEIR HEELS."
"THEY BELIEVE THEIR HOME IMMUNE TO WHAT COMES NEXT. GODS AND KINGS... THE SOURCE OF SO MUCH MISINFORMATION."
"KILLING THE ELF HAS FINALLY FREED ME."
"THANK YOU."
ALLOW ME TO RETURN THE FAVOR...
GIVE ME THAT BOOK.
WAIT! JUST WAIT A SECOND!
MARGARET, WHAT ARE YOU--?
WE NEED TO BUY HIM TIME, UNDER-STAND?
NOW, WREN!
THERE'S AN ATTRACTIVE SILVER LINING HERE THAT YOU'RE NOT--
LISTEN TO ME, WILL--
-- WE'RE SENDING YOU AWAY SO YOU'LL HAVE TIME TO WORK THE SPELL!
OKAY, I'M CLOSING IT!
WHA--? OOF!
NO!

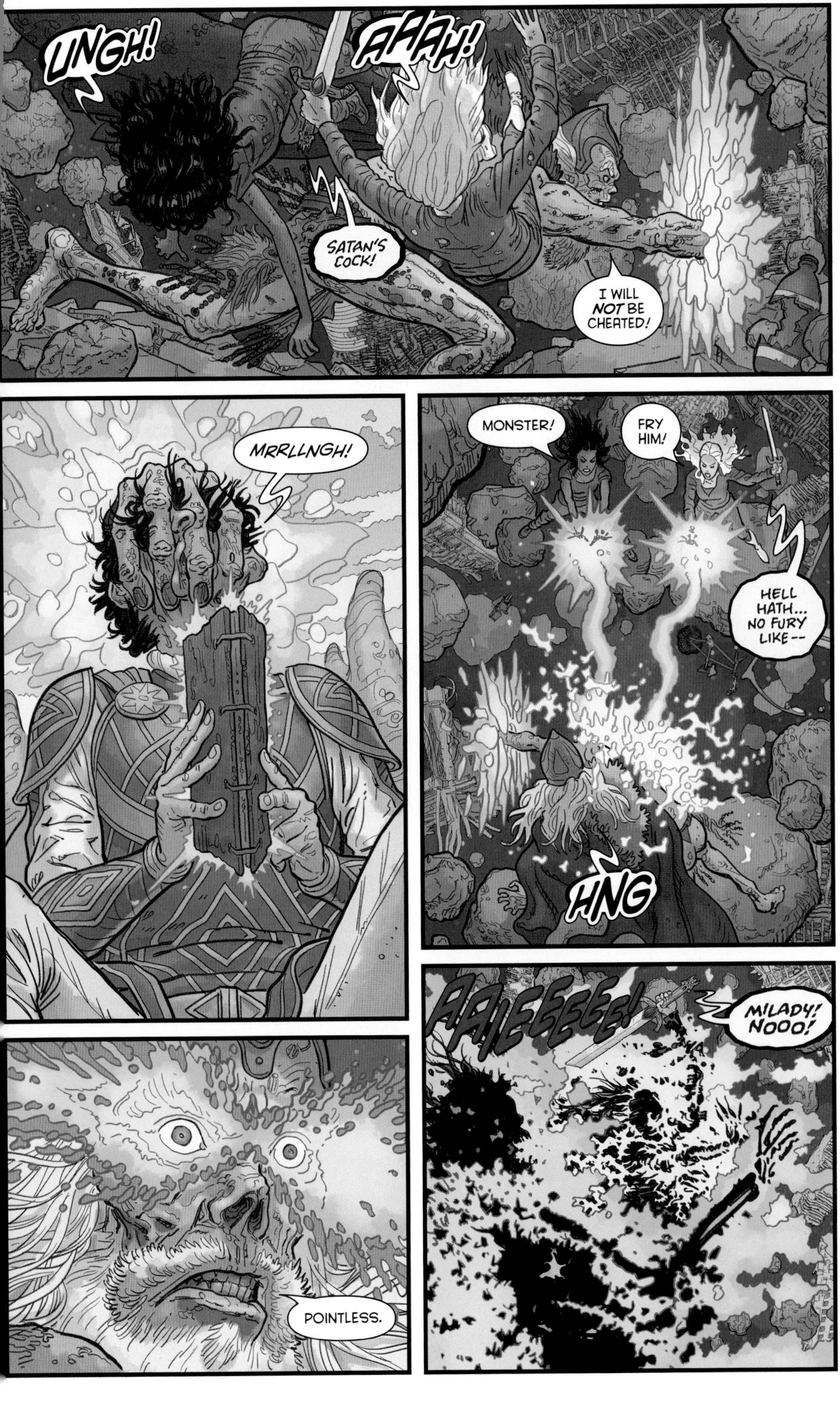
UNGH!
AAAAH!
SATAN'S COCK!
I WILL NOT BE CHEATED!
MRRLLNGH!
MONSTER!
FRY HIM!
HELL HATH... NO FURY LIKE--
HNG
POINTLESS.
AAIEEEEE!
MILADY! NOOO!

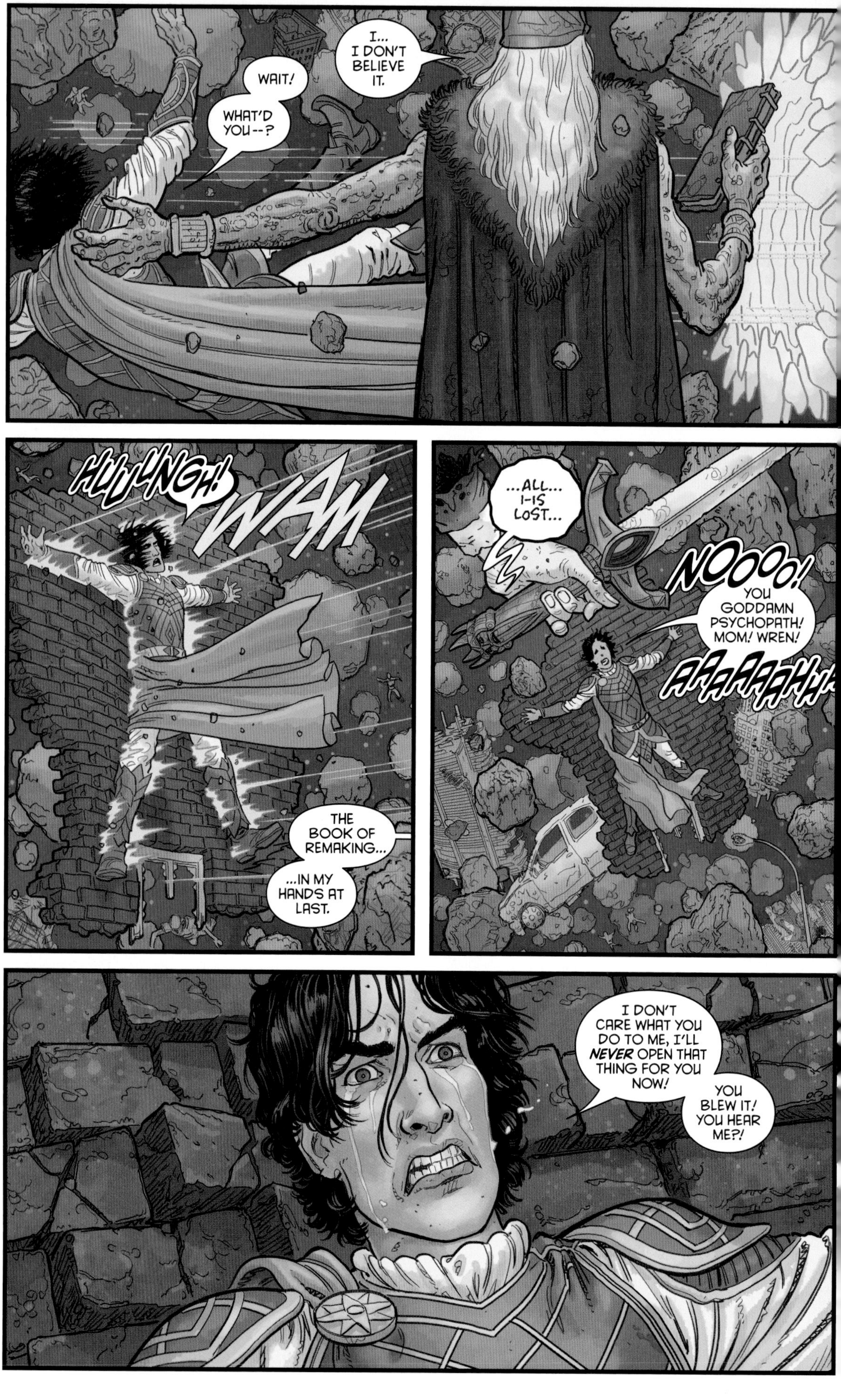
WAIT!
WHAT'D YOU--?
I... I DON'T BELIEVE IT.
HUUUNGH!
WAM
THE BOOK OF REMAKING...
...IN MY HANDS AT LAST.
...ALL... I-IS LOST...
NOOOO!
YOU GODDAMN PSYCHOPATH! MOM! WREN!
AAAAAAHH
I DON'T CARE WHAT YOU DO TO ME, I'LL ***NEVER*** OPEN THAT THING FOR YOU NOW!
YOU BLEW IT! YOU HEAR ME?!

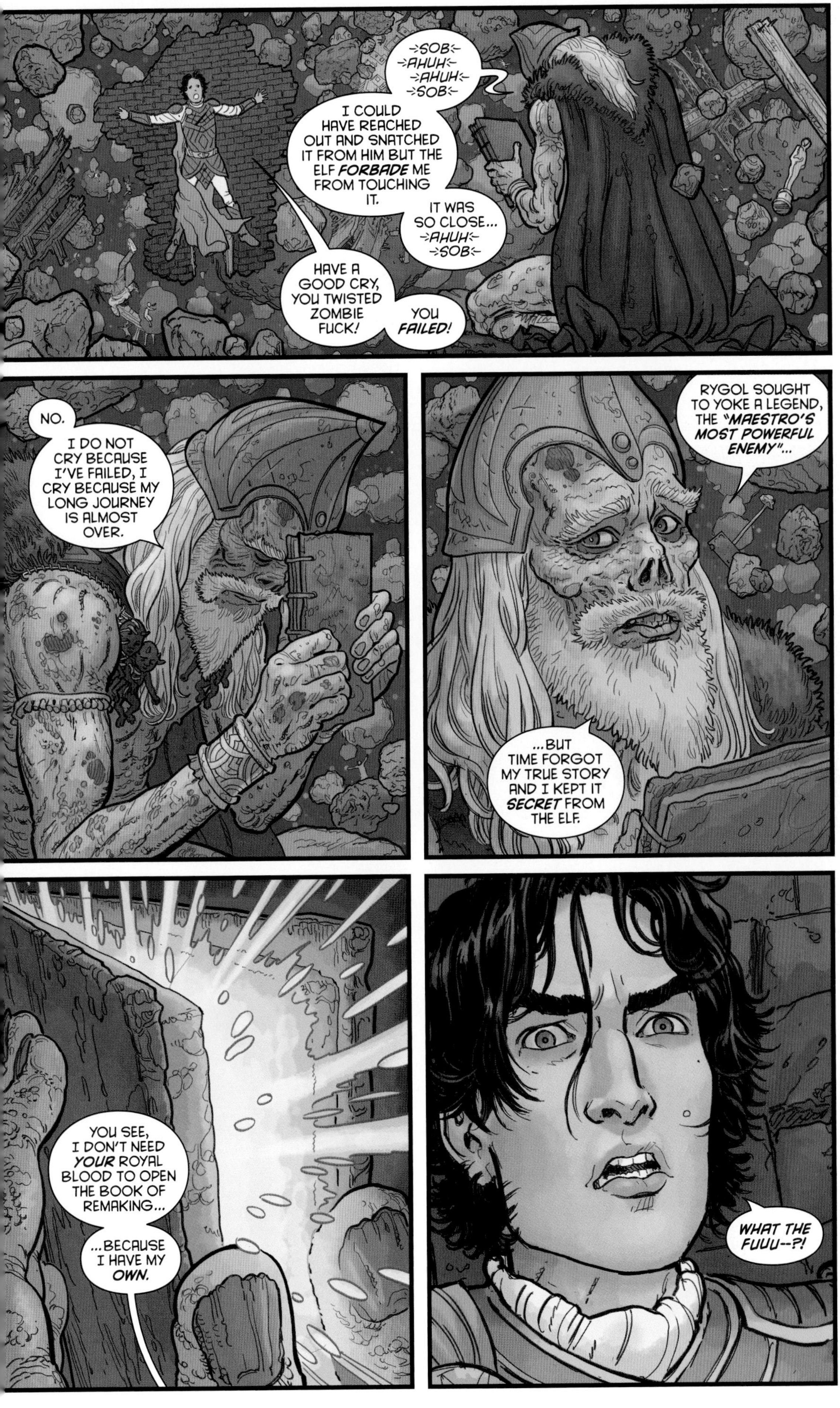

-SOB- -AHUH- -AHUH- -SOB-
I COULD HAVE REACHED OUT AND SNATCHED IT FROM HIM BUT THE ELF FORBADE ME FROM TOUCHING IT.
IT WAS SO CLOSE... -AHUH- -SOB-
HAVE A GOOD CRY, YOU TWISTED ZOMBIE FUCK!
YOU FAILED!
NO.
I DO NOT CRY BECAUSE I'VE FAILED, I CRY BECAUSE MY LONG JOURNEY IS ALMOST OVER.
RYGOL SOUGHT TO YOKE A LEGEND, THE "MAESTRO'S MOST POWERFUL ENEMY"...
...BUT TIME FORGOT MY TRUE STORY AND I KEPT IT SECRET FROM THE ELF.
YOU SEE, I DON'T NEED YOUR ROYAL BLOOD TO OPEN THE BOOK OF REMAKING...
...BECAUSE I HAVE MY OWN.
WHAT THE FUUU--?!

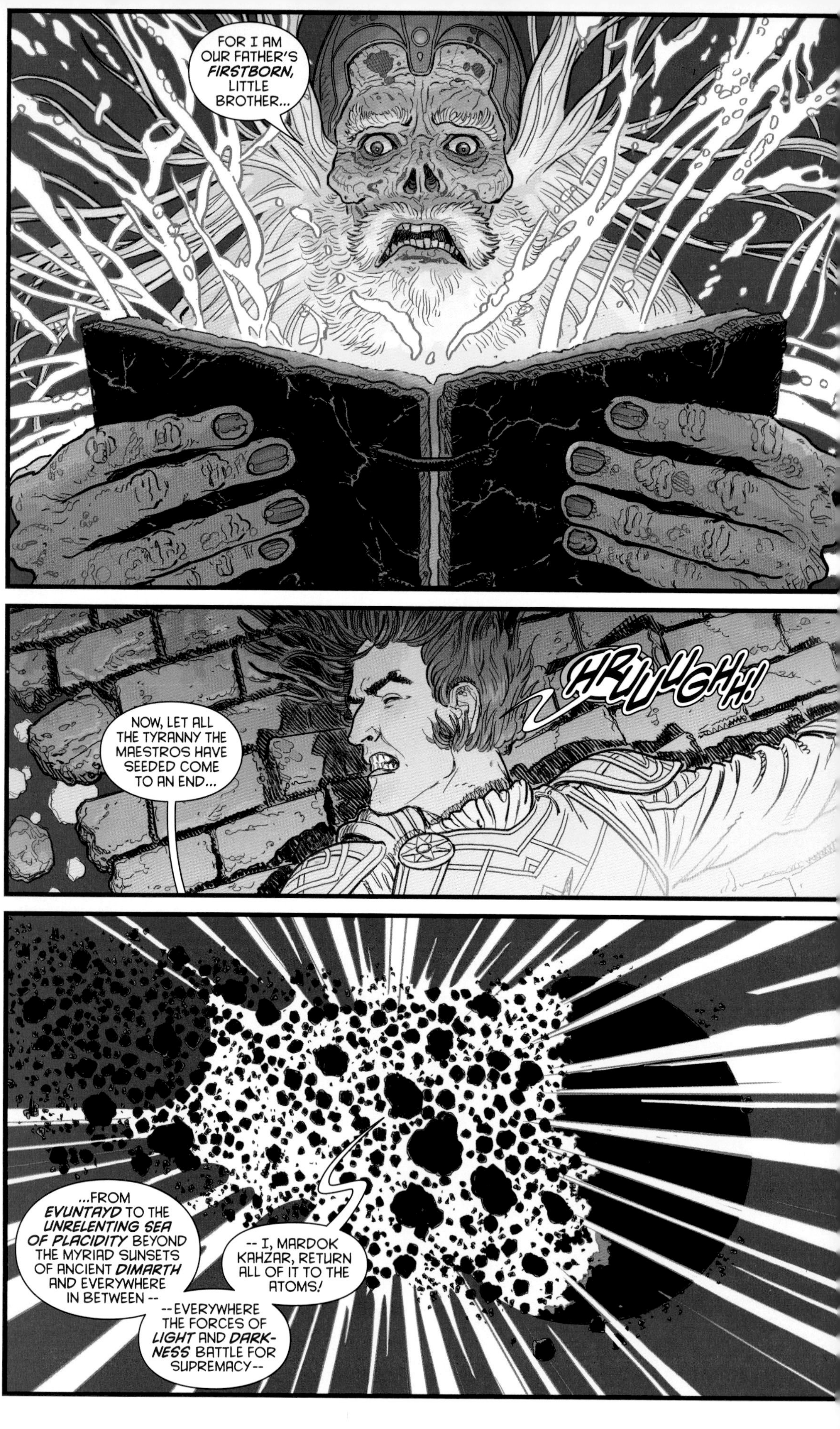
FOR I AM OUR FATHER'S *FIRSTBORN,* LITTLE BROTHER...
HRUUGHH!
NOW, LET ALL THE TYRANNY THE MAESTROS HAVE SEEDED COME TO AN END...
...FROM *EVUNTAYD* TO THE *UNRELENTING SEA OF PLACIDITY* BEYOND THE MYRIAD SUNSETS OF ANCIENT *DIMARTH* AND EVERYWHERE IN BETWEEN --
--EVERYWHERE THE FORCES OF *LIGHT* AND *DARK-NESS* BATTLE FOR SUPREMACY--
-- I, MARDOK KAHZAR, RETURN ALL OF IT TO THE ATOMS!

LET CREATION BE UNMADE.

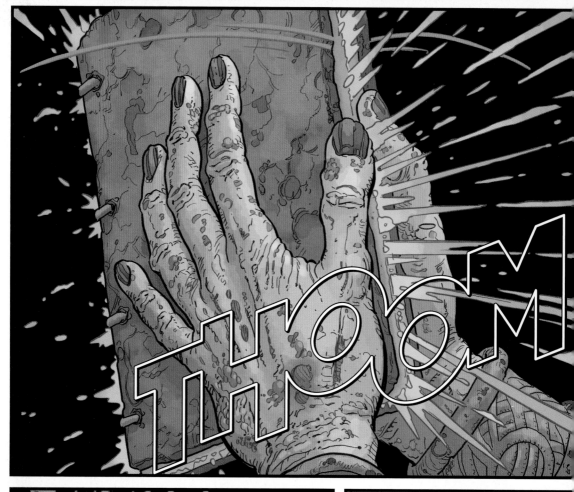

THOOM

IT WASN'T ALL MEANINGLESS TO ME...

...BUT IT'S BETTER THIS WAY.

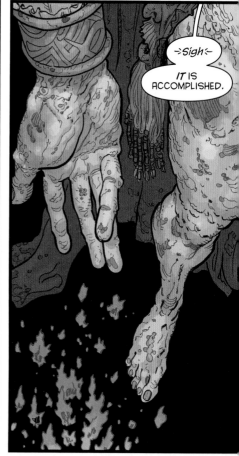

~Sigh~

IT IS ACCOMPLISHED.

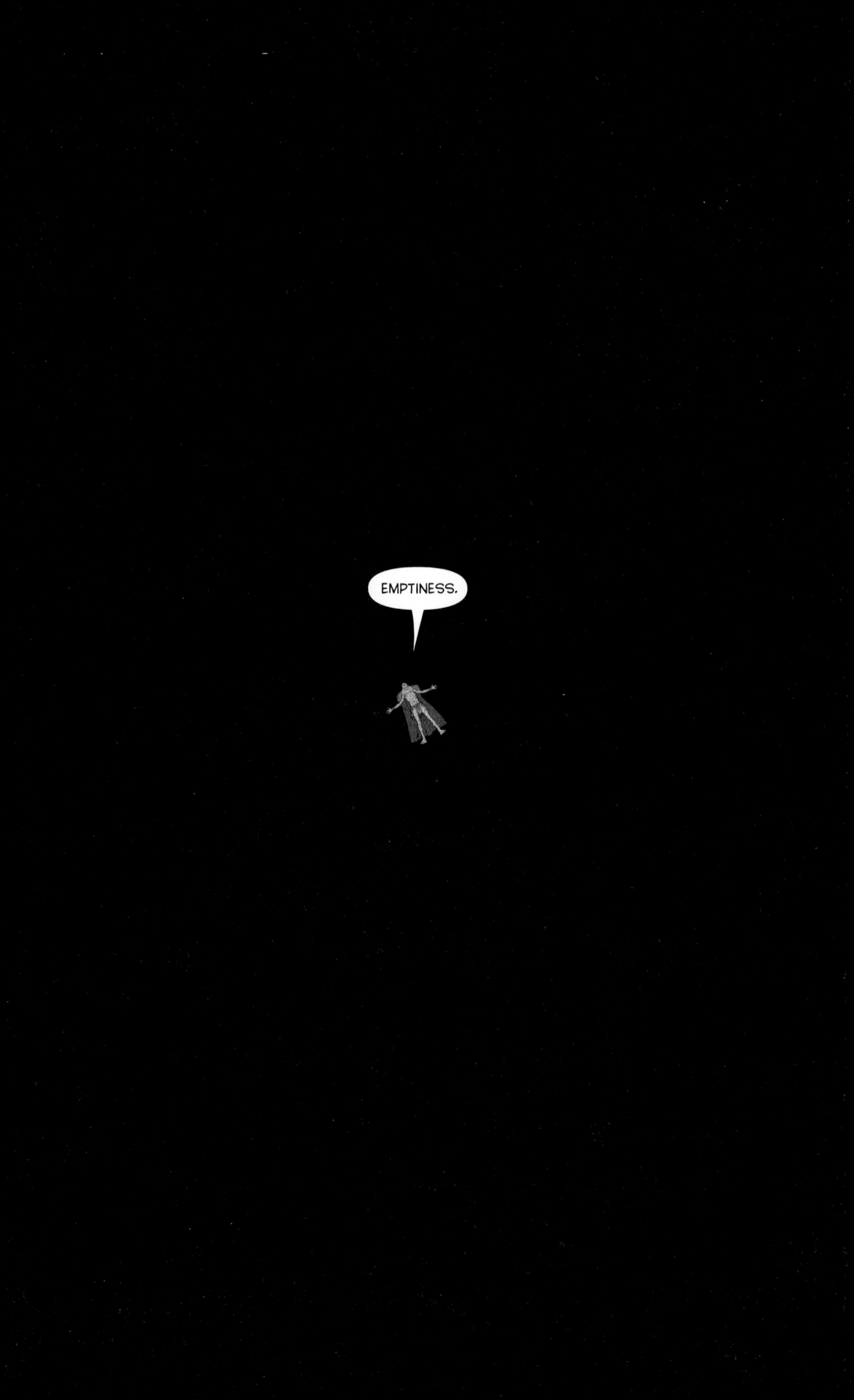
EMPTINESS.

CHAPTER SEVEN

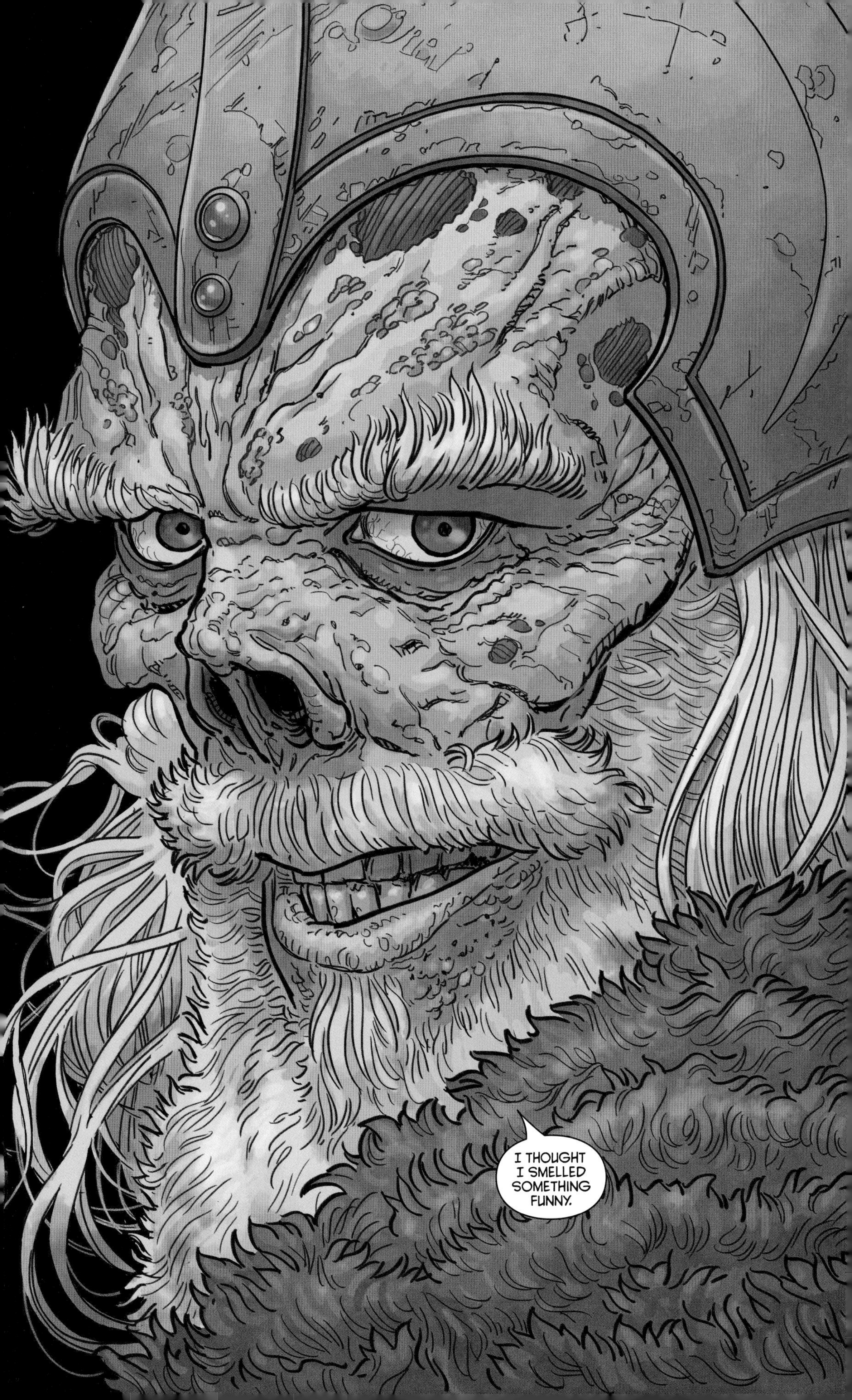
I THOUGHT I SMELLED SOMETHING FUNNY.

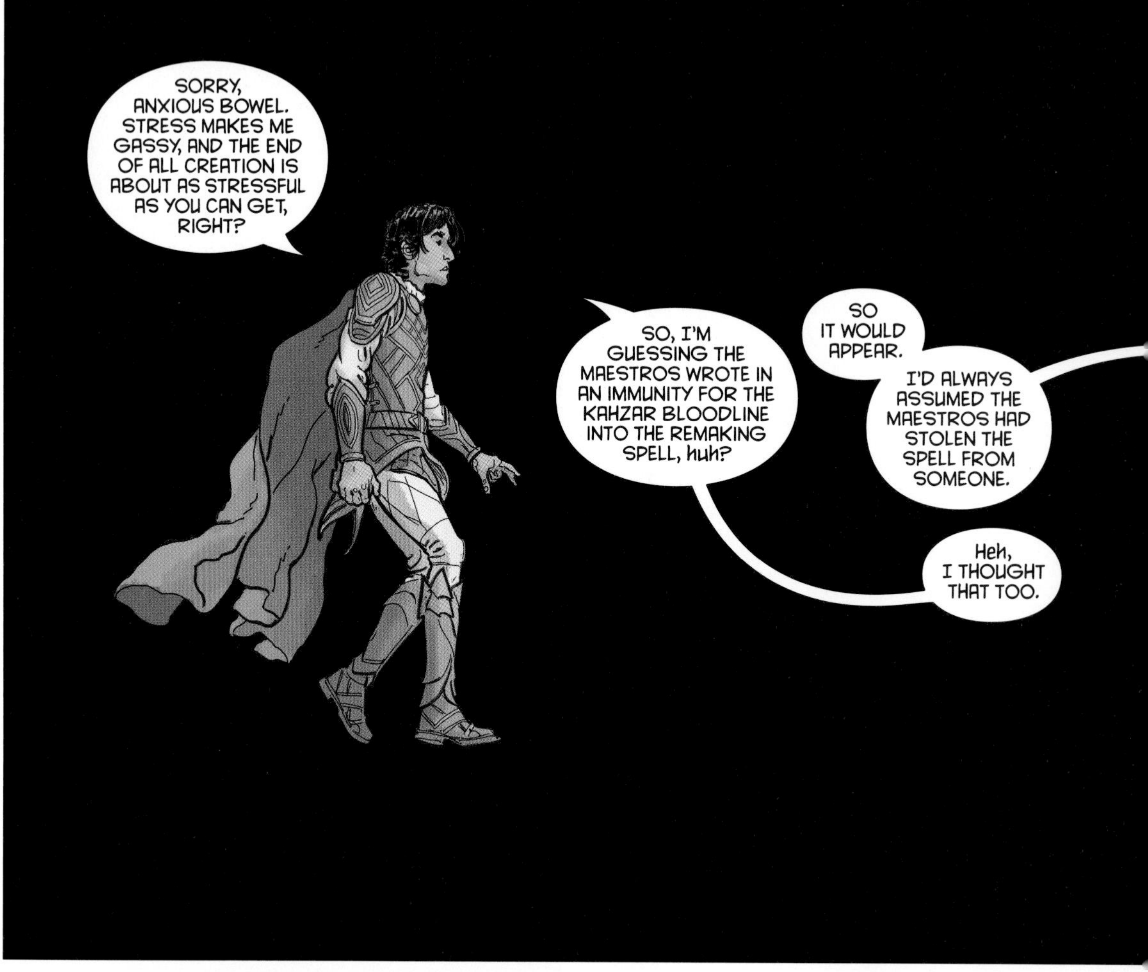
SORRY, ANXIOUS BOWEL. STRESS MAKES ME GASSY, AND THE END OF ALL CREATION IS ABOUT AS STRESSFUL AS YOU CAN GET, RIGHT?
SO, I'M GUESSING THE MAESTROS WROTE IN AN IMMUNITY FOR THE KAHZAR BLOODLINE INTO THE REMAKING SPELL, huh?
SO IT WOULD APPEAR.
I'D ALWAYS ASSUMED THE MAESTROS HAD STOLEN THE SPELL FROM SOMEONE.
Heh, I THOUGHT THAT TOO.

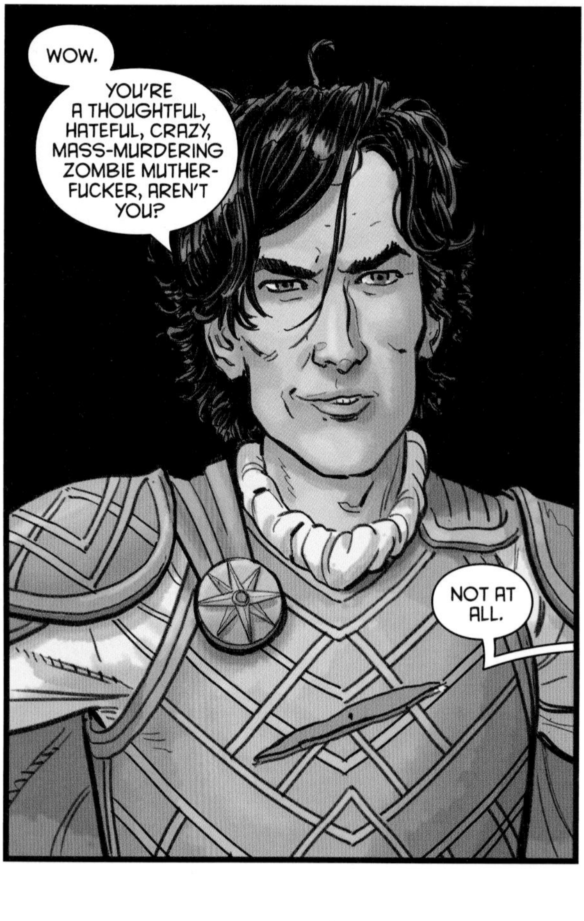
WOW.
YOU'RE A THOUGHTFUL, HATEFUL, CRAZY, MASS-MURDERING ZOMBIE MUTHER-FUCKER, AREN'T YOU?
NOT AT ALL.

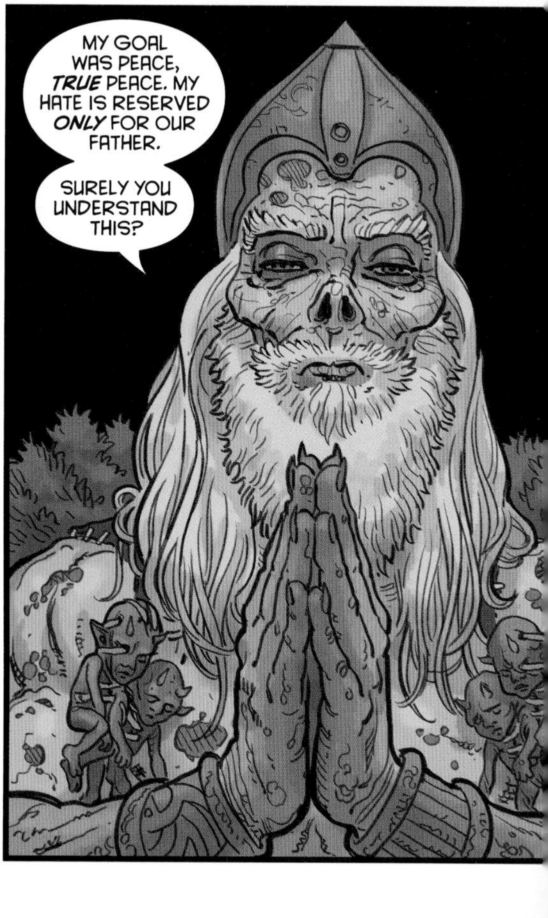
MY GOAL WAS PEACE, ***TRUE*** PEACE. MY HATE IS RESERVED ***ONLY*** FOR OUR FATHER.
SURELY YOU UNDERSTAND THIS?

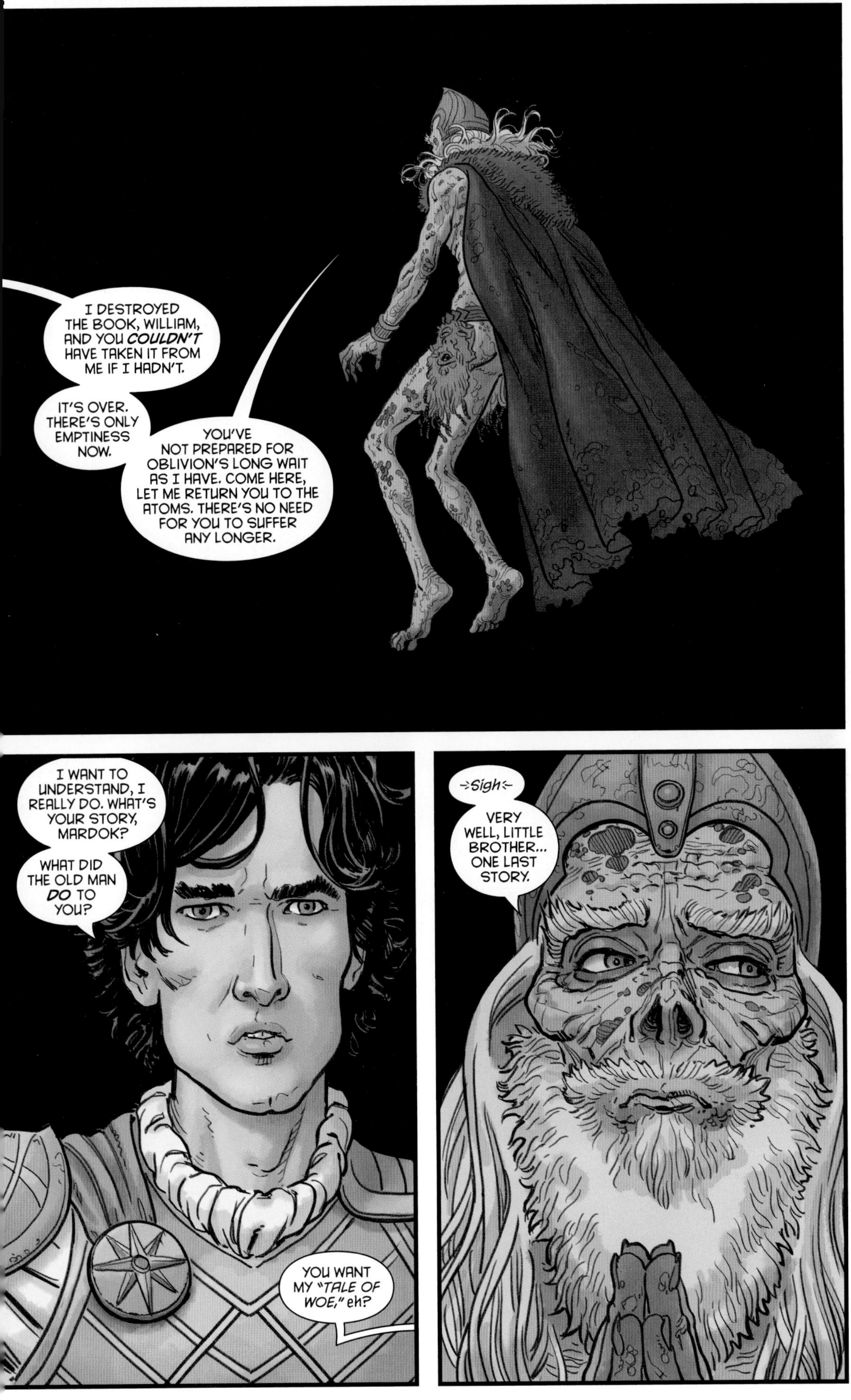
I DESTROYED THE BOOK, WILLIAM, AND YOU COULDN'T HAVE TAKEN IT FROM ME IF I HADN'T.
IT'S OVER. THERE'S ONLY EMPTINESS NOW.
YOU'VE NOT PREPARED FOR OBLIVION'S LONG WAIT AS I HAVE. COME HERE, LET ME RETURN YOU TO THE ATOMS. THERE'S NO NEED FOR YOU TO SUFFER ANY LONGER.
I WANT TO UNDERSTAND, I REALLY DO. WHAT'S YOUR STORY, MARDOK?
WHAT DID THE OLD MAN DO TO YOU?
YOU WANT MY "TALE OF WOE," eh?
Sigh
VERY WELL, LITTLE BROTHER... ONE LAST STORY.

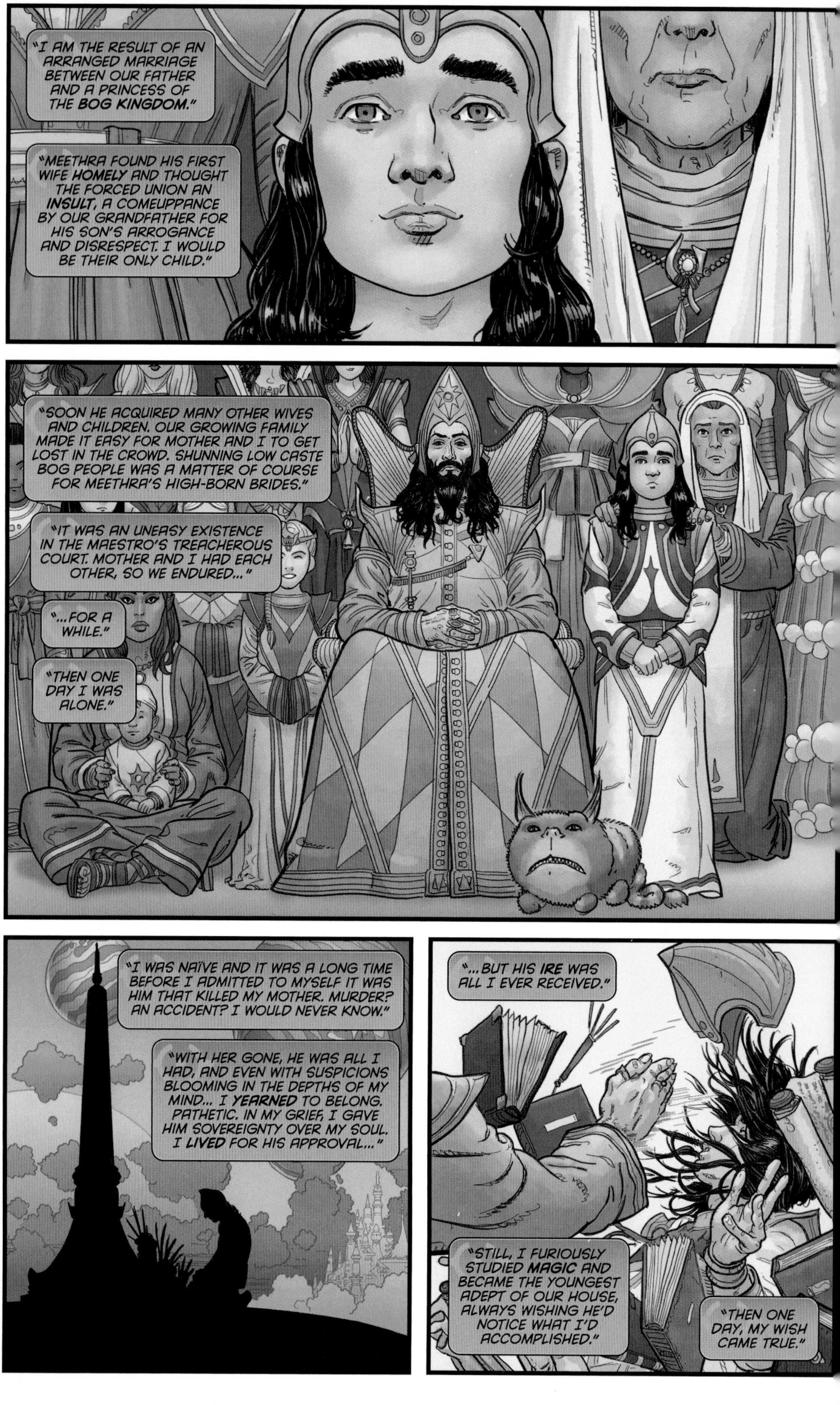
"I AM THE RESULT OF AN ARRANGED MARRIAGE BETWEEN OUR FATHER AND A PRINCESS OF THE BOG KINGDOM."
"MEETHRA FOUND HIS FIRST WIFE HOMELY AND THOUGHT THE FORCED UNION AN INSULT, A COMEUPPANCE BY OUR GRANDFATHER FOR HIS SON'S ARROGANCE AND DISRESPECT. I WOULD BE THEIR ONLY CHILD."
"SOON HE ACQUIRED MANY OTHER WIVES AND CHILDREN. OUR GROWING FAMILY MADE IT EASY FOR MOTHER AND I TO GET LOST IN THE CROWD. SHUNNING LOW CASTE BOG PEOPLE WAS A MATTER OF COURSE FOR MEETHRA'S HIGH-BORN BRIDES."
"IT WAS AN UNEASY EXISTENCE IN THE MAESTRO'S TREACHEROUS COURT. MOTHER AND I HAD EACH OTHER, SO WE ENDURED..."
"...FOR A WHILE."
"THEN ONE DAY I WAS ALONE."
"I WAS NAÏVE AND IT WAS A LONG TIME BEFORE I ADMITTED TO MYSELF IT WAS HIM THAT KILLED MY MOTHER. MURDER? AN ACCIDENT? I WOULD NEVER KNOW."
"WITH HER GONE, HE WAS ALL I HAD, AND EVEN WITH SUSPICIONS BLOOMING IN THE DEPTHS OF MY MIND... I YEARNED TO BELONG. PATHETIC. IN MY GRIEF, I GAVE HIM SOVEREIGNTY OVER MY SOUL. I LIVED FOR HIS APPROVAL..."
"...BUT HIS IRE WAS ALL I EVER RECEIVED."
"STILL, I FURIOUSLY STUDIED MAGIC AND BECAME THE YOUNGEST ADEPT OF OUR HOUSE, ALWAYS WISHING HE'D NOTICE WHAT I'D ACCOMPLISHED."
"THEN ONE DAY, MY WISH CAME TRUE."

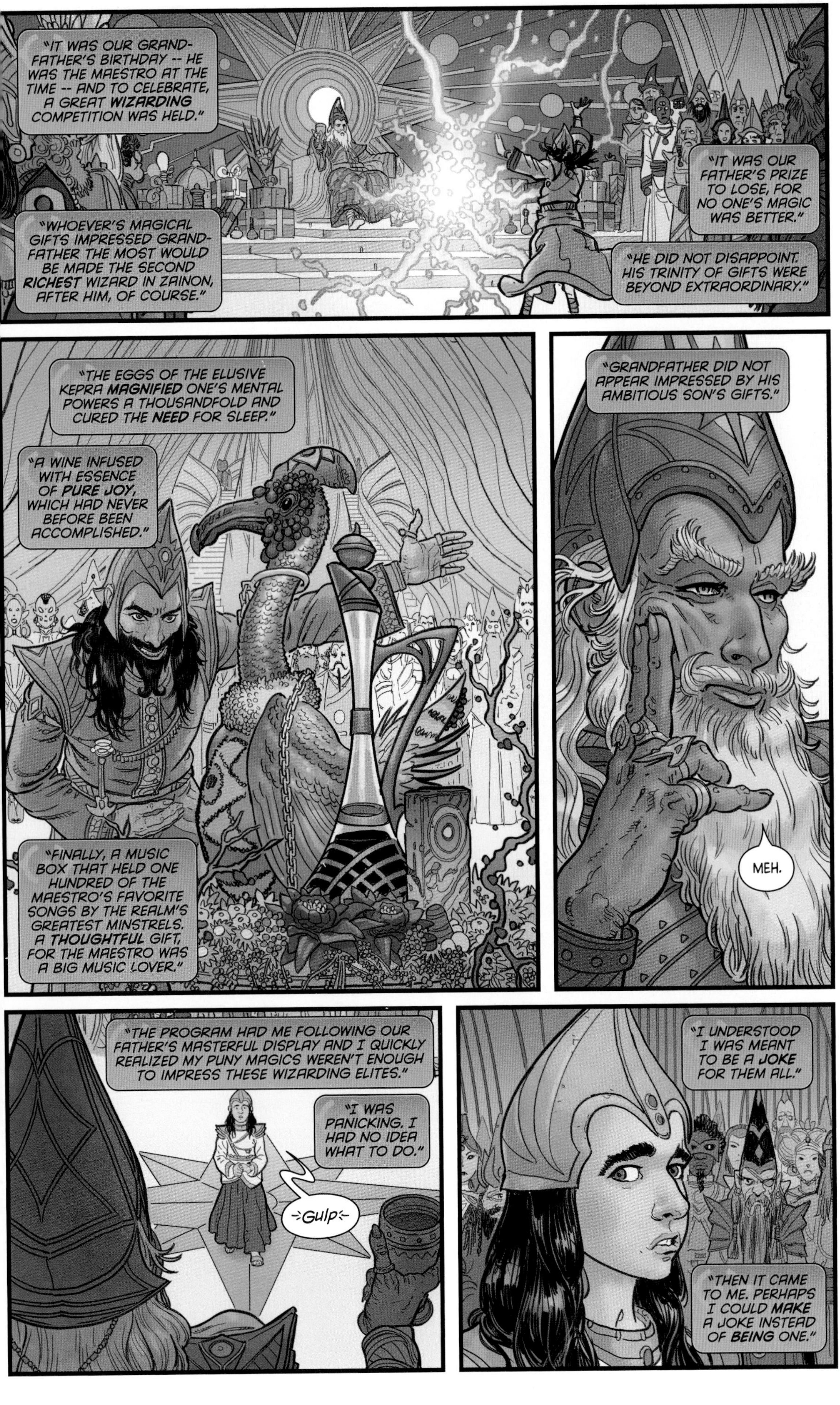
"IT WAS OUR GRAND-FATHER'S BIRTHDAY -- HE WAS THE MAESTRO AT THE TIME -- AND TO CELEBRATE, A GREAT WIZARDING COMPETITION WAS HELD."
"WHOEVER'S MAGICAL GIFTS IMPRESSED GRAND-FATHER THE MOST WOULD BE MADE THE SECOND RICHEST WIZARD IN ZAINON, AFTER HIM, OF COURSE."
"IT WAS OUR FATHER'S PRIZE TO LOSE, FOR NO ONE'S MAGIC WAS BETTER."
"HE DID NOT DISAPPOINT. HIS TRINITY OF GIFTS WERE BEYOND EXTRAORDINARY."
"THE EGGS OF THE ELUSIVE KEPRA MAGNIFIED ONE'S MENTAL POWERS A THOUSANDFOLD AND CURED THE NEED FOR SLEEP."
"A WINE INFUSED WITH ESSENCE OF PURE JOY, WHICH HAD NEVER BEFORE BEEN ACCOMPLISHED."
"FINALLY, A MUSIC BOX THAT HELD ONE HUNDRED OF THE MAESTRO'S FAVORITE SONGS BY THE REALM'S GREATEST MINSTRELS. A THOUGHTFUL GIFT, FOR THE MAESTRO WAS A BIG MUSIC LOVER."
"GRANDFATHER DID NOT APPEAR IMPRESSED BY HIS AMBITIOUS SON'S GIFTS."
MEH.
"THE PROGRAM HAD ME FOLLOWING OUR FATHER'S MASTERFUL DISPLAY AND I QUICKLY REALIZED MY PUNY MAGICS WEREN'T ENOUGH TO IMPRESS THESE WIZARDING ELITES."
"I WAS PANICKING. I HAD NO IDEA WHAT TO DO."
Gulp
"I UNDERSTOOD I WAS MEANT TO BE A JOKE FOR THEM ALL."
"THEN IT CAME TO ME. PERHAPS I COULD MAKE A JOKE INSTEAD OF BEING ONE."

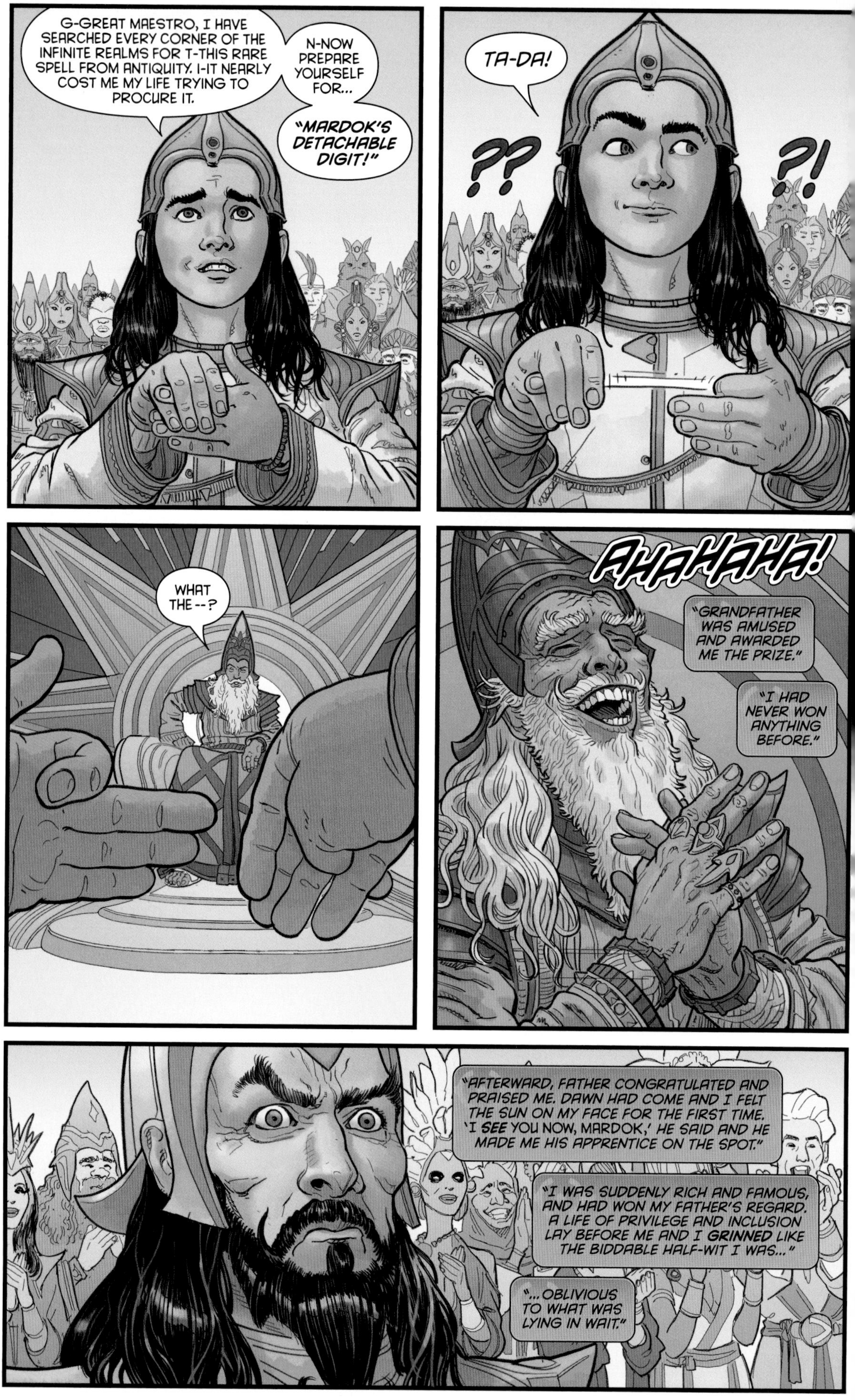
G-GREAT MAESTRO, I HAVE SEARCHED EVERY CORNER OF THE INFINITE REALMS FOR T-THIS RARE SPELL FROM ANTIQUITY. I-IT NEARLY COST ME MY LIFE TRYING TO PROCURE IT.
N-NOW PREPARE YOURSELF FOR...
"MARDOK'S DETACHABLE DIGIT!"
TA-DA!
??
?!
WHAT THE--?
AHAHAHA!
"GRANDFATHER WAS AMUSED AND AWARDED ME THE PRIZE."
"I HAD NEVER WON ANYTHING BEFORE."
"AFTERWARD, FATHER CONGRATULATED AND PRAISED ME. DAWN HAD COME AND I FELT THE SUN ON MY FACE FOR THE FIRST TIME. 'I SEE YOU NOW, MARDOK,' HE SAID AND HE MADE ME HIS APPRENTICE ON THE SPOT."
"I WAS SUDDENLY RICH AND FAMOUS, AND HAD WON MY FATHER'S REGARD. A LIFE OF PRIVILEGE AND INCLUSION LAY BEFORE ME AND I GRINNED LIKE THE BIDDABLE HALF-WIT I WAS..."
"...OBLIVIOUS TO WHAT WAS LYING IN WAIT."

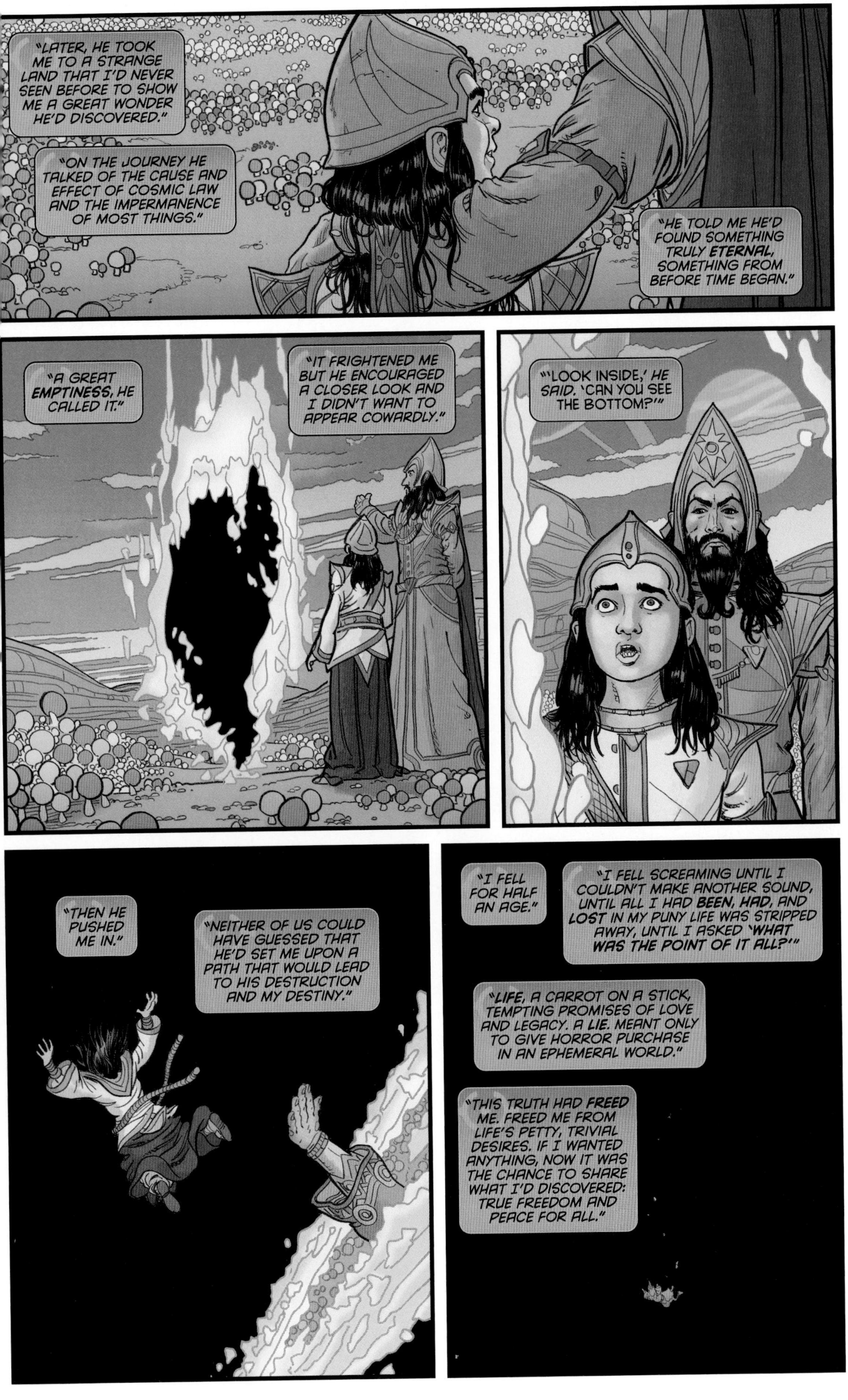
"LATER, HE TOOK ME TO A STRANGE LAND THAT I'D NEVER SEEN BEFORE TO SHOW ME A GREAT WONDER HE'D DISCOVERED."
"ON THE JOURNEY HE TALKED OF THE CAUSE AND EFFECT OF COSMIC LAW AND THE IMPERMANENCE OF MOST THINGS."
"HE TOLD ME HE'D FOUND SOMETHING TRULY ETERNAL, SOMETHING FROM BEFORE TIME BEGAN."
"A GREAT EMPTINESS, HE CALLED IT."
"IT FRIGHTENED ME BUT HE ENCOURAGED A CLOSER LOOK AND I DIDN'T WANT TO APPEAR COWARDLY."
"'LOOK INSIDE,' HE SAID. 'CAN YOU SEE THE BOTTOM?'"
"THEN HE PUSHED ME IN."
"NEITHER OF US COULD HAVE GUESSED THAT HE'D SET ME UPON A PATH THAT WOULD LEAD TO HIS DESTRUCTION AND MY DESTINY."
"I FELL FOR HALF AN AGE."
"I FELL SCREAMING UNTIL I COULDN'T MAKE ANOTHER SOUND, UNTIL ALL I HAD BEEN, HAD, AND LOST IN MY PUNY LIFE WAS STRIPPED AWAY, UNTIL I ASKED 'WHAT WAS THE POINT OF IT ALL?'"
"LIFE, A CARROT ON A STICK, TEMPTING PROMISES OF LOVE AND LEGACY. A LIE. MEANT ONLY TO GIVE HORROR PURCHASE IN AN EPHEMERAL WORLD."
"THIS TRUTH HAD FREED ME. FREED ME FROM LIFE'S PETTY, TRIVIAL DESIRES. IF I WANTED ANYTHING, NOW IT WAS THE CHANCE TO SHARE WHAT I'D DISCOVERED: TRUE FREEDOM AND PEACE FOR ALL."

"THEN... MY DESCENT HALTED."

UHN!

"HANGING THERE IN THE DARKNESS, I FELT A PRESENCE."

"IT WAS THE ENTITY THAT HAD SUSTAINED ME THROUGHOUT MY LONG DROP."

"IT WAS THE ESSENCE OF MY NEW TRUTH. 'IT IS NOT TOO LATE,' EMPTINESS SAID. 'WE CAN STILL BRING TRUE *PEACE* TO ALL CREATION... TOGETHER.'"

"IT OFFERED ITS HAND TO ME..."

"...AND I TOOK IT."

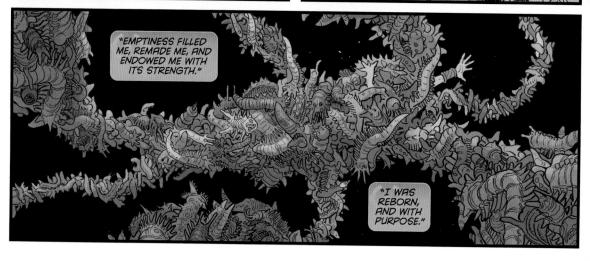

"EMPTINESS FILLED ME, REMADE ME, AND ENDOWED ME WITH ITS STRENGTH."

"I WAS REBORN, AND WITH PURPOSE."

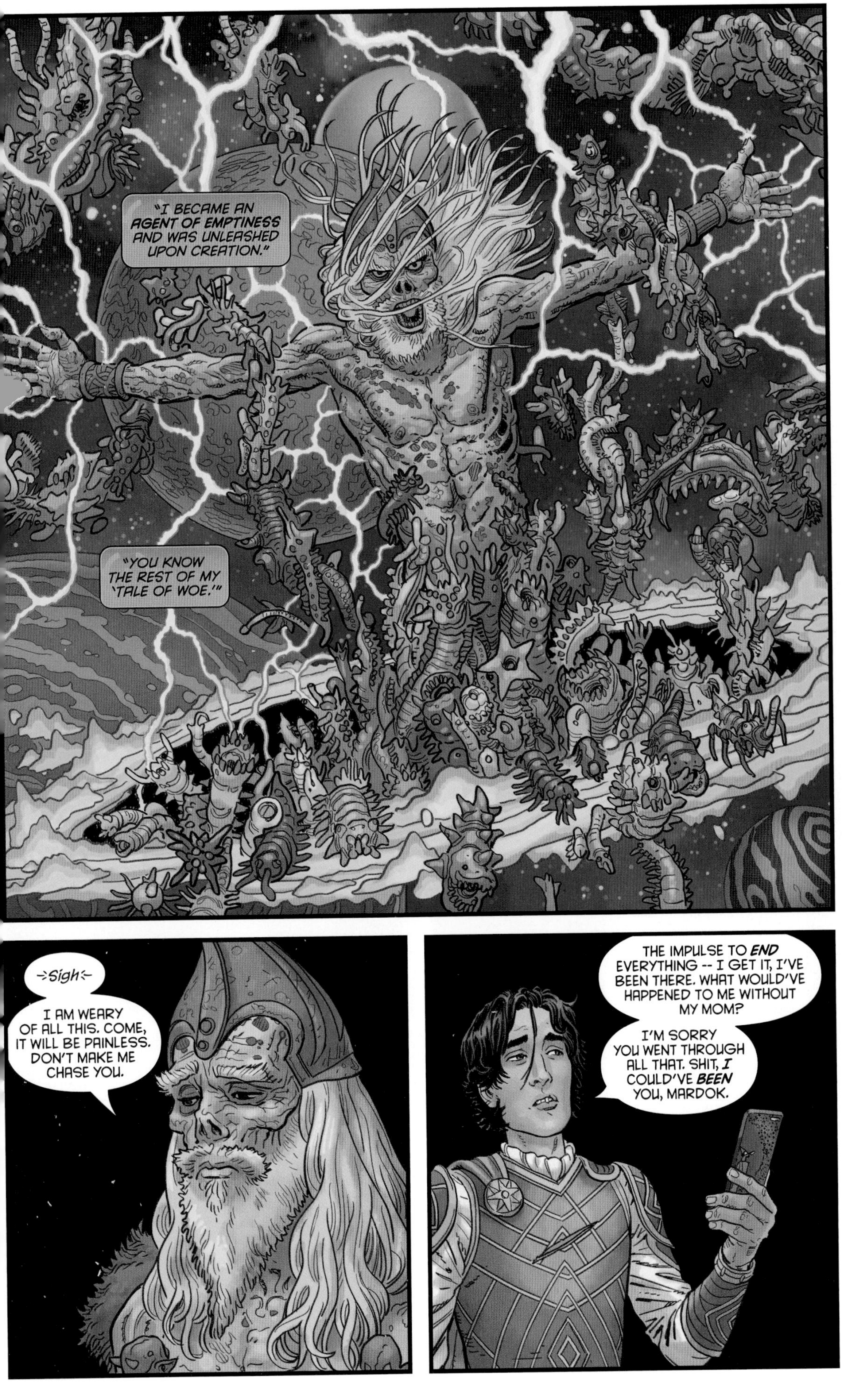
"I BECAME AN AGENT OF EMPTINESS AND WAS UNLEASHED UPON CREATION."
"YOU KNOW THE REST OF MY 'TALE OF WOE.'"
-SIGH-
I AM WEARY OF ALL THIS. COME, IT WILL BE PAINLESS. DON'T MAKE ME CHASE YOU.
THE IMPULSE TO END EVERYTHING -- I GET IT, I'VE BEEN THERE. WHAT WOULD'VE HAPPENED TO ME WITHOUT MY MOM?
I'M SORRY YOU WENT THROUGH ALL THAT. SHIT, I COULD'VE BEEN YOU, MARDOK.

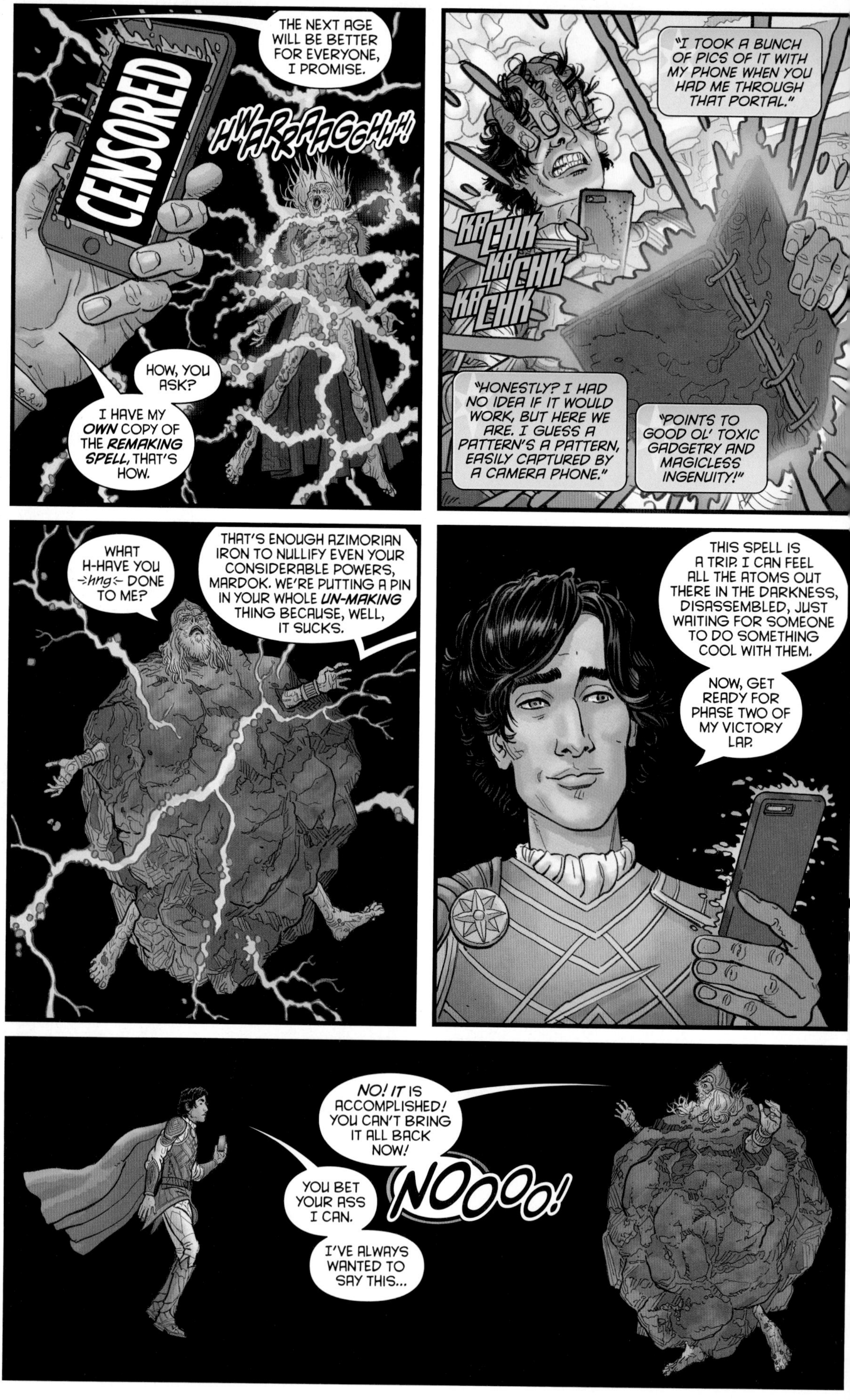

THE NEXT AGE WILL BE BETTER FOR EVERYONE, I PROMISE.
CENSORED
HWARRAAGGHH!
HOW, YOU ASK?
I HAVE MY OWN COPY OF THE REMAKING SPELL, THAT'S HOW.
"I TOOK A BUNCH OF PICS OF IT WITH MY PHONE WHEN YOU HAD ME THROUGH THAT PORTAL."
KACHK KACHK KACHK
"HONESTLY? I HAD NO IDEA IF IT WOULD WORK, BUT HERE WE ARE. I GUESS A PATTERN'S A PATTERN, EASILY CAPTURED BY A CAMERA PHONE."
"POINTS TO GOOD OL' TOXIC GADGETRY AND MAGICLESS INGENUITY!"
WHAT H-HAVE YOU -hng- DONE TO ME?
THAT'S ENOUGH AZIMORIAN IRON TO NULLIFY EVEN YOUR CONSIDERABLE POWERS, MARDOK. WE'RE PUTTING A PIN IN YOUR WHOLE UN-MAKING THING BECAUSE, WELL, IT SUCKS.
THIS SPELL IS A TRIP. I CAN FEEL ALL THE ATOMS OUT THERE IN THE DARKNESS, DISASSEMBLED, JUST WAITING FOR SOMEONE TO DO SOMETHING COOL WITH THEM.
NOW, GET READY FOR PHASE TWO OF MY VICTORY LAP.
NO! IT IS ACCOMPLISHED! YOU CAN'T BRING IT ALL BACK NOW!
NOOOOO!
YOU BET YOUR ASS I CAN.
I'VE ALWAYS WANTED TO SAY THIS...

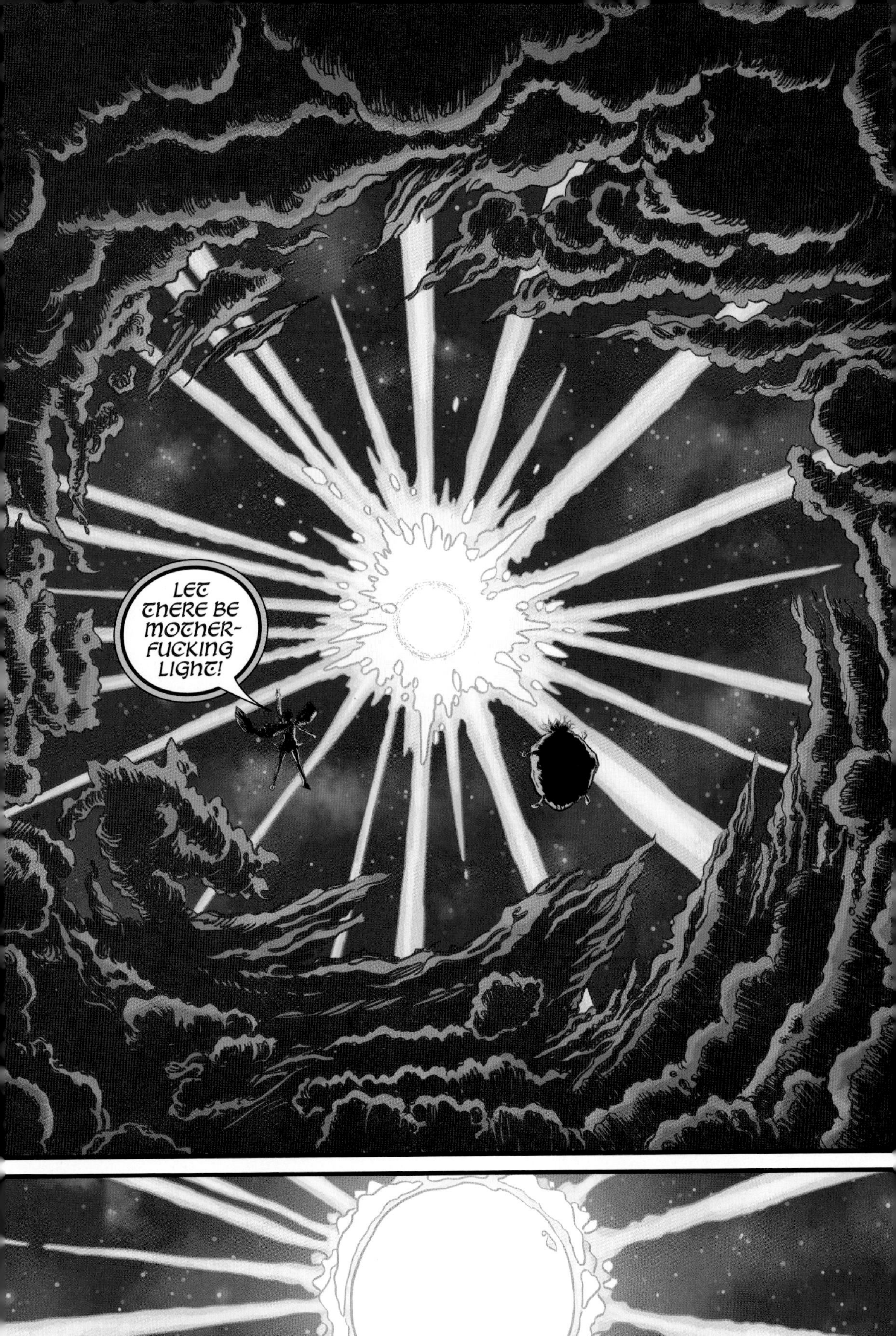
LET THERE BE MOTHER-FUCKING LIGHT!

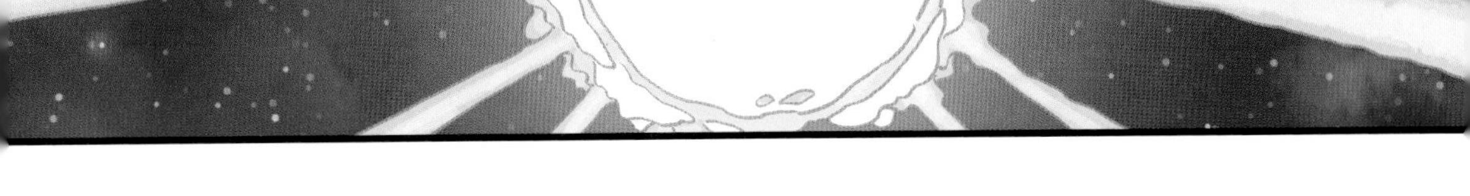

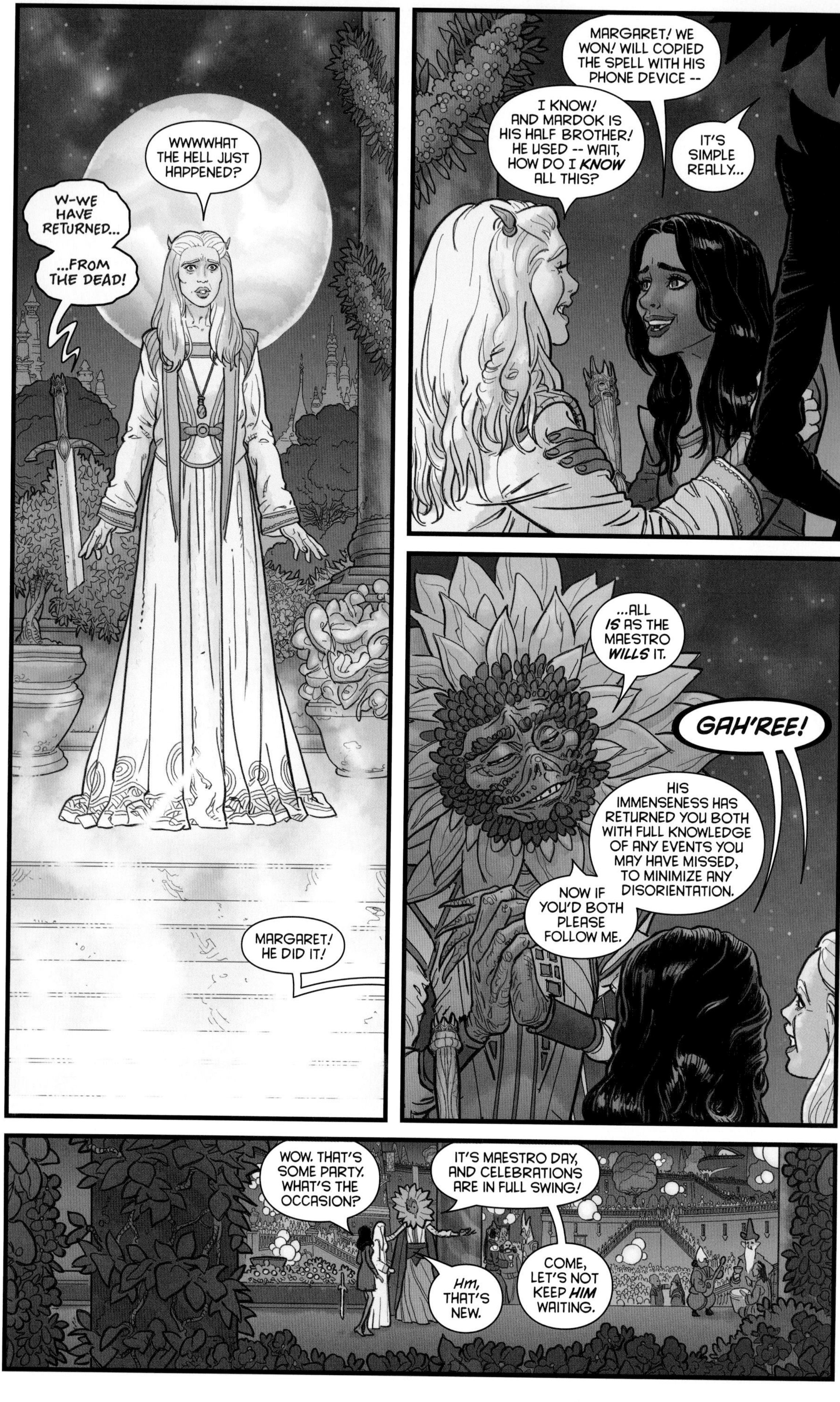
WWWWHAT THE HELL JUST HAPPENED?
W-WE HAVE RETURNED...
...FROM THE DEAD!
MARGARET! HE DID IT!
MARGARET! WE WON! WILL COPIED THE SPELL WITH HIS PHONE DEVICE --
I KNOW! AND MARDOK IS HIS HALF BROTHER! HE USED -- WAIT, HOW DO I KNOW ALL THIS?
IT'S SIMPLE REALLY...
...ALL IS AS THE MAESTRO WILLS IT.
GAH'REE!
HIS IMMENSENESS HAS RETURNED YOU BOTH WITH FULL KNOWLEDGE OF ANY EVENTS YOU MAY HAVE MISSED, TO MINIMIZE ANY DISORIENTATION.
NOW IF YOU'D BOTH PLEASE FOLLOW ME.
WOW. THAT'S SOME PARTY. WHAT'S THE OCCASION?
IT'S MAESTRO DAY, AND CELEBRATIONS ARE IN FULL SWING!
Hm, THAT'S NEW.
COME, LET'S NOT KEEP HIM WAITING.

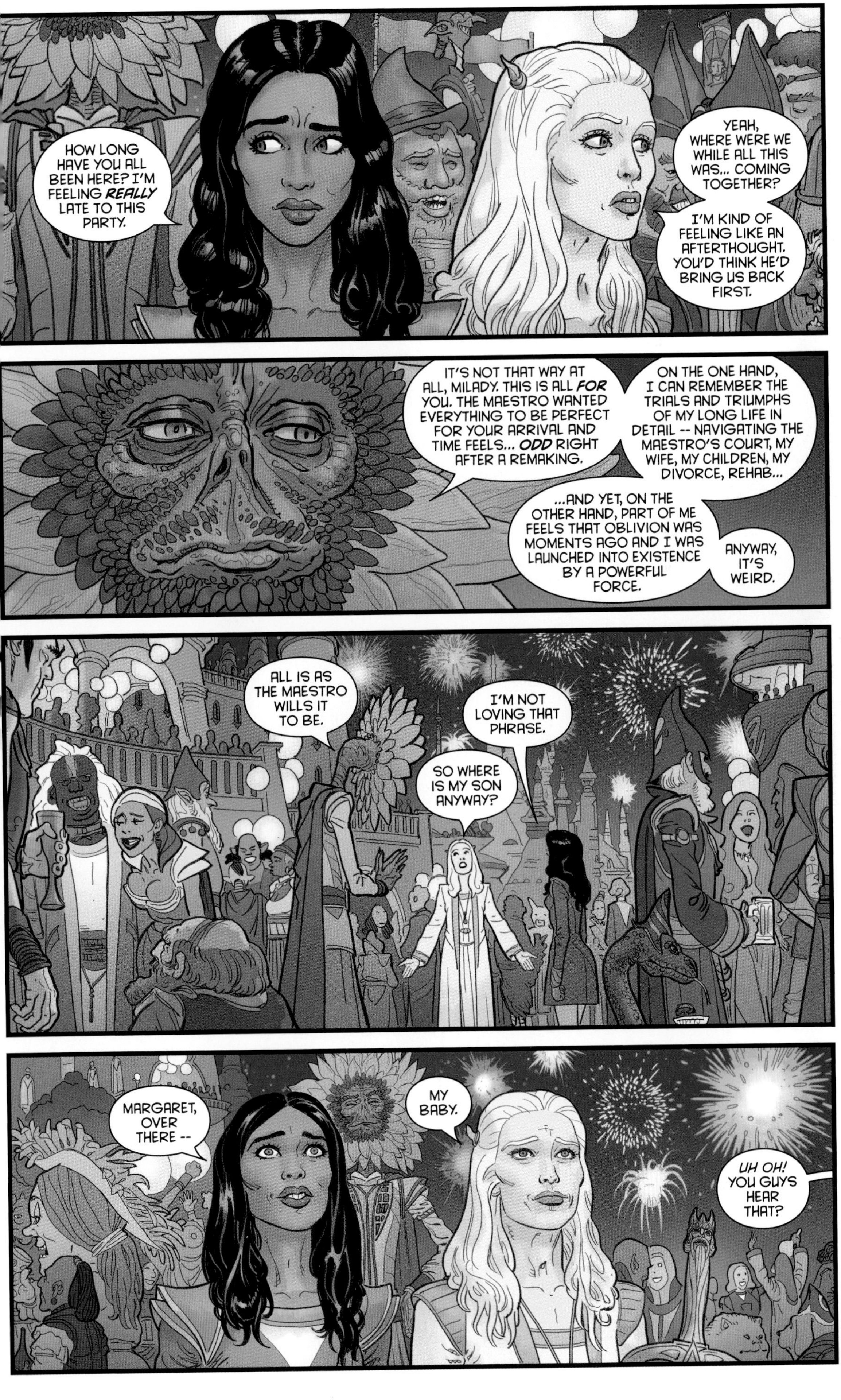
HOW LONG HAVE YOU ALL BEEN HERE? I'M FEELING *REALLY* LATE TO THIS PARTY.
YEAH, WHERE WERE WE WHILE ALL THIS WAS... COMING TOGETHER?
I'M KIND OF FEELING LIKE AN AFTERTHOUGHT. YOU'D THINK HE'D BRING US BACK FIRST.
IT'S NOT THAT WAY AT ALL, MILADY. THIS IS ALL *FOR* YOU. THE MAESTRO WANTED EVERYTHING TO BE PERFECT FOR YOUR ARRIVAL AND TIME FEELS... *ODD* RIGHT AFTER A REMAKING.
ON THE ONE HAND, I CAN REMEMBER THE TRIALS AND TRIUMPHS OF MY LONG LIFE IN DETAIL -- NAVIGATING THE MAESTRO'S COURT, MY WIFE, MY CHILDREN, MY DIVORCE, REHAB...
...AND YET, ON THE OTHER HAND, PART OF ME FEELS THAT OBLIVION WAS MOMENTS AGO AND I WAS LAUNCHED INTO EXISTENCE BY A POWERFUL FORCE.
ANYWAY, IT'S WEIRD.
ALL IS AS THE MAESTRO WILLS IT TO BE.
I'M NOT LOVING THAT PHRASE.
SO WHERE IS MY SON ANYWAY?
MARGARET, OVER THERE --
MY BABY.
UH OH! YOU GUYS HEAR THAT?

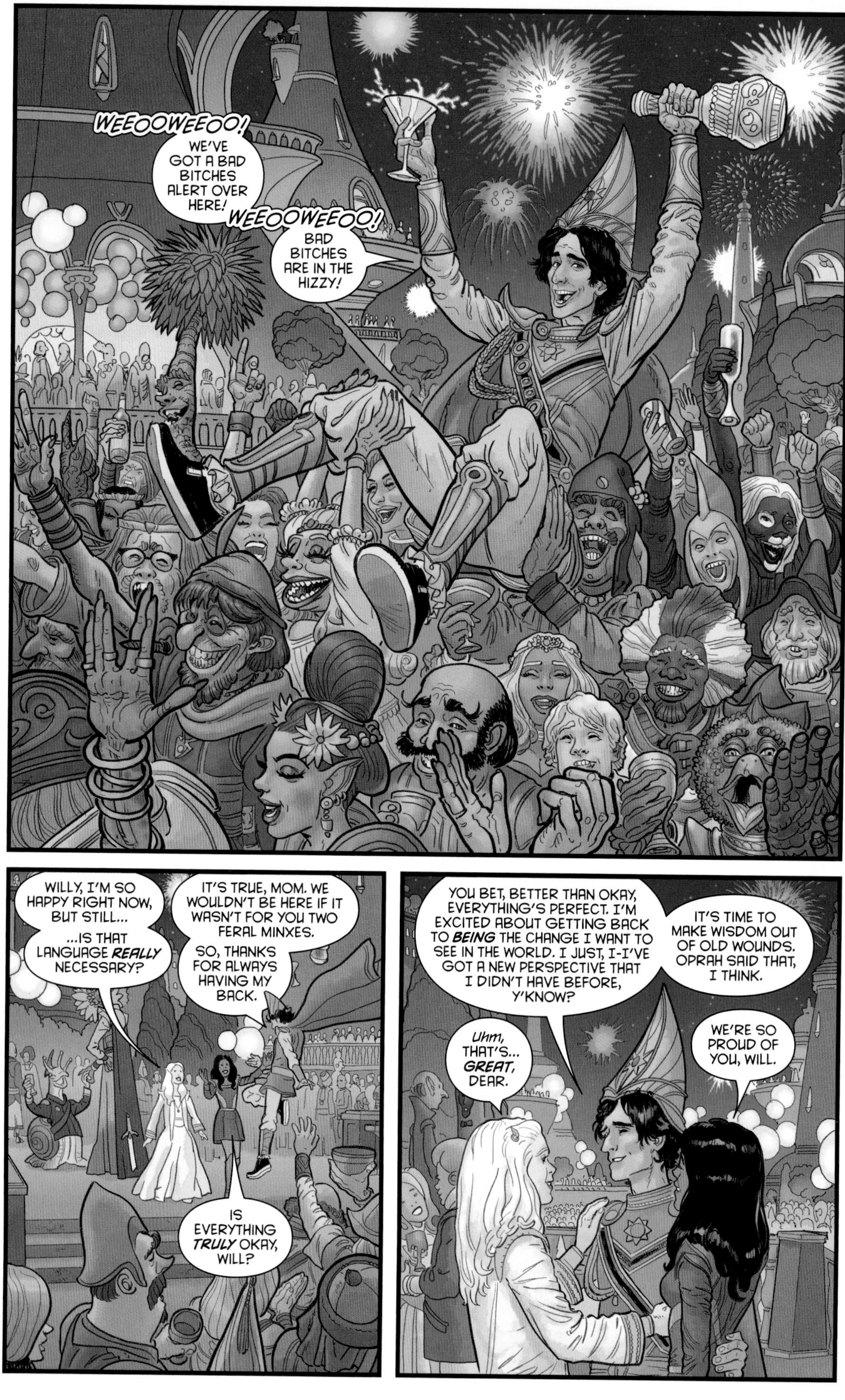
WEEOOWEEOO!
WE'VE GOT A BAD BITCHES ALERT OVER HERE!
WEEOOWEEOO!
BAD BITCHES ARE IN THE HIZZY!
WILLY, I'M SO HAPPY RIGHT NOW, BUT STILL...
...IS THAT LANGUAGE *REALLY* NECESSARY?
IT'S TRUE, MOM. WE WOULDN'T BE HERE IF IT WASN'T FOR YOU TWO FERAL MINXES.
SO, THANKS FOR ALWAYS HAVING MY BACK.
IS EVERYTHING *TRULY* OKAY, WILL?
YOU BET, BETTER THAN OKAY, EVERYTHING'S PERFECT. I'M EXCITED ABOUT GETTING BACK TO *BEING* THE CHANGE I WANT TO SEE IN THE WORLD. I JUST, I-I'VE GOT A NEW PERSPECTIVE THAT I DIDN'T HAVE BEFORE, Y'KNOW?
IT'S TIME TO MAKE WISDOM OUT OF OLD WOUNDS. OPRAH SAID THAT, I THINK.
*Uhm, THAT'S... **GREAT**, DEAR.*
WE'RE SO PROUD OF YOU, WILL.

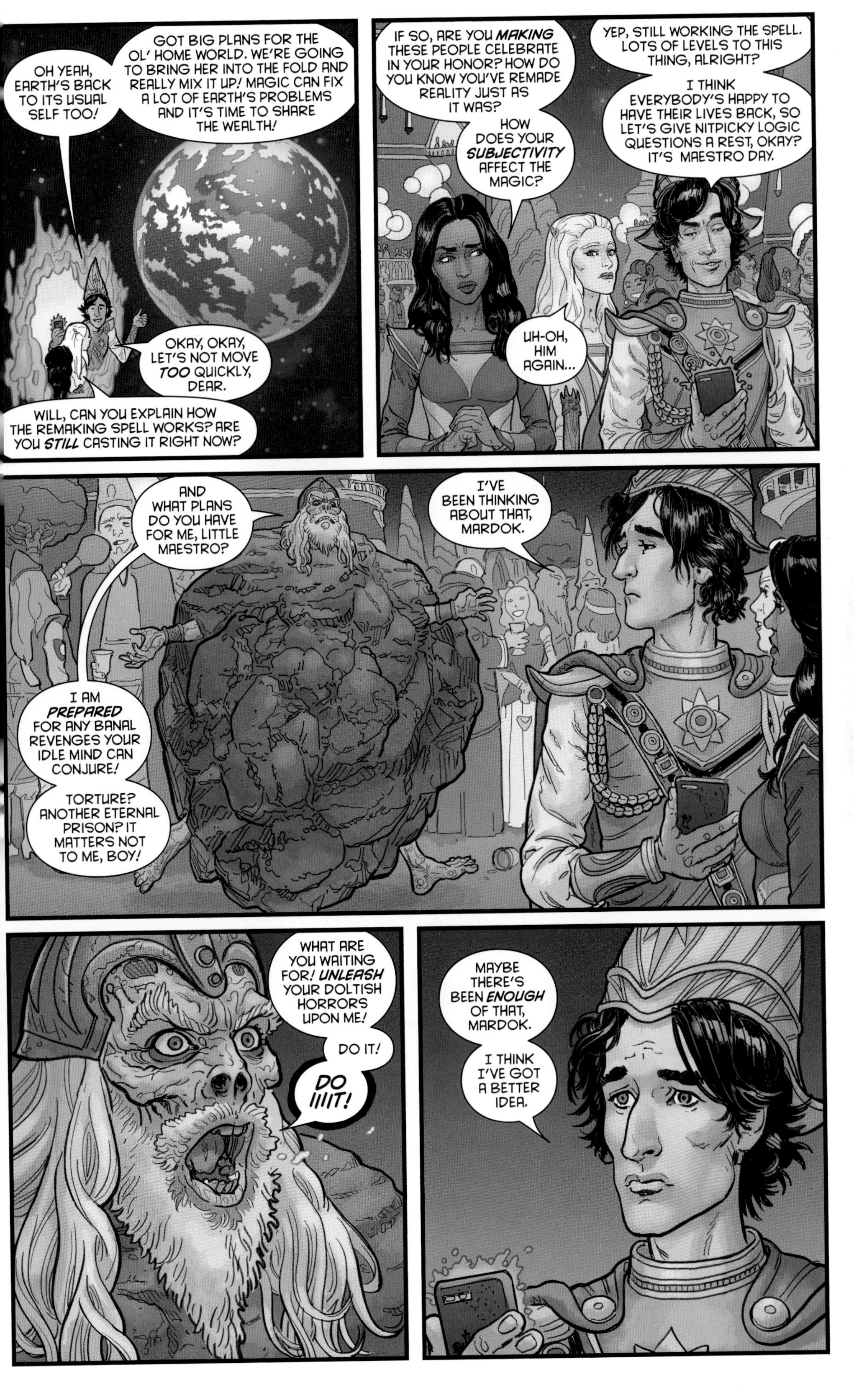
OH YEAH, EARTH'S BACK TO ITS USUAL SELF TOO!
GOT BIG PLANS FOR THE OL' HOME WORLD. WE'RE GOING TO BRING HER INTO THE FOLD AND REALLY MIX IT UP! MAGIC CAN FIX A LOT OF EARTH'S PROBLEMS AND IT'S TIME TO SHARE THE WEALTH!
OKAY, OKAY, LET'S NOT MOVE *TOO* QUICKLY, DEAR.
WILL, CAN YOU EXPLAIN HOW THE REMAKING SPELL WORKS? ARE YOU *STILL* CASTING IT RIGHT NOW?
IF SO, ARE YOU *MAKING* THESE PEOPLE CELEBRATE IN YOUR HONOR? HOW DO YOU KNOW YOU'VE REMADE REALITY JUST AS IT WAS?
HOW DOES YOUR *SUBJECTIVITY* AFFECT THE MAGIC?
YEP, STILL WORKING THE SPELL. LOTS OF LEVELS TO THIS THING, ALRIGHT?
I THINK EVERYBODY'S HAPPY TO HAVE THEIR LIVES BACK, SO LET'S GIVE NITPICKY LOGIC QUESTIONS A REST, OKAY? IT'S MAESTRO DAY.
UH-OH, HIM AGAIN...
AND WHAT PLANS DO YOU HAVE FOR ME, LITTLE MAESTRO?
I AM *PREPARED* FOR ANY BANAL REVENGES YOUR IDLE MIND CAN CONJURE!
TORTURE? ANOTHER ETERNAL PRISON? IT MATTERS NOT TO ME, BOY!
I'VE BEEN THINKING ABOUT THAT, MARDOK.
WHAT ARE YOU WAITING FOR! *UNLEASH* YOUR DOLTISH HORRORS UPON ME!
DO IT!
DO IIIIT!
MAYBE THERE'S BEEN *ENOUGH* OF THAT, MARDOK.
I THINK I'VE GOT A BETTER IDEA.

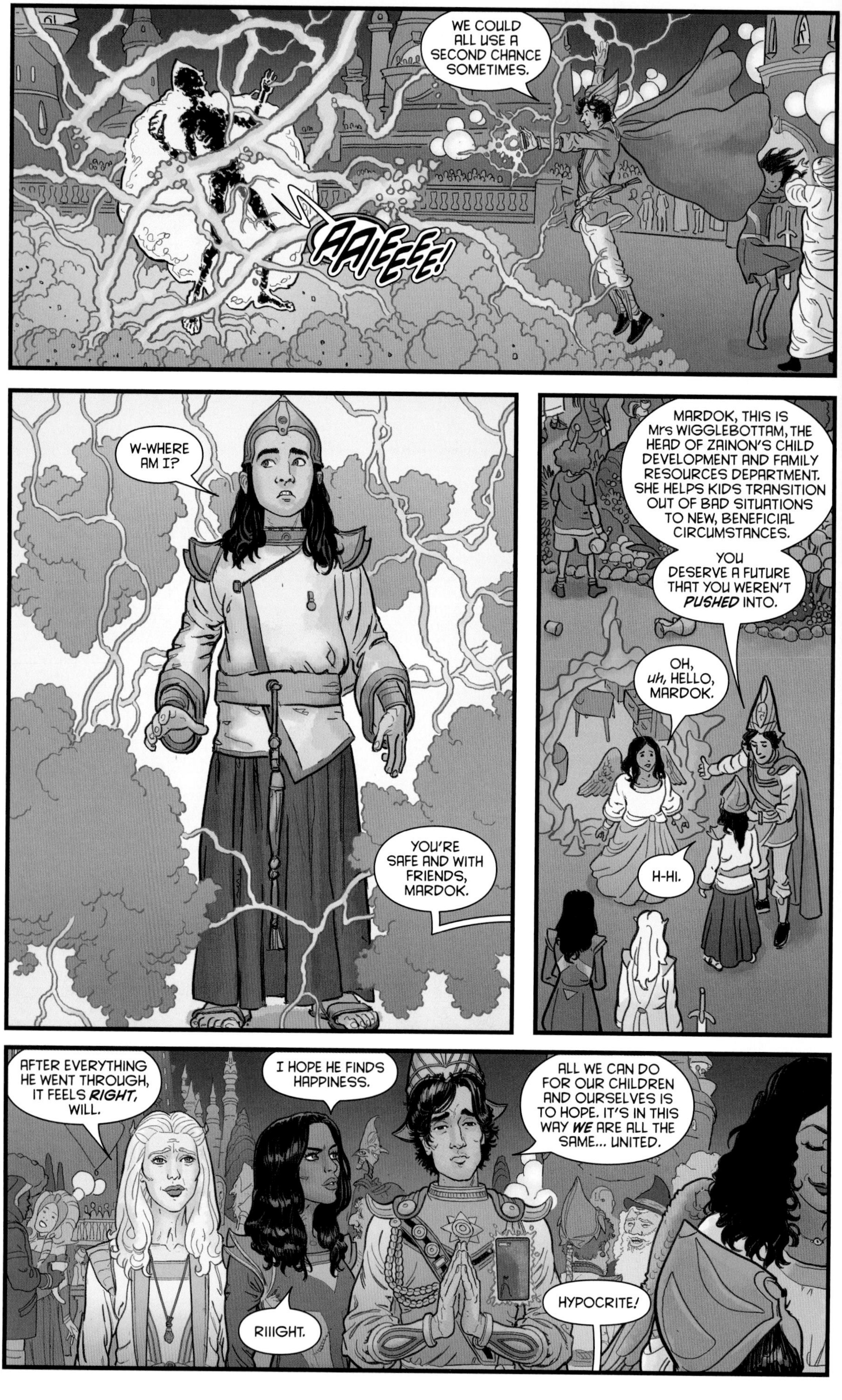
WE COULD ALL USE A SECOND CHANCE SOMETIMES.
AAIEEEE!
W-WHERE AM I?
YOU'RE SAFE AND WITH FRIENDS, MARDOK.
MARDOK, THIS IS Mrs WIGGLEBOTTAM, THE HEAD OF ZAINON'S CHILD DEVELOPMENT AND FAMILY RESOURCES DEPARTMENT. SHE HELPS KIDS TRANSITION OUT OF BAD SITUATIONS TO NEW, BENEFICIAL CIRCUMSTANCES.
YOU DESERVE A FUTURE THAT YOU WEREN'T *PUSHED* INTO.
OH, *uh,* HELLO, MARDOK.
H-HI.
AFTER EVERYTHING HE WENT THROUGH, IT FEELS *RIGHT,* WILL.
I HOPE HE FINDS HAPPINESS.
ALL WE CAN DO FOR OUR CHILDREN AND OURSELVES IS TO HOPE. IT'S IN THIS WAY *WE* ARE ALL THE SAME... UNITED.
RIIIGHT.
HYPOCRITE!

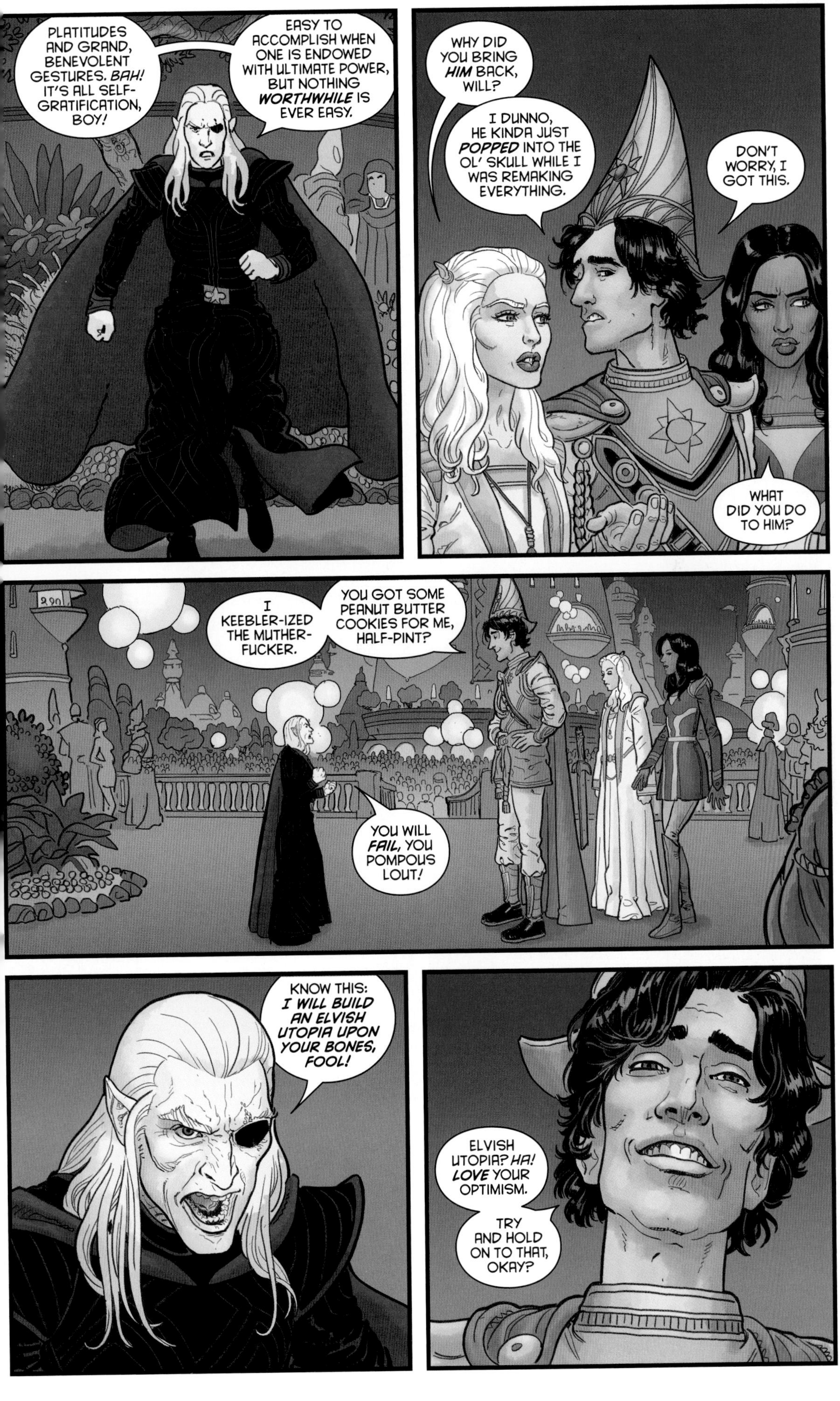

PLATITUDES AND GRAND, BENEVOLENT GESTURES. *BAH!* IT'S ALL SELF-GRATIFICATION, BOY!
EASY TO ACCOMPLISH WHEN ONE IS ENDOWED WITH ULTIMATE POWER, BUT NOTHING ***WORTHWHILE*** IS EVER EASY.
WHY DID YOU BRING ***HIM*** BACK, WILL?
I DUNNO, HE KINDA JUST ***POPPED*** INTO THE OL' SKULL WHILE I WAS REMAKING EVERYTHING.
DON'T WORRY, I GOT THIS.
WHAT DID YOU DO TO HIM?
I KEEBLER-IZED THE MUTHER-FUCKER.
YOU GOT SOME PEANUT BUTTER COOKIES FOR ME, HALF-PINT?
YOU WILL ***FAIL,*** YOU POMPOUS LOUT!
KNOW THIS: ***I WILL BUILD AN ELVISH UTOPIA UPON YOUR BONES, FOOL!***
ELVISH UTOPIA? *HA!* ***LOVE*** YOUR OPTIMISM.
TRY AND HOLD ON TO THAT, OKAY?

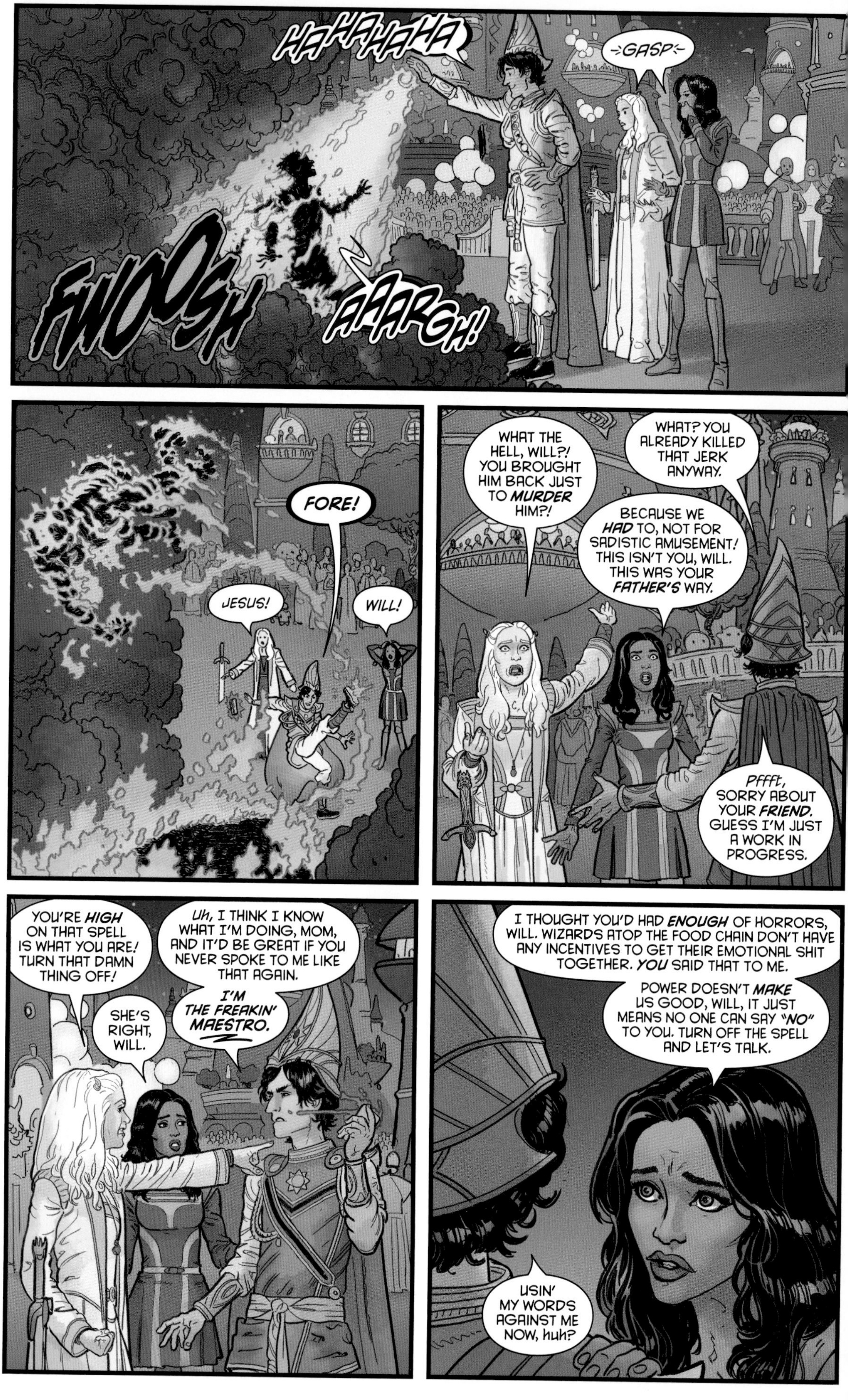
HAHAHAHA
-GASP-
FWOOSH
AAARGH!
FORE!
JESUS!
WILL!
WHAT THE HELL, WILL?! YOU BROUGHT HIM BACK JUST TO MURDER HIM?!
WHAT? YOU ALREADY KILLED THAT JERK ANYWAY.
BECAUSE WE HAD TO, NOT FOR SADISTIC AMUSEMENT! THIS ISN'T YOU, WILL. THIS WAS YOUR FATHER'S WAY.
Pffft, SORRY ABOUT YOUR FRIEND. GUESS I'M JUST A WORK IN PROGRESS.
YOU'RE HIGH ON THAT SPELL IS WHAT YOU ARE! TURN THAT DAMN THING OFF!
SHE'S RIGHT, WILL.
Uh, I THINK I KNOW WHAT I'M DOING, MOM, AND IT'D BE GREAT IF YOU NEVER SPOKE TO ME LIKE THAT AGAIN.
I'M THE FREAKIN' MAESTRO.
I THOUGHT YOU'D HAD ENOUGH OF HORRORS, WILL. WIZARDS ATOP THE FOOD CHAIN DON'T HAVE ANY INCENTIVES TO GET THEIR EMOTIONAL SHIT TOGETHER. YOU SAID THAT TO ME.
POWER DOESN'T MAKE US GOOD, WILL, IT JUST MEANS NO ONE CAN SAY "NO" TO YOU. TURN OFF THE SPELL AND LET'S TALK.
USIN' MY WORDS AGAINST ME NOW, huh?

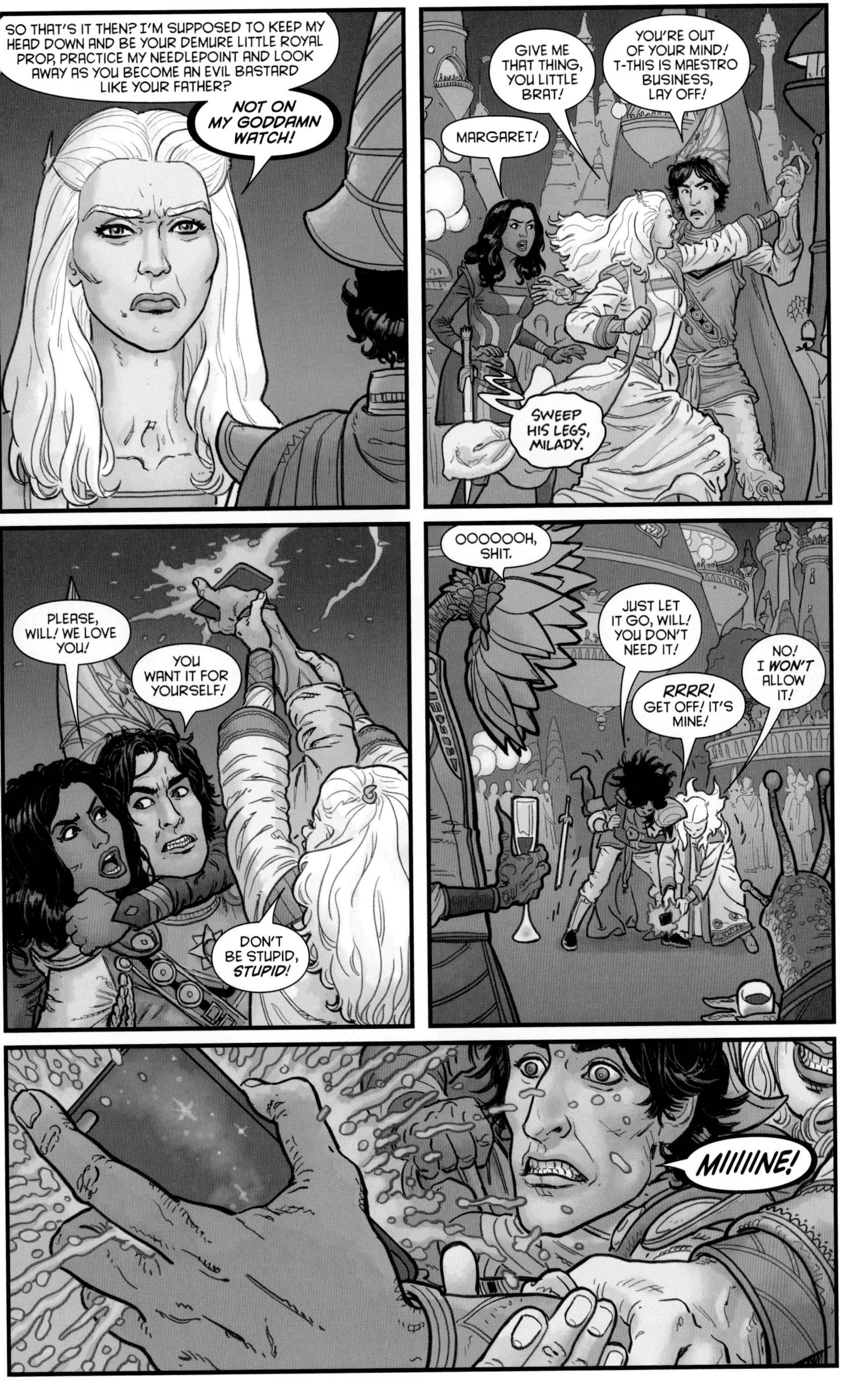
SO THAT'S IT THEN? I'M SUPPOSED TO KEEP MY HEAD DOWN AND BE YOUR DEMURE LITTLE ROYAL PROP, PRACTICE MY NEEDLEPOINT AND LOOK AWAY AS YOU BECOME AN EVIL BASTARD LIKE YOUR FATHER?
NOT ON MY GODDAMN WATCH!
GIVE ME THAT THING, YOU LITTLE BRAT!
YOU'RE OUT OF YOUR MIND! T-THIS IS MAESTRO BUSINESS, LAY OFF!
MARGARET!
SWEEP HIS LEGS, MILADY.
PLEASE, WILL! WE LOVE YOU!
YOU WANT IT FOR YOURSELF!
DON'T BE STUPID, STUPID!
OOOOOOH, SHIT.
JUST LET IT GO, WILL! YOU DON'T NEED IT!
RRRR! GET OFF! IT'S MINE!
NO! I WON'T ALLOW IT!
MIIIIINE!

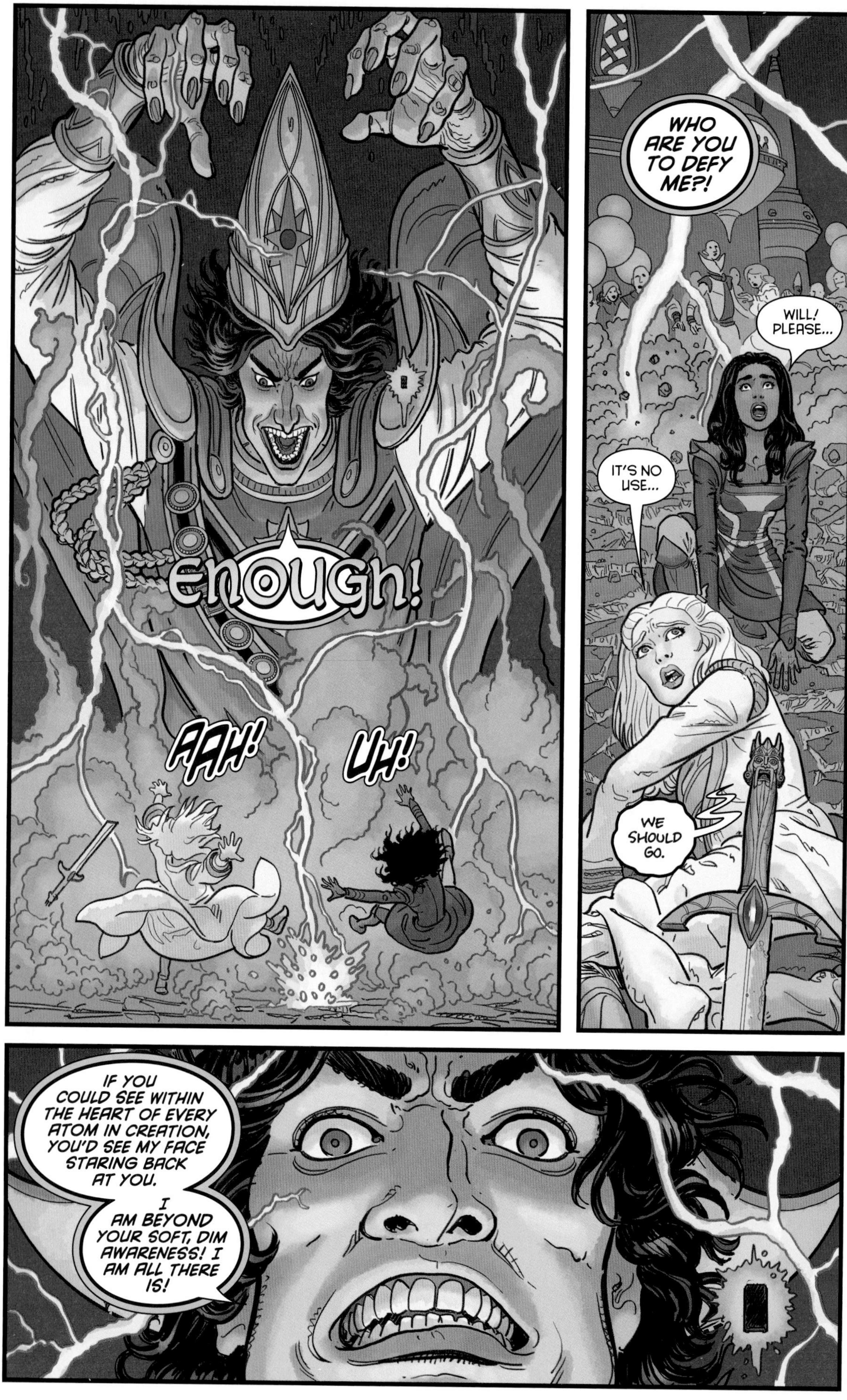
ENOUGH!
AAH!
UH!
WHO ARE YOU TO DEFY ME?!
WILL! PLEASE...
IT'S NO USE...
WE SHOULD GO.
IF YOU COULD SEE WITHIN THE HEART OF EVERY ATOM IN CREATION, YOU'D SEE MY FACE STARING BACK AT YOU.
I AM BEYOND YOUR SOFT, DIM AWARENESS! I AM ALL THERE IS!

NO, NO, NO. *PLEASE.* NOT LIKE THIS.

I DON'T KNOW WHAT TO DO...

REMAKING IT ALL AS IT WAS, WAS A MISTAKE! I CANNOT IGNORE ITS FLAWS ANY LONGER.

A NEW REMAKING IS IN ORDER. ONE OF TRUE VISION!

NOOOo! AAAHH!!

RRRUMMMBBBLLE

PZZT

HUH?

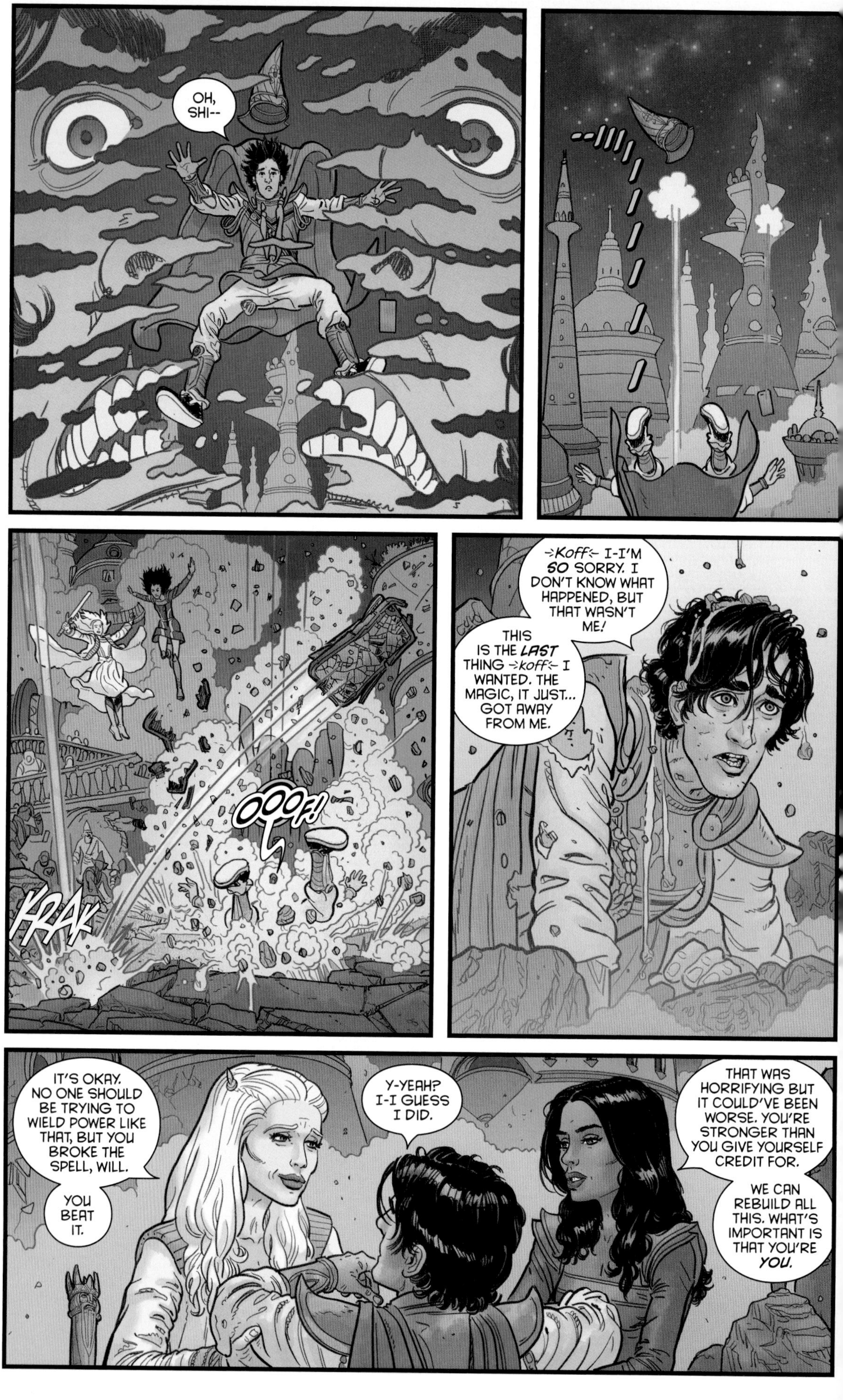
OH, SHI--
--!!!!!!!!!
OOOF!
KRAK
⇒Koff⇐ I-I'M SO SORRY. I DON'T KNOW WHAT HAPPENED, BUT THAT WASN'T ME!
THIS IS THE LAST THING ⇒koff⇐ I WANTED. THE MAGIC, IT JUST... GOT AWAY FROM ME.
IT'S OKAY. NO ONE SHOULD BE TRYING TO WIELD POWER LIKE THAT, BUT YOU BROKE THE SPELL, WILL.
YOU BEAT IT.
Y-YEAH? I-I GUESS I DID.
THAT WAS HORRIFYING BUT IT COULD'VE BEEN WORSE. YOU'RE STRONGER THAN YOU GIVE YOURSELF CREDIT FOR.
WE CAN REBUILD ALL THIS. WHAT'S IMPORTANT IS THAT YOU'RE YOU.

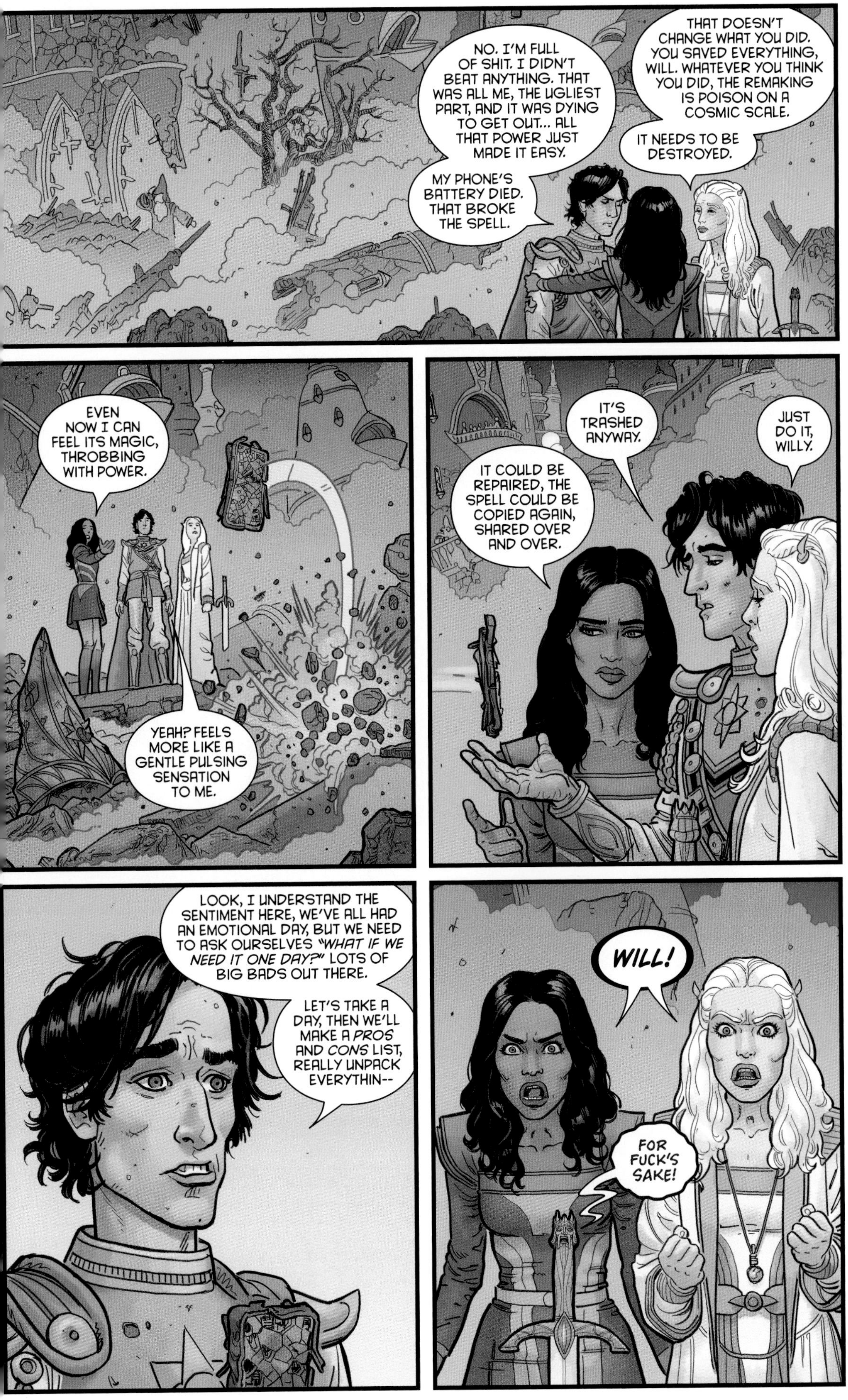
NO. I'M FULL OF SHIT. I DIDN'T BEAT ANYTHING. THAT WAS ALL ME, THE UGLIEST PART, AND IT WAS DYING TO GET OUT... ALL THAT POWER JUST MADE IT EASY.
MY PHONE'S BATTERY DIED. THAT BROKE THE SPELL.
THAT DOESN'T CHANGE WHAT YOU DID. YOU SAVED EVERYTHING, WILL. WHATEVER YOU THINK YOU DID, THE REMAKING IS POISON ON A COSMIC SCALE.
IT NEEDS TO BE DESTROYED.
EVEN NOW I CAN FEEL ITS MAGIC, THROBBING WITH POWER.
YEAH? FEELS MORE LIKE A GENTLE PULSING SENSATION TO ME.
IT'S TRASHED ANYWAY.
IT COULD BE REPAIRED, THE SPELL COULD BE COPIED AGAIN, SHARED OVER AND OVER.
JUST DO IT, WILLY.
LOOK, I UNDERSTAND THE SENTIMENT HERE, WE'VE ALL HAD AN EMOTIONAL DAY, BUT WE NEED TO ASK OURSELVES *"WHAT IF WE NEED IT ONE DAY?"* LOTS OF BIG BADS OUT THERE.
LET'S TAKE A DAY, THEN WE'LL MAKE A *PROS* AND *CONS* LIST, REALLY UNPACK EVERYTHIN--
WILL!
FOR FUCK'S SAKE!

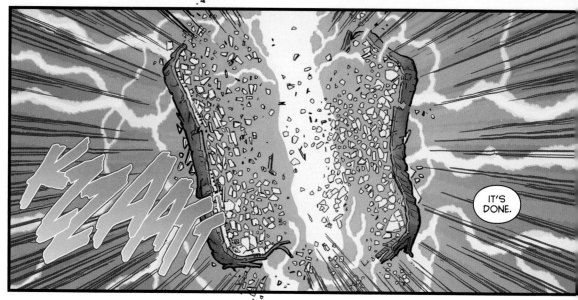

KRRAKT

IT'S DONE.

WE ALL HAVE OUR UGLY PARTS, WILL. THE PART THAT *ACTS* IS WHAT MATTERS.

DON'T REMIND ME.

WIIILL... DON'T BE GRUMPY.

MAESTRO! A MOMENT, PLEASE!

MIRACULOUSLY, THERE WERE NO CASUALTIES.

ALSO, RECONSTRUCTION AND MEDICINAL MAGI RESOURCES ARE ALREADY AT WORK. YOUR... *THE* INCIDENT WILL BE RECOUNTED AS A MAGICAL DISPLAY GONE AWRY.

Phew! DIDN'T WANT TO HAVE TO *BRING* ANYONE BACK.

YOU'RE AMAZING, GARY. TAKE THE REST OF THE WEEK OFF.

IT'S PRONOUNCED *GAH*-- →sigh← THANK YOU, GREAT ONE.

HEY! *CHIOPINO'S?* EIGHT O'CLOCK? TABLE BY THE BIG WINDOW?

THAT SOUNDS AMAZING.

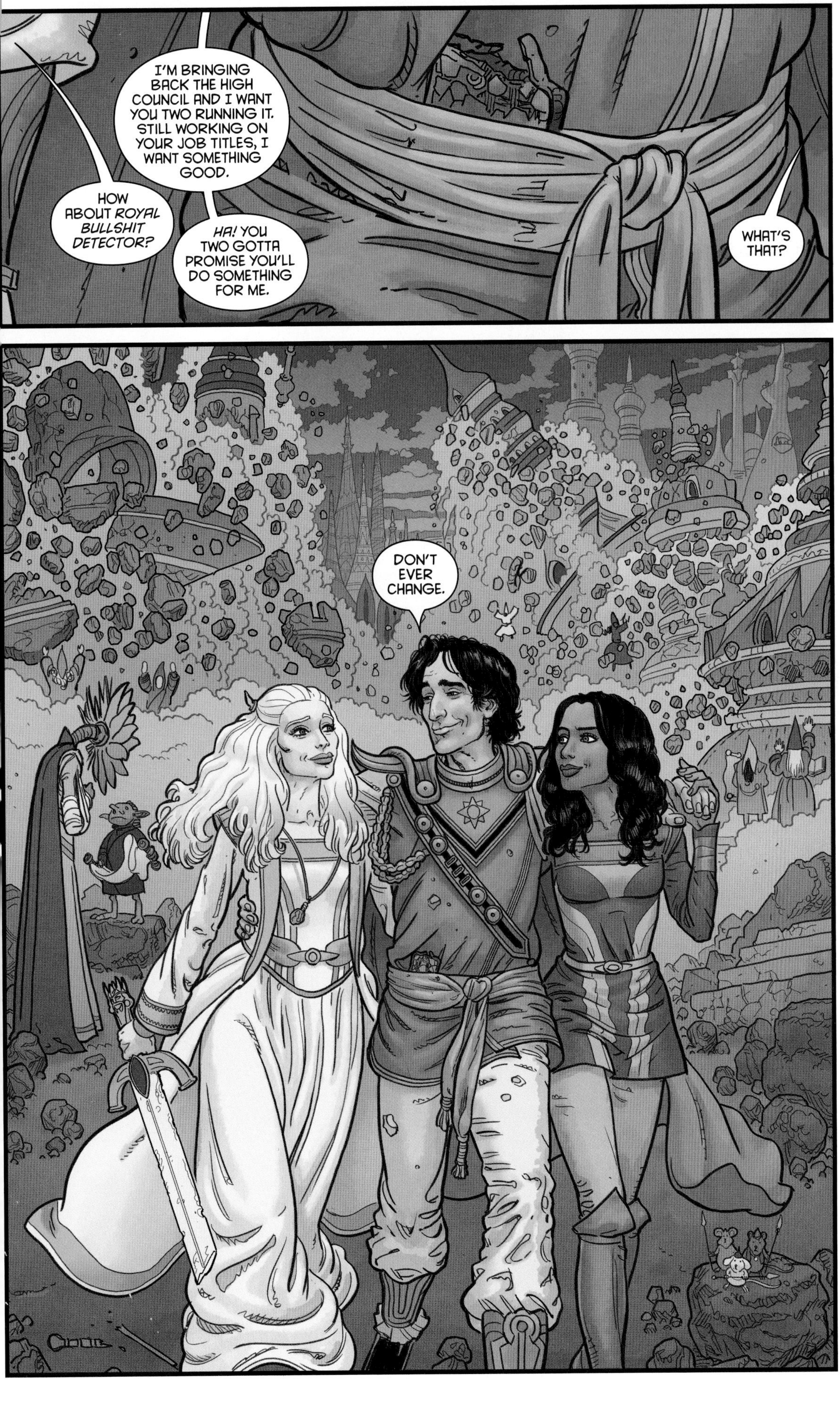
I'M BRINGING BACK THE HIGH COUNCIL AND I WANT YOU TWO RUNNING IT. STILL WORKING ON YOUR JOB TITLES, I WANT SOMETHING GOOD.
HOW ABOUT *ROYAL BULLSHIT DETECTOR?*
HA! YOU TWO GOTTA PROMISE YOU'LL DO SOMETHING FOR ME.
WHAT'S THAT?
DON'T EVER CHANGE.

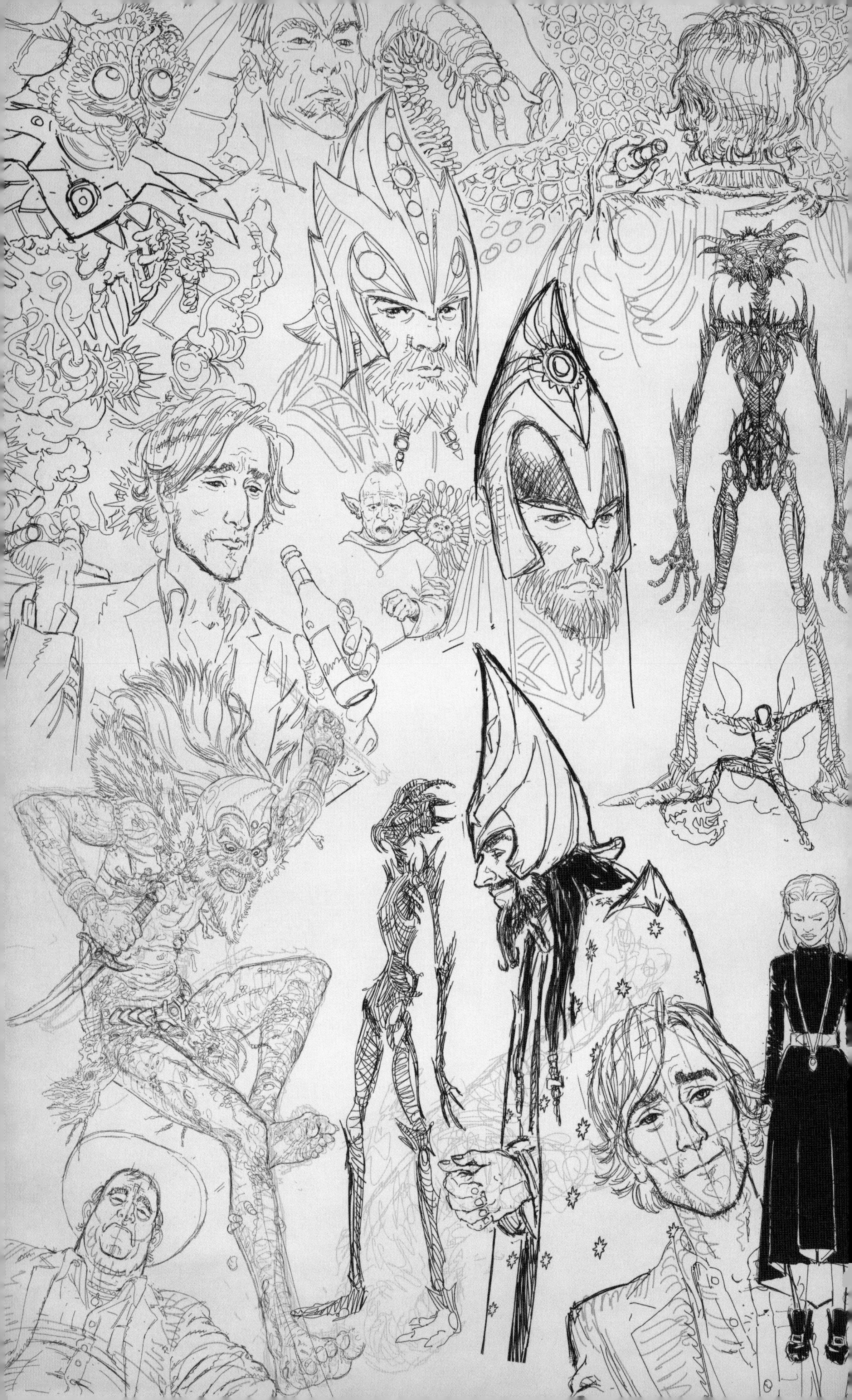

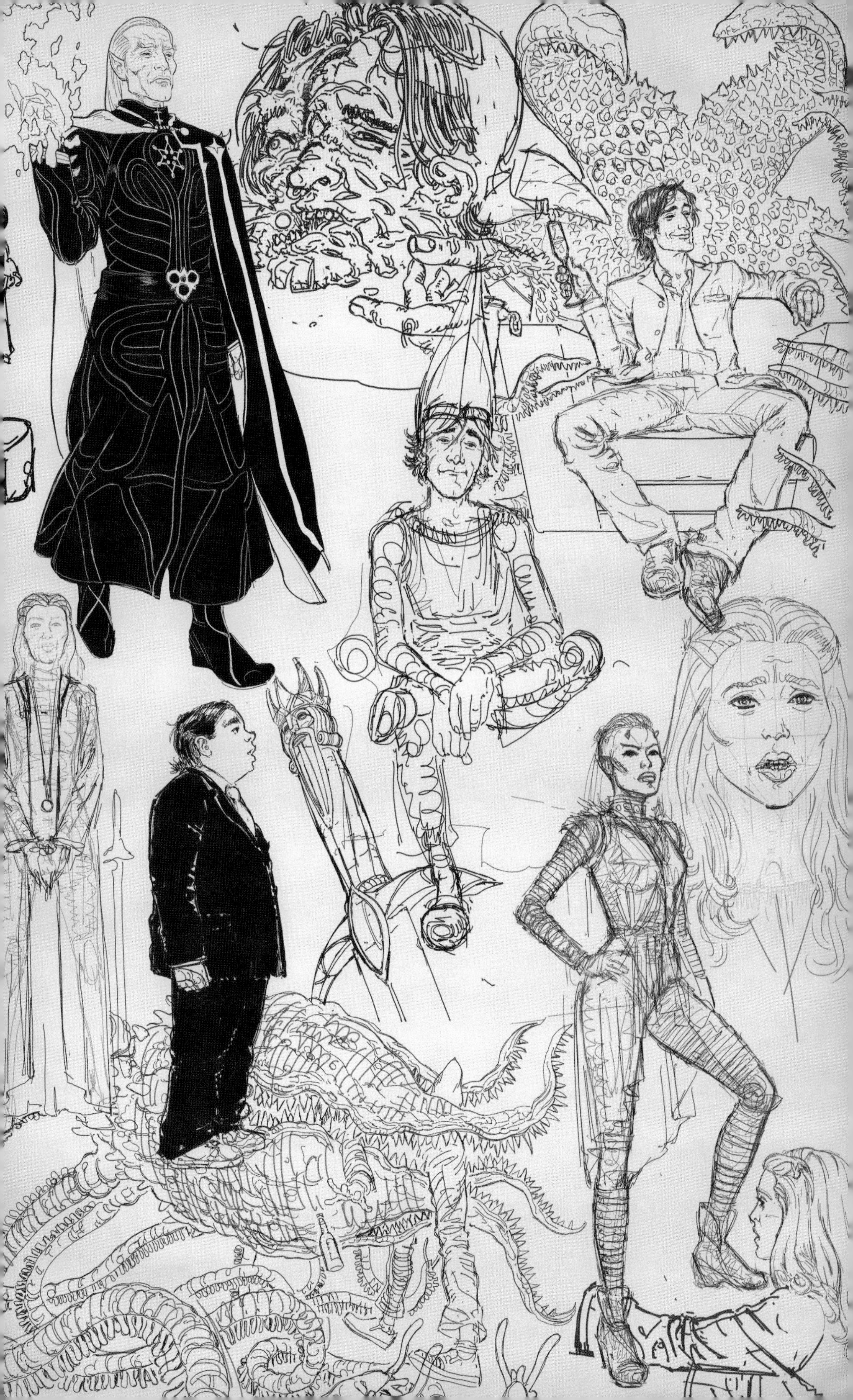

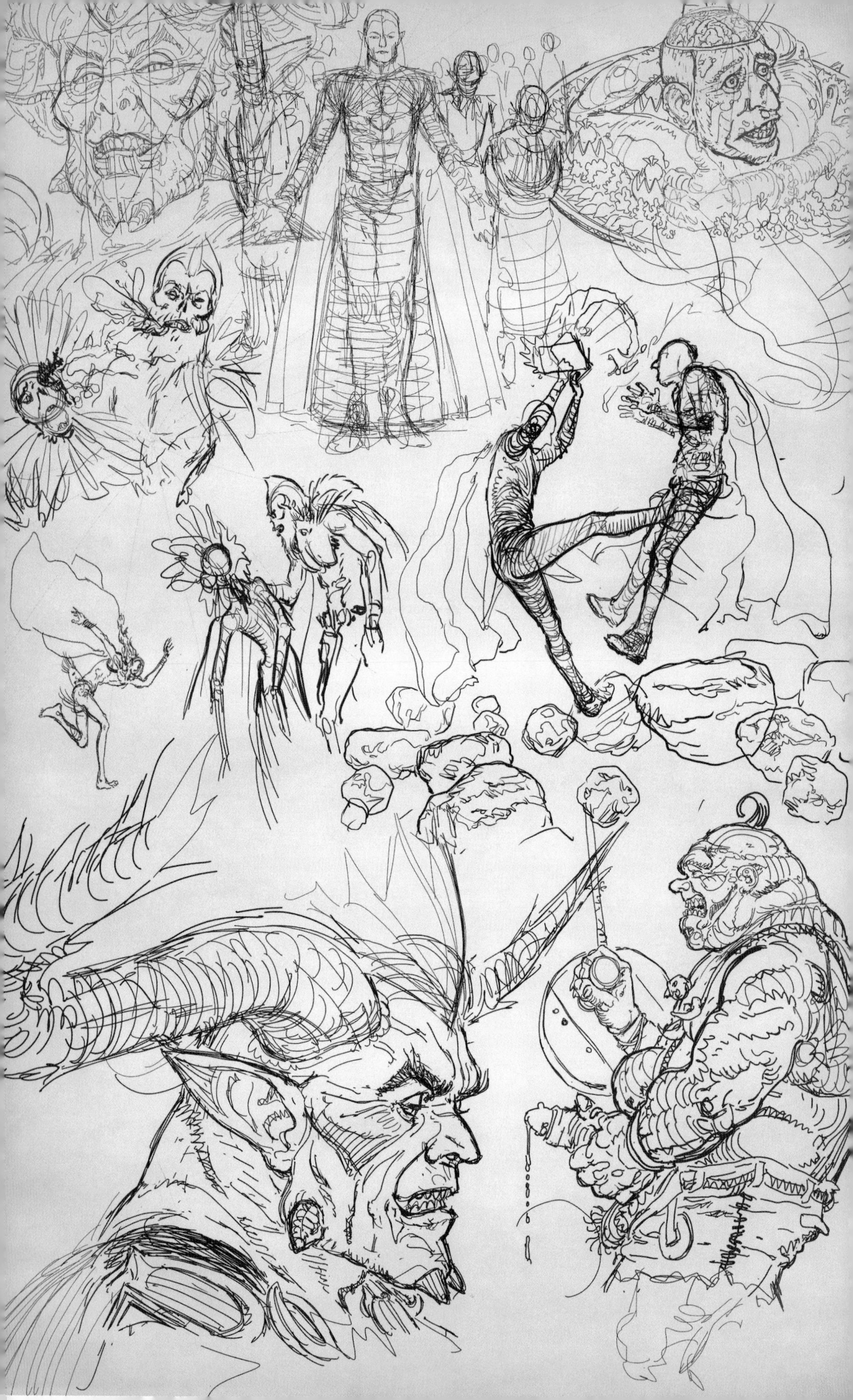

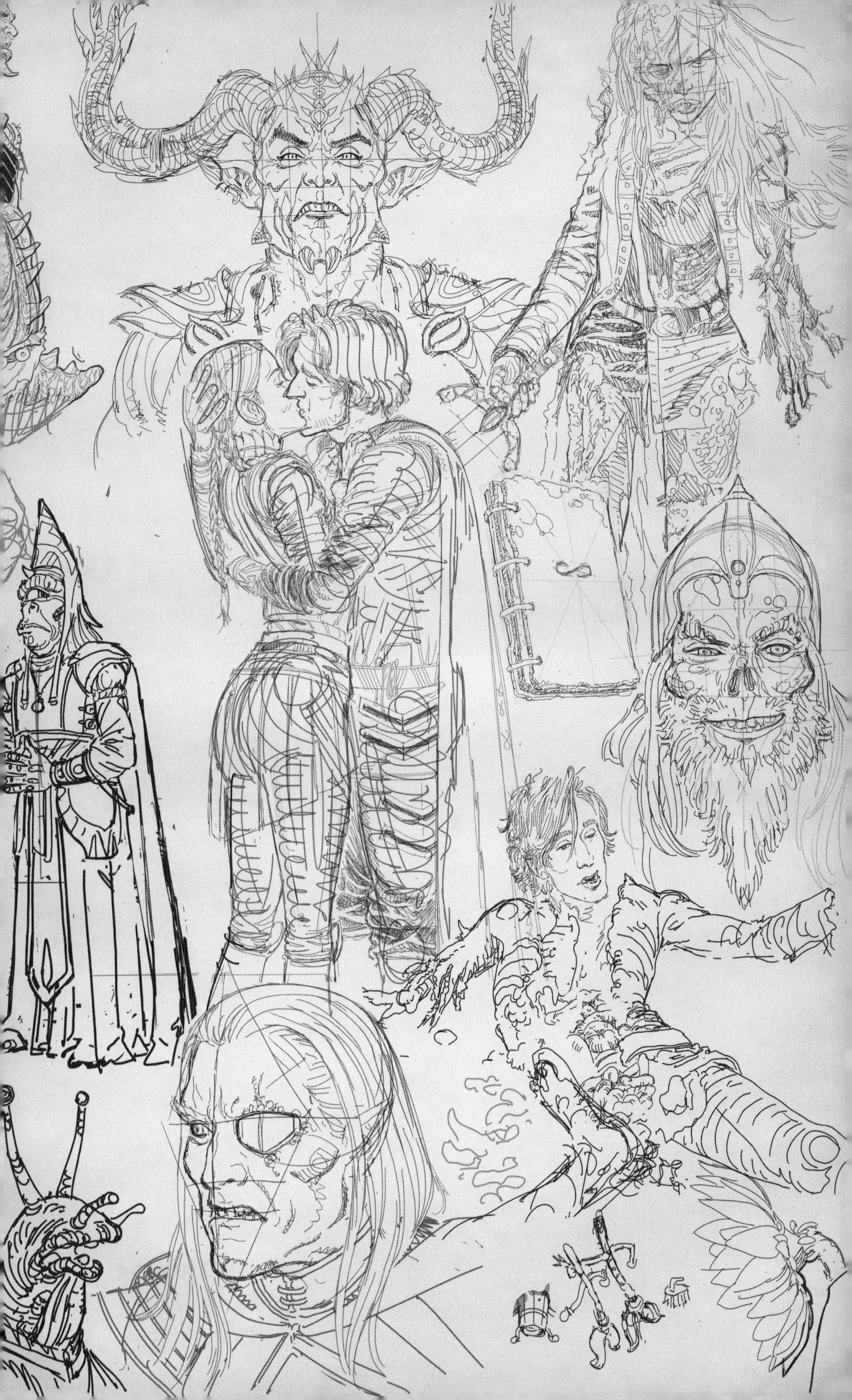

STEVE SKROCE worked at Marvel Comics for a decade on *Spider-Man*, *Cable*, and *Wolverine* before starting a career as a movie storyboard artist, working on films like *The Matrix* trilogy among others. He returned to comics in 2016 with WE STAND ON GUARD written by Brian K. Vaughan and is currently creating a new post-apocalyptic series for Image before his next MAESTROS series. Steve lives with his wife and two children in Vancouver, B.C.

DAVE STEWART is a multi Eisner Award-winning colorist who has worked for DC, Marvel, Dark Horse, and Image Comics. Some of his award-winning works include *Hellboy*, *Star Wars*, *Human Target*, *Daredevil*, *Ultimate X-Men*, *Captain America*, *Superman*, *BPRD*, *The Goon*, *Body Bags*, and FATALE.

FONOGRAFIKS is the banner name for the comics work of designer Steven Finch, which includes the Image Comics series NOWHERE MEN, INJECTION, WE STAND ON GUARD, CEMETERY BEACH, and the multi-award-winning SAGA. He lives and works, surrounded by far too many books, in the north east of England.